T3-BGV-783

The Noir Thriller

Crime Files Series

General Editor: **Clive Bloom**

Since its invention in the nineteenth century, detective fiction has never been more popular. In novels, short stories, films, radio, television and now in computer games, private detectives and psychopaths, prim poisoners and overworked cops, tommy gun gangsters and cocaine criminals are the very stuff of modern imagination, and their creators one mainstay of popular consciousness. Crime Files is a ground-breaking series offering scholars, students and discerning readers a comprehensive set of guides to the world of crime and detective fiction. Every aspect of crime writing, detective fiction, gangster movie, true-crime exposé, police procedural and post-colonial investigation is explored through clear and informative texts offering comprehensive coverage and theoretical sophistication.

Published titles include:

Ed Christian (*editor*)
THE POST-COLONIAL DETECTIVE

Paul Cobley
THE AMERICAN THRILLER
Generic Innovation and Social Change in the 1970s

Lee Horsley
THE NOIR THRILLER

Susan Rowland
FROM AGATHA CHRISTIE TO RUTH RENDELL
British Women Writers in Detective and Crime Fiction

Crime Files
Series Standing Order ISBN 0–333–71471–7
(*outside North America only*)

You can receive future titles in this series as they are published by placing a standing order. Please contact your bookseller or, in case of difficulty, write to us at the address below with your name and address, the title of the series and the ISBN quoted above.

Customer Services Department, Macmillan Distribution Ltd, Houndmills, Basingstoke, Hampshire RG21 6XS, England

The Noir Thriller

Lee Horsley
Senior Lecturer in English
University of Lancaster

palgrave

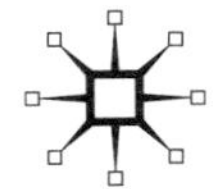

First published 2001 by
PALGRAVE
Houndmills, Basingstoke, Hampshire RG21 6XS and
175 Fifth Avenue, New York, N. Y. 10010
Companies and representatives throughout the world

PALGRAVE is the new global academic imprint of
St. Martin's Press LLC Scholarly and Reference Division and
Palgrave Publishers Ltd (formerly Macmillan Press Ltd).

ISBN 0–333–72045–8

This book is printed on paper suitable for recycling and made from fully managed and sustained forest sources.

A catalogue record for this book is available from the British Library.

Library of Congress Cataloging-in-Publication Data
Horsley, Lee, 1944–
The noir thriller / Lee Horsley.
p. cm.
Includes bibliographical references and index.
ISBN 0–333–72045–8
1. Detective and mystery stories, American—History and criticism. 2. Detective and mystery stories, English—History and criticism. 3. American fiction—20th century—History and criticism. 4. English fiction—20th century—History and criticism. 5. Literature and society–-United States—History—20th century. 6. Suspense fiction—History and criticism. 7. Crime in literature. I. Title.

PS374.D4 H65 2000
813'.087209—dc21

00–040453

10 9 8 7 6 5 4 3 2 1
10 09 08 07 06 05 04 03 02 01

Printed and bound in Great Britain by
Antony Rowe Ltd, Chippenham, Wiltshire

In Memory of
Hilda Drewery,
1919–1998

Contents

List of Illustrations

Acknowledgements

My aim in this study has been to include a range of the literary noir published in America and Britain between 1920 and the present. I wanted to cast my net as widely as possible, and this necessitated drawing in a large number of novels that are not currently in print. In my search for old editions, I have been given much help by a small group of British dealers in second-hand and vintage paperbacks, most of whom belong to the British Association of Paperback and Pulp Book Collectors. Two whom I particularly want to thank are Maurice Flanagan, whose Zardoz Books is one of the largest postal suppliers of second-hand crime paperbacks, and David Hyman, who has been very helpful indeed in looking for books on my wants list. I also feel a general sense of indebtedness, as presumably do most British crime-fiction enthusiasts, to Maxim Jakubowski, for his republication of noir classics and his encouragement of new British crime-writing, as well as for establishing the Murder One bookstore.

During the early stages of research and writing I was given extremely useful suggestions by Clive Bloom, general editor of this series, by John Morris of Brunel University and by two of my Lancaster colleagues, Tess Cosslett and Jonathan Munby (who, in addition, kindly loaned me videos from his large collection of *films noirs*). I benefited as well from discussions with the enthusiastic graduate students who have taken 'The Noir Thriller' as a University of Lancaster MA module, especially with those who have been working on related dissertations. I am also grateful to Steve Holland (author of *The Mushroom Jungle*, an essential text for students of British paperback publishing) and Paul Duncan (co-editor of *Crime Time* magazine), both of whom gave me valuable advice on British crime fiction.

I am indebted to the University of Lancaster Committee for Research and to the English Department for their generous contribution towards the cost of a research trip to the United States in 1998, and to the University of Lancaster for giving me sabbatical leave to write this book. I also want to thank the staff of the British Library and of the libraries I visited during my American research trip: Harvard's Widener Library, Boston University's Mugar Library, the Library of Congress and the New York Public Library all provided me with indispensable material.

Most of all, I want to express my thanks to the members of my family, without whose encouragement this book could not have been written. Tony Horsley has, as always, been a patient and percipient reader of the manuscript, as has my daughter, Katharine Horsley, who also collaborated with me in writing one of the articles published while this research was in progress. Both have given me invaluable help and advice. The entire family has greatly added to my pleasure in the project by sharing my enjoyment of neo-noir films, and my sons, Daniel and Samuel, have been a constant source of useful suggestions (Have you read David Huggins? Charles Higson?) and interesting questions (Why isn't *Total Recall* noir?) that have extended the range of the study. Finally, I want to express my gratitude to their grandmother, Hilda Drewery, to whom this book is dedicated. Until her death in 1998 she was a mainstay of the household and her unstinting support and love sustained us all.

Introduction

> Murder. Lust. Greed. Despair . . . And Literary Criticism. No wonder they called it the Waste Land.[1]

The noir thriller is one of the most durable popular expressions of the kind of modernist pessimism epitomised in *The Waste Land*. This relationship is wittily suggested by Martin Rowson's comic-book version of the poem, conflating Eliot's vision of modern life with the quest of a hard-boiled detective. Condensed into Rowson's opening page of 'Burial of the Dead' (see Figure 1) are fragmentary hints of common themes: death without renewal, the past, memories and 'old desires', the mysterious clues and fractured narratives that are part of the atomised urban scenes of modernity, plus a glance back ('Marlowe, Chris Marlowe') to an earlier period of disillusionment and alienation, the darkly violent world of revenge tragedy. As a parodist, Rowson is taking advantage of a noir iconography that can be reduced to the immediately recognisable elements of the private eye and the mean streets, the scene evoked by Chandler's famous pronouncement that 'Down these mean streets a man must go who is not himself mean, who is neither tarnished nor afraid.'[2] The extent to which the image is ripe for parody is evidence of its wide currency. So potent an icon is the private eye that it sometimes seems difficult to detach the popular conception of noir from the compelling figures of Marlowe and Spade and – uniting the roles – Humphrey Bogart. Even in academic studies, a recurrent problem (weakening efforts to analyse later adaptations of the form) is that the tradition of the noir thriller is identified wholly with the tough, resilient individualism of the hard-boiled detective who acts to reconstitute order. I wish in this study to establish a much broader understanding of literary noir and of the many different protagonists who go down

Figure 1 Martin Rowson, *The Waste Land* (1990)

small-town Main Streets and country roads as well as down mean streets and dark alleyways. Private eyes play a part, but so do transgressors and victims, strangers and outcasts, tough women and sociable psychopaths. These are characters who *are* tarnished and afraid, and who find it difficult or impossible to escape from the 'bleakness, darkness, alienation, disintegration', the 'sense of disorientation and nightmare' that are associated with the modernist crisis of culture.[3]

The influence of various strands of European cinematic modernism on American *film noir* has been extensively analysed. Critics have stressed the impact of the visual style of German Expressionist cinema and of French Poetic Realism, with its 'poetry of wet cobblestones, of nights in the faubourgs and of bleak dawns'; they have related the American phenomenon to European representations of criminal psychology and working-class crime and to the '*noir* dynamics' of the British films of Hitchcock.[4] James Naremore, in his recent analysis of the contexts of *film noir*, suggests that the French critics who, in the mid-1940s, first applied the term *film noir* might well have agreed on a formulation that defined noir as 'a kind of modernism in the popular cinema'.[5] Modernism might seem to be separated from both Hollywood and pulp fiction by such qualities as its formal complexity and technical display, its aesthetic self-consciousness, its association with high culture and its rejection of classical narrative. But with its 'extraordinary compound' of apparently contradictory elements, modernism did encompass many impulses that found natural expression in a popular genre engaged in undermining the essentially optimistic thrust of other popular forms, such as detective and action adventure stories.[6] Thematic links are the most apparent. Words associated with noir, such as 'angst, despair, nihilism',[7] echo standard summations of modernism. 'The idea of the modern', as Bradbury and McFarlane define it, is 'bound up with consciousness of disorder, despair, and anarchy', with 'the intellectual conventions of Plight, Alienation, and Nihilism'. Strindberg's description of his characters in *Miss Julie* (1888) can, they suggest, be taken to express the modernist sense of fragmentation and discontinuity: 'Since they are modern characters, living in an age of transition . . . I have drawn them as split and vacillating . . . conglomerations of past and present . . .'.[8] Although the aesthetic sophistication and deliberate difficulty of the modernist response was not appropriate to a popular genre, modernist techniques as well as themes helped to shape literary noir, encouraging, for example, the use of irony, non-linear plots, subjective narration and multiple viewpoints.

The two modernist writers whose names are most often invoked in discussions of literary noir are Eliot and Conrad. The influence of Eliot is very evident, for example, in the work both of Graham Greene ('Greeneland' has been called' 'a province of the Waste Land') and of Dashiell Hammett, 'the earliest and most radical of the popular modernists', who was reading Eliot at the time that he wrote *The Glass Key* and talked at length about Eliot with Lillian Hellman.[9] One of the most striking postwar examples of the 'Waste Land' theme is William Lindsay Gresham's *Nightmare Alley* (1946), which uses Eliot's lines on Madam Sosostris as an epigraph and has chapters named for the Tarot cards. Conrad more directly contributed to the development of the noir thriller. Aside from some of his own literary ancestors (for example, Dostoevsky and Dickens), Conrad, who both exemplifies emergent modernism and combines this with a leaning towards popular culture, is the most notable of the pre-World War One novelists to produce proto-noir fiction. *Heart of Darkness* (1902) is the novel most cited in relation to noir themes like otherness and the crossing of boundaries into dark, forbidden zones. Marlow's withholding of the truth from Kurtz's Intended presupposes an unbridgeable gap between hard masculine sensibilities and the sheltered gentility of the 'feminine' middle classes,[10] and his show of masculine fortitude in confronting disturbing realities is part of the ethos behind the creation of the noir thriller as a 'tough', male-dominated popular genre. *The Secret Agent* (1907) anticipates popular literary noir even more plainly. It is a text that goes some way towards defining noir sensibility and narrative techniques, with its ironic presentation of the perceptions of guilty and vulnerable characters, its non-linear structure and inconclusive ending. Although it was published near the beginning of the century, *The Secret Agent* was a novel more in accord with the mood of the interwar years. In his 1920 'Author's Note', Conrad looks back on the reasons for the criticisms that were initially made of it. He confesses that he had not guessed how disturbed earlier audiences would be by the 'sordid surroundings and the moral squalor' of a tale dealing with 'the poignant miseries and passionate credulities of a mankind always so tragically eager for self-destruction' (*The Secret Agent*, 7–8).

In a study that begins with *The Secret Agent* as an early example of the defining elements of noir and ends with the 'future noir' of the nineties, I am inevitably parting company with those analyses which see noir as narrowly time-bound. As will also become clear, I do not see it as an exclusively American phenomenon.[11] Many critics of *film noir* have maintained that the label can legitimately be applied only to a specific cycle of post-World War Two Hollywood films, the limits of which are most often fixed as 1941 (the year of John Huston's film of *The Maltese Falcon*) and 1958 (with Welles' *Touch of Evil* marking the end of the cycle). Such firm national and chronological boundaries are problematic even for the classic cycle of *film noir*. Reflection on an unrealised Welles project suggests some of the difficulties. Had Welles fulfilled his intention of filming *Heart of Darkness* in 1940, it might now have been regarded as 'the first example of American film noir'.[12] It might equally, because of its date, setting and subject matter, have been relegated to the margins of canonical *film noir*, rather in the way that Greene's Conrad-influenced *The Third Man* (Carol Reed, 1949) and Alfred Hitchcock's adaptation of *The Secret Agent* have been. The latter, released as *Sabotage*, was directed by Hitchcock in pre-World War Two England (1936) and usually finds no place in studies of *film noir*. But Raymond Durgnat's 'Paint It Black: the Family Tree of the *Film Noir*',[13] which is one of the early (1970) Anglo-American essays responsible for introducing the concept of noir to an English-speaking audience, does include Hitchcock's film amongst a large number of other European *films noirs*. These movies – French, Italian, German and English – are all, Durgnat maintains, comparable to the Hollywood *films noirs* of the forties and fifties. Nevertheless, they are commonly excluded from standard studies of the phenomenon. In extending his range of films, Durgnat argues that noir should be viewed as 'perennial' rather than historically limited and that it should be seen as part of a much wider Western literary tradition.

In recent years, critics have increasingly followed Durgnat 's example. The motivation for a chronological broadening of the term has not only been to draw in pre-World War Two examples (as Durgnat does) but to expand the category sufficiently to include the burgeoning phenomenon of 'neo-noir', which was already beginning to appear at the time that American critics first adopted the French label. Silver and Ward, for example, in their *Film Noir: an Encyclopedic Reference to the American Style*,[14] choose as their first film the 1927 *Underworld*, directed by Josef von Sternberg – 'the first modern gangster film in which the heroes are actually criminals'. At the same time, they push their analysis forward, including in their list of canonical *films noirs* a movie as recent as Scorsese's 1976 *Taxi Driver*, and separately discussing neo-noir films up to 1992 (21 films in that year alone, including Tarantino's *Reservoir Dogs*). The 1996 *Film Noir Reader* (edited by Silver and Ursini) reprints essays that range over noir from Borde and Chaumeton's seminal piece of the mid-1950s to, for example, a 1990 Todd Erickson article arguing that noir really only becomes a genre (neo-noir) in the eighties, when it emerges from its 'embryonic' state in the sixties and seventies. One of the best recent analyses, Naremore's *More Than Night*, explores 'noir and its contexts' from the classic 1940s films to *L. A. Confidential* (1997). In terms of its national character, Naremore sees noir as occupying 'a liminal space somewhere between Europe and America': both its relationship to European modernism and the extensive current use of the term suggest that it is 'a phenomenon that transcends national boundaries'.[15] Arguments remain for emphasising American pre-eminence in the creation of noir: the majority of influential films and novels are American, and literary noir, like *film noir*, has developed in ways closely related to the social, cultural and political history of the United States. But this is only part of the story, and it in no sense detracts from the 'American character' of much that is best in literary and cinematic noir to consider this body of work in relation to other lines of development.

This broadening of the term, of course, complicates one of the questions that critics continue to debate. That is, what kind of classification *is* 'noir'? Is it a visual style, a tone, a genre, a generic field, a movement, a cycle, a series – or just a helpful category? Naremore argues that having a 'noir category' serves an important function, and his position over the matter of generic status serves also for this study. Even if it is not, strictly speaking, a genre (in the sense that, say, the western or science fiction or the detective story are genres), it is a label that at the very least invokes 'a network of ideas' that is valuable as an organising principle. Such is the 'flexibility, range, and mythic force' of the concept of noir that it belongs 'to the history of ideas as much as to the history of cinema' and is too useful to abandon as a means of textual classification. Whatever its generic status, the word 'noir' has become widespread both in academic discourse and as 'a major signifier of sleekly commercial artistic ambition'.[16] In the cinema alone, there have been over 300 noir-influenced films released since 1971, and the term is applied not only to films and novels but to television programmes, comics and video games, a growth in usage that has spawned 'fusion phrases' such as 'cable noir', 'TV noir', 'pop noir', 'cyber noir', 'tech noir', 'future noir' and 'digital noir'.[17]

This study analyses the noir crime fiction of both America and Britain, where the established tradition of the 'serious thriller' (Conrad, Greene, Ambler), the postwar efforts to create British versions of American popular fiction and the distinctively British thrillers of recent decades have all added to the evolution of literary noir. The discussion begins with American 'hard-boiled' noir thrillers of the 1920s and takes in a wide range of American and British literary noir through to the end of the 1990s. I consider both constant elements and changing patterns in the noir thriller and work towards a definition of noir applicable to the range of texts that have been included. In his study of the narrative structures of *film noir*, J. P. Telotte argues that noir is 'a narrative form with specific conventions and concerns which bulk beyond the cinema's limited confines'; these conventions and concerns are evident not just in films but in the novels of writers like Hammett, Chandler, James M. Cain, Cornell Woolrich, Jim Thompson, David Goodis and Dorothy B. Hughes.[18] As Telotte says, a definition appropriate to novels as well as to films must be based on something other than the 'look' of noir. It has to go beyond the visual and other specifically cinematic elements on which discussions of classic *film noir* have often centred,[19] and instead take account of such things as themes, mood, characterisation, point of view and narrative pattern.

This study will also, for reasons I return to in Chapter 1, separate the definition of noir from literary style, in particular from the distinctive stylistic attributes of hard-boiled fiction. Like the visual style of *film noir*, the hard-boiled style is only one means of expressing the noir vision. The popularly recognised stylistic traits of noir that Rowson draws on for his parody are the look (the dark shadows and claustrophobic scene) and the tough manner ('the old dame in the doorway coming in like a mean martini'). These signal what are clearly important forms of noir – classic *film noir* and hard-boiled fiction – but they by no means exhaust the possibilities. There are many other settings, from sun-drenched small towns to snow-bound mountains, and many other styles of speech. Cornell Woolrich, for example, in *Waltz into Darkness* (1947), concludes his despairing final scene with the lines, 'The soundless music stops. The dancing figures wilt and drop. The Waltz is done' (310). Patricia Highsmith, describing her murderer-to-be, Ripley, as he embarks for Europe, writes: 'His mood was tranquil and benevolent, but not at all sociable. . . . He was courteous, poised, civilized and preoccupied' (*The Talented Mr Ripley* [1955], 31), and the style of her narrative is always in keeping with her protagonist's aspirations to poise and civility. The narrator of J. G. Ballard's *Cocaine Nights* (1996) assures us that 'Nothing could ever happen in this affectless realm, where entropic drift calmed the surfaces of a thousand swimming pools' (35). Although they are no less 'noir', there is little in the style of such passages to connect Woolrich, Highsmith and Ballard with Hammett and the tough-guy 'hard-boilers' of the thirties.

In this study (as the reader will have observed from the title) 'noir' is coupled with 'thriller'. A label such as 'the noir crime novel' also describes the texts I have included: as defined by Julian Symons, the crime novel (as distinct from the classic detective story) need not have a detective (and hence does not need clues or forensic details), makes characters and their psychological make-up the basis of the story and often radically questions 'some aspect of law, justice or the way society is run'.[20] All of these characteristics are to be found in the texts discussed, and 'crime novel' will be used interchangeably with 'thriller'. 'Thriller' also, however, carries other connotations which perhaps make it the more apposite term. The definition set out in Martin Rubin's recent book, *Thrillers*, suggests how closely related the concept of the thriller is to noir, and how the addition of the adjective 'noir' can be seen as intensifying some of the defining characteristics of the thriller. In Rubin's formulation, the identifying marks of the thriller include: excess, feeling and sensation, as opposed to the rationality implicit in the structure of the classic detective story; suspense, arising from the involvement of the protagonist in menacing events (in contrast to the detachment of the traditional detective); the evocation of fear and anxiety; the creation of contrasts due to threatening eruptions in the normal; ambivalence; vulnerability; and a sense of being carried away (control–vulnerability being 'a central dialectic of the thriller, closely related to sadism–masochism').[21] In reflecting on the meanings of 'noir', it will be apparent how inextricably linked it is to this idea of the thriller, and how noir accentuates fear and anxiety, ambivalence and vulnerability (for example, by the destabilising of roles and emphasis on the protagonist's weakness and limitations). The main elements in my own definition of noir are: (i) the subjective point of view; (ii) the shifting roles of the protagonist; (iii) the ill-fated relationship between the protagonist and society (generating the themes of alienation and entrapment); and (iv) the ways in which noir functions as a socio-political critique.

Silver and Ward's observation that 'The most consistent aspect of film noir, apart from its visual style, is its protagonists'[22] could be taken to imply that in literary noir it is the creation of the protagonist that is of paramount importance. Two things should be brought into focus here. The first is the representation of the protagonist's subjectivity – his perceptions (both accurate and deluded), his state of mind, his desires, obsessions and anxieties; the second is the nature of the roles assumed by the protagonist, that is, the extent to which he functions as victim, transgressor or investigator. The need for attending to the handling of perspective in *film noir* is concisely summed up in Fritz Lang's explanation of his subjective camera work: 'You show the protagonist so that the audience can put themselves under the skin of the man'; by showing things 'wherever possible, from the viewpoint of the protagonist' the film gives the audience visual and psychological access to his nightmarish experiences.[23] In literary noir, this effect is often discussed in relation to the use of first-person narration, many noir thrillers being narrated by the protagonist. It is more to the point, however, to say that, whether the narrative is first- or third-person, it is kept close to the mind of the character who is immersed in the action and struggling to make sense of what is happening. The noir narrative is frequently focused through the mind of a single character who is bemused or disingenuous; it ironises his evasions and disguises; it calls into question his judgements; it foregrounds the difficulties of interpreting a mendacious society. Alternatively, noir writers create several unreliable narratives: Kay Boyle's *Monday Night* (1938) presents the stories of supposed murderers which turn out in the end to be the fabrications of a mad 'dispenser of justice' (133); Jim Thompson, in *The Criminal* (1953) and *The Kill-Off* (1957), employs multiple narrators who contend for control of the narrative and in the end leave the reader unsure of the truth of the matter, suggesting the futility of trying to arrive at any objective understanding of events. The disturbing subjects of *film noir* are made doubly so by the fact that crime, corruption, psychosis and desire are channelled, as Telotte says, 'into an unprecedented concern with *how* we see, understand, and describe our world'.[24]

As in Conrad's *The Secret Agent*, noir plots turn on falsehoods, contradictions and misinterpretations, and the extent to which all discourse is flawed and duplicitous is a dominant theme. 'Like high art,' James Sallis writes, 'these stories . . . unfold the lies society tells us and the lies we tell ourselves.'[25] Although Conrad's complex prose and his chilly, detached third-person narration differ greatly from the immediate, colloquial style of the American hard-boiled writers, he in fact achieves a similar effect by allowing us to see events from multiple viewpoints. Each character's angle of vision is ironised, but we are nevertheless given extended insights into the highly subjective perceptions of Verloc, Winnie, Ossipon, the Chief Inspector and so on. Conrad builds to scenes of complete and blackly comic mutual incomprehension: 'He wished only to put heart into her. It was a benevolent intention, but Mr Verloc had the misfortune not to be in accord with his audience' (203). The sustained irony of style serves not just to make us aware of characters' misjudgements and misconceptions but, in the broadest terms, to create a picture of a society in which everyone is a 'secret agent' and no one is to be taken at face value, in which no appearances actually correspond to realities and in which supposed order is revealed to be anarchy.[26]

The unsettling effect of the manipulation of point of view is heightened by the unstable position of the protagonist. The iconic figures of noir are more complex and ambiguous than the traditional detective, the cowboy or the action hero. In *Story*, Robert McKee writes that the subgenres of crime story 'vary chiefly by the answer to this question: From whose point of view do we regard the crime?' Noir, he suggests, is characterised by the 'POV of a protagonist who may be part criminal, part detective, part victim of a femme fatale'.[27] The femme fatale is a stereotype more prevalent in *film noir* than literary noir (and victimisation certainly need not be at her hands), but this in other respects succinctly captures one of the essential aspects of noir narrative. That is, we are brought close to the mind of a protagonist whose position vis-à-vis other characters is not fixed. Treacherous confusions of his role and the movement of the protagonist from one role to another constitute key structural elements in noir narrative. The victim might, for example, become the aggressor; the hunter might turn into the hunted or vice versa; the investigator might double as either the victim or the perpetrator. Whereas the traditional mystery story, with its stable triangle of detective, victim and murderer, is reasonably certain to have the detective as the protagonist, noir is a deliberate violation of this convention.[28] In noir, victim, criminal and investigator can all act as protagonists: combinations or reversals of roles and the destabilising of identities mean that, as McKee's brief formulation suggests, it is rare for central characters to occupy single fixed positions in the narrative. So, for example, another of the distinctly noirish qualities of Conrad's *The Secret Agent* is the way in which changing roles undermine any sense of a traditional character triangle. Even the most innocent or altruistic action (Winnie's sisterly protection of Stevie, her mother's self-sacrificing removal of herself) contributes to death and disaster; a victim (Winnie) becomes a murderer; the inadvertent murderer of Stevie (Verloc) becomes Winnie's victim; the motives of the investigator are suspect, his apparently miraculous insights are in large part accidental, and he precipitates deaths (Verloc's, Winnie's) in ways he could never have anticipated. Guilt for the disasters that befall is distributed amongst the characters: since virtually everyone is guilty, there is no single 'guilty party' as there is in the classic detective novel. An exploration of guilt is at the core of noir, and there can be no clear distinction between guilt and innocence.

Shared guilt is often the only common bond amongst noir characters, who are usually doomed to be isolated and marginalised. The main themes of the noir thriller are generalisations of the ill-fated relationship between the protagonist and his society. Characters suffer either from failures of agency (powerlessness, immobilising uncertainty) or from loss of community (isolation, betrayal). Obsessed, alienated, vulnerable, pursued or paranoid, they struggle with fatality, suffering existential despair as they act out narratives that raise the question of whether they are making their own choices or following a course dictated by fate. The forces affecting the protagonist can be perceived as a manifestation of the world's randomness and absurdity. But the historical dimension of noir fatality is strong. The protagonist feels his course to be shaped by society's injustices, failures, prejudices or pressures, and this historical specificity accounts for marked changes over time in the nature of the noir narrative. The forces controlling the lives of the characters are conceived in terms of the dominant conceptions of social-political determinants. Thus, in the interwar years, characters' fates are repeatedly seen as the result of deprivation – economic injustice obviously being a primary concern. In the post-World War Two period fate is recurrently associated with difference, with alienation or exclusion from a conformist and prejudiced society. Although both of these patterns are still to be seen in contemporary noir, there has been a tendency, particularly post-1980s, to think of an individual's fate less as the result of deprivation or difference than as a consequence of dependence on a consumer society. Instead of being tempted into a dangerous *demi-monde*, protagonists are lured by a seductive commodity culture and a society of spectacle. Collusion, complicity and assimilation become significant sources of anxiety.

The noir narrative confronts the protagonist with a rift in the familiar order of things or (particularly in contemporary noir) with a recognition that apparent normality is actually the antithesis of what it seems to be: it is brutal rather than benign, dehumanised not civilised. In the course of the story, it becomes clear that the things that are amiss cannot be dealt with rationally and cannot ultimately be put to rights. The protagonist is often, at best, offered (like Conrad's Marlow) a 'choice of nightmares' (*Heart of Darkness*, 89); he has 'no exit, no options'.[29] This entrapment is frequently conveyed through surreal images of being imprisoned by irrational impulses or external compulsions. Marlow, telling his listeners in *Heart of Darkness* that he is trying to convey 'that notion of being captured by the incredible which is the very essence of dreams' (39), evokes the oneiric quality that noir often possesses. In those plots set in motion by the sudden intrusion of the 'incredible' into ordinary experience, the protagonist becomes involved in a futile effort to restore order to a life that has been captured by the forces of unreason. As readers, our own sense of disorientation may be reinforced by the fact that we only gradually, by means of a non-linear narrative, discover causes and consequences.

Our piecemeal discovery of information corresponds to the protagonist's difficulties in arriving at any secure knowledge by means of orderly enquiry. The bloody and fragmentary remains of Stevie, whose violent disintegration is the central event of *The Secret Agent*, can only gradually be interpreted by characters who, like Conrad's readers, have not witnessed the tragedy. The impact of this event in turn shatters what had seemed (to those who did not enquire too deeply) a safe society and a stable domestic world, which, like Stevie himself, can never be reassembled: the novel ends with Ossipon still struggling to interpret the 'impenetrable mystery' of Winnie's death, her 'act of madness or despair' (249). What has broken through an apparently secure social structure is the criminality, cruelty and brutality which in the noir vision are always there. They are not just the 'dark secret' of respectable society but an inescapable part of it, only thinly disguised by civilised pretence. The dispersal of guilt, the instability of roles, and the difficulties of grasping the events taking place all mean that there can be no 'simple solution'. Even if there is a gesture in the direction of a happy ending, the group reformed is damaged and cannot return to prior innocence. It is in the nature of noir that guilt never disappears, and any resolution will be coloured by the 'cynical, existentially bitter'[30] attitude that is generally taken to be one of the hallmarks of noir, creating a tone that can be blackly comic but that, if it modulates too far towards light humour, or becomes upbeat or sentimental, will lose its 'noirish' quality.[31]

The guilt represented in the noir thriller is both individual and social, and the narrative is thus both transgressive and critical. Noir is 'the voice of violation', acting to expose the inadequacy of conventional cultural, political and also narrative models. It expresses fears and anxieties but also has the potential for critique, for undermining complacency and illusions (the false promises of the American dream; the hypocrisy of the British establishment). The fact that *film noir* was created in the postwar United States is often attributed to an atmosphere in which American society 'came into a more critical focus'.[32] More generally, the noir sensibility may come to the fore at any time of discontent and anxiety, of disillusionment with institutional structures and loss of confidence in the possibility of effective agency. The transgressions represented can be a mirror, the damaged self as an image of the society that caused the deformation or the unbalanced mind as a metaphor for society's lunacy (the burden of the past carried into the future as inescapable fatality). They can also be a protest, an attack on corruptions or injustices in the wider community. Each section of this study will sketch in the social, political and cultural circumstances to which noir thrillers were responding – for example, the unprecedented disruptions brought by two world wars, economic crises, the rise of aggressive ideologies, racial conflicts, Cold War paranoia, the emergence of the consumer society, the Thatcher–Reagan years. The noir thriller is rooted in its own time and place. Social realism and the choice of contemporary society as subject, a sceptical attitude towards received opinions and established institutions, and a strong satiric edge are all characteristic features. The ironies can, of course, be relatively unsophisticated, operating to expose obvious discrepancies between appearance (admired establishment figures and law enforcers) and reality (underlying criminality). In much literary noir, however, more subtle ironies proliferate and produce an essentially modernist undermining of conventional values and 'moral meaning', unsettling confidence in our ability to interpret and judge the world, and broadening the noir critique, prompting a sceptical distrust of the whole of society. Literary like cinematic noir often moves towards a universal sense of absurdity – towards what Alfred Appel calls noir's 'black vision of despair, loneliness and dread – a vision that touches an audience most intimately because it assures that their suppressed impulses and fears are shared human responses'.[33] But the immediate causes of pessimism and despair are grounded in the lies and corruptions of a particular milieu. The outcome of the noir narrative may be the utter disintegration of the human – imaged in Stevie's violent death. Its substance, though, is almost invariably a specific, time-bound struggle with doubtful meanings in a world of deliberate deceptions. This constant theme is epitomised in the question that rises in Stevie's mind when Winnie persuades him that the metropolitan police are not 'a sort of benevolent institution for the suppression of evil': 'What did they mean by pretending then? Unlike his sister, who put her trust in face values, he wished to go to the bottom of the matter' (143–4).

Part I

1920–45

Sudden violence signifies a radical disruption of normal existence. Horace McCoy's *They Shoot Horses, Don't They?* opens with the gentle and non-violent narrator recalling the moment at which he fired a bullet into Gloria's head; in Paul Cain's *Fast One*, Gerry Kells just wanted 'to be let alone', but has been 'mixed up in five shootings in the last thirty-two hours' (58, 67); in Dashiell Hammett's *Red Harvest*, after 16 murders in less than a week, the Continental Op says that he fears he himself is going 'blood-simple' (139). Only half-jokingly, Raymond Chandler suggested that the main principle of construction in the hard-boiled thriller was 'When in doubt, have a man come through a door with a gun in his hand.'[1] His comments on the role of the man with a gun are a reflection on the reading public's appetite for violent action, but Chandler also argues in the same essay that the 'smell of fear' generated by such stories was evidence of their serious response to the modern condition:

> Their characters lived in a world gone wrong, a world in which, long before the atom bomb, civilization had created the machinery for its own destruction and was learning to use it with all the moronic delight of a gangster trying out his first machine-gun. The law was something to be manipulated for profit and power. The streets were dark with something more than night.[2]

The noir thriller began to develop as a popular form in the aftermath of one devastating war and came to maturity in the two decades that terminate in a second world war. In its most characteristic narratives, some traumatic event irretrievably alters the conditions of life and creates for its characters an absolute experiential divide between their dependence on stable, predictable patterns and the recognition that life is, in truth, morally chaotic, subject to randomness and total dislocation. In the best-known parable of ordinary life disrupted, Dashiell Hammett's Sam Spade tells the story of Flitcraft, who comes to realise life's arbitrariness and absurdity when he is nearly killed by a falling beam. The thrillers of the period repeatedly represent the sort of transformation that leaves the protagonist feeling, as Flitcraft does, that 'someone had taken the lid off life and let him look at the works' (*The Maltese Falcon*, 429). In one of Benjamin Appel's stories, 'Brothers in Hell's Kitchen' (1935), two brothers fail to understand one another because only the elder has gone through World War One and therefore 'couldn't be the same inside'; the younger, at the end, thinks he has gained the upper hand over the brother who is 'all wiped up', but then reflects, 'ME, I'm younger, I got something ahead of me. What, he thought, another war?' (*Hell's Kitchen*, 124–5). This sense of disillusionment in the years between the wars was heightened by political and economic disasters for which people were wholly unprepared. In America there was the folly of Prohibition and its attendant gangsterism, as well as growing evidence of illicit connections between crime, business and politics in American cities. Crises afflicted both American and European economies, bringing the stock market crash of 1929 and the Great Depression, which Keynes saw as the worst catastrophe of modern times. With the failure of parliamentary governments in Europe and the rise of totalitarian dictatorships, there was the spectre of another war.

In the noir fiction of this period, the anxious sense of fatality is usually attached to a pessimistic conviction that economic and sociopolitical circumstances will deprive people of control over their lives by destroying their hopes and by creating in them the weaknesses of character that mark them out as victims. In post-World War Two thrillers, a protagonist's fate is most often linked to difference from others, to an isolating inability or refusal to conform to conventional expectations. Interwar thrillers, on the other hand, incline to economic determinism, stressing the pressures exerted by an economically unjust and fragmenting society. Where the psychology of the characters is explored, it is predominantly in terms of ordinary human shortcomings. For example, obsession with success, aggressive drives, self-deception and lying to others are presented as weaknesses of character that precipitate disaster under the strain of adverse socio-economic conditions. The thrillers of this period are frequently described as 'harshly realistic', but their focus on the real conditions and problems of interwar society is repeatedly joined to the fantastic and the symbolic. Violence itself, though it is sometimes no more than 'thriller sensationalism', can take on symbolic force, as, for example, in Hammett's *Red Harvest* or Paul Cain's *Fast One*. There are heightened, sometimes surreal descriptions of threatening and oppressive scenes or of destruction and viciousness. Amongst the most memorable images of the period's thrillers are the hellishness of Daly's Satan Hall stories and of Hammett's *Red Harvest*, the terrible brutality of a corrupt society encountered in Burnett's *Little Caesar* and Armitage Trail's *Scarface*, the blackly satiric or tragic scenes of entrapment by misfortune that dominate McCoy's novels and the work of James M. Cain. This combination of abrasive realism and satiric intensification is a hallmark of tough-guy writing. As David Madden argues in *Tough Guy Writers of the Thirties*, these are novels that provide 'stylised exaggeration of very real traits in the American character ... the nightmare version of the American Dream'.[3]

The preoccupation with characters goaded or defeated by adversity was often interpreted, by interwar critics of both the tough thriller and *film noir,* as an acceptance or even encouragement of moral bankruptcy. It was seen as a form of collusion in the neurosis and violence of the world depicted. George Orwell, for example, in 'Raffles and Miss Blandish' (1944), attacked James Hadley Chase (René Raymond) and his 'half-understood import from America' as a debased expression of the 'moral atmosphere' of the age that witnessed the rise of fascism:

> In his imagined world of gangsters Chase is presenting, as it were, a distilled version of the modern political scene, in which such things as mass bombings of civilians, the use of hostages, torture to obtain confessions, secret prisons, execution without trial, floggings with rubber truncheons, drownings in cesspools, systematic falsification of records and statistics, treachery, bribery and quislingism are normal and morally neutral, even admirable when they are done in a large and bold way.

The essay complains that 'lowbrow fiction' has followed modernist literature and the 'serious novel' (Lawrence, for example) in abandoning all sense of 'a sharp distinction between right and wrong and between legality and illegality'. It is one thing for the intelligentsia to think in this way, but quite another for the mass of the population: now that 'Freud and Machiavelli have reached the outer suburbs', the 'common people' will lose completely their moral bearings.[4]

Orwell's criticism is echoed in John Houseman's often quoted disparagement (in 1947) of *film noir* as lacking in moral energy, giving in to 'fatalistic despair' and representing people 'groping their way through a twilight of insecurity and corruption'.[5] Like Chandler's assertion of the 'authentic power' of such thrillers, the comments of Orwell and Houseman focus on social and political content – on the fact that these films and novels refer to a world in crisis, destabilised by one war and moving into another. Orwell's protest is a backhanded acknowledgement of the relevance of the newer kind of crime novel to events in Europe (a relevance made clear, for example, in Brecht's or Graham Greene's use of mythologised gangsters as emblems of fascist violence). What Orwell in effect denies is that such fiction can do more than 'express' the disintegrating moral atmosphere of the time. To take his own example, the truth of the matter is that, beneath the surface of the American tough-guy pastiche, Chase *is* exploring the pressing question (one raised by many British thrillers of the thirties), that is, the extent to which passivity should be judged culpable in the face of psychopathic violence. For most writers of the time, such themes are much more to the fore than they are in *No Orchids for Miss Blandish*. In taking as their subject what Ezra Pound called 'disillusions never told in the old days', 'serious' thriller writers of the interwar period judge the society portrayed. In breaking with the existing conventions of the detective novel, they provide, from the early twenties on, a form of popular fiction that deals critically with the 'wrongness' of 'a world gone wrong' and that confronts the catastrophes brought about by the intrusion of violence, the betrayal of trust and the corrupt exercise of power.

The noir thriller had its forerunners (Conrad, Dickens, Dostoevsky, amongst others), but the 1920s was the period in which it became firmly established as popular fiction. The label 'hard-boiled' began to be applied, distinguishing this departure in crime-writing from the classic detective story. The most important publication of the twenties in encouraging and marketing the new kind of crime story was *Black Mask*. The magazine was founded in 1920 by H. L. Mencken and George Jean Nathan, who sold it after half a year, and from then on it was given over to crime, adventure and western stories. In the early 1920s, Dashiell Hammett and Carroll John Daly began writing for *Black Mask*, and the identity of the magazine became more sharply defined when the editorship was taken over in 1926 by Captain Joseph T. Shaw. Shaw encouraged a high standard of colloquial, racy writing, favouring 'economy of expression' and 'authenticity in character and action',[6] all of which are important features of the hard-boiled style. Shaw greatly increased the circulation of *Black Mask*, and other pulp magazines (for example, *Dime Detective, Detective Fiction Weekly, Black Aces*) were soon competing in some numbers. Several of the writers discussed in this section were amongst the regular contributors to *Black Mask*: in addition to Daly and Hammett, Frederick Nebel, Raoul Whitfield, Paul Cain (George Sims), Raymond Chandler, Horace McCoy.

Although much 'hard-boiled' fiction is in essential respects closer to the traditional adventure story than to 'noir', there is considerable common ground. In examining the development of literary noir, I will begin with a discussion of the American hard-boiled investigator – a tough, independent, often solitary figure, a descendant of the frontier hero and cowboy but, as reimagined in the 1920s, a cynical city-dweller: 'He finds no way out. And so he is slugged, shot at, choked, doped, yet he survives because it is in his nature to survive.'[7] He can achieve a degree of control, but, unlike the classic Holmesian detective, he cannot restore order and set all to rights. The basic narrative pattern pits this lone investigator against brutal criminals, often in league with a corrupt power structure. His function is in some respects analogous to that of the satirist:[8] he exposes and punishes, though by no means always claiming the moral high ground. One of the main contrasts I will look at in the hard-boiled stories and novels of this period is that between two types of investigators: on the one hand, those who possess some form of moral superiority (Chandler's Marlowe comes first to mind); on the other, those who are more implicated in the world of corruption, depicted as entering into a scene of disorder and acknowledging their own anarchic tendencies and capacity for violence (as in the novels of Hammett, Paul Cain and Raoul Whitfield). These 'compromised' investigators are key figures in the evolution of literary noir, which, as it develops in the late 1920s and the 1930s, turns to the portrayal of deeply flawed, transgressive, often criminal protagonists.

In the thrillers of this time it is the character of the male protagonist that has the clearest relationship to the novel's theme and structure. In contrast to the post-World War Two period, the roles of female characters tend not to be of determining importance. The women represented are often defined primarily as the helpers of the men, either as, say, the gangster's moll or as the basically tough, good girl who helps the downtrodden gangster or endangered victim (for example, Marie in Burnett's *High Sierra*, Keechie in Anderson's *Thieves Like Us*, the character of Midnight in Woolrich's *Black Path of Fear*, the Communist heroine in *No Pockets in a Shroud* and Grandquist in *Fast One*). There are some notable examples of the femme fatale in Chandler's novels and occasionally in the work of Hammett and James M. Cain, but it is only really with the post-World War Two boom in paperback thrillers that this iconic figure comes into her own. My main subject in this section, then, will be the shifting representations of the male protagonists. The second and third chapters will deal, respectively, with the criminal and the victim. In Chapter 2, I look at the novels of Paul Cain, James M. Cain, W. R. Burnett, Armitage Trail (Maurice Coons), Benjamin Appel, Edward Anderson and Ernest Hemingway, and consider the various ways in which crime-centred narratives use the rebellious figure of the criminal and the hierarchical structure of the criminal organisation both to challenge and to ironise capitalism and the business ethic. Having made a career of illegality, the gangster functions as the dark double of 'respectable' society, undermining its claims to legitimacy and parodying the American drive to succeed. Chapter 3 focuses on the ordinary man as victim, wrongly persecuted or finding himself doomed to failure in the commission of a crime. A weak and ineffectual character, the victim-protagonist lacks the survival skills of the investigator or gangster; he can serve a purpose within the novel comparable to that of the satiric naif who acts as foil to those who are corruptly competent. In the American novels included here (by, for example, Horace McCoy, James M. Cain, Richard Hallas [Eric Knight] and Cornell Woolrich) economic determinism is often very pronounced, as it is, of course, in other naturalistic fiction of the time. Characters have little scope for effective action, and the narratives tend towards bleak, suicidal pessimism.

The second and third chapters also include British thrillers of the interwar period. At a time when the main threat of violence seemed to come from the rise of aggressive continental political ideologies, writers of serious British thrillers – Eric Ambler, for example, and Graham Greene – tended to cast the armed gangster in the role of fascist thug and to represent the victim-protagonist as a man who hesitates to act against fascist violence for fear of losing his own humanity. In novels such as these, narratives are often constructed in a way that foregrounds Orwell's equation of criminal brutality with the atrocities of the 'modern political scene'. They aim, however, not simply to shock but to explore the dangerous dilemmas faced by those accustomed to what Orwell, in another essay of the time ('Wells, Hitler and the World State'), called 'the sheltered conditions of English life'.[9]

1
Hard-boiled Investigators

At the end of *The Maltese Falcon* (1930), Brigid O'Shaughnessy asks Sam Spade whether he would have treated her differently if he had received his share of the money from the sale of a genuine falcon. '"Don't be too sure I'm as crooked as I'm supposed to be,"' Spade replies. '"That kind of reputation might be good business – bringing in high-priced jobs and making it easier to deal with the enemy."' His answer suggests the ambivalent position of the archetypal hard-boiled investigator. Self-aware and self-mocking, he acknowledges that he is often seen as indistinguishable from the crooks with whom he has to deal. However, while he readily admits looking after his own financial interests, he is not ultimately motivated by greed. In spite of his apparent amorality and tough cynicism, Spade does have at least some standards – a personal code against which unscrupulous 'enemies' and the disorder they create can be judged. The label 'hard-boiled' is often used synonymously with 'noir'.[1] Although this is to some extent misleading, there is substantial overlap, and much of the best noir crime fiction is unquestionably hard-boiled. Both labels connote the use of crime stories to provide insights into the socio-political disorders and moral dilemmas of the time in which they are written; they look critically at the illusions and hypocrisy, the rotten power structures and the brutal injustices of a superficially respectable society. Protagonists tend to be isolated and estranged, existing on the margins of society and, as outsiders, capable of seeing with a satirist's eye. As much as anything, it is the investigator's ability to strip away pretence and reveal the sources of corruption that gives him his effective agency, enabling him to survive in (and giving him a kind of freedom within) a hazardous environment.

'Hard-boiled' and 'noir' can both refer to narratives that have as their protagonists predators or victims as well as investigators. It is the tough, independent investigator, though, who is most strongly associated with the hard-boiled tradition. Most accounts of this figure begin with the *Black Mask*, which from 1923 on printed the kind of tough crime stories in American settings that became one of the key points of origin for American hard-boiled writing. The focus of these stories is on the activity of exposure, but this activity involves much more attendant danger and moral uncertainty than there is in the orthodox detective story, with its puzzle-solving sleuths analysing clues and providing rational solutions. The hard-boiled investigator not only enquires into entrenched power structures but engages in combat against them and can choose to inflict punishment. This enforcer element, the individualist ethic of taking things into one's own hands, is particularly marked in some of the early *Black Mask* stories. In the retrospective investigations of the 'Golden Age' of crime fiction, the detectives of Agatha Christie, Dorothy Sayers or S. S. Van Dine are themselves insulated from the crime that has taken place. In the characteristic *Black Mask* story, on the other hand, every case becomes part of an ongoing sequence of violent events. The time of the crime and the time of the investigation are no longer separate. Narratives are commonly, though not invariably, in the first person, and the narrator's own sense of control is always open to challenge: he is 'caught in a narrative that writes him as much as he writes it',[2] and thus cannot have the aloofness and detachment of the classic detective. There are, however, a variety of positions from which such an investigation can be conducted, and narratives can be classified in terms of the psychological and moral distance of the protagonist from the world of crime investigated.

The archetypal hard-boiled character is, of course, the private eye. He is the figure most often analysed in comparisons between hard-boiled crime fiction and classic detective fiction, to the extent that comparisons with the white male hard-boiled tradition (for example, in analyses of female-authored or black crime fiction) are generally constructed solely with reference to Hammett's Sam Spade or Chandler's 'crusader/knight' of the mean streets. The private eye, in a way no less than the traditional detective, can function as a very positive figure. Many private eyes, adhering to an individualistic core of values, are distanced from the world investigated by qualities that ultimately distinguish them from those 'on the wrong side of the fence'.[3] Their characterisation can be seen as based in 'romantic images of the lone male – strong, brave, independent – a compendium of the *macho* values apparently so popular in American society'.[4] This summing up of the nature of the private eye is a fair enough description of the kind of protagonist popularised by Chandler and his heirs (for example, Howard Browne, Richard S. Prather and Robert B. Parker) and by such contemporaries as Frederick Nebel, Carroll John Daly and George Harmon Coxe. These are writers who created a gallery of breezily macho action heroes whose hard-boiled manner gives a tough veneer either to fairly traditional detection or to high-spirited adventure tales, rather than compelling us to enter the despondent, morally insecure world of noir.

The romantic crusader image does not, however, apply nearly so well to other investigative figures of the thirties. Hammett, for example, can be credited with the inauguration of an altogether less comfortable kind of crime fiction. He introduced characters who much more nearly conform to the description of the private eye as 'half gangster' – a man whose innocence has become so tarnished as to be no longer visible, and who is a close relation of the crook-as-investigator protagonists who emerge in other thrillers of the early thirties. The range of investigators, then, is considerable. At one end of the scale, often presented in a lightly comic manner, is the Marlowe-like private eye of unshakeable integrity, together with such honourable private eye substitutes as tenacious reporters and newspaper photographers, and the triumphantly pugnacious action hero. At the other end are Hammett's decidedly unknightly Continental Op on his more turbulent days and other protagonists who lack even the legitimate credentials of private eyes and news hounds – the ex-cons or the hard-bitten strong-arm men to be found in the work of Raoul Whitfield and Paul Cain. As is evident even from the cover art of the period (see Figure 2), criminals and investigators can often appear to be indistinguishable.

From pulp heroics to Poisonville

The divergent possibilities within hard-boiled fiction – in terms of tone, narrative resolution, characterisation and moral vision – are apparent from the outset in the work of 'the *Black Mask* boys', sometimes within the work of a single writer. So, for example, Frederick Nebel, a good friend of Hammett's and one of the most popular of the early *Black Mask* contributors,[5] uses grim urban settings and writes in a tough style ('"Now pipe this, you eggs . . ."'[6]). His stories and novels often darkly delineate a Depression America that is greedy, politically corrupt and morally chaotic, in which only the tough can survive. In his first novel, *Sleepers East* (1933), a journey brings together people involved in concealing a murder that has serious political ramifications, leaving characters caught up in 'a vast contraption whose existence depended on

Figure 2 The hard-boiled investigator: Pocket Books 1943 edition of Dashiell Hammett's *The Glass Key*

the co-ordination of all the other cogs' (113). One of his stories was adapted as a film, *The Bribe* (Robert Z. Leonard, 1949), which contains enough noir elements (pervasive corruption, a sense of defeat and betrayal) to bring it within canonical *film noir*.[7] His 'Tough Dick' Donohue can be counted as one of the main successors to Hammett's Op: a man who 'had seen crime in its many strata',[8] Donohue is the protagonist in a series of violent and cynical stories published in *Black Mask* in the early thirties. In many of Nebel's stories, however, especially those using the series characters of MacBride and Kennedy, his light-hearted prose carries him towards a more thoroughly comic world of knockabout antics and whimsical humour. Humour (the wisecrack in particular) is a basic ingredient of much hard-boiled writing, but when the dominant tone becomes genially comic the effect tends to be protective and reassuring. Kennedy, ace reporter and falling-down drunk, reels through more than 30 droll *Black Mask* tales in which he alternately aids, annoys and is propped up by Captain John MacBride and his fellow policemen: 'The reason I'm holding him up, Cap, is that the souse can't stand. He fell out of a taxi, fell over the curb and started crawling up the path . . .'.[9] The same combination of pulp heroics and a jaunty, humorous tone is to be found in Nebel's later Cardigan stories, published in *Dime Detective*, one of *Black Mask*'s most important rival magazines, which first appeared in November 1931. 'Kick Back' (April 1934), for example, begins with a grey-coated gunman disarmed after he slips on a banana peel and ends in an exchange of light comic banter, with the good guys 'bickering all the time, like a couple of kids'.[10]

Another of the early *Black Mask* writers whose work shifts between different hard-boiled tones is Carroll John Daly, Hammett's most important co-contributor and at first the more popular of the two.[11] His stories are crudely written and, for the most part, are not notably akin to noir. They do, however, break sharply from traditional detective fiction in being more violent and urban and in establishing a partial prototype of the hard-boiled investigator.[12] Daly's December 1922 story, 'The False Burton Combs', is often taken to be the first of *Black Mask*'s hard-boiled stories. It contains, like most Daly stories, little by way of serious social criticism, partly because what is represented is the intrusion of a gang into an orderly community, rather than (as, say, in Hammett) a whole community that is corrupt. But 'The False Burton Combs' does offer its share of cynical one-liners – as when the narrator observes that 'There ain't nothing in government unless you're a politician. And as I said before, I ain't no crook.'[13] Also, though he is an 'adventurer' rather than a detective, the narrator uncovers wrongdoing from a position that he locates between the crook and the policeman. It is this 'middleman' position that is most obviously related to the development of hard-boiled detection. Daly's investigative figure, the nameless first-person narrator, is both morally ambivalent and dangerously implicated. Guilty and vulnerable, he occupies, at different stages of the story, the three roles kept carefully separate in most classic detective fiction, that is, victim, murderer and detective. He is paid to impersonate a potential victim (the 'false' Burton Combs). Although he is wrongly accused of being a professional killer, he believes that it is 'good ethics' to shoot a man down after he has been duly warned (if 'you happen to have my code of morals'[14]). By the end of the story, however, his public image has been transformed from that of 'desperate criminal' to heroic detective, credited with the confident agency of the traditional heroic protagonist. When the narrator tells the reader, '"I guess I'll take that job – if it pays enough to get married on,"'[15] it is clear that the story has been resolved by an optimistic and romantic conclusion which henceforth disqualifies the hero from the role of the lone investigator.

In Daly's writing, rather than the light-hearted, resilient humour that characterises Nebel's stories, it is all-conquering, two-fisted action that distances his protagonist from the corrupt world he enters. His first series character and his most famous creation, Race Williams, can be regarded as 'the true progenitor of the American private eye'.[16] Well armed and well paid for fearlessly tackling brutal gangsters and master criminals, Race dispenses rough justice when the situation seems to call for it: '"Call it murder if you like – a disregard for human life. I don't care. I'll run my business – you run yours."'[17] The Race Williams stories (over 30, published in *Black Mask* between 1923 and 1934) occasionally probe sources of socio-political corruption, but the boastful exploits and rugged individualism of the hero closely connect him to such traditional action heroes as the frontiersmen and gunfighters of the American West.[18] For Race Williams, being situated between cops and crooks mainly implies a willingness to resort to violent means and to proceed without formal legal sanction. His violence of response in part functions as a critique of violence in society, and as means of bringing to light hidden corruptions (in such a society, the implication is, only violent means are effective). But, like the earlier American dime novel heroes, Race acts out fantasies of revenge against popular scapegoats, like foreign master criminals. Excessive evil is routinely vanquished, as in the Race Williams novel *The Snarl of the Beast* (1928),[19] which ends with the dispatching of 'the Beast', a 'notorious English criminal' with 'flaming eyes' and 'great hairy hands' (49 and 280).

From the point of view of literary noir, the more interesting Daly series character, appearing in *Detective Fiction Weekly* from the early 1930s,[20] is Satan Hall, a policeman, but one whose methods isolate him within the force in much the same way that the private eye is isolated. Published at the height of the public obsession with gang warfare and city corruption, the Satan Hall series aims for a degree of verisimilitude in its social and political references. At the same time, though, the stories contain strong elements of ironic inversion and satiric fantasy. In contrast to the Race Williams stories, the nature of the crimes portrayed has shifted towards contemporary relevance and the investigative figure is pushed much further towards moral ambivalence. Instead of concentrating on devious criminal masterminds and foreign villains, Daly focuses on the corruption of local politics. Society is shown to be at war because the forces of destabilisation and threat are within. In *Satan Sees Red* (1932), for example, 'the system' and 'the racket' are treated as synonymous, and the cause of both is said by the world-weary captain to lie in 'crooked politics, stupid laws and human nature' (40). Bowers, a big racketeer closely involved in the political life of the city, is in origin just a local 'gangster and gunman' hunting his enemies in the 'dark alleys'. The description of the grotesquely caricatured Daggett, in *Satan Laughed* (1934), epitomises the way in which Daly represents the relationship between city political power and organised crime: the ironised 'great man' has 'worked his way into control. Gangster, racketeer, politician. Now a power behind the throne; the throne of evil that dominates all too often in many large cities' (220–1).

Satan Hall, as his name suggests, is also a larger-than-life figure. All of the details of his appearance and manner associate him with his evil namesake, from the sinister curves of his thin lips to his hot breath and a 'steady tread' – the 'Footsteps of Doom' – associated with the inexorable fate that awaits malefactors (*Adventures of Satan Hall*, 16, 31). His character, in contrast to that of more ordinary detectives, is defined in terms not of duty but of passion and obsession, the embodiment of a barely contained 'pent-up force' capable of sweeping away the corrupt (52). Daly plays sardonically with the metaphoric possibilities of 'Satan' Hall, the fallen angel who is without the blessing of those who sit in judgement, as the only effective opponent of 'the infernal system' (14), the 'lower city' controlled by Bowers and his kind. The predecessor of later avengers like Mike Hammer and Dirty Harry, Satan has to go into the dark doorways and dismal streets, keeping 'close to the gutter' and dispensing his own form of justice: it might be murder in the eyes of the state law but not in the light of 'The criminal's law. Satan's law' (92–3).

In spite of Daly's greater renown at the time, it is, of course, Dashiell Hammett whose reputation has survived and who has much the stronger claim to be seen as the progenitor of literary noir. In 1923, eight years before Daly's creation of Satan Hall, Hammett introduced in *Black Mask* a protagonist, the Continental Op, who was a much more plausible inhabitant of the territory 'close to the gutter'. The Op was followed in 1929 by Sam Spade and in the next year by Ned Beaumont, an investigative figure who is himself the associate of racketeers and corrupt politicians. Hammett's immense influence is due in part to his superior ability in creating a distinctive voice, a true 'hard-boiled' style that is in itself an implicit rejection of bourgeois hypocrisy and conventional values. His spare, unembellished prose is appropriate to his no-nonsense protagonists. Hammett is often praised as a realist, and unquestionably part of his superiority to a writer like Daly lies in his greater verisimilitude. His flawed, vulnerable narrators and his hard, direct representation of contemporary material give him an ability to lay bare the 'heart, soul, skin and guts' of a corrupt town (*Red Harvest*, 12). As a phrase like this suggests, Hammett does share something of Daly's fondness for mythologising,[21] though not for the kind of insistent patterning that characterises the Satan Hall stories. What really distinguishes Hammett from Daly, however, are the qualities which have led critics to label him a modernist and which also identify him as a more obviously noir writer: his development of more sophisticated ironies, his ambiguity and complexity, his disruption of reliable narrative and of binary oppositions between good and evil, order and disorder. The ambivalence of Hammett's stories is not produced (as it is in Daly's Satan Hall stories) just by playing with moral inversions but by injecting into his writing a thoroughgoing scepticism that affects themes, structure and narrative techniques.

In creating his most famous protagonist, Sam Spade, Hammett uses the image of a 'blond satan' (*Maltese Falcon*, 375) which may well, of course, have influenced Daly's creation of Satan Hall. Spade (like Satan) is the 'good guy' who is also capable of killing without much compunction, and the emphasis on his satanic appearance leads us to reflect from the outset on his 'wicked' side. In contrast to Daly, however, Hammett uses the image in passing, rather than as a means of shaping and colouring the whole story. The comparative subtlety of Hammett's narrative methods is evident in the fact that it is only in the final pages of *The Maltese Falcon* that we discover the full deviousness of Spade's character. It is only at this juncture that the reader realises not just that he was hired by the woman who murdered his partner but that he has been aware of her guilt from the beginning and has nevertheless made love to her and played along with her until the end. It is typical of Hammett that this crucial piece of information emerges without comment or explanation, so that it is readers themselves who must work out what has been revealed (that is, if Spade knows now he must have known all the time) and who must think through the implications for their assessment of Spade's character. Repeatedly in Hammett novels the protagonist's closest alliances turn out to be with those who are most guilty and who have most to conceal. In *Red Harvest*, the Op is working for the Willsson family, hired by the son of the man who is at the centre of the town's corruption and who himself hires the Op only when he is persuaded that his gangster associates mean to murder him as well. In *The Dain Curse* (1929), it turns out that the Op has been collaborating with the murderer, Fitzstephan, and it emerges that Ned Beaumont, in *The Glass Key* (1931), is working for Madvig, who in turn works for the murderer. Nick Charles, in *The Thin Man* (1934), is relying on the information of another friend and killer, Macaulay. All of these are connections that are hidden from the reader until the end.

What the reader is certain of from the first in Hammett's novels are his protagonists' imperfections, their human weaknesses and self-distrust. Fat and middle-aged, the Op often has to cope with things that undermine his strength and competence. In 'The Gutting of Couffignal' (*Black Mask*, 1924), for example, his loss of masculine effectiveness is imaged in his lameness – a defect for which he compensates by stealing a crutch from a cripple. More like Conrad's Marlow than Chandler's Marlowe, the Op has no higher motivation than dedication to his job. His work ethic makes him painstaking, patient and dogged. Tough when necessary, the Op never glorifies toughness: he admits that there is a certain attraction in brutality, but is self-doubting enough to be worried by this. There are arguably some 'knightly' qualities in the Op, particularly in *The Dain Curse*, in which his compassion for and rehabilitation of the mistreated damsel in distress (Gabrielle) is much more to the fore. But on the whole he is deliberately created as the antithesis of a knightly hero. In the 1927 *Black Mask* stories later published as *Blood Money*,[22] for example, he is situated between characters who represent opposing types of ally, the romantic boy, Jack Counihan, and the hardened criminal, Tom-Tom Carey, a contrast used to define the choices the Op himself has to make. The young operative Counihan, at first teased by the Op for his self-image of 'youthful gallantry' (382), must ultimately be condemned for the romantic vanity that leads him to think he can play the part of 'a desperate suave villain' (411), so betraying the Op, who goads him into a response that ensures his death. Carey, on the other hand, traffics in guns, booze, dope and illegal immigrants, and is capable of torturing information out of a man in a most grisly fashion ('ribbons of flesh had been cut loose' [387]). He is, however, a much less treacherous ally because honest about his greed and villainy. In *Red Harvest*, where the Op's own character is 'infected' with the poison of violence, he plays all factions against one another and abandons himself to the violent atmosphere in full awareness of the corruption of his own character and motives: 'It makes you sick, or you get to like it' (139). Ned Beaumont, in *The Glass Key*, lacks even the partial legitimation of the private eye, since he is merely the henchman of a prominent racketeer and politician. Beaumont is a gambler who is capable of being thoroughly unscrupulous, for example, of planting evidence; he is a man of dubious values and cloudy motives, telling harsh truths about some things and lying about others.

One of the essential characteristics of noir is a preoccupation with the problems of seeing and speaking the truth, evident in its exploration of new narrative forms and its tendency towards narrative fragmentation, subjectivity and unreliability. This tendency is fundamental to Hammett's novels. Instead of simply (as Daly and Nebel do) aiming to expose the falsity of public discourse and to bring out the hidden connections between the criminal and the official, Hammett creates narratives in which lying and deceit undermine and erode all human relations and all of the fictions sustained by respectable society. Like Conrad, Hammett depicts society as a network of secret agents, men and women concealing their true identities and past crimes, telling false stories that leave them entangled in a web of lies. Macaulay, one of the more accomplished deceivers in *The Thin Man*, only succeeds as well as he does because so many others are also dishonest, so acting as his unwitting accomplices. False narratives are not just the means by which the powerful establish their ascendancy, but are often the only way for victims to try to protect themselves and for the investigator-protagonists to gather information and survive. The duplicity is so pervasive that it appears to typify the whole nature of discourse in the modern world.

Hammett's involvement in leftist politics in the mid-thirties, a few years after he published his last novel, has led some critics to read back into his novels (particularly *Red Harvest*) a Marxist political agenda.[23]

The critique he develops is in many respects left-wing, for example in its hostility to the greed and exploitation he associates with unrestrained capitalism. The economic structure of capitalism appears, however, to be more an effect than a cause. Hammett expresses a pessimistic vision that is essentially political without being programmatic. In this he again resembles Conrad, conveying a sense of irremediable human flaws, abuses of power, inescapable violence and death, rather than a hope that changing the structure of society will bring a utopian transformation. The atmosphere of ubiquitous deceitfulness is such that moral chaos and betrayal seem the norm rather than the exception. Anarchic human appetites – sometimes sexual, but more often the lust for wealth or power – disorder all relationships from the most personal to the political and economic. In *Blood Money*, the title itself underlines the symbolic coupling of money and violence. Surreal confusion follows the gathering of 150 gangsters in San Francisco for an assault on The Seaman's National and The Golden Gate Trust, after which (with trust shattered) murderous greed seems to infect the houses of the city, filling them with death and betrayal: 'All the house held was fourteen dead men' (340); 'Larrouy's home was pregnant with weapons' (354). In *Maltese Falcon*, the initial pretence of a quest for the restoration of family harmony – 'Miss Wonderly's' search for a sister whose loss would kill 'Mama and Papa' (376–7) – is rapidly replaced by the real names and actual motivation, the quest for fabulous wealth. The all-devouring Gutman, whose history of the Falcon is a tale of the universal pursuit of riches, is the father-figure of a grotesque family group constituted by its lust for the Falcon. In seeking its possession Gutman will do anything, whether it is killing others or quite readily agreeing to the sacrifice of his surrogate son Wilmer.

In other novels, instead of creating treacherous criminal confederacies as analogues for the unchecked materialism of the larger society, Hammett devises narratives in which those who are most apparently respectable maintain their position in conventional society. They do so by creating intricate lies to conceal their exploitation of everyone associated with them, so revealing their readiness, like Gutman, to betray those closest to them. All bonds of trust disintegrate, making orderly, sustaining social relationships impossible. Whether it is in the tortured relationships of *The Dain Curse* or the broken families of *The Thin Man*, family members in Hammett novels routinely damage one another. Men of power safeguard their careers by sacrificing their children: Senator Henry, in *The Glass Key*, betrays his daughter by using her attractions to secure the support of Paul Madvig, and, having killed his own son, shows himself willing to kill Madvig so that he would carry the blame for the earlier crime. Children cannot conceive of the perfidy of their fathers. In *Red Harvest* an idealistic son begins a newspaper campaign against the corruption of Personville, unaware of how deeply involved his own father is in these crimes. None of these are problems that seem susceptible of a solution. The powers of destruction are too entrenched. If the end of the novel appears to bring resolution, it is a brief point of equilibrium after which things will return to the same sort of conflicts which set the plot in motion. At the end of *Red Harvest*, when the Op leaves Personville after a frenzy of cleansing and retribution, he has merely given the town back into the same hands as before. Personville is 'all nice and clean and ready to go to the dogs again' (181), and the Op is under no illusion that he has achieved something of lasting value. Similarly, at the end of *The Glass Key*, as Ned Beaumont prepares to depart, he stares 'fixedly' through an open door, and we are left pondering the open question of whether Madvig stands any chance of 'cleaning house' and ultimately managing to 'get the city back' (783).

Instead of remediable political–economic ills, there is a sense of deep-seated moral disorder in the patterning of Hammett's novels, reinforced by symbolic suggestions of randomness, disorder and loss of control. So, for example, the town of Personville has an element of historical specificity. A mining town of about 40 000 people, it had a strike in 1921 that led to the influence of criminal elements. The resident criminals have helped to put down the strike but cannot be kept in check by Elihu Willsson, himself implicated in their corrupt methods. Hammett also, however, makes extensive use of the naming of the town, which is known by two names, both metaphoric. As 'Personville' it suggests a representative population and, in terms of the power structure, one man's presumption in taking over the whole town, making it in every respect his personal property ('Elihu Willsson was Personville'). The insidious nature of the corruption he presides over gives rise to the town's other name, 'Poisonville', with its suggestions of crookedness and violence spreading like a toxin through the body politic, not just in one small town but (given the representative nature of the name) through the whole of American society. Hammett's titles very often point towards a symbolic reading: the horrific violence of a 'red harvest'; the 'glass key'[24] that suggests a liminal passage into darker experience through a door which, once opened, cannot be locked again; the fetishised falcon which, valueless in itself, is invested with meaning by those who seek to possess it; the 'thin man' who symbolises man reduced to a financial resource, 'as thin as the paper in that cheque', alive only 'on paper', as an asset to those whose greed leads them to feed off him. Meanings are amplified by inset dreams and parables, hinting in one way or another at the dark truths that cannot be contained: the falling beam in the Flitcraft parable, which makes it seem as though someone has 'taken the lid off life'; the snakes that cannot be locked up again in the dream Janet Henry tells Ned Beaumont; the story of cannibalism in *The Thin Man*, which supports the wider theme of insatiable greed by describing in gruesome detail an isolated man's reversion to primitive impulses, to a savagery that cannot ultimately be concealed by his 'conflicting stories'.

Beautiful manners and flawless English

Hammett's most famous successor, Raymond Chandler, started writing for *Black Mask* in December 1933, shortly after Hammett published *The Thin Man*, his final novel. Aside from the tale of cannibalism, *The Thin Man* has a lightness of tone that has led critics to dissociate it from the body of his earlier work. This dissociation was strengthened by the series of 'Thin Man' films originating with the novel, in which the 'thin man' came to be identified as Nick Charles, so that the darker implications of Hammett's imagery of rapacity were forgotten. The work of Chandler is characterised by a much more consistent lightness of tone. Chandler combines witty detachment with an underlying sentimentality that is also there in some film adaptations, heightened, for example, in a romanticised adaptation like *The Big Sleep* (Howard Hawks, 1946). Hawks' film foregrounds the relationship between Marlowe and Vivian Sternwood which, like that between Nick and Nora Charles, seems capable of withstanding the threatening and corrupting forces of the noir underworld.[25]

Of other Hollywood adaptations of Chandler novels, the most 'canonically noir' is *Murder, My Sweet* (Edward Dmytryk, 1944), adapting *Farewell, My Lovely* (1940), and it is in a way this film that best suggests why Chandler is usually regarded as Hammett's heir.[26] The place of Hammett and Chandler within the *film noir* canon has led many critics to overemphasise the relationship between the two, and their names, of course, are routinely linked as creators of the private eye, with the image of Bogart playing both Spade and Marlowe acting as iconic confirmation of their union. The novels themselves, however, are very different in style, themes, narrative patterns and attitudes to action. There are unquestionably noir elements in Chandler's work, and these are accentuated in Dmytryk's film adaptation. Dmytryk underscores the 'quintessentially noir' role of the femme fatale and the immersion of a vulnerable protagonist in a world gone wrong, peopled by grotesque characters. He creates an atmosphere of paranoia, heavy with threat and violence. An 'uncompromising vision of corruption and decay' is intensified by surreal, expressionistic distortions.[27] *Murder, My Sweet* is, however, a film that destabilises Chandler's world, undercutting the comparative detachment and superiority that Marlowe preserves in the text through verbal wit. Limits to his masculine competence and insight are suggested, for example, by expressionist shooting, with its attendant sense of disorientation and vulnerability, as well as by Marlowe's symbolically bandaged eyes in the framing interrogation.

Wider social and political concerns of the sort voiced in Hammett's novels are sometimes more evident in the stories Chandler published between 1933 and 1939 than in his novels. 'Finger Man' (*Black Mask*, 1934), for example, an early story which Marlowe narrates, does little to develop the character of the private eye, focusing instead on the machinations of 'a big politico' who is willing to go to great lengths to 'fix' things in his territory.[28] Another short story, 'Guns at Cyrano's' (*Black Mask*, 1936), ultimately reveals the consequences of the unscrupulous behaviour of 'that thin cold guy', a corrupt state Senator.[29] And in 'Trouble is My Business' (*Dime Detective*, 1939) the real villain of the piece is old man Jeeter, who ruined people during the Depression 'all proper and legitimate, the way that kind of heel ruins people', driving them to suicide while never having 'lost a nickel himself'.[30] The crimes of power-hungry politicians, the clandestine alliances of government officials with gangsters and the criminality of 'legitimate business', often supported by brutally corrupt policemen, are preoccupations to be found in Chandler's novels as well, where such themes provide a public dimension to the narrative. Chandler has not, however, always convinced his readers of his serious commitment to exposing corruption in high places. Docherty, for example, argues that the 'big bosses' – the corrupt businessmen and political manipulators – are often perceived by Marlowe as 'presentable and decent', Chandler perhaps being more inclined to exculpate gangsters than to imply that all businessmen are really gangsters. It is certainly true that, in comparison to Hammett, the reader is not immersed in a sense of nightmarish urban corruption, and figures like Eddie Mars and Laird Brunette do remain 'civil' and 'presentable'. It might be said that the keyword here, though, is 'presentable'. A characteristic Chandler trope is the picture of a beguiling surface, of a scene that can remain 'presentable' even after we have returned from the subterranean horrors of finding the body in the lake. Part of the point about his smooth businessmen-gangsters is that they retain their façade of gentlemanly respectability, and having succeeded in this they do, in fact, go unpunished, because that is the nature of the society portrayed. Chandler depicts a world of 'respectability', but one should not underrate the disturbing elements lurking just out of sight. The suburban Dad that Marlowe conjures up in *The Little Sister* (1949) is sitting 'in front of a picture window', but it gives him no view of 'the big money, the sharp shooters, the percentage workers, the fast dollar boys . . .' (202–3). Even those who play down the socio-political dimension in Chandler's novels see in them a modernist sense of urban anomie and moral disintegration.

There are, however, several aspects of Chandler's work which muffle his critique of American society. Most important is his use of the same first-person narrator, which, combined with some recurrent features of style, means that his novels are considerably more homogeneous than those of Hammett. When Marlowe develops beyond the sketchily realised narrator of 'Finger Man', the fictional world created is always reliably mediated by the voice of a protagonist who unfailingly combines honourable conduct with penetrating judgement and self-mocking humour. Though Marlowe is caught up in plots of notorious complexity (and is significantly less in control than, say, the figure of the classic detective) he continues to provide the reassurance of a stable and trustworthy perspective. His detachment places him much closer to the masculine competence and 'rightness' of traditional detective fiction, and so moves him away from a noir sense of uncertainty.

The protective presence that Marlowe establishes is above all stylistic. The witty, ironic aloofness of his narrative acts to evaluate and to contain the moral disorder of the society he investigates. When Hammett's Op is shot in *Red Harvest*, he issues a declaration of war on Poisonville and on 'fat Noonan', the chief of police: '"Now it's my turn to run him ragged, and that's exactly what I'm going to do. Poisonville is ripe for harvest. It's a job I like, and I'm going to do it . . . I've got a mean disposition. Attempted assassinations make me mad"' (64). This mood of aggression, leading the Op to fight the corruption in Poisonville by means of violence and brutality, provides *Red Harvest* with the distinctively noir element of immersion in a world gone wrong. It is very unlike Marlowe's response to extreme provocation. Both Marlowe and the Op speak with a satirist's mocking insight, but Marlowe's insights are not the savage ironies of the Op. Instead, his habitual form of self-defence is teasing, elegantly phrased and ironically guarded. In *Farewell, My Lovely*, for example, when Marlowe tries to make Anne Riordan see the rottenness of Bay City, he says, '"Sure, it's a nice town. It's probably no crookeder than Los Angeles. But you can only buy a piece of a big city. You can buy a town this size all complete, with the original box and tissue paper. That's the difference. And that makes me want out"' (295). The effects of this quip are characteristically double. Marlowe is urging Anne (and the reader) to see the realities of local corruption, and his irony underscores his fastidious taste and the weary cynicism of his disillusioned gaze. The sarcastic use of 'nice' (a recurrent feature of Marlowe's style) and the reductive image of the whole town gift-wrapped combine to satirise the deceptiveness of decent appearances and the ease with which powerful coalitions can buy and sell influence. The satirical diminishment and the arch manner also, however, provide a distancing humour, removing both Marlowe and his audience from the brutal scene just experienced and making it clear why he 'wants out'. Indeed, even when he is being physically coerced, Marlowe's self-ironising manner simultaneously acknowledges his limitations and draws attention to his separateness: '"Don't make me get tough," I whined. "Don't make me lose my beautiful manners and my flawless English"' (*Farewell, My Lovely*, 289). Marlowe's superiority to his environment is not, though he is resilient, a matter of physical prowess but of a subtle intellect that can manage a self-deprecating joke even when he has been sapped and imprisoned and 'shot full of dope and locked in a barred room' (288). Unlike the Op, Marlowe would never 'go blood-simple'. What we most remember in Chandler's novels is not the narrator losing himself in a violent, crowded scene but the wry voice of the satirist, scathing, defensive or appalled, but ultimately disengaged.

The high degree of stylistic control, it has been argued, goes with an 'authoritarian romantic core'.[31] It can be seen as reflecting the bourgeois individualist's distaste for and essential separation from the sordid world he investigates. As critics have often observed, when Marlowe does enter into conflict with the depraved society around him, his preferred role is that of the questing knight. This sentimentalised figure engages in encounters that simultaneously propel him on and test his skill in arms, challenging his fearlessness and integrity and leading him to a more sophisticated understanding of his moral make-up. Marlowe's knightly qualities are everywhere apparent, from the history of his naming ('Mallory' in the early *Black Mask* story, 'Blackmailers Don't Shoot', with 'Marlowe' as its 'coded version') to Chandler's own description of the man of honour, 'good enough for any world', who must go down 'these mean streets'.[32] When Marlowe contemplates the stained-glass window in the Sternwood house, he reflects that the knight rescuing the lady looks so ineffectual 'that if I lived in the house, I would sooner or later have to climb up there and help him' (3). Chandler is seen as promoting the positive side of the 'Great Wrong Place' myth, the American dream of the 'last just man' whose alienation is the guarantee of his integrity. In addition, however, his idealised representation of the private eye has led many to psychoanalyse the 'real' nature of both Marlowe and his creator and to search for unintentional revelations of Marlowe/Chandler's own obsessions and neuroses. One might in fact argue that it is this inadvertent revelation of inner weaknesses that has been most responsible for making adaptations of Chandler's work of such interest to critics of the classic *film noir* cycle. Marlowe's isolated knightly superiority can be interpreted as a hedge against his own neurotic unease. His inner-directed, intellectualising defensiveness in such a reading acts as a compensation for paranoid fear and inadequacy.[33] *Murder, My Sweet*, in particular, with Dmytryk's expressionistic suggestions of paranoia, its strongly subjective flashback structure and its shadowed, dreamlike distortions of perception, can be taken to reveal personal aversion and crisis – noir sexual anxiety, the destabilising of masculine authority and the placing of the protagonist in a situation of impairment and powerlessness. The romantically admirable knight, then, can be read as an ideal of mastery generated by a tortured self whose fears of losing control are projected, for example, in the fascinated disgust he expresses for effeminate men like Marriott, Lavery and Geiger.[34]

Marlowe's neurotic alienation, his fears about loss of agency, about violations of self and fragmenting identity are expressions of characteristically modernist anxieties. In comparison to Hammett's modernism, however, Chandler's involves shifting the focus of his thrillers away from wider socio-political disorder and corruption, and towards terrors that are more inward. His novels bring together the public and the personal: the crimes of crooked policemen, businessmen and politicians provide an outer structure within which more private crimes are enacted. Part of Chandler's point is that these personal wrongs are inextricably related to the larger controlling forces at work in early twentieth-century society: as Marlowe says in *The Big Sleep*, 'it all ties together' (158–9). But it is equally evident that the intrusive forces of urban criminality function more as background than as foreground. The kinds of intrusion Marlowe himself seems to find most disturbing and repellent are those that surface in personal relationships, particularly those which threaten bodily violation, as encounters with sexually attractive, dynamic women do. Chandler is one of the few writers of this period to make substantial use of the figure of the femme fatale – in fact, to habitually place the femme fatale at the centre of his plots. Critics often take this to be an individual neurotic response to the sexy manipulative woman. Women are always associated with 'the nastiness' of which Marlowe fears he has become part, and against which he protects himself both with humour ('"I'm the guy that keeps finding you without any clothes on"'; 'It wasn't a game for knights') and, at times, with astonishing ferocity: 'I put my empty glass down and tore the bed to pieces savagely' (*Big Sleep*, 163–4 and 111–13).

'The hardest of the hard-boilers'[35]

Chandler often refers to Marlowe's marginality. It is part of his claim to integrity that, for no more than 'twenty-five dollars a day and expenses', he is willing to risk getting himself 'in Dutch with half the law enforcement of this country' (*Big Sleep*, 81). But however at odds he is with 'law-abiding society', Marlowe does not occupy any position outside the law other than that of lowly independence. Unlike many another 'loogan' ('a guy with a gun'), though he may sit on the fence, he never falls on to the wrong side of it (*Big Sleep*, 105). Chandler did allow one or two protagonists who were more tarnished than Marlowe,[36] but on the whole his chosen perspective is poor but ostentatiously honest. Amongst Chandler's fellow *Black Mask* writers, on the other hand, there were some who gave much more scope to morally ambiguous protagonists, to men whose position 'outside the law' gave them an angle of vision very different from that of the essentially pure Marlowe. Like Daly's Satan Hall and Hammett's Ned Beaumont, such figures are characteristic of the early thirties – of a time, that is, when the gangster (both real and imagined) had become one of the most easily recognisable emblems of the changes afflicting urban America. One of the significant developments in the *Black Mask* writing of this period is the creation of investigative figures who are more clearly tainted by the corrupt milieux they are investigating. In terms of respectable society, they are marginalised by their criminal connections rather than by their shabby integrity. Corruption is judged, but there is no secure position within the text constituting a moral high ground.

Two of the most notable *Black Mask* contemporaries of Chandler, Paul Cain and Raoul Whitfield,[37] both moved their investigative figures nearer to criminality, emulating the 'tougher' strains in Hammett's writing, particularly in *Red Harvest* and *The Glass Key*. Their protagonists fulfil the functions of the private eye and are not altogether without scruple. But they are exposing the underside of a society from which they cannot themselves be dissociated. Whitfield, who wrote nearly a hundred stories (of varying quality) for *Black Mask* between 1926 and 1930, published (starting in December 1929) 'The Crime Breeders', a story sequence reissued in 1930 as a novel called *Green Ice*. The narrator, Mal Ourney, is an ex-con. As in Hammett's *Woman in the Dark* (1933), in which the protagonist, Brazil, has just been released from prison, the status of the ex-con creates a dubious kind of freedom. He is a character technically free but unable to dissociate himself from the way in which society has defined him. Unlike the private eye, who is often said to be a man without a past, the ex-con has a past that is of determining importance. Ourney, like Brazil, is not a true criminal, having gone to jail because he has taken the blame for a death caused by the driving of his drunken girlfriend, but neither is he blameless ('She'd been drinking my liquor'). He is, in relation to real killers, an outsider, that is, 'not a crook' in comparison to those 'inside' the criminal fraternity. On the other hand, much more like the Op or Ned Beaumont than Marlowe, he has criminal connections and risks becoming a crook by using unscrupulous methods. For example, he taunts and psychologically torments a hospitalised criminal in order to get a name out of him: 'It wasn't easy to do – not with the woman-faced fence dying on the bed' (142–3).

Mal Ourney sees himself as a crusader, but of rather a rough and pragmatic kind. Crimes are interpreted and judged from the perspective of the aggrieved underdog rather than from the moral vantage point of the knight errant. Whitfield shared what was, in the Depression years, a common conviction that the source of many social ills lay in the exploitation of the small and weak by the large and greedy. The object of Ourney's crusade is to bring down some of the big crooks who are 'the breeders – the few who rope in the dumb ones, the weak ones' (*Green Ice*, 31). He generalises his objectives to include exposure of all those who use others, making explicit the 'greed and exploitation' theme that lies behind much of the writing of this period: 'I got the idea that just a few humans were using a lot of other humans as they wanted, then framing them, smashing them . . . I'd like to smash some of the ones who use the others up' (65). A cynical and not overly optimistic friend of the underdog, Whitfield's protagonist identifies with the small crooks, the human debris that is presented as the cost of profit-making on the part of the criminally rich and unscrupulous:

'It's a dirty street all the way, but some of the debris is important – to me' (29).

What *Green Ice* shares with Hammett's fiction is a narrative movement that draws the protagonist ever deeper into a densely crowded scene of corruption. As the earlier title, 'Crime Breeders', implies, there is a proliferation of the forces of corruption. In contrast to Chandler, who confessed that a 'crowded canvas' bewildered him,[38] Whitfield used the frenetic, apparently disconnected movements of his large cast of characters to express the nature of a society in which deceit and betrayal, framing and double-crossing, are the norm. The intricacy of the connections in itself suggests the web of urban corruption and the intractable difficulty of knowing the truth: 'I spent most of the time trying to separate lies from truths. After a while I gave it up' (159). The movement associated with Ourney is 'blundering' (133), and the confusion of his quest is underscored by the image of 'green ice', the emeralds that everyone is after. Fetishised by those who greedily compete for them, they are in reality cold and deadly. The pursuit is ultimately of death itself, of stones that are 'perfectly cut. Something like a coffin' (179). The trope of the emeralds as coffin/death is an irony compounded by the fact that the 'five big ones' are, like the falcon in Hammett's novel, fake – intrinsically worthless symbols of the fabulous wealth that motivates treachery in remote places and an endless chain of betrayals. This 'unending' quality is one of the most noir aspects of the novel. The climax of the plot is a shoot-out at a funeral, which is again heavy with the sort of irony that attaches to the theme of wealth and death. Gunmen rise out of the flowers and kill for emeralds that are 'fused glass. . . . Cold as – death' (191). In the end, Ourney thinks back over the list of the dead and acknowledges that he has only stopped two of the 'crime breeders'. As the 'New York dick' says, '"You didn't do so damned much reforming, Ourney"' (191).

The stories of Paul Cain are similarly grim and downbeat, centring on morally dubious protagonists who are closely involved with the corruption they investigate. Cain, whose real name was George Sims, started writing for *Black Mask* a year before Chandler's first story appeared. William F. Nolan dubbed him 'the hardest of the hard-boilers'. The effectiveness of his stories, however, is due to more than just their sheer toughness. What is most unsettling is the use Cain makes of morally equivocal perspectives to disorient the reader. This is reinforced by his use of delayed recognition. Cain often suppresses, for example, the identity of the narrator and his relationship to the violent scene he is investigating, which, when ultimately revealed, is invariably compromised. The protagonist is never just a detached investigator. Through first- or close third-person narration, Cain provides fragmented descriptions of violent scenes, encounters with both criminals and corpses that are made strange by a focus on what at first seem to be disconnected details or disconnected body parts. In 'Black', for example, we first witness three apparently unrelated people: a dying man, the narrator and a cabby. These men seem to have been thrown together by chance but are, we eventually learn, all players in the same violent and complicated set of rivalries. The way that the reader and the protagonist find out information is fragmentary and apparently haphazard: the narrator looks through a small window, with the rain drumming, hearing the conversation inside as a buzz that does not mean anything. As in Hammett, the corrupt interests controlling a small town are a microcosmic version of big city corruption, and, like the Op, the narrator controls the unravelling of guilt and stage-manages punishment. In contrast to the Op, however, this narrator is not employed as an investigator but as a hired gun, sent by his boss to seek revenge. His function, as he moves silently through the small town, is to bring together those who are corruptly and secretly connected. Having offered to work for each of the rival factions, the narrator forcibly brings the parties in the dispute together and then ironically proposes that he accept money from both and kill them both: '"I'm auctioning off the best little town in the state . . ." . . . I was having a swell time' (11–12). As elsewhere, the hallmarks of Cain's writing are black humour and a laconic manner, the stylistic equivalent of the narrator's blunt vision and methods.

Images of showmanship and game-playing dominate Cain's stories, with the implication that success and indeed survival in such a world are entirely dependent on luck, cunning and an ability to manipulate appearances, though Cain avoids suggesting that a tough masculinity and aggressive individualism will invariably prevail. In 'Murder in Blue', for example, the protagonist, Doolin, is a young man retained as a bizarre kind of showman to organise a violent entertainment for a dying villain. He orchestrates assorted killers to perform in his show with the same element of playing both ends against the middle as in 'Black'. His plans as a showman, however, are made in ignorance of secret connections, and he finds himself an unwilling actor in a grotesque, dehumanised final scene of violence. This denouement is presented to us as Doolin sees it, like strips of motion picture film, with surreal laughter and automaton-like characters killing and dying. Doolin himself only fortuitously survives to tell the tale. Cain develops in an extreme form the undermining of trust that is a recurrent feature of the thrillers of this period. The ironies of his stories spring from a widespread tendency to trust the wrong people, or to distrust 'everybody except the guy who was holding the knife' (181). Characters often make errors of this sort, and there is *always* someone with a knife. Paranoia is on the whole structural rather than clinical: if someone has come to the view that everyone was trying to double-cross them, then 'Everybody probably was' (184–5). As readers, we cannot even feel sure that the narrator is trustworthy, since he is as likely as any other character to be guilty. In 'Parlor Trick', for example, we appear at first to be reading another narrative describing the entry of the narrator-protagonist into what we suppose is an alien and threatening environment. We share what we think is his shock at seeing Frank with 'a thin knife-handle sticking out of one side of his throat' (52). The first twist in the story comes with the revelation that the narrator himself has put the thin knife in Frank's throat; the second reversal occurs when he has resigned himself to being taken away for execution by 'the boys' but finds that the gun is turned instead on one of his supposed executioners: 'Frank's number has been up for a long time' and McNulty was 'in it with him' (61). Cain thus turns what at first looks like an investigative structure into the narrative of a criminal.

This transformation of the protagonist into the criminal is much more than an isolated narrative trick for creating suspense and surprise. In September 1930, *Black Mask*'s editor, Joseph T. Shaw, argued, in defence of his magazine, that *Black Mask* had published only one story, the serialised parts of Hammett's *The Glass Key*, in which 'the gangster was in any sense "the hero"' and this, he said, was justified as a representation of the alliance between corrupt politicians, public officials and organised crime. It was a demonstration of 'one of the most serious illnesses, to put it mildly, that our body politic has ever suffered from'.[39] During the course of the thirties, however, in *Black Mask* and elsewhere, the use of criminal protagonists and very often the abandonment of an investigative structure became increasingly common in narratives of both private and public crimes. The next chapter looks at the stories of the very public careers of gangsters. In these narratives, the tensions apparent in Paul Cain's 'Parlor Trick' are often central, with the business rivalries of powerful gang bosses and the powerlessness of the small-time crook epitomising the imbalance and 'illness' of Depression America.

2
Big-shot Gangsters and Small-time Crooks

Roy Earle, a gangster on the run in W. R. Burnett's *High Sierra* (1940), throws his newspaper down in disgust and launches into an indignant tirade against society's injustices. He assails a system that defines and severely punishes John Dillinger as a criminal but does little to deter the corrupt policeman, the banker who loses the depositors' money in the stock market, the judge who takes bribes to fix cases, the preacher who gyps his congregation, or the big-shot official who sells jobs. 'Why do people stand it?' Earle demands. 'A few guys have got all the dough in this country. Millions of people ain't got enough to eat. Not because there ain't no food, but because they got no money. Somebody else has got it all' (150–1). Even when their criminal protagonists do not voice such forthright criticisms, the gangster-centred novels of the time are implicitly concerned with the issues raised by Roy Earle (himself a character whom Burnett based on Dillinger).[1] Gangster novels repeatedly depict the cripplingly hierarchical nature of society, with its divisions between the haves and the have-nots, and draw attention to the similarity between apparently respectable businessmen and those whom society defines as criminals. The mythologised gangster can only be understood in relation to the wider society, whether he is cast as a villain whose actions confirm the need for law and order or as an outlaw hero admired for the toughness and energy with which he defies the system.

The popular appeal of the American gangster figure during the thirties was divided. Cinema audiences experienced the double satisfaction of vicarious participation in gangster violence and of seeing violence turned against the gangster himself. This enabled them, on the one hand, to identify with criminal rebellion against a corrupt, hypocritical society, and, on the other, to enjoy revenge fantasies against criminals who could be cast as 'the root of evil'. The Hollywood gangster story was conventionally placed in a retributive frame,[2] and the negative side of the gangster myth could be seen as the reinforcement of a belief in the 'public enemy'[3] as an explanation of the collapse of morality, discipline and order in American society. This villainising of the gangster is most apparent post-1935, when a 'war against crime' was waged in vigilante and G-Men movies exempt (because of their law-and-order bias) from the anti-violence provisions of the Hays Office production code that had, by 1934, 'all but outlawed the gangster movie'.[4] A moralising frame is also sometimes to be seen in the crime novels of the time, but it is more usual to find complex portrayals of gangsters who are typed as representative rather than aberrant. From the late twenties on, fictional American gangsters are no longer the crudely vilified 'defectives' and physical monsters to be found in earlier representations (for example, in the films of Lon Chaney or in early 1920s cartoons of grotesque, diminutive criminals skulking like creatures apart). Nor are they drawn as the kind of psychopathic gangster later epitomised by Ralph Cotter in Horace McCoy's *Kiss Tomorrow Goodbye* (1948), played by James Cagney as an unbalanced sadist in the 1950 film adaptation.[5] The prewar British thrillers discussed in the final section of this chapter associated gangsterism with fascism, and accordingly tended to type the violent gangster as a dehumanised psychopath. American gangsters of the period, however, are instead characterised by their normality: 'Criminals thought, looked, and, for the most part, even acted like respectable Americans. The *Saturday Evening Post* suggested the ordinariness of one criminal in the pseudonym it assigned him: John Doe.'[6]

If the criminal is seen as essentially normal, then fictionalisations of his career can act as wide-ranging critiques of American society and economic structures. A high-profile gangster, like any man trying to live out a public identity, poses the question of what drives such a man to succeed and what qualities ultimately undermine his power. A struggling, unsuccessful gangster is only another of the innumerable small men who are put under pressure by (and have their characters determined by) hostile forces, whether bigger businessmen-gangsters or the political establishment, or the two in league together. Sharing so much common ground with respectable, law-abiding citizens but at the same time functioning outside the law, the gangster serves both as a figure admirable for his toughness and energy, defying an unjust system, and, looked at from another angle, as a parallel in his activities to the criminality of supposedly honest society. He both collides with and replicates this society's legitimate structures. As the protagonist says in Benjamin Appel's *Brain Guy* (1934), having lost his job in the Depression he has gone into crime 'like a business man': 'It's nothing. The world's full of crooks, but some are called millionaires' (157–8).

Many types of criminal, from the urban ethnic gangster to the poor farm boy who has drifted into crime, acquire, in the Depression, cross-class and cross-ethnic appeal.[7] Both types become symbols of a rebellion impossible for ordinary law-abiding citizens to enact. The heroic rebel image was reinforced by the Hollywood versions of the myth, featuring performances of great verve and energy. Movie gangsters such as Cagney and Edward G. Robinson were heroes 'of dynamic gesture', strutting, snarling and posturing, possessing a blatant, anarchic appeal. Standing outside the law in a period when Depression America was cynical about all sources of moral authority, they were 'awe-inspiring . . . grand, even in death'.[8] At the same time, however, they were a reflection of legitimate society. The criminal big shot, viewed in the distorting mirror of the satirist, is a parody of the American dream of success, ironising the business ethic by the illegality of his methods as well as by his ultimate defeat. The fallen gangster or the small-time crook (really just an average man trying to avoid ruin) figures the failures of laissez-faire capitalism during years of great economic hardship. The inevitable fall of the big-time gangster creates a sense of entrapment in an economically determined reality. He is the victim of a society in which everyone is corrupt: they are all 'thieves like us'. The foundering criminal, like the law-abiding no-hoper, is the product of a faulty economic system. As Burnett wrote, 'if you have this type of society, it will produce such men'.[9] In looking at American examples of the criminal-centred narratives written in the years between 1929 and the outbreak of World War Two what we see is a range of strategies for challenging, mimicking and reproaching a society that has ceased to operate in a legitimate way, in which, as Roy Earle says, 'somebody else has got it all'.

It is usual for film criticism to distinguish the classic gangster film from *film noir*. Silver and Ward argue that there are fundamental differences in narrative attitude. They see the glorification of the gangster in early, Prohibition-era films such as *The Underworld* (von Sternberg, 1927) and *The Racket* (Lewis Milestone, 1928) as still present in the 'demented idealism' and egomania of Rico in *Little Caesar* (Mervyn LeRoy, 1930) and Tommy Powers in *Public Enemy* (1931). This romanticising is evident as well in the emphasis on action and the flamboyant nature of the violence, with its staccato rhythms and blazing machine-guns. Silver and Ward do concede, however, that gangster films and *films noirs* also share iconic and narrative characteristics, and that they can both be viewed as part of a larger, 'underworld film' phenomenon, with slightly later gangster films like *Scarface* (Howard Hawks, 1932) closer to the dark mood, the ironies and the sense of claustrophobic entrapment that characterise noir.[10] Other recent critics have argued persuasively against seeing any sharp disjuncture. Most notably, Jonathan Munby, in *Public Enemies, Public Heroes*, presents a strong case for viewing *film noir* as a development of a 'repressed but established formula'. Noir, in this interpretation, is an infusion of modernist stylistic attributes which enabled the earlier, 'potentially seditious' crime cycle to negotiate the censors.[11]

The connections between 'gangster' and 'noir' thrillers are even more apparent in fiction than film. For one thing, the kind of periodisation familiar in film cycles does not operate in fiction to nearly the same extent. There is also a quite different chronological relationship between gangster novels and other types of crime story than there is between gangster films and canonical *film noir*. Whereas, in looking at Hollywood films, we see a cycle of 1930s gangster films followed by the classic cycle of *films noirs* that starts in the 1940s, there is no such divide in the fiction of these decades. Several of the texts that formed the basis of classic *film noir* (for example, Hammett's *Maltese Falcon*; James M. Cain's *The Postman Always Rings Twice*) were written during the same period (1929–34) that saw the production of the most famous gangster films and the creation of such seminal gangster novels as Burnett's *Little Caesar* (1929), Armitage Trail's *Scarface* (1930) and Paul Cain's *Fast One* (1932). Most of Chandler's better-known novels, the other major novels of James M. Cain and the early novels of Cornell Woolrich date from the period (1939–44) when Burnett wrote *High Sierra* (1940) and *Nobody Lives Forever* (1943). In looking at literary noir what one sees is the simultaneous development of investigative and criminal-centred thrillers, with many common features and with modernist traits (for example, subjective narration, the expression of existentialist anxiety and a sense of claustrophobic entrapment) as evident in gangster novels as they are in those narratives that became the basis for classic *films noirs*.

What is distinctive about the criminal-centred narratives discussed in this chapter is that the perspective is located within organised crime. In contrast to novels whose protagonists are 'private' criminals, the solitary transgressors caught up in very personal tragedies who are the subject of Chapter 3, these are stories involving some form of organised crime, or at least involving more than one criminal, engaged in a structured criminal enterprise. They therefore tend to be directly concerned with economic competition, the exercise of power and the dominance of strong over weak interests. One of the features of ordinary criminal life most thoroughly explored by fictional accounts of gangsters is the development of elaborate hierarchies of authority.[12] Conventional society may try to consolidate its boundaries by defining and excluding the gangster, but its divisions and its strategies of exclusion are in fact reflected in a highly competitive underworld that has its own oppressors and oppressed. Within criminal-centred narratives, tensions are generated both by the gangster's conflict with the larger society and by the conflicts amongst the various levels of the criminal power structure, with different types of novel corresponding to the level the protagonist occupies in the hierarchy. Whereas an investigative figure like the Continental Op or Marlowe is primarily seen engaging in combat with the corrupt powers-that-be, criminal protagonists, both large and small, are competing within a well-defined pecking order. In investigative narratives, irony emerges from the contrast between appearance and the reality discovered in supposedly respectable society. The stories of gangster protagonists additionally ironise the gaps between seeming success and an inevitable fall, between aspiration and reality, and between apparent and real destiny – powerful sources of irony in Depression years, when the national sense of the discrepancy between dream and reality was at its greatest.

It is sometimes said that the gangster does not himself suffer from a hypocritical disjuncture between what he is and what he appears to be, and that this sets him apart from the more 'noirish' criminal protagonist. This is much too sweeping a generalisation, particularly given the historical movement of the gangster into legitimate business and political activity. The representation of this process in fiction often centres on the need for shifts in public image. Books like Paul Cain's *Fast One* (1932) and James M. Cain's *Love's Lovely Counterfeit* (1942) are much taken up with the need to suppress the publication of unwelcome truths about the gangsterism of those in power. Other crime novels of the period also concern themselves with the problem of public image, whether encountered in the process of establishing one's own image (for example, in *Little Caesar* and *Scarface*) or in coping with the publication of journalistic vilifications (as in *High Sierra* and *Thieves Like Us*). These are all novels that are in part *about* the self-publicising and the public interpretation of the gangster and about the nature of the myth-making. They explore the desire for legitimation and recognition on the part of the gangster. Such desires make the gangster vulnerable to the destabilisation of identity that afflicts the insecure, self-divided protagonist of canonical *film noir*, with the gangster often suffering from a splitting of identity that is evident, for example, in his doomed efforts to acquire the trappings of social success (flash cars, stylish suits) and to achieve upward mobility.[13]

Gutter Macbeths

Benjamin Appel, many of whose stories were published in non-genre magazines such as *Esquire* and *Colliers*, was one of crime writing's hardest-hitting social critics.[14] His condensed version of the rise of gangsterism, a 1935 short story ironically titled 'Movie of a Big Shot', concisely illustrates the way in which underworld activities could be used to image the injustices and vicissitudes of American economic life, with its illusions of upward mobility, its preoccupation with image-building and its hierarchy of exploiters and exploited. Appel's *Hell's Kitchen* stories of the late thirties[15] all centre on the downtrodden and dispossessed. Like Paul Cain's 'Parlor Trick', Appel's 'Movie' views the business rivalries of powerful gangsters from the vantage point of a criminal who is on one of the lower rungs of the organisation – not a Macbeth but one of the Murderers, priding himself on his fierceness. In just a few pages, Appel takes in the years from 1916 to the mid-1930s, creating a protagonist, Franky, who is the embodiment of dogged and naive aggression. He is the common man of crime, the sort of 'prize dope' with a head of 'solid bone' who would have been willing cannon-fodder in World War One – anxious to enlist but encouraged instead, in the parallel life of the underworld, to satisfy his patriotic aggression by beating up 'Dutchies' and Jews (85–7). Franky's potential is recognised by one of the eventual gangland bosses, who values him for his physical toughness and makes him part of a gang which is given 'a new lease on life' by Prohibition (89). Soon everybody 'wallowed in money'. Franky, however, with his strong-arm methods, is oblivious to the fortunes being made by the businessmen of the gang who control everything. He is 'the toughest guy in the world', but he is not 'the guy' (90–4). Ironically, despite all his physical strength, he is a victim, fancying himself admired by all in the role of a big shot but, with the approach of repeal, needed less and less in a society in which crime has established itself as 'business first, last and always' (95). Gangsters had already, before the Crash of 1929, been seen as businessmen, and in the years following the Crash they were portrayed as feeling the effects of economic adversity like any other capitalist enterprise: 'As a business, crime was subject to general economic forces.'[16] In these Depression years, the business of crime has to cut down on shaky assets like Franky. The story of the gangster struggling to consolidate his ill-gotten gains and to move into legitimate society is, as we have seen, a story of the desire 'to be somebody', and for Franky the fantasy of status achieved is so powerful that he never guesses that he is on the skids, 'practically nobody now' (97).

By taking a violent man too simple-minded to rise to anywhere near the top, Appel makes his 'Movie' an exercise in counter-mythologising. He presents the myth of the heroic gangster as a dream of success beyond the grasp of most ordinary men. If the gangster saga is, as has been argued, a version of the Horatio Alger myth, the career of a character like Franky suggests that in a time of economic catastrophe the old 'rags-to-riches' narratives should be revealed for the sham they are. By focusing on the delusions of a man who could never have been 'destined' for greatness, Appel is revising the myth behind such novels as Burnett's *Little Caesar* and Trail's *Scarface*, and the early thirties gangster films based on them. In these narratives, the eponymous heroes, just like their counterparts in respectable society, fulfil their destiny by showing themselves able to achieve upward mobility, becoming the apotheosis of a heroic and amoral capitalistic drive.

If the novels of W. R. Burnett were to be judged on the basis of their influence, he 'would undeniably be numbered amongst the most important writers of his time'.[17] Burnett saw himself as the writer most responsible for the shift towards depicting crime from the point of view of the criminal himself. *Little Caesar* was, he said, 'the world seen through the eyes of the gangster. It's commonplace now, but it had never been done before then. . . . The criminal was just some son-of-a-bitch who'd killed somebody and then you go get 'em.'[18] *Little Caesar* stands at the start of a period of fascination with the criminal's own perspective, not only in gangster narratives but in the other central noir roles of investigator (as in the work of Whitfield and Paul Cain) and victim (the destitute young outlaws of *Thieves Like Us* or the love triangle murderers of James M. Cain's novels). Written in 1929 and filmed in 1930, *Little Caesar* was the most influential of the gangster sagas. It was imitated in dozens of early thirties films and novels,[19] amongst them *Scarface* by Armitage Trail, who wanted Edward G. Robinson, star of *Little Caesar*, to play the role of Scarface in the film adaptation. Like Tony Guarino in the Trail novel, Burnett's Rico ('Little Caesar') is obsessed with scaling the heights of power. Burnett analyses at some length, as Trail does, the qualities that enabled his hero to rise. In comparison to Trail, however, Burnett gives closer attention to the flaws in his protagonist's character that bring about his downfall, a preoccupation which also distinguishes his novel from most gangster films. The dynamism caught on screen in the performances of Robinson, or Cagney in *Public Enemy*, is outweighed in a novel like *Little Caesar* by the flaws and insecurities that both motivate and finally bring down the gangster.

Burnett's gangsters are driven by a sense of social inferiority and, in the case of Little Caesar, by an overwhelming ambition that made him, in Burnett's eyes, akin to the heroes of tragedy, 'a gutter Macbeth'.[20] As the novel's title suggests, the central theme is the parallel between the gangster and the man of power. It is an analogy that works to ironise the 'great man' in a way which was to become, for European writers like Brecht and Greene, one of the more potent aspects of American gangland mythology. Rico is from the outset referred to as a 'great man', which raises (as it does, for example, in Henry Fielding's *Jonathan Wild*) the question of what actually constitutes political 'greatness' in the society being portrayed. In Burnett, in contrast both to European versions and to a purely satirical elaboration of the comparison, there is pathos in the conception of Rico. Burnett probes his aspirations and dreams. He lingers, for example, on Rico's reverie whilst reading the story of a rich society girl who seems 'remote and unreal to him' (44–5), and he conveys Rico's sense of wonderment at the way he is climbing the ladder.

Rico has the illusion that he cannot be stopped, but under the confident surface there is always a sense of isolation and despair. His meetings with 'bigger shots' invariably make him feel anxiously inadequate. Deliberately created as an unromantic figure, Rico is small, pale and quiet, in contrast to 'legendary' figures who were outwardly more impressive. Although in many respects Rico is the antithesis of the 'impaired' noir protagonist, Burnett's study dwells, sympathetically throughout, on the inner weaknesses that undermine his confident masculine authority, especially his 'dangerous' lapses of drive and energy (70–1, 84–5). Like many other noir protagonists, Rico associates his vulnerable states with women and their 'ability to relax a man, to make him soft and slack' (81–4). In spite of his role in organising and manipulating others, he is in key respects isolated. As he struggles to consolidate his power, Rico begins to weaken physically and to suffer increasingly from self-doubt: 'He was nobody, nobody. Worse than nobody' (132). Forced into exile, hiding out with men who do not know his true identity, Rico cannot bear his insignificance and suffers alienation as 'a lonely Youngstown yegg in a hostile city without friends or influence' (141). Like *Scarface*, *Little Caesar* moves towards an end in which irony derives from the contradictions within the protagonist's identity. Rico must hide all knowledge of his past in order to survive, but it is this past that he longs to reassert and, in the end, he is psychologically unable to resist resuming his old identity. His urge to have people know his 'real' (recognisable) identity is his undoing, and the novel ends with Rico seeing the death of the public self he has so carefully created: '"is this the end of Rico?"' (158).

The historical figure who most influenced the conception of the big-time gangster was, of course, Al Capone, who had by the end of the 1920s become the symbol of American gangsterism. Capone was accepted as 'a force in American life that government was powerless to control', his phenomenal rise to power in Chicago's underworld having made him not only feared and hugely wealthy but a substantial political influence and an example of how a gangster could make a business asset of his reputation.[21] Burnett's Little Caesar was partly modelled on Capone, but the most famous fictionalisation of his career was undoubtedly Trail's *Scarface*, in which Tony Guarino, the Capone figure, is both protagonist and scapegoat.

Armitage Trail (the pseudonym of Maurice Coons, who had been a detective-story and Hollywood script writer) immersed himself in Chicago's gangland whilst he was writing, researching the book by getting to know Sicilian gangsters. But he also stood back from his material, incorporating numerous passages designed to establish a normative moral perspective and insisting that, as an exemplary figure, the gangster supplies a cautionary tale rather than a glamorous role model.[22] From his opening descriptions to the moralising end of the novel, Trail presents the celebrated career of Scarface as a rebuke to the society that produced him and a lesson that will help in the restoration of decent government. Before he dies, moved by 'the social impulse', Tony Guarino writes a 'damning indictment' of the system of which he has been a part, and the publication of this indictment ultimately leads to 'a complete reorganisation of the government and police administration' (177–8). It is significant that it is Scarface himself who is given the 'great vision' of the corrupt system that has facilitated his rise and of the amoral, treacherous man who has been created (170). Nor is this entirely out of character, since it is his insights into the nature of power that have enabled him to attain dominance in the first place. What differentiates the big-time gangster from other noir protagonists is this skill as a political manipulator. Scarface is not altogether dissimilar to the private eye. Like the archetypal hard-boiled investigator, he is separated from his past and his family. He has a sense of chivalry and pride in keeping his word, and he possesses as well a vitality and masculine competence that set him apart from the small-scale, defeatist, unheroic noir transgressor. What most distinguishes him from other noir protagonists, heroes and anti-heroes alike, is his drive for power, sustained by a combination of efficient violence and efficient business. Contrasted with an old prewar 'strong-arm' type, Tony is a dapper, efficient, postwar gangster who goes in for 'regular business administration in crime' and who ultimately feels 'like many another millionaire' that success is easily achieved if you are not too squeamish (74–5, 147–8).

Like Appel's 'Movie', the story of Scarface charts a series of developments that start before the First World War. Tony's first killing is just before the war, at a time before violence was a natural recourse in gangland, and the actual war forges his character, not only confirming his qualities as a leader but earning him medals for the art of murder. Although violence is only one of the means necessary for the achievement of his political ends, warfare is a dominant image in *Scarface*, and the scar itself takes on symbolic importance, constituting his new identity (since 'Tony Guarino' is reported as killed in action). It is his curse as well as his destiny, and, together with his gun, it signifies the inescapability of violence. He is 'a marked man', and the scar leaves him unrecognisable to the family he was close to in earlier life, so guaranteeing his separation from the past and from warm humanity. The noir identity crisis dominates the end of the novel as it does *Little Caesar*, except that here it is the protagonist's human rather than his public identity that is fatal to him. Scarface must confront his own brother, a policeman, and the question is whether his past or his present identity will prevail. He dies at the moment when his past (his human identity) resurfaces in his mind and stops him from using the gun that has constituted his male authority as a gangster. The end is brought about by his knowing more than 'respectable society' knows. Decent folk like his brother cannot see him for who he is, whereas he 'knows' them and, like Conrad's Marlow at the end of *Heart of Darkness*, he keeps the truth from them. He has previously hidden from his mother, for example, knowledge of events that would kill her and of the real nature of the society that has recreated her son as Scarface: 'What a blessing it was that most people actually knew so little' (155).

Also-rans, has-beens and other losers

The 'tragic hero' potential of the protagonists of rise-and-fall gangster sagas is harder to discern in the more unequivocally noir stories of criminals who never make it to the top, or of once successful men whose last vestiges of power are eroded by time and exhaustion. Marginalised in the competition for wealth and position, such characters provide writers with the underdog's perspective on hierarchy. Paul Cain's *Fast One* and James M. Cain's *Love's Lovely Counterfeit* are both structured around underworld struggles for ascendancy. They focus on attempts to seize power on the part of men who aspire to be political manipulators but whose flaws of character and errors of judgement bring them down long before they can consolidate their power. In such narratives, ambition is a driving force, and the protagonists, like Rico and Scarface, embody the capitalist obsession with success. During the course of their ill-fated campaigns, however, they never quite cease to be victims. In other thrillers of the period (for example, in the work of Appel, Anderson and Hemingway, and in the early forties novels of Burnett) protagonists are not clawing their way to the top but are in the main just struggling to survive. It is in novels like these that we see the strongest protests of the little man against the whole of the social and economic structure and the clearest assertions of economic determinism – of deprivation as a form of noir fatality.

Paul Cain's *Fast One*, one of the most brutal and compelling of the unheroic gangster novels, was originally written, starting in March 1932, for *Black Mask*. Cain's first piece of fiction and his only novel, *Fast One* is the ultimate expression of Chandler's half-jesting suggestion that hard-boiled writers use the simple expedient of having a man come through the door with a gun whenever the action threatens to flag. Followed faithfully, the method produces an image of a savage and random universe. In fact, the fluctuating fortunes that determine the rhythms of the gangster saga change with such relentless speed in Cain's novel that it has sometimes been seen as a parody. Although this is clearly far from being Cain's only purpose, *Fast One* does foreground some of the more easily parodied qualities of hard-boiled fiction, and the title itself has a distinct air of generic knowingness. It refers to the novel's countless lies and multiple betrayals (pulling a fast one) and to Kells' (kills) speed as a gunman and his sudden rise to a temporary position of strength. It also, however, seems intended to refer to the novel itself: that is, of all the hard-boiled thrillers, this is indeed the 'fast one', moving so rapidly that the reader has barely had time to adjust to one turn of events before another incident propels the story in a new direction.

The dizzying complexity of the betrayals and the randomness of the unanticipated deaths in *Fast One* make the effects achieved hypnotic and surreal. Violence is presented in a manner that is *so* laconic it is like some bizarre accident glimpsed from the corner of the eye whilst speeding past. The protagonist, Gerry Kells (assuming, in a novel abounding with false narratives, that his own story of his life is a reliable one), has a background of war, drug addiction and criminal convictions (40). Partly because of the proliferation of dishonest narratives, characterisation of Kells and others is minimal, leaving readers sure only that duplicity and toughness are fairly evenly shared around. What Cain does is to involve the 'rise to power' plot of the earlier gangster novel with patterns more closely associated with other types of protagonist, that is, with the pursued, wrongly accused victim and the investigator whose negotiating position and indeed survival depend on his ability to find out what is actually going on. The opening pages quickly take Kells through the 'reluctant participant' and 'wrong man' plot possibilities. Although he says at the outset that he does not 'want to be a part of *anything*' (4), he is soon a wanted man, and continues to be, in part wrongly, pursued by the police throughout. His behaviour becomes increasingly 'mad', in the sense of stop-at-nothing vengefulness. We sympathise with him, but he is in many ways a very disturbing figure, used to embody the capacity of violence to destabilise: 'a kind of soft insanity came into his eyes'; 'the grin was a terrible thing on his bloody face' (22–3). Having 'helped eliminate a lot of small fry', Kells survives sundry attempts on his own life (100–4, 110), only to meet an end in darkness, pain and loss that is one of the most pointedly grim of any noir protagonist, with the rain, the torn body and the broken earth suggesting that an elemental violence has claimed him.

Love's Lovely Counterfeit was James M. Cain's only novel with a strongly explicit political dimension. Like *Fast One*, it has a plot centring on the revelation of damaging information about political figures – information that will demonstrate to the public the extent of political corruption in the city, revealing the 'alliance between crime, the mayor, and the police' (22). The novel is set in an 'imaginary metropolis', like Hammett's Personville a representative American city. The protagonist, Ben Grace, is basically a non-violent man who defines himself as 'just in between' a chiseller and a crook (17) and who tries to gain ascendancy by cleverness and control of information. He is also used as an example of power corrupting. When scandal surfaces and the bigger crooks leave town, Grace is opportunistic and unscrupulous enough to see his own chance to wield some power and, as he makes his move, his whole manner changes. There is a pretence of cleaning up the city, but in reality Grace has become 'callous, calm and cold' (77). He develops skills at bullying, recognising that 'a big operator, he runs it or he don't operate' (101), but at the end of the day, his identity has not been sufficiently transformed and he is not quite corrupt enough to make a go of it.

Many other crime stories of the thirties and early forties share this plot dynamic, moving towards the eventual or rapid self-destruction of flawed characters engaged in a criminal journey along the American 'road to success'. In *Love's Lovely Counterfeit*, the protagonist is motivated initially by the wish to extricate himself from a menial job with a notorious racketeer, and the 'big man's' refusal to release him generates the characteristic Depression-era sense of entrapment by circumstances that cannot be altered. As so often in James M. Cain stories, actions perversely produce the opposite of the desired effect, with Grace's drive to free himself and to attain some form of financial autonomy leading only to his death.

This ironic pattern is also evident in Benjamin Appel's *Hell's Kitchen* stories, which generally centre on the ill-fated ambitions of vulnerable, poverty-stricken young criminals. Appel carefully establishes the normal humanity of the 'suckers' he portrays. They are all mother's sons. This does not have the Oedipal implications that it might have in later noir, but instead serves only to place his protagonists firmly in a social and human context. Appel plays with perspective in order to challenge dehumanising stereotypes of criminals, so that even the one vaguely psychopathic character he includes, a murderous young thug in a story called 'Oh, Mother . . .', dies murmuring '"Mama, mama . . ."' (41). As Hammett does in *Red Harvest*, but from the opposite side of the conflict and more sentimentally, Appel subverts the distinction between the hunter and the hunted. The detective in 'Oh, Mother . . .' hunts 'this killer who was hunting him'; both are, at a moment of total isolation, thinking of their families, and as the detective listens to the boy's voice, he suddenly himself feels 'utterly lonely, as if he also lay dying' (40–1). More often the stories involve protagonists who are driven by hardship into a world of organised crime where they are remorselessly destroyed. In 'Crazy Kid', the kid thinks he can 'hijack himself into being a big-shot' but is swiftly executed by the gangsters he holds up (83); in 'Ask Anybody', the good-natured Bittsy, failing to find any work, agrees to be the driver in a hold-up planned by two other boys, and the story ends with Bittsy's mother protesting that '"My boy is a good boy. It isn't right he should be killed in the chair"' (133). In his *Dock Walloper* stories as well,[23] Appel writes movingly about the loss of human dignity forced on his characters by necessity and human cruelty. The bum in 'Night

Court Monologue', deprived of his human identity, wants only to be acknowledged as a man, but is worn down by the indifference or contempt of everyone he encounters: 'it was no use thinking I was a man when all of them said I wasn't' (125). These are *essentially* stories of the Depression, insisting on a recognition that fate is economically determined, and driving home the human cost. As the rich kid narrating 'Red Mike, Mabel and Me' comes to understand the perspective of Red and Mabel he, too, sees that 'Things happen. And that's all. The poor guy. No luck, no breaks' (*Hell's Kitchen*, 62). Appel reiterates his 'there but for the grace of God' theme as a challenge to the categorisation of the criminal as other. Whereas the 'big shot' like Rico or Scarface enjoys his short-lived heroic moment when he seems to have achieved the American dream of success and power, the career of the small-time crook embodies the impotence of the ordinary man trapped at the bottom of the system.

One of the novels of the late thirties in which this harshly deterministic economic fate is most effectively used to structure a crime story is Edward Anderson's *Thieves Like Us*, published in 1937 and adapted for the cinema by Nicholas Ray in 1948 as *They Live by Night* and by Robert Altman (as *Thieves Like Us*) in 1973. Like Appel, Anderson pays close attention to the social origins of crime and uses the small-time crook as the measure of 'respectable' society – of its criminality, its want of humanity, and its failure to recognise that this society itself is constituted by 'thieves like us'. These are characters destined to be fleeced not only by respectable society but by the bigger crooks as well, an emblem of the defeat of the decent small man. The choice of bank robbers as protagonists is, in the context of the time, a way of generating sympathy, since hostility towards banks, which were often blamed for the Depression, was widespread in the 1930s.[24] The bungling young crooks are used throughout to provide a perspective on the economic disparities that produce crime. Anderson underscores the irony of the poor allowing themselves to be persuaded that small-time criminals are deserving of punishment in a system in which 'the great criminals' never go to prison at all (341–2). His protagonists are products not of urban squalor but of the rural dust bowl: in Bowie's description of his 'people', for example, we see him as 'just a big old country boy' who has found that a gun is necessary just 'to make a piece of money' (233). But there is little nostalgia for the old rural America, except perhaps as it is embodied in the moral natures of the protagonists themselves. They are motivated by a combination of altruism and by a simple wish to have some semblance of the good life, such as the house, home cooking and little luxuries that they experience when they are briefly in 'Clear Waters' (273). As in Appel's 'Movie', there is an ironic miscasting of the small-time criminal by the newspapers. Bowie and his girlfriend Keechie dream of getting away somewhere and forgetting about 'Bowie Bowers', a fantasy of escape in which there would ultimately just be 'the real Bowie Bowers' (301–3), the man submerged by the myth of the gangster created by a hostile world.

In the same year that Anderson published *Thieves Like Us*, Ernest Hemingway produced *To Have and Have Not*. Himself an influence on the hard-boiled style, Hemingway also wrote the short story that was the basis of one of the quintessential films noirs, Robert Siodmak's *The Killers* (1946). *To Have and Have Not*, however, was his closest approximation to the hard-boiled thriller. The strong relationship between small-time crook narratives and more mainstream thirties literature of social criticism is very evident in Hemingway's adaptation of the genre. Harry Jordan is another ordinary man, older and endowed with more Hemingway-style toughness than Anderson's thieves, but equally a victim of an unjust economic system. His life is a constant reminder of the central thematic contrast between the immunity of the rich and the persecution of the poor. As in Anderson, economic circumstances are presented as fate. Harry reflects, 'I don't want to fool with it but what choice have I got? They don't give you any choice now' (75). Also as in Anderson, his indignation is sentimentalised by his genuine love of his wife and by having a needy family, and his crimes are put into perspective by representations of the destructive criminality of the upper classes. There is the old grain broker, for example, worrying about the Inland Revenue investigators and incapable of remorse or pity for those he had ruined, who jumped to their deaths or shot themselves with 'those admirable American instruments . . . so well designed to end the American dream when it becomes a nightmare' (167). Harry is an independent operator rather than a gang member, but, driven by want into illegal activity, he forms temporary alliances and takes on questionable and dangerous customers, running liquor and smuggling aliens to earn enough to keep body and soul together. His loss of an arm, coupled with his inability to have sons and his inability to earn anything, make him feel less than a man, but, particularly in comparison to those who engage in pseudo-intellectual parlour politics, he has a fund of stoical and manly strength. Though he is 'no radical' (60–9), his mute suffering and the touching simplicity of his final inchoate ramblings as he lies dying are meant to stand as a radical protest: 'No matter how a man alone ain't got no bloody fucking chance' (158).

Burnett's fiction of the early forties creates a very similar image of the criminal in relation to society. Transgressions are explained by reference to social and economic circumstance, and ordinary men are shown being villainised by a press that never exposes bankers and financial manipulators as 'real criminals'. *High Sierra* (1940) and *Nobody Lives Forever* (1943) are, like *To Have and Have Not*, novels of middle age rather than youth, with protagonists who are not battling for ascendancy or doomed to remain at the bottom but who have already had a measure of success in the criminal world and are now entering a period of decline. Burnett turns from the myth of the rapid rise and sudden catastrophic fall of the ambitious gangster, which perhaps had its greatest resonance at the time of the Crash and its immediate aftermath. Instead, these are novels of exhaustion: protagonists are worn down by years of struggle and poverty and filled with nostalgia for commonplace life at a time when they no longer have the energy to hope for the success of the 'big-time'. The nostalgia for a vanished American dream of opportunity and peaceful sufficiency is explored, but as a sustaining myth rather than a lost reality: 'the morning of the world, a true Golden Age' remembered by an early twentieth-century farm boy, is contrasted with the struggles of a middle-aged man headed towards 'an ambiguous destiny in the Far West' (5). As he experiences the bitterness and moral ambiguity of the present, Roy Earle comes to realise his mistake in thinking that there was ever a past that constituted a 'good place'. Roy's appearance is that of the archetypal tough guy, but he is in fundamental ways an innocent, possessing warm human impulses.[25] Burnett juxtaposes Roy's character with that of the crook as capitalist exploiter ('Big Mac', bossing and buying him) and confronts him with the class unfairness of Tropico Springs, the goal of the robbery and a 'dream-oasis' of riches and leisure. Roy refuses to be a 'chump' who lets the big guys push him around (60), and his self-assertion is an implicit form of social protest.

Death, old age and fear of confinement also haunt *Nobody Lives Forever*, another novel that assimilates a strong sense of social injustice to a more cosmic sense of human absurdity. Four 'hungry guys', all 'has-beens' (157, 71), plan a con that is doomed to fail. At the same time it leads the 'big guy', Jim, to experience a transforming sense of human responsibility. Burnett reinforces his central theme by including a gangster who reads Shakespeare and also by inserting the story of Tom Rodney, another 'aged king' figure, admired and envied, but meeting a cautionary end of the 'paths of glory lead but to the grave variety'. Rodney had seemed to Jim, as a boy, all-powerful, a dream of greatness who 'owned the world'. At the finish, however, he is 'a filthy, stinking old man', becoming the central figure in the nightmares in which Jim envisions himself becoming a figure of scorn, old, alienated and alone (28–9).

Britain's armless bandits

The essential normality of the protagonist in Burnett's *Nobody Lives Forever* is confirmed by the presence of a character called Doc, the gangster as psychopath. Doc is a twisted, deformed schemer who feels menaced by 'the dark future'; he is a man of no principle and a violator of the criminal code of honour. Doc cherishes images of destruction, hoping the Jap bombers will 'blast the hell' out of Los Angeles and declaring that he would 'split with Hitler if I couldn't work it any other way' (65, 17). The kind of division one sees here, between an essentially non-violent man like Jim and the twisted, violent psychopath, was a crucial one for British thriller-writers of the late thirties and early forties. Unlike their American counterparts, British writers like Graham Greene and Eric Ambler were never inclined to give a sympathetic role to the armed gangster and were much more likely to class any violent criminal as a psychopath, the man excluded from the human community. There was a deep-rooted sense that criminality and violence were inherently un-British. In comparison to America, with its more visible urban crime and its Prohibition gangsterism, British criminals were decidedly low profile, providing little material for a romanticised gangster mythology. Involved mainly in activities like protection, racecourse racketeering and street-betting, they were not known for shootings and machine gun battles, tending instead to sort out their quarrels with chivs, knives and bottles. It was only in the 1940s, after taking advantage of wartime opportunities for organising rationing, gambling and prostitution, that 'spivs and racketeers entered the public consciousness and . . . began to appear in films and novels'.[26] There are some notable crime-centred British novels written before 1945, but criminals who are largely sympathetic are also unarmed and undangerous, and violent psychopaths are distinctly un-British. Most often, in fact, they are the kind of men who would unhesitatingly 'split with Hitler'.

Passing references to Hitler aside,[27] the main political thrust of the American gangster novel during this period is domestic. In England and often also in continental Europe, on the other hand, the 'great man' as 'great gangster' analogy was recurrently related to the rise of fascism. In Germany such comparisons were quickly suppressed. Banned without delay after the Nazi take-over, Fritz Lang's *Testament of Dr Mabuse* (1933) was made, according to Lang, 'as an allegory to show Hitler's processes of terrorism' by putting Nazi slogans, doctrines and paranoid ambitions into the mouths of criminals.[28] Brecht, in *Arturo Ui*, cast a comically deromanticised gangster as a man of power, but again this was clearly not a work likely to find favour in Nazi Germany. Written in 1941 but not performed for nearly two decades (1958), Brecht's 'parable play' satirises Hitler's rise to power as the take-over of a Chicago gangster, 'the biggest gangster of all times' following 'the call of destiny', securing peace with machine guns and rubber truncheons (8, 95). For British writers of this period, living in a country dominated by the fear of an impending war, violence was not generally admitted as an understandable response to economic deprivation and powerlessness. Instead, there was the nightmare image of the 'civilised normality' of England menaced by the unnatural monstrosity of fascist violence.

As is apparent in Orwell's response to James Hadley Chase's *No Orchids for Miss Blandish*, in the context of the late thirties, even the non-political representation of the psychopathic gangster tends to be read in relation to continental political violence. Chase's novel struck Orwell as a debased American import that unwittingly expressed the moral atmosphere of fascism. Immensely popular, selling over a million copies in the first five years,[29] *No Orchids* was adapted first for the theatre and then for the cinema (by St John L. Clowes in 1948). The film raised an outcry both because of its obvious debt to American gangster films and because of its sex, perversion and sadism. [30] The most obvious influence on Chase's conception was Popeye in Faulkner's *Sanctuary* (1931), with his jerking hat and 'vicious cringing' look, a misbegotten, impotent embodiment of pathological violence quite unlike the very human criminals of most American thrillers of the thirties and early forties. In popular film and fiction, there were (as in the character of Doc in *Nobody Lives Forever*) minor psychopathic characters lurking at the margins, but the 'psychologising' of the gangster-protagonist is mainly, in the United States, a postwar phenomenon, evident in such Cagney films as *White Heat* (1949) and *Kiss Tomorrow Goodbye*. In *No Orchids*, the violent gangster, Slim, is a mother-dominated psychopath comparable to Cagney in *White Heat*, but without any of the romantic rebel overtones. He is an 'idiot' who is 'mean and bad right through'. The explanation of his having a background 'typical' for a 'pathological killer' (28) bears more than a passing similarity to Popeye's profile. The descriptions of Slim in the act of killing are used to evoke horror. As his idiot mask slips to reveal the killer, the reader is told that he feels 'the same odd ecstasy' he always felt when killing (34). The social critique implicit in Chase's novel is quite different from that in the American gangster novels we have examined. Slim is not a product of his society but, like any threatening external force, he is a test of its resolve. Whereas American writers of the time use the rise of the gangster and his violent aggression as an analogue for the ambitious careers of those at the top, Chase presents Slim as a perverted and monstrous creature who is dangerous because modern 'good time' society lacks the moral fibre to stand against him. As Miss Blandish says of being held in captivity by Slim, 'I'm a person without any background, any character or any faith . . . I haven't believed in anything except having a good time' (155–6).

Writers of more 'serious' thrillers than those of Chase used the figure of the gangster to engage explicitly with the political dangers and tensions of the late thirties. Graham Greene, in particular, uses psychotic, dehumanised criminal types to image the extremity of brutally aggressive behaviour.[31] In *Gun for Sale* (1936) and *Brighton Rock* (1938) Greene associates violence with those who are on the margins of society, literally and symbolically homeless and untutored in English decency and 'respectability'. Both Raven and Pinkie are characterised as immature. They do not possess the kind of redeeming innocence of, say, Anderson's young outlaws but are distorted personalities, born to violence and 'doomed to be juvenile',[32] and thus beyond all possibility of growth or change. In *Gun for Sale*, Raven's name, his background and his physical appearance all mark him out as wholly other. He is less than human, with his harelip, his ugliness, his 'bitter screwed-up figure', his inner coldness and his failed sexuality (5). Greene does include in the novel two caricatured figures (Major Calkin and Buddy Fergusson) whose behaviour suggests the presence within Britain of the home-grown masculine aggression traditionally associated with the sensational thriller and adventure story. But whereas these men are linked to fantasy violence, Raven is the thing itself. He is an abomination metaphorically paired with his gun, 'dark and thin and made for destruction' (13).

An altogether more complex character, Pinkie is explained in both socio-economic and theological terms. He possesses a viciousness that is a consequence of social injustice and exploitation but is also a central actor in Greene's drama of good and evil. Having begun with the intention of producing a crime story, Greene shifted the novel towards a theological vision that required a conception of evil going far beyond a socially conditioned corruption of values, and the fact that he was able to incorporate the young gangster in such a vision suggests how completely he had detached his violent criminal from human normality. Pinkie, like Scarface, is scarred, but in his case the scarring is not simply the mark of initiation into the world's violent realities but part of a cluster of physical and psychological traits that conventionally distinguish the dehumanised villain. Again, what we see is a stunted appearance, sexual abnormality and a diseased pathological violence manifested in minutely detailed sadism. These are the signs that ensure Pinkie's 'capacity for damnation' but also, on a more secular level, make it natural for Greene to relate his gangland aspirations to continental political threats. The power Pinkie wants for himself is that wielded by Colleoni, boss of 'the great racket', whose expansive gestures map 'the World as Mr Colleoni visualised it'. Pinkie, challenging his power, is imaged as 'a young dictator' of unlimited ambition, his breast aching 'with the effort to enclose the whole world' (132–5).

The psychopathic gangster/fascist continued to make appearances in British crime fiction after the war as well, in, for example, Gerald Kersh's *Prelude to a Certain Midnight*. Written in 1947 but set in the mid-1930s, Kersh's *Prelude* contains a character, until the end identified simply as 'the Murderer', who fantasises about worshipping or being an 'Ideal Man – the Leader' and reflects that 'Good must be pitiless . . . and although it was not expedient to say so, he saw Herr Hitler's point. The pure man must be strong . . .' (119–20). The point behind such a comparison is not dissimilar to the one that Chase makes in passing in *No Orchids*. That is, the Murderer is moving through a society too weakened in its resolve to resist fascist atrocities: '"Yet is it not a fact that in Germany Hitler has been in power for over two years. . . . And are you up in arms? No! You recognise Hitler, you honour Hitler . . ."' (149–50).

In novels that separated crime from violence, it was much easier for British writers to convey a sense of the criminal's own humanity and status as a victim, and of his wrongdoing as the product of hardship and of a brutalising environment. Some of the most striking examples are to be found in the work of James Curtis, an actively left-wing writer who was involved with both communist and socialist movements in the 1930s.[33] Curtis often uses characters who have just been released from or broken out of jail, for example in *The Gilt Kid* (1936) and *Look Long upon a Monkey* (1956). In *They Drive by Night* (1938),[34] Shorty, another small-time crook just out of jail, is suspected of a murder of which he is innocent. Chapters in which we share his perspective are interspersed with chapters in which we enter the mind of the actual murderer, an anonymous man in a shabby raincoat who has killed the girl Shorty is thought to have murdered. Shorty's traumatic experiences bring him to reflect repeatedly on the deprivations that grind down the ordinary man or woman and on official indifference and callousness: when she was alive, 'they hadn't bloody well bothered their heads' about the 'poor kid' who was murdered, except to arrest her for soliciting. Shorty himself, downtrodden, hounded and 'messed and bitched about from pillar to bloody post', feels his kinship with the rest of society's victims: 'It was a bastard all ways up. . . . Blokes worked and what did they get? Nothing but bloody misery . . .' (83, 38–9). The murderer on the prowl, however, thinks only of himself and his own isolation from a society he despises, in reveries that act to confirm his madness rather than lending him the tragic dignity of Burnett's Little Caesar.

Less wholeheartedly sympathetic with the petty criminal, Gerald Kersh, in *Night and the City* (1938), nevertheless presents his wide-boy protagonist as an entirely human character. Adapted for the cinema in 1950 by Jules Dassin, *Night and the City* is one of two British-set 'spiv movies' of the period in which the spiv is the central character (the other is John Boulting's 1947 film of *Brighton Rock*).[35] Harry Fabian is some distance from Curtis's romanticised small man, but however sleazy he is, we are not moved to outright condemnation, in part because he so utterly fails to match up to his fantasies about having connections with the famous gangsters of the American underworld. Like Appel, Kersh uses the small-time crook's unsuccessful imitation of the mythologised gangster to make a point about the ways in which social conditions circumscribe most human ambitions. But in contrast to Appel and other left-wing writers of the Depression (including Curtis), Kersh represents his unfortunate protagonists as choosing their lots and indeed as inviting the fates that befall them. Fabian has elected to inhabit 'the shifting frontier between the slough of small business and the quagmire of the underworld' (51–2), and Kersh deliberately counters a socially deterministic explanation of his criminal activity by having Fabian's own brother, Bert, revealed to us at the end of the novel as the salt of the English earth. A good-hearted, hard-working Cockney costermonger, Bert provides a chorus-like commentary on Harry Fabian's scummy activities, and Kersh's addresses to the reader underscore the irony of a man like Harry, who 'could have devoted such keenness, such perseverance, and such energy to something legitimate', instead becoming 'a creature of the gutters, sniffing after a trail along the dank and shadowy roads of the night, hunting somebody down' (27).

The satirical nature of Kersh's writing is strongly marked, but the satire is directed against the human types portrayed. A grotesquely distorted society is cast less as the cause of crime than as its punishment. In place of the mythic gangster-hero or psychopathic monster of violence, Kersh creates human examples of moral disintegration who are condemned to drift in 'silent putrefaction' in the 'nightmare-land' of a London landscape of surreal and hellish degradation, epitomised in Bagrag's Cellar, a place into which daylight never penetrates, 'on the bottom of life . . . the penultimate resting place of the inevitably damned' (31, 114). In the Dassin film of *Night and the City*, this entrapping underworld is so powerfully established that Fabian himself becomes a somewhat more sympathetic figure. The imprisoning buildings, dark alleyways and threatening shadows give the audience an overwhelming sense of the protagonist's own view of his environment, and the desperation and despair of the noir protagonist are evident throughout in Richard Widmark's performance as Fabian. The film adds, at the very end, one unselfish gesture (his insistence that Mary claim the price on his head) that gives him something of the pathos of the doomed figure of the American gangster. Even in the opening sequence, when Widmark's Fabian pauses for breath after having been pursued through the London streets, he is metaphorically in the position that characterises the compassionately viewed criminal protagonist, 'caught halfway, transfixed between top and bottom and trying to catch his breath'.[36]

3
Victims of Circumstance

Both the hard-boiled investigator and the career criminal have the kind of masculine competence that enables them to achieve some degree of mastery in a hostile world, however temporary and limited it might be. Even Harry Fabian, though he is in most respects a failure, can, like Rico or Scarface, be compared to counterparts in the world of business, gifted with energy, perseverance and enough nous to enable him, in his small way, to thrive: 'He was not quite an ordinary person: he had highly developed intuitions, proceeding from long cumulative experience of the customs of the City' (21). He knows what he is doing, and is single-minded in the pursuit of his own interests. Like most other criminal protagonists, he will end as a victim, but he will at least have put up a plausible fight before becoming a casualty in the conflict. In many noir thrillers of the period, however, the protagonist is a victim throughout, one of the uninitiated who has acquired neither the special competence of the private eye nor the underworld knowledge and sharply focused survival instincts of the seasoned criminal: 'and then,' says one of Horace McCoy's narrators, 'I said something to myself I had never said before (but which I now knew had always been in the back of my mind): *I should have stayed home* . . .' (142). The cover of this McCoy novel, *I Should Have Stayed Home* (1938 – see Figure 3), catches exactly the sense of resignation and defeat so often felt by the characters in his novels. Listless and immobile, the man slumps in a posture of hopelessness. Although the woman in the picture reveals the requisite cover cleavage, the man is not gazing at her but looking away with an expression of blank despair. He holds a movie magazine containing dreams now recognised as unobtainable. Its false images, we eventually discover, are the cause of death by disillusionment.

The ordinary man who has strayed into disaster, who is essentially

Figure 3 The noir victim: Signet Books 1951 edition of Horace McCoy's *I Should Have Stayed Home* (artist: Ray Pease)

innocent or bemused or just thinking of something else (distracted by love, or driven by sexual obsession) is one of the most familiar protagonists in *film noir*. Vulnerable, insecure, inept, he is acutely aware of being in an inferior position, unable to assert his masculine authority or to feel that he is in control of his fate. Whether he is up against a ruthlessly aggressive capitalist system or (as in the thrillers of Eric Ambler and Graham Greene, for example) confronting violent political ideologies, the victim protagonist acts in desperation. Ill-equipped for such a world, he feels trapped and doomed, filled with so many misgivings that life seems an intolerable prison. James M. Cain, Horace McCoy, Eric Knight (writing as Richard Hallas), Cornell Woolrich and Patrick Hamilton all create characters who feel suicidal and may actually kill themselves or force others to kill them – and whereas murder, as Norman Mailer writes in *An American Dream*, 'has exhilaration within it', suicide 'is a lonely landscape with the pale light of a dream'.[1] 'Victim noir' narratives are amongst the most frequently analysed patterns in canonical *film noir*. Dramatising the insecurity of normal existence, such narratives are full of 'wrong men' pursued for crimes they did not commit; men whose lives are subject to random reversals and who seem to be the sport of a malign fate; men who may reveal latent criminal capacities but who do not approach the status of competent criminals; weak men worn down by the pressures of environment, floundering in a world of corruption that they cannot quite grasp or betrayed by the women who seem equally incomprehensible.[2] The solving investigator and the heroic gangster, if sufficiently in the ascendancy, may carry a narrative away from what one would strictly class as noir. The noir victim, on the other hand, can be so far reduced to hopelessness and fatalistic inertia that his narrative ceases to be recognisably a 'thriller'. McCoy's *I Should Have Stayed Home*, James M. Cain's *Mildred Pierce* and, in a later period, David Goodis's *The Blonde on the Street Corner* are all examples of this tendency.

It might be said that victim noir serves less often as a vehicle for specific socio-political criticisms of, for example, the criminality of the local political machine or the gangsterism of the businessman. Since these are largely narratives of individual struggles or sexual triangles, they tend not to turn on the kind of direct confrontation with public wrongdoing that is central to other forms of noir thriller. Nevertheless, they function as some of the most powerful critiques of contemporary society, using the weak protagonist either as a foil to corruption or as the embodiment of pervasive enervation and moral or intellectual confusion. As a foil, the protagonist functions rather in the way that the satiric naïf does, his innocence or good nature throwing into relief the brutality of the society that persecutes and destroys him. McCoy's novels provide the most obvious examples here. Even McCoy's naive victims, however, are not so innocent as to be morally blameless, and in their encounters with harsh realities they reveal traits that can be taken to represent more widespread tendencies towards self-deception, loss of will, despondency and passivity. In contrast to the 'stranger-outcast' figures of the mid-century, most Depression era victim-protagonists are not essentially isolated or different. Instead they are 'like anyone else', just trying to fulfil a modest dream of love or security but finding circumstances such that (just as for the gangster protagonist) the action they hope will attain their objective is what ultimately dooms them.

American dreams

California seemed the last hope for a place that might not be subject to 1930s forces of economic determinism. Nathaniel West, in *Day of the Locust* (1939), describes Los Angeles as 'the final dumping ground', with the Hollywood studio lot 'in the form of a dream dump. . . . And the dump grew continually, for there wasn't a dream afloat somewhere which wouldn't sooner or later turn up on it . . .' (99). The narrator of Eric Knight's parodic *You Play the Black and the Red Comes Up* (1938) reminisces about his childhood belief that moving westward 'over those golden mountains' would bring his family to the promised land. The relatively little-known Knight produced only the one crime novel, though he did subsequently make his mark by writing *Lassie, Come Home*. But in the early thirties, when Knight came to write scripts in Hollywood, two other prospective screenwriters also arrived whose output was larger and whose influence was much greater: James M. Cain and Horace McCoy. All three writers are preoccupied with California as what Mike Davis in *City of Quartz* calls 'the nightmare at the terminus of American history'. Each in his way conveys something of the 'new vision of evil' that in the 1930s 'rushed in upon the American consciousness' in southern California, 'a *bad* place – full of . . . victims of America'.[3] The first novels of Cain and McCoy, *The Postman Always Rings Twice* (1934) and *They Shoot Horses, Don't They?* (1935), can be seen as the real starting place of the Los Angeles novel, the fictional undermining of a frontier myth in which California figures as the fabled land of opportunity. In place of this myth, a new image emerges, with California as the site of disappointment and failure, of disastrous endings for rootless characters who arrive at a dead end of hopelessness.[4] It is a mood captured, for example, in Edgar G. Ulmer's 1945 film, *Detour*, in which the journey of Al Roberts (Tom Neal) across America to Los Angeles leads only to murder, entrapment and despair. Sometimes – for example, in Cain's *Double Indemnity* (1936) and *Serenade* (1937) and in a 'non-California' Cornell Woolrich novel, *Black Path of Fear* (1944) – the need to escape or to continue their quest draws characters beyond American borders, often south, to South America or Cuba, remote and exotic locations that nevertheless turn out to offer no more liberating a fresh start than does California.

James M. Cain and Horace McCoy were yoked together in Edmund Wilson's essay on the 'boys in the back room', which classed both of them as 'hard-boiled'. McCoy, in response, objected to the comparison of his work to that of 'the Cain school', and there in fact seems little likelihood that they influenced one another.[5] It is possible that McCoy, like Chandler, felt some distaste for, or at least wanted to dissociate himself from, the shock value of novels like Cain's, which were much more open in their representation of sexuality than most other writers of the time, Cain being in this respect more like post-1945 writers.[6] Cain offers compelling early versions of the femme fatale, most fully in *Double Indemnity*. McCoy's women, if sometimes fatal to themselves and others, are never primarily important as objects of sexual obsession. McCoy is clearly very much like Cain, however, in focusing social criticism through individual tragedy, and also in writing genre novels that modify and transcend the conventional form. Neither liked to be labelled as hard-boiled,[7] and both are in a sense straining away from generic categorisation.

Dismissed as pulp novel hacks by many American critics of the time, both Cain and McCoy were treated by European critics as the equals of Hemingway and Faulkner. This European acclaim is in fact one of the most important links between the two writers, both of whom were cited as influences by French existentialists. Existentialism as a philosophical movement only really became well known in America after the war, when the writings of Sartre and Camus gained attention, but Cain and McCoy seemed to European audiences to have anticipated absurdist themes. They represented isolation, alienation, loneliness and dread. They chose 'insignificant' protagonists under sentence of death, struggling to make sense of a random and unstable world, epitomised in Los Angeles, with its 'population of strangers drifting about, surrendering to heedless impulse'.[8] The earliest screen adaptations of Cain's novels were in fact French, Camus cited *Postman* as an inspiration for *L'Étranger* and McCoy's *They Shoot Horses, Don't They?*, hailed as an American masterpiece, was circulated 'among underground readers by the French literati' before and during World War Two.[9]

McCoy, who started writing stories for *Black Mask* in 1927, was a contributor contemporary with Hammett, Paul Cain and Chandler. He depicted decent, gullible, ineffectual protagonists, ill-equipped to cope with the world. Firmly embedding his wider absurdist themes in American life of the thirties, he was one of the crime writers to capture most starkly the deprivation experienced in the years of the Great Depression. Although his work is very unlike the gangster sagas of Burnett, it has affinities with, for example, a narrative like *High Sierra*, in which violent death constitutes a form of choice and freedom for a protagonist who finally 'crashes out' of life when travel in the 'hopeful' westward direction is no longer possible, and in which the condemned criminal is seen as far less brutal than those who organise so unjust a society. The private, everyday world of McCoy's novels is one in which violence and corruption seem matter of course. He develops what is essentially a radical, left-wing critique of American society, economic injustice and (in *No Pockets in a Shroud*) native fascism, though without developing any kind of overt, programmatic political position (in *They Shoot Horses*, he actually edited out topical references).[10] Like Hammett, Anderson and the proletarian writers of the thirties, McCoy shows clearly the socio-economic factors producing the world he describes. So, for example, the dance marathon of *They Shoot Horses* can be seen as having both 'universal' and historically specific meanings. It is an absurdist parable, a picture of a deadening and dehumanising contest so self-enclosed and denatured that you are disqualified if you open a door to the outside. With its circular movement, the marathon signifies that 'There is no new experience in life' (53). Futile repetition is interrupted only by random violence, like the shooting that closes down the marathon, or Gloria's suicidal decision to 'get off this merry-go-round' (120). The novel is also, however, a protest against the casual viciousness of the American economic and social system, and against the pursuit by so many in the thirties of illusory goals, only to end by having their fragile hopes (that they might, for example, be 'discovered' in Hollywood) worn away by weariness and defeat.

They Shoot Horses is framed by the death sentence passed on the protagonist, broken into sections that precede each chapter, with the type becoming larger and larger as his final doom is read out. There is a savagely ironic juxtaposition of the utterly cold, formal, deterministic frame of the sentence with the puzzled, innocent first-person narrative of how Robert Syverten actually came to shoot Gloria, his 'very best friend', because she has asked him to kill her. The enclosing of the narrative in the judicial death sentence sets up two discourses, with the strong implication that the remorseless legal judgement omits all that is humanly important and that the individual is punished for sins that are the responsibility of society. There is no possible *legal* answer to the question of 'why sentence should not now be pronounced', but the human reasons are compelling, and the gap between these two discourses constitutes the condemnation of official morality. Like Willeford and Goodis later, McCoy uses the genre to censure a whole society. His iconic figures are both victims, neither carrying guilt. The 'femme fatale', Gloria, is guilty only of despair, a pathos-filled version of the woman-as-temptress, tempting the narrator not to sex but to nihilism and death. The 'killer', Robert, is touchingly bemused ('I try to do somebody a favour and I wind up getting myself killed' [15]). In terms of noir fatality, their narrative is doubly doomed. The opening phrase of the legal pronouncement ('The prisoner will stand') starts a run-on sentence that acts throughout as an increasingly insistent reminder of the fate that awaits Robert. At the same time, there is a close-up (everything 'plain as day') of the murder itself, with Gloria smiling for 'the first time' when Robert is forced to agree that the only act of friendship to someone in so alienated and friendless a state must be to shoot them.

In *I Should Have Stayed Home* as well, the functioning of the judicial system demonstrates official unwillingness to bring corruption to light and the pervasive wrongness of the society (a judge, for example, releases Mona, but only because he is running for re-election). Hollywood's rich and powerful make the laws and own the courts and so 'coerce and browbeat and violate all the laws . . .' (96). The crushing circularity of the plot is established by the protagonist's sense, at the end as well at the beginning of the novel, that he cannot move on from the level of Hollywood society signified by a modest rented bungalow in the kind of neighbourhood where you lived 'when you first started in pictures', hoping to gradually work your way 'westward to Beverly Hills, the Promised Land' (8). On the opening page, Ralph Carston sits at home, so afraid of what evils the sun will reveal to him that he waits 'for the darkness' (5). In the end, he lingers on in the same place, still nursing vague hopes but no longer caring 'what [the sun] would show me'. Mona, the movie extra with whom he has shared his bungalow, is convinced that there is 'no escape' and 'proves it' by marrying through a *Lonesome Hearts* magazine, going back to what 'she had desperately tried to run away from' (142). As in the earlier novel, suicidal impulses are never far from the surface. In an unpublished version of the novel, McCoy had Ralph Carston kill himself.[11] In the published version, what remains is the suicide of Dorothy Trotter, who 'never would have stolen all that stuff if [she] could have got work in pictures' (61). Her death represents for Mona and Ralph the destructiveness of a system designed to generate illusions and feed dreams that cannot be fulfilled. Mona props up movie magazines as 'the instrument of death' (98–100). Another of McCoy's innocents abroad, the callow Ralph is used to provide a perspective on 'the most terrifying town in the world', though he is also culpable in his simple-mindedness. Altogether too willing a victim of exploitation, he reflects, when he first accepts money from the appalling Mrs Smithers, that with a 100 dollar bill in his pocket he feels he is beginning to appreciate that 'You had to kiss you-know-whats . . . you have to play ball to get anywhere' (33–4).

Published in the same year as McCoy's *I Should Have Stayed Home, You Play the Black and the Red Comes Up* is the only crime novel published by 'Richard Hallas' – the pseudonym of Eric Knight, who was born in England and only emigrated to the United States in his teens, and hence was regarded by some critics as an 'imitation' hard-boiled writer. Knight unquestionably used his tough-guy manner with at least some degree of parodic intent, allowing the satiric impulses in the noir thriller to come to the fore by caricaturing not just an absurdly corrupt and foolish society but an absurdly unfortunate protagonist, whose 'bad luck' ironically consists in not having the bad luck he desires.[12] Like Hammett's *Dain Curse*, Knight's novel satirises form and content at the same time. He mocks Hollywood endings and the darker ironies of noir but also exposes the lunacies of southern Californian society and politics.[13] 'Dick' is the only name given to a protagonist who, though not particularly bright, possesses a kind of simple-minded integrity. The deadpan voice of this 'uninitiated' narrator records all of the political events of the novel with a kind of amused resignation to the 'goofiness' of everyone who has crossed the mountains into California. When the audience for those spreading 'the gospel of Ecanaanomics' applauds rather than giving Sister Patsy the horse laugh, he decides that they all must be 'so slap happy they couldn't have told the difference between Thursday and a fan dancer' (65).

The flourishing of strange cults is just one manifestation of the fact that California takes in its throngs of dust-bowl migrants (like Dick's father, who arrived from Oklahoma the year 'everyone went broke') and offers them nothing more substantial than demented schemes and the 'fake plot(s)' of Hollywood films (8, 123–4). Dick's own story seems set to become grist to the Hollywood mill when he tells it to a movie director, Quentin Genter, who retells it to another audience as a 'tragedy', a piece of 'stark Americana . . . raw and vital', 'brutal folklore': '"It was about a man, hungry, exhausted from lack of sleep, a magnificent animal, puzzled and hurt by outrageous arrows of fortune . . . "' (54). There is a kind of blackly comic excess about *You Play the Black*, especially in the last chapters, in which Dick, trying to lose his 'guilty money', discovers that the usual gambler's jinx, 'you play the black and the red comes up', will not work for him when he wants to lose (31). He then vainly tries to lose his life. Having escaped a death sentence for killing by accident the woman he loves, he begs the system to condemn him for various other transgressions but is 'laughed out of court': '"You've had your headlines, brother"' (130). In Knight's version of the existential choice of death, it is life as adapted for Hollywood – 'like a Hays-office ending to a movie plot' – that is the intolerable prison from which the protagonist longs to escape, and 'fatality' is not dying but remaining in it against his will.

The promised land is more obsessively sought in the novels of James M. Cain. McCoy's Robert Syverten, motivated by weariness and compassion, only kills Gloria on the spur of the moment. Knight's narrator, much too incompetent to accomplish the murder he plans, only manages to kill inadvertently the woman who seemed to him to give his life meaning. In Cain's novels, on the other hand, the protagonists do murder, not quite with professional proficiency but successfully and with malice aforethought. In spite of this, his transgressors – bums, drifters, seedy salesmen – are sympathetically drawn. Cain, who did not write for *Black Mask* or the other crime pulps (publishing instead with Knopf), described his novels not as genre fiction but as tragic depictions of the 'force of circumstance' driving characters to commit some 'dreadful act'.[14] Although Cain does not offer sustained social criticism, the Depression years are mentioned in passing or taken as given, a constant determinant in characters' actions and movements. *The Postman Always Rings Twice* (1934) opens with Frank Chambers, who is bumming along the California roads, thrown off of a hay truck he has sneaked a ride on. In 'Brush Fire' (a short story of the mid-thirties) the young drifter is paid for the 'torture' of fire fighting with the first money he has earned for two years, after he had 'begun this dreadful career of riding freights, bumming meals, and sleeping in flop-houses'.[15] *Double Indemnity* (1936), in Cain's words, 'really belongs to the Depression',[16] as does *Mildred Pierce* (1941), in which the iron resolution of Mildred is embodied by her assertion that '"I can't take things lying down, I don't care if we've got a Depression or not"' (333). Cain presents his characters as victims of a society traumatised by national economic disaster but nevertheless driven by myths of limitless opportunity, success and unhampered self-determination. They follow the ignis fatuus of the American dream, and when they have (opportunistically) attained their wishes they find that all they have really secured is defeat and entrapment. As Frank says to Cora towards the end of *Postman*, '"We thought we were on top of a mountain. That wasn't it. It's on top of us, and that's where it's been ever since that night"' (79).

Two years after the huge success of *Postman*, Cain sold to *Liberty* magazine a serialisation of *Double Indemnity*, which is in many ways a reworking of his earlier novel. A man falls for a strong, sexually knowing woman. He plans, with her help, to kill her husband and, when the murder has been accomplished, finds himself ensnared by a relationship in which the bond of death has replaced that of sexual attraction. This is a version of one of the most recognisable of *film noir* plots[17] and, as adapted for screen by Billy Wilder (1944), *Double Indemnity* became one of the classics of the genre. Because Cain was writing for the family magazine market, he was already working within the kind of restrictions that shaped post-Code Hollywood films.[18] This meant both that the sex scenes in *Double Indemnity* were less steamy and brutal than those in *Postman* and that the woman's actions and motives in the murderous affair were such that they could be more unequivocally censured. Rather than being a sympathetic figure like Cora, Phyllis Nirdlinger is, as Walter Huff is finally told, '"a pathological case. . . . The worse I ever heard of"' (316). She has not just killed Nirdlinger's first wife but has also murdered at least eight other people in her care while she was a nurse, some of them in order to get their property, others just to '"cover up the trail a little"' (317). This element of melodramatic excess was removed in Wilder's film, in which Phyllis is only found to have murdered the first wife. It is a change that simplifies and improves the plot but which, of course, also has the effect of making the femme fatale even more culpable, scheming, manipulative, not excused by madness and, as played by Barbara Stanwyck, the first real example of 'one of the enduring archetypes of the American screen, the *noir* female'.[19] As created by Cain, however, Phyllis Nirdlinger becomes, in her deadly derangement, an emblem of despair. Less touching than McCoy's Gloria and not presented as a product of Depression deprivation, she is nonetheless a pitiable figure, seeking her own destruction as well as symbolising death's inescapable presence at the end of the protagonist's quest. Cain's novel, unlike the film, closes with Walter apparently having been given a chance to start again. He has a ticket on a steamer leaving for Balboa 'and points south'. He discovers, however, that Phyllis is also on the cruise ship, smiling 'the sweetest, saddest smile you ever saw', preparing to meet her 'bridegroom' Death (322–3).

The ending of Wilder's film, with Walter (Fred MacMurray) dying in a scene that reaffirms his father–son bond with the chief claims investigator, Keyes (Edward G. Robinson), is generally regarded as neater and more satisfactory than Cain's own ending. This is a fair judgement, though what Cain's resolution does offer is an altogether darker and more mocking image, ironically echoing the American dream of moving on to a new life. Walter sits on the steamer, sliding by the coast of Mexico, and, in the final twist of the plot, his feeling that he is not 'going anywhere' is confirmed by the realisation that he is accompanied by Phyllis, an intimate of Death who knows with certainty that '"There's nothing ahead of us"' (322). The need for onward movement, whether to find escape or fulfilment, makes California seem the promised land. It also motivates still more desperate searches beyond American borders for some place not bound by the laws of harsh reality and remorseless retribution. This is often, when westward movement fails, 'points south'. Occasionally *film noir* will offer its audience a glimpse of the imagined idyll, such as the meeting in Peru at the end of the film version of *Dark Passage*. More characteristically, though, and obviously more noir, there are the conclusions in which destinations beyond American borders are no more likely than California to erase the past or to conform to the promises of the travel brochure. When Frank Chambers sets out for South America with a puma trainer (feeling free of Cora, 'made of gas' and able to 'float off somewhere') he gets as far as Ensenada and then realises 'that Nicaragua wouldn't be quite far enough' (67–70); Walter and Phyllis are eaten by sharks off the coast of Mexico; Johnny, in Cain's *Serenade* (1937), finds Guatemala to be indistinguishable from California, and the final return to Mexico leads to Juana's death and Johnny's recognition that he will never sing again.

Hollywood occupies a pivotal point in the structure of *Serenade*. The setting is the world of music rather than film, but its function as an embodiment of false hopes and sordid commercial realities is unchanged. Even more explicitly than Cain's earlier novels, *Serenade* is a fable about capitalism and the corrupt exercise of financial power – treating others as possessions, buying a voice or a person. Although the role of Juana is very different from that of Phyllis, she, too, symbolises a reality that undermines all transitory notions of success. Equated with Earth and Mother, she is both dangerous and vital, a source of Johnny's power as a singer (142–3, 169, 195). Johnny's voice is what he loses when he sells himself, a loss literalised (he cannot sing any more) as a central element in the narrative. From the outset his singing is associated with his male identity. When he is unable to sing, Juana laughs at him and rejects him; when they come together on non-commercial terms, he regains his voice, and with it his masculine competence. Ironically and inevitably, this competence restores his economic status and the 'power' of his voice takes them back, disastrously, into the commercial world, first to Hollywood, then to New York, where he becomes even more ensnared by the commercial forces that assert ownership of his voice. The most sinister embodiment of these forces is Winston Hawes, who schemes to re-establish the economic (and sexual) control that he once had over Johnny: Winston 'didn't care about art. . . . He wanted to *own* it. Winston was that way about music. He made a whore out of it.' There is obviously a sense in which Johnny's artistic sterility is caused by his latent homosexuality, but the nature of the relationship with Winston is also, and equally, characterised by its economic nature. Ownership by an older man who makes a whore of your music is presented as analogous to the ownership of Juana by the politico from whom Johnny has earlier saved her. In the end, as the narrative circles back to Guatemala and Mexico, both Juana and Johnny are defeated by the world they have tried to defy.

Such circular, aspiration-defeating tales of victimisation by the rich and powerful need not, of course, revolve around Hollywood. Cornell Woolrich, for example, in the fifth of his 'black' novels, *The Black Path of Fear* (1944),[20] creates a sexual triangle similar to those in Cain's early novels, with an older, wealthier man, a discontented wife and an insufficiently cautious lover. Here, however, the centre of power is Miami and the escape route leads to Havana, which turns out, like Cain's South American destinations, to be not quite far enough for freedom. It is still a place in which the pursuer can accomplish his vindictive ends by remote control, a place as close to death as anywhere else. The overpowering feelings of dread and entrapment are characteristic of Woolrich, who more than any single writer created the atmosphere that is associated with canonical *films noirs*, several of which were based on Woolrich novels and stories.[21] The 'path of fear' is one that turns back on itself, eventually drawing the protagonist, Bill Scott, to return to Miami, where he is at the outset, only now knowingly walking towards death, his cold-blooded revenge, rather than love. The established male power, Eddie Roman, a vicious night-club owner and drug dealer, had viewed his wife, Eve, as a commodity, and speedily arranged her death and the framing of Scott when the lovers ran off. There are limits, however, to the power of his wealth. Though Roman in the end offers Scott his entire fortune, it does not enable him to buy his own survival, any more than he can accomplish the resurrection of Eve: '"All I want [Scott says] is just Eve. Just arrange to have her brought back. . . . That should be easy for a guy like you, used to pulling wires"' (148).

European nightmares

Two images dominate the end of *Black Path of Fear*: the journey that for Bill Scott ends as it began, in an encounter with violent death; and the walls built around Roman's Miami house, which 'hadn't been good enough to keep death out' (152–4). Roman cowers in his estate because he is a gangster gone soft (decidedly 'un-Roman'), but the walled sanctuary is perhaps more often associated with the innocent victim, the man who, in order to avoid death, is forced to venture out and confront aggressors on their own terms. As W. M. Frohock argues in *The Novel of Violence in America*, 'the novel of destiny' (his label for the kind of novel in which the predicament of the hero can only be resolved by violence, which in turn brings his own destruction) was more characteristic of American than other writers, and England 'did not follow suit' in the sense of producing novels as saturated with violence as the tough thrillers of the American thirties.[22]

In their own way, however, English writers *were* preoccupied with the question of whether 'violence is man's fate'. As I argued in the previous chapter, with the rise of continental fascism in the thirties, writers of the 'serious' British thriller increasingly turned their attention to violence. They used the gangster as an embodiment of alien aggression, but more often they centred their plots on the dilemmas of the protagonist who seems to be left no option other than violent action. In such novels, violence is often figured as the terminus of a journey or as a response to violation of boundaries that turn out not to have been 'good enough to keep death out'. In one of the more memorable crime novels of the period, Patrick Hamilton's *Hangover Square* (1942), the boundaries are internal. The apparently civilised man's relationship to violence is imaged as a psychic split, with repressed violence surfacing at a terrible cost. The thrillers of Graham Greene and Eric Ambler also locate in their British characters a long-suppressed capacity for violent action, but the internal struggles of their protagonists are only part of the story.[23] The action in their novels is always precipitated by 'the other', most commonly the representative of fascist aggression. Violence is a foreign menace, intercepting the protagonist on his journey or invading his sanctuary, Britain itself – the fortified estate that turns out to be all too vulnerable.

There are, as Chapter 2 points out, elements within some American thrillers of the thirties (Burnett's *Nobody Lives Forever*, for example) that hint at links between European fascism, or native American manifestations of fascist tendencies, and the thuggery of American gangsterism. Horace McCoy also responded very directly to fascist violence in his 1937 novel, *No Pockets in a Shroud*. This was a novel for which he did not succeed in finding an American publisher until 1948, and even then in so altered a version that the political dynamic was wholly transformed, with its passionately left-wing heroine changed from a Communist to a sexual pervert. Its 1937 publication, only somewhat altered, was in fact in London (by Arthur Barker), and in Europe this novel was more widely translated and better known than any of McCoy's other fiction.[24] In comparison to the defeated victim-protagonists of other thirties novels, McCoy's protagonist, the crusading journalist Michael Dolan, is assertive and effective, exposing the corruption of the 'political high-binders . . . the big-time thieves' (9). In some ways he is heir to the radical principles and indignation of such early twentieth-century naturalistic novels as Upton Sinclair's *The Jungle* (1906). Dolan's sense of political purpose and his determined integrity make this a less wholeheartedly pessimistic novel than *They Shoot Horses* and *I Should Have Stayed Home*, but he is up against forces of oppression in comparison to which he is weak and doomed.

Resembling less the tough private eye or successful gangster than British protagonists of the thirties thriller, Dolan is principled but ill-suited to a confrontation with armed brutality. Placed, like Hammett's Op, in a representative city, 'typical and symbolic of the whole rotten mess', he tackles a range of corruption, most daringly a fascist, Klan-like, secret political organisation (125–30), entering their territory dressed as they are, suffering a savage beating and ultimately murdered for having 'blasted this town wide open' (170). Like the unwilling protagonists of the British thrillers of the period, Dolan is confronted with a choice between withdrawal and resistance, and must suppress the 'panicky and helpless' (11) feeling that only retreat is sensible. Throughout the novel, there are explicit comparisons between the strong-arm bullying of the corrupt American men of power and Hitler or Mussolini, together with the heavy ironising of the 'wonderful paradise' of the United States, where 'a man can say what he pleases . . . the hell he can' (90–1). Dolan denies that he is a Communist (or 'If I am, I don't know it' [162]) but in determining to fight the Crusaders he has woken up to a sense of purpose, sustained in the face of his certain knowledge that his actions will not only be unrewarded but fatal: 'there's no pockets in a shroud' (132).

In Britain in the late thirties and early forties, writers like Eric Ambler, Graham Greene and Patrick Hamilton repeatedly explored the question of how a man who is by nature civilised, cautious and restrained is to respond to violent political forces that threaten to plunge civilisation into barbarism. For writers who felt that they were much more immediately confronting the possibility of another war, there was even more at stake than there was for a man like Dolan, wavering between prudence and dangerous journalistic boldness. Dolan briefly experiences what it is to become 'indistinguishable' from his enemies when he disguises himself to attend their meeting. For British writers, there was a fear of becoming like the enemies in a far more thoroughgoing way, that is, of becoming brutal in order to oppose brutality. The memory of the horrors of World War One had reinforced pacifist feeling in Britain and strengthened the determination to stay out of continental political conflicts, dominated by what seemed to most Britons to be utterly alien political ideologies. Orwell, in 'Wells, Hitler and the World State', argued that 'the sheltered conditions of English life' had led many liberal humanists to dissociate themselves to the point of incomprehension from the repellent, 'anachronistic' emotions aroused by fascist militarism. This made it difficult for them to come to terms with the fact that, to stand against Hitler, it was necessary to bring into being 'a dynamic not necessarily the same as that of the Nazis, but probably quite as unacceptable to '"enlightened" . . . people'.[25] Forster, in 'The 1939 State', described the same 'hideous dilemma', which left 'intelligent and sensitive people' torn by 'messages from contradictory worlds, so that whatever they do appears to them a betrayal of something good'.[26]

This dilemma, Forster suggested, produced a kind of paralysis, and the thrillers of the period repeatedly create characters who suffer from a sense of immobilising contradiction. An unwilling protagonist hesitates to act lest he lose his own humanity and take on the qualities of his opponents. In order to defend his cherished culture and core of values, he must cross the boundary between innocence and guilt, risking separation from the culture he is trying to protect: 'It was extraordinary how the whole world could alter after a single violent action' (*Confidential Agent*, 121). In both its structure and its imagery, the British thriller of the thirties expresses this sense of being divided from oneself, of paradoxically becoming what one is not. Whereas Dolan arrives at his crucial decision to risk journalistic aggression in the early pages of McCoy's novel, the British thriller often involves its protagonist in prolonged hesitation, a deferral of violent response until no other option remains. Like the victim-protagonists in the American thriller, these are figures who never really achieve competence, who may finally act in desperation but who are always at a disadvantage compared to the world of 'real' violence.

Eric Ambler's prewar thrillers are on the whole too optimistic to be classed as noir. In the novels written before 1940, armaments themselves tend to be viewed as the cause of conflict, and his plot resolutions accordingly offer salvation in the form of conflict averted, with war becoming less likely as a result of the dismantling of weapons of destruction. The protagonists of novels such as *Uncommon Danger* (1937) and *Cause for Alarm* (1938), generally ineffectual innocents, struggle to comprehend the world of violent action, and very reluctantly move from detachment to involvement during the course of the narrative. Kenton (*Uncommon Danger*) and Marlow (*Cause for Alarm*), like McCoy's Dolan, have their resolution strengthened by the alliances they form with a sympathetic Communist. In both novels, this is the Russian agent Zaleshoff, whose idealistic left-wing views are tacitly supported by plots that move towards the possibility of utopian transformation, of fascism thwarted, not without toughness, but without recourse to brutalising violence.

Ambler only created a noir version of this basic plot pattern when the avoidance of war had ceased to be a possibility. *Journey into Fear* (1940) was the first Ambler novel adapted as a *film noir*, if a somewhat marginal noir, in which a less isolated protagonist moves towards a more reassuring resolution than Ambler himself supplies.[27] The last novel Ambler published before himself joining the army, *Journey into Fear* propels its ill-equipped engineer-hero, Graham, into an irretrievably dark and violent world, awaiting 'a bloody spring' (10). The novel is set on board a ship from which the protagonist cannot escape, a miniature of the looming European conflict. Unsupported by a competent Communist ally, Graham has to come to terms with the fact that his only option is armed combat. His survival on board the ship (which is carrying him home to assist in the work of re-equipping the Turkish navy) depends on his willingness and ability to handle a gun. He is completely cut off from all of the props of normal life: wife, home and friends 'had ceased to exist. He was a man alone, transported into a strange land with death for its frontiers' (132). Without a revolver, he would be 'as defenceless as a tethered goat in the jungle' (59). The journey, meant to carry him back to civilisation, has ironically carried him into a regressive world of primitive animal violence and to avoid his own destruction Graham has to throw civilised restraint aside. At the climax of the novel he unleashes his own aggressive impulses in a blind fury. He does emerge alive from his ordeal, but he has unequivocally crossed the border between peace and war: 'life was never going to be quite the same again' (23).

The thrillers that Graham Greene wrote during the late thirties and early forties are more uniformly pessimistic than those of Ambler. The left-wing grounds for hope that underpin the optimism of Ambler's thirties thrillers are absent in the novels of Greene, whose tendency is always to subvert the distinctions of political rhetoric. Like Ambler, Greene develops his novels around the theme of lost innocence, but in his work innocence is most often blighted from the start, and there is no innocent or ideal future to be conjured from 'what we are'.[28] As war approached, Greene's response to the political conflicts of the time became increasingly direct, moving away from his tendency, evident in *Brighton Rock* (1938), for example, to think in terms of eternal rather than merely national salvation. In *Confidential Agent* (1939), written after the Munich Agreement, when 'trenches were being dug on London commons' and the approach of war seemed certain,[29] and in *Ministry of Fear* (1943), written in the midst of war, he is preoccupied with the unequal contest between fascist violence and an opponent weakened by civilised scruples.

In *Confidential Agent*, Greene creates in 'D' a protagonist who, though nominally a Spanish agent caught up in the animosities and betrayals of the Spanish Civil War, embodies the very 'English' qualities that also mark out Ambler's protagonists. He is a gentle and civilised man 'pushed around' by the pressures of political violence, his humanistic responses (compassion, basic decency, a preference for non-violence) invested with a fundamental sense of rightness, in spite of which he seems doomed to defeat. The dilemmas faced by the principled man as he moves from impotent passivity to reluctant aggression are central to Greene's theme. D's initiation into violence had taken place when he was buried alive in a cellar, an experience of total powerlessness which permanently altered his sense of the probable and the permissible: 'you couldn't be buried in a bombed house for fifty-six hours and emerge incredulous of violence' (32). Eventually, D and his companion, Rose Cullen, feel themselves propelled into a repugnant course of action, a revolt against the 'passive past' requiring 'a violence which didn't belong to them' (145). As in Ambler, the decision not to be passive marks a turning point in the plot, reversing the direction of the pursuit. Going on the offensive means a complete break with the graspable order of a passive past: 'the blind shot . . . in the bathroom of a strange woman's basement flat. How was it possible for anyone to plan his life or regard the future with anything but apprehension?' (156). Though the context of war of course transforms its legal–political meaning, such an action, like the shot the narrator fires in McCoy's *They Shoot Horses*, signifies an irreversible self-transformation. It is also a violation of the calm stability that Greene associates with peacetime England. As in his earlier novels, Greene both ironises and views nostalgically the English sense of immunity from violence. Running like a refrain through the novel are phrases suggesting that in England violence seems tasteless and improbable. When a young girl who has helped D is murdered, he thinks of her as having become 'by the act of death . . . naturalised in his own land. . . . His territory was death' (128). The journeys by ship at the beginning and end of *Confidential Agent* reinforce our sense of Britain's actual vulnerability, an island that is like a frail fortress surrounded by death. In D's hesitant confrontation with danger and in his final defeat, Greene encapsulates British anxiety on the eve of war. His mission having failed, D is 'powerless' in more than one sense: he returns home without the power (coal) essential for his side to continue, and we know that his own half-hearted aggression will give him a poor chance of survival.

Greene's last novel of the war years, *Ministry of Fear*, is his most searching representation of the emergence of the ordinary individual into a world in which violence seems inescapable. The protagonist, Arthur Rowe, is not 'innocent' (he is technically guilty of the mercy killing of his sick wife). He is already isolated from ordinary society and feels himself 'an exile' from 'the old peaceful places' (47). The function of his earlier crime, however, is to establish a central contrast between, on the one hand, a regretful involvement in violence, motivated by love and mindful of suffering, and, on the other, the malignant aggression associated with fascism. Britain's involvement in the war is figured in Rowe's anxiety over what he had, after all, done for the best of motives. The unsuspecting Rowe must undergo further transformations as he is drawn into this darker world of political violence. The first crucial transformation takes place when he agrees to deliver a suitcase to a room in a hotel in which you can lose yourself – a labyrinthine wilderness of darkness and danger in the heart of London. The blast from a bomb in the suitcase leaves Rowe with amnesia and a new identity, recovering in a shell-shock clinic which restrains all violence, taking it to be a form of madness. In the 'madhouse' of Europe, the clinic seems to be an 'arcady' in which Rowe feels the inexplicable happiness of someone 'relieved suddenly of some terrible responsibility' (111). Paradoxically, however, this state of regression is also one in which Rowe is able, with the romantic exhilaration of the boyhood state of mind that seems most real to him, to act in an uncharacteristically vigorous way. When his personality is finally, at the end of the novel, reintegrated, his new 'wholeness' contains the tensions and contradictions of English involvement in violence. Like Graham at the end of *Journey into Fear*, he feels that he is returning to a home that is irretrievably altered: it was impossible to retreat, closing the door 'as if one has never been away'. He is at war and, knowing not to expect peace, he has joined the 'permanent staff' of the 'Ministry of Fear'. More forcefully than any other British thriller of the period, *Ministry of Fear* expresses the anxiety that the recourse to violence will in itself 'ruin' what is defended. Earlier, when Rowe contemplates London in ruins, he says that what frightens him is 'how I came to terms with it before my memory went . . . God knows what kind of ruin I am myself. Perhaps I *am* a murderer?' (163).

In contrast to Ambler and Greene, Patrick Hamilton uses a much more inward domestic drama to express the confrontation of the ordinary English self with an 'other self' that is all too familiar with emptiness, meaninglessness and impending violence. Hamilton's best-known novel, *Hangover Square*, represents the almost unbridgeable gap between civilised man and destructive man as a case study in schizophrenia. His protagonist, George Bone, is the very type of the victim-transgressor. His lapses from his socially constructed self into his 'insane' other self resemble the liminal experiences of Greene and Ambler protagonists: men cross over into a zone in which normal civilised inhibitions no longer apply. The zone of danger, with which both gangsters and private eyes are thoroughly acquainted, is the 'other side' of a boundary demarcating a world in which violent, unexpected things routinely happen, in which beams fall and any 'softness', whether on the part of a Sam Spade or a Rico, puts one's life in jeopardy. Bone is established as someone who has been 'a noticeably uncruel boy in that cruel and resounding atmosphere' of his school days (96–7), alienated from the outset, persecuted for his 'dotty' moods, but a wholly 'human' and sympathetic figure – touching, simple, direct, vulnerable (99). Even in his 'normal' state Bone is an outsider, though one who pathetically tries to fit in and follow the rituals of the world into which he is drawn by his obsession with one of noir's most completely disagreeable femmes fatales, the 'loathsome' Netta (79). Bone's murderous response is in a sense not just to Netta, with whom he decides he is 'in hate' (29), or to 'Darkest Earl's Court in the Year 1939' (Hamilton's subtitle: the novel begins in December 1938) but to the viciousness, nastiness and pointlessness of the whole of the prewar world. Bone's private hell is seen in relation to the post-Munich period of suspense about whether there will be a war, with Bone reflecting that a war is perhaps what he's waiting for, to 'put a stop to it all' (31). Part of the atmosphere of the time that Hamilton creates is to do with the belief that the peace would never break and the bombs never fall (101). Bone's 'shilly-shallying' (169) about killing Netta and Peter is, like the delays and evasions in Greene, an image of the state of mind of decent, kindly Britain in the aftermath of Munich.

There are also, however, forces of evil within Britain itself. The violence of the social world to which the gentle Bone belongs is seen very clearly, for example, by Bone's old friend Johnnie, to whom the fascist Peter is 'a scornful, ultra-masculine man' with a cruel face who singles himself out by wearing a kind of 'uniform', and Netta is someone who wears her attractiveness 'as a murderous utensil' (104, 124, 127). The alliance between Netta and Peter is explicitly analysed in terms of a blend of social snobbery and 'blood, cruelty, and fascism', not an ideological commitment but a 'feeling for violence and brutality', for 'the pageant and panorama of fascism' (128–31). Bone's eventual act of murder coincides more or less exactly with the outbreak of war: it is 3 September 1939 when he finally puts his own plan into motion. He goes through his task with conscientious thoroughness, but afterwards, in Maidenhead, realises that if he were to wake from his dream state and look back on events of the morning he would 'be faced with some inconceivable horror of the mind such as he could not bear' (278), such as war is for a previously secure England. The symbolic function of Maidenhead is similar to that of the mythic simplicity of the American farm or small town. As Bone's imagined final destination all through the novel, it is associated with childhood and innocence and is, of course, fated to disappoint his expectations. There is no return to innocence or release from the sadness and incomprehensibility of existence, so for someone as ingenuous as Bone, death is the only option. The 'virginal' state symbolised by Maidenhead turns out to be 'no good at all', and probably never was: 'It wasn't, and never could be, the peace, Ellen, the river, the quiet glass of beer, the white flannels, the ripples of the water.' Bone was 'wrong about Maidenhead' (278–80).

Part II
1945–70

The years immediately following the end of World War Two marked the start of a crucial phase in the creation, definition and popularising of both literary and cinematic noir. There were several concurrent developments: the Hollywood production of a growing number of pessimistic, downbeat crime films, the postwar release in Europe of a large backlog of American films, the publication in France of a new series of crime novels and the appearance in America of a new kind of book, the paperback original. Films released in America just before the end of the war, such as Billy Wilder's *Double Indemnity* and Edward Dmytryk's *Murder, My Sweet* (both 1944), were taken as evidence, when they appeared in France, that 'the Americans are making dark films too'.[1] In 1945, under the editorship of Marcel Duhamel, Gallimard started publishing its translations of British and American crime novels in the *Série Noire*. In 1946, echoing the Gallimard label, the French critics Nino Frank and Jean-Pierre Chartier wrote the two earliest essays to identify a departure in film-making, the American *'film noir'*. Although they were not thought of in the United States as *films noirs* (the French label did not become widely known there until the 1970s), numerous postwar Hollywood movies seemed to confirm the French judgement that a new type of American film had emerged, very different from the usual studio product and capable of conveying an impression 'of certain disagreeable realities that do in truth exist'.[2]

The Hollywood releases of 1945 included Edgar G. Ulmer's *Detour*, Michael Curtiz's *Mildred Pierce* and three *films noirs* directed by Fritz Lang – *Ministry of Fear*, *Scarlet Street* and *The Woman in the Window*. In 1946 David Goodis published the first of his crime novels, *Dark Passage*, and Delmer Daves began filming it; in the spring and summer months of 1946 alone, Hollywood released *Blue Dahlia* (George Marshall), *Dark Corner* (Henry Hathaway), *The Postman Always Rings Twice* (Tay Garnett), *Gilda* (Charles Vidor), *The Killers* (Robert Siodmak) and *The Big Sleep* (Howard Hawks). In the same year Gallimard brought out French translations of two of Horace McCoy's novels, the first American novels to be included in the *Série Noire*.

American publishing was itself being transformed by the introduction of the paperback. By 1946 there were over 350 softcover titles in print (three times as many as in 1945), with Pocket Books, Avon, Popular Library, Dell and Bantam all publishing in the paperback format and replacing the pulp magazines on the news-stands.[3] Several of the best postwar crime novelists (Goodis, Jim Thompson, John D. MacDonald, Mickey Spillane, Charles Williams, Gil Brewer) were about to begin writing paperback originals, though, as is usual in noir narratives, some of the characters were confronted with failure and many were in the dark about what others were doing. Thompson, who was spending much of his time drinking and doing odd jobs, was as yet unsuccessful in establishing himself as a crime writer. He had started writing his first crime novel in 1932 but it was only in 1949, after 17 years of 'fighting that book', that *Nothing More Than Murder* was finally published in hardcover by Harper's.[4] Spillane was living in a tent and trying to build his own house. Needing 1000 dollars for the materials, he wrote *I, the Jury,* which only sold about 7000 copies in hardcover but, as a Signet paperback, sold over 2 million copies in two years,[5] an achievement that 'electrified and inspired the softcover book industry'.[6] Gold Medal saw the possibility of publishing paperback originals, and they were soon providing an entirely new kind of market for crime writers, whose work could now for the first time go directly into cheap softcover editions. MacDonald, Williams and Brewer, none of whom had previously published novels, all began to write for Gold Medal in 1950–1. Goodis, after the success of *Dark Passage,* had a brief career as a Hollywood script writer, and when this collapsed at the end of the forties he retreated to his home town of Philadelphia and started writing his bleak paperback originals, the first of which, *Cassidy's Girl,* was a best-seller for Gold Medal in 1951. Thompson's first paperback original, *The Killer Inside Me,* was published in 1952 by a competing house, Lion Books, 'the most offbeat of paperback imprints'.[7] As the boom grew, the struggling, often isolated crime writers fed both the 'gloriously subversive era'[8] of American paperback publishing and a burgeoning output from Hollywood of films that would in due course be grouped together under the name French critics had given them: as Nino Frank described them, '. . . these "dark" films, these films noirs, [which] no longer have anything in common with the ordinary run of detective movies . . .'.[9]

Nino Frank's article reflects the difficulty of finding a suitable label for these 'dark films'. The films he is discussing, he writes, all 'belong to what used to be called the detective film genre, but which would now be better termed the crime adventure, or, even better yet, the crime psychology film'.[10] American film critics, without a unifying term at their disposal, settled for such phrases as 'murder melodrama', or 'brass-knuckled thriller' or 'hard-boiled, kick-em-in-the-teeth murder cycle'.[11] The search for a satisfactory description itself gives some indication of the diversity of noir. Both French and American critics emphasised the indebtedness of these films to hard-boiled investigative novels, which provided the basis for some of the most memorable of early *films noirs*: Hammett's *Maltese Falcon* and *The Glass Key* had both been adapted in the early 1940s; Chandler's *Farewell, My Lovely*, *The Big Sleep* and *Lady in the Lake* were all adapted in the mid-1940s, and Bogart's performances as Sam Spade in *The Maltese Falcon* and as Marlowe in *The Big Sleep* established him as the iconic private eye. Revisions of the detective story were, however, only one element in the phenomenon, and Bogart's place as 'a key iconographic figure in all of film noir'[12] was secured by the fact that he was cast, as well, in a range of non-investigative *films noirs*, such as *High Sierra* (1941), *Dark Passage* (1946) and *In a Lonely Place* (1950). These films were based, respectively, on novels by W. R. Burnett, David Goodis and Dorothy B. Hughes, and Bogart's roles in them suggest the different forms noir took as it developed during the forties. In addition to the weary integrity of the private eye, there was the pathos of the ageing gangster (Roy 'Mad Dog' Earle in *High Sierra*), the desperation of the 'wrong man' (the escaped convict wrongly accused of his wife's murder in *Dark Passage*) and the violence of the suspected psychopath (the self-destructive writer in *In a Lonely Place*).

In creating *film noir*, Hollywood drew on the work of a wide range both of earlier writers and of the late forties–early fifties crime novelists who were writing crime fiction that very often had no role for the private eye. Amongst those whose work was adapted during this period, along with Burnett, Goodis and Hughes, were William Lindsay Gresham, Horace McCoy and William P. McGivern, all of whom produced novels that had as their protagonists violent, self-deceived men, criminals, crooked cops, killers, psychotics. Cornell Woolrich was another of the writers whose work, very different in style from the hard-boiled tradition, became closely identified with the noir sense of helplessness and paranoia. Between 1942 and 1949, there were 11 Woolrich novels or stories made into films, the protagonists of which include a man hypnotised into thinking he is a murderer (*Fear in the Night*) and a mind-reader who predicts his own death (*Night Has a Thousand Eyes*), as well as alcoholics, amnesiacs, hunted men and fall guys. Private eye films continued, of course, to be made, but if investigative figures were included, they tended to become increasingly vulnerable and flawed – for example, Bogart's confused, hunted Rip Murdoch in John Cromwell's *Dead Reckoning* (1947), Robert Mitchum as the traumatised Jeff Markham in *Out of the Past* (Jacques Tourneur, 1947), Edmund O'Brien as the dying protagonist hunting his own killers in Rudolph Maté's *D.O.A.* (1950).[13]

Many of the writers whose work was adapted by the Hollywood

studios were also translated for Gallimard's *Série Noire*: Chandler, Hammett, Burnett, McGivern and Goodis were all added to Duhamel's list between 1948 and 1953. He included many of the American writers whose work was central to the development of paperback crime writing from the 1950s on. So, for example, in addition to Goodis, he published Jim Thompson, John D. MacDonald, Gil Brewer, Harry Whittington, Charles Williams and Lionel White. If, however, one wants to arrive at a coherent definition of literary noir, it would have to be said that a full list of the novels Duhamel chose for his *Série Noire* would not be the best basis. Amongst the huge number of *Série Noire* offerings (getting on for 300 American, British and French crime novels in the first ten years alone) many would be unlikely to be included in any late twentieth-century reprinting of classic *romans noirs*. This is particularly true of the sizeable number of French and British imitations of the American style, which were generally published under assumed names that were meant to sound more American.[14] British thrillers were mainly represented by the novels of Peter Cheyney and James Hadley Chase. The latter wrote several satisfyingly noirish novels, for example *Eve* and *More Deadly Than the Male*, both in the mid-forties.[15] Cheyney, however, is a prime example of the tone of light-hearted hard-boiled pastiche that often found its way into imitation American thrillers. He created pacy and violent novels that are exaggerated, present-tense versions of the stories produced by such *Black Mask* writers as Carroll John Daly. Cheyney's Lemmy Caution is an American G-man who first appeared in novels like *Dames Don't Care* (1937), *Can Ladies Kill?* (1938) and *You'd Be Surprised* (1940). Caution's style and character can perhaps be gauged from his banter on the last page of *Dames Don't Care*: '"Listen lady," I tell her . . . "I am one tough guy. I am not the sorta guy who you can trust around the place havin' breakfast with a swell dame like you. Especially if you are good at makin' waffles"' (192). As the upbeat comic tone here suggests, the Caution novels are imitation hard-boiled without being noir, exemplifying, especially in the French film versions, the parodic impulse that is never far from the idea of the tough-guy investigator.[16]

The defining characteristics of the American *roman noir* and *film noir* can more easily be deduced from French critical discourse, which was in general less focused on what was, by the fifties, the fading role of the investigator than on the other narrative patterns that were becoming increasingly dominant, in which morally ambivalent victims and criminals served as centres of consciousness. The French admiration for such interwar writers as Horace McCoy and James M. Cain continued to be apparent in the postwar period, particularly amongst French existentialists, who responded to the protoabsurdist qualities of the earlier American thrillers. As Naremore writes, both before and after the war, 'when the French themselves were entrapped by history', critics influenced by existentialism were attracted to *film noir* 'because it depicted a world of obsessive return, dark corners, or *huis-clos*'.[17] The crises that had shaken France since the 1930s – the period of war, occupation, resistance and collaboration described by the French as 'les années noires' – led many to share the existentialist preoccupations, and to appreciate the darker strains in recent American literature and film.

The Americans, for their part, were increasingly absorbing European intellectual influences. In the postwar years, the work of the French existentialists became more widely known in the United States as a response to the absurdity of modern life and an articulation of the need for existential self-definition: 'Auden [*Age of Anxiety*] was not alone in seeing wartime and postwar America as a place where the existential anxieties of modern Europe found a second home.'[18] The existentialist novels of Sartre and Camus, *La Nausée* and *L'Étranger*, were gaining an American audience, and mainstream American writers were beginning to express a sharper sense of distance between self and community. They evoked feelings of estrangement, displacement and dislocation with their representations of fearful, isolated anti-heroes, such as the rebels and victims of writers like Saul Bellow, Bernard Malamud, Richard Wright and Ralph Ellison. Existentialism had a particularly strong appeal for black American writers like Wright and Chester Himes,[19] for whom existentialist themes seemed closely allied to the expression of a racially derived sense of alienation and of the outsider's need to become visible and assert his own reality.

In the United States, the postwar years were, of course, a time of prosperity. The economy continued to expand and the country established both its military and economic power, with real incomes soon doubling. Unprecedented affluence made it seem that the Depression had been a historical aberration.[20] Increased affluence, however, was accompanied by materialism and conformity to an ideal embodied in the family home, the 'site of integration into the cultural order'.[21] This was a period in which many felt that the individual was powerless against the large-scale forces of industrial and technological mass society, and during which the pressures towards conformity were heightened by a national mood of self-righteous aggressiveness, directed not just against communism abroad but against those at home who were regarded as seditious or subversive of 'the American way'. Cold War apprehensions and suspicions and McCarthyite witch-hunts helped create the atmosphere of fear and paranoia that is so strongly present in both the cinematic and the literary noir of the fifties.[22]

The representation of postwar America as a 'consensus society' has been challenged in recent years by those who argue that the domestic scene, both during and after World War Two, was 'a site of disagreements, of oppressions, and, often, of the careful and carefully hidden deployment of new modes of power and power-alliances'.[23] Literary noir develops its own narratives of disagreement and its exposures of oppression, debunking the dominant myth of a unified, happily conformist America. Liberal critics of the time often focused on the ways in which American society hunted out difference and suppressed and marginalised dissent. They were concerned with explaining a postwar malaise characterised by caution, repression and intellectual retreat.[24] These preoccupations can be seen in the work of the many critics who were beginning to assail the conformist ethos. Norman Mailer, for example, attacked what he saw as a new totalitarianism in a culture that stifled dissent, and Irving Howe, in an essay called 'The Age of Conformity', complained that the nation's intellectuals were becoming moderate and 'tame'.[25] Sociological analysis which flourished in the late fifties and early sixties, like that of David Riesman in *The Lonely Crowd* (1950), identified the bland 'other-directed' character type that seemed to be emerging in America's affluent consumer culture.[26] Much other analysis focused on the problems of consent and conformity, on the negative effects of private affluence (J. K. Galbraith on *The Affluent Society* [1958]) and on the manipulation of people by advertising men (Vance Packard, in *The Hidden Persuaders* [1957] and *The Status Seekers* [1959]). William H. Whyte, in *The Organization Man* (1956), argued that the successful men who ran the large organisations that increasingly dominated corporate America were themselves run by the organisations, tested and monitored by corporations that fostered conformist mediocrity. C. Wright Mills, in *White Collar* (1951), maintained that white-collar workers sold not only their work but their personalities. As Bradbury and Temperley write, 'Despite the Eisenhower equilibrium, the romanticization of anarchic unreason, and the insistence that a conflict rather than a consensus model of society was necessary, were central themes of the Fifties', laying the basis for the protests of the sixties against social and sexual repression, against injustice to minorities and the power of the military–industrial complex.[27]

Amongst popular genre writers, it was the noir novelists who issued the most effective challenge to optimistic portrayals of American life.

Rejecting the pervasive 'vocabulary of normality', noir thrillers offered portraits of maladjustment – what David Riesman called 'Tales of the Abnorm'.[28] The inset film plot in Charles Willeford's *The Woman Chaser* (1960) epitomises the contrast: 'Mr Average American', with an average family and 'the dullest job imaginable . . . Deadly', causes a fatal accident and, in consequence, is isolated completely from his conventional existence. Execrated and hunted and doomed, he ceases to be 'a nobody' and, 'all alone on Highway one-oh-one – a good place to work in some symbolism', is suddenly someone of importance, 'a man against the world' (80–2). In studies of noir, both cinematic and literary, the sixties are often sharply divided from the fifties, but there is as much continuity as discontinuity. The sixties were no more uniformly rebellious than the fifties were 'uniformly conservative', and indeed in looking at the popular literature of the period, there is no radical break. The heyday of the paperback originals, with their lurid cover art and sensational cover copy, was over by the early sixties.[29] But some of the most notable paperback writing careers spanned the period, extending from the immediate postwar years through the sixties and beyond. Gil Brewer, David Goodis, John D. MacDonald, Peter Rabe, Jim Thompson, Lionel White, Harry Whittington and Charles Williams, all of whom were writing in the early to mid-fifties, were still producing novels in the late sixties and early seventies (in the case of John D. MacDonald, much longer). The same is true of several other noir crime novelists who published in hardback, such as Stanley Ellin, Patricia Highsmith, Ross Macdonald, William McGivern, Margaret Millar and Helen Nielsen.

In the work of these and other American writers of the period, there is, in comparison to the novels of the interwar years, a new emphasis on 'difference' as a key determinant in the lives of the characters. The sense of disillusionment and the theme of economic deprivation remain, but in contrast to the archetypal noir protagonist of the interwar years, the alienated figures of the post-World War Two period are less likely to be victims of economic failure and deprivation than of exclusion and displacement. The social background against which they are defined is more often characterised as one of material prosperity and cultural conformity; characters' anxieties more commonly spring from pressures towards loyalty and uniformity. This is not just a matter of the McCarthyite themes that run through many novels. It can also be seen, for example, in relation to the more insistent use of a small town environment, which acts as a locus for exploring hostility to deviance, stereotyping, moral platitudes, social and racial prejudice. Jim Thompson's novels are particularly associated with the satiric dissection of the closed community, but many other writers of the time (such as Harry Whittington, John D. MacDonald, Day Keene and Charles Williams) produced comparable critiques. As the protagonist of Day Keene's *Notorious* (1954) is warned, '"The eyes of your fellow citizens in Bay Bayou are on you"' (91).

The chapters in this section examine three types of character recurrently found in the novels of 1945–70. The protagonist killer, the femme fatale and the stranger or outcast are all used by their creators to probe and subvert what they see as the complacent conformity of the time. The protagonist killer is a man acting to change a given set of circumstances (compared to many other noir protagonists, he does possess agency). He acts to change things through revenge, 'cleansing' society or righting a wrong; he murders in order to profit or to achieve upward mobility, that is, to change his economic and social circumstances. If he is more radically alienated from 'normality', the killer may act to undermine the whole social order. The avengers, in comparison to earlier figures like the Op and Satan Hall, are more isolated and may themselves be trying to escape from the demands for conformity to a particular code or organisational loyalty (as in Stark [Westlake], Rabe and McGivern). Those who kill for profit (for example, in Whittington's *Web of Murder*) frequently function as satiric representations of capitalist enterprise and greed. Their willingness to kill to achieve their ends exposes the brutality of a widely upheld business ethic. The killer might be a psychotic figure who sees himself as a saviour, and whose aggression leads him towards the insights of the savage satirist: Thompson's novels furnish the most striking instances here, but notable examples are also found in the work of Vin Packer and Patricia Highsmith. The psychopath embodies the flaws hidden by a conformist society – Thompson's Lou Ford, for example, whose mocking adherence to social pieties hides the latent sadism which prompts him to punish as well as to expose.

It is really only in the post-World War Two period that the femme fatale becomes a significant part of noir narratives. In Hollywood, as Frank Krutnik points out, the iconic figure of the fatal woman became much more central from the mid-forties on. Studios producing hard-boiled thrillers introduced or increased the importance of the love-story element, so that, instead of being merely one aspect of the protagonist's quest (as in *Maltese Falcon*), the entanglement with a woman complicates the whole of the action and undermines the masculine ethos of the investigative thriller.[30] Fatal women also begin to appear much more frequently in literary noir, and in more diverse roles than was possible in the cinema. Publishers had quickly recognised that more sex brought higher sales, and the new paperback originals aimed not just for 'gritty realism' but for frank eroticism, 'lacking in . . . conventional morality, and with an iconoclastic eagerness to explore the controversial and the taboo'.[31] Inevitably in fifties America there were expressions of public outrage at the liberties taken, with the result that the paperback industry was investigated in 1952 by the House Select Committee on Current Pornographic Materials. However, although pressures continued, there was no overt censorship.[32] The less predictable representation of women in literary than in cinematic noir may in part be due to the fact that Hollywood, subservient to the Production Code, was more straight-jacketed. Film-makers, though capitalising on the appeal of the sexually dangerous woman, were forced to make concessions to conventional morality. The stereotypical strong woman plot was given its most characteristic shape in *film noir* by the general requirement that such women were to be punished or otherwise excluded by the end of the narrative. This pattern is also, of course, present in the literary noir of these decades, and both films and novels can be read as expressions of male anxiety about the independent woman. In the novels, however, there is much more scope for variation and for playing against conventional expectations. Although, as a glance at the cover art makes clear, the greater measure of freedom could scarcely be said to have done away with the stereotypical representation of women, paperback narratives were less constrained than films by notions of acceptable plots, and many of the novels that give central roles to women explicitly confront the issue of gender stereotyping. Narratives are centred, for example, on the overturning of social expectations, about, say, the relationship between a woman's appearance and her character. Writers such as Thompson, Williams and Brewer satirise male views of women. Others, like Bardin and Millar, challenge conventional images by creating female protagonists who fulfil the functions traditionally assumed by male characters, whether as investigative figures or as protagonist killers whose actions are an implicit criticism of the male world that shaped them.

The novels of the period are also less constrained than *film noir* in their representation of social and racial marginality, developing a wide-ranging critique of the treatment of those who are outside 'normal', prosperous, white, middle-class society. The marginalised white protagonists are more often portrayed as alienated from the whole idea of a cohesive, normative social structure, as, for example, in the novels of

Goodis. Several other white writers of the time take the step of choosing black protagonists who are racially outcast, persecuted, prejudged and shut out by the dominant society. In some cases a character's marginality is self-imposed, as in Goodis novels like *Cassidy's Girl* or *Down There*, in which a protagonist deliberately circumscribes his own life. Many characters, however, are represented as imprisoned by an inherited past of class or racial marginality. As French critics of the period perceived, there was an intersection between tough-guy and black protest writing, which had natural affinities with the left-wing existentialism of Sartre and others,[33] and one of the things I will consider most closely in Part II (Chapter 6) is the way in which difference and exclusion become central themes in the absurdist Harlem cycle of Chester Himes.

My emphasis in Part II will be strongly American. The combination of Hollywood *film noir* and the hugely creative energy that went into the rapidly expanding pulp fiction market were the most important contributions of the time to the phenomenon of the noir thriller. The American literary noir of this period was unmatched. Writers like Thompson, Goodis, Williams and Willeford, amongst many others, produced some of the classics of the genre. Although the links with British writing do not disappear, the hundreds of crime paperbacks published in postwar Britain were primarily imitations of American tough-guy and gangster pulps. In addition to the novels of Cheyney and Chase, there were the even more rapidly produced, pseudonymous novels put out by the numerous small 'mushroom' publishers that sprang up to feed the British mass paperback market, a phenomenon very fully documented by Steve Holland in *The Mushroom Jungle*.[34] The appetite for American hard-boiled crime thrillers had started to grow in the forties. Encouraged by the huge success of *No Orchids for Miss Blandish*, which sold over a million copies between 1939 and 1944, writers like Frank Dubrez Fawcett, Harold Kelly and Stephen Frances (writing under the names, respectively, of Ben Sarto, Darcy Glinto and Hank Janson, but under other names as well) had by the mid-forties started to produce an astonishing array of low-priced crime paperbacks.[35] Written at speed and printed on rationed paper, these short novels were unashamedly aimed at the mass market. Using a variety of catchy pen-names, the British gangster novelists churned out versions of every available American plot: the young man who is in too deep with gangsters or who eventually seizes his chance to go straight (Al Bocca's *She Was No Lady*; Darcy Glinto's *Protection Pay-Off*); the amateur crook who gets involved with big-time criminals (Hank Janson's *Don't Cry Now*); the crumbling of a mob and the exposure of 'every rat in town' (Al Bocca's *City Limit Blonde*); gangsters double-crossing one another (Duke Linton's *Dames Die Too!*) or falling out over a woman (Hank Janson's *Flight from Fear*); wrong-man narratives (Janson's *Menace* and *Play It Quiet*); first-person accounts of a gangster's ill-fated career (Janson's *Devil's Highway*) or of involvement in graft and corruption (Sammy Coburn, *Uneasy Street*); small-town iniquities (Janson's *Hellcat*); the white slave trade (Janson's *Mistress of Fear* and Glinto's *Lady – Don't Turn Over*).

Because of the imitative nature of most British noir during the period, these are novels that tend not to confront specific socio-political concerns, although they often create lively variations on the key themes of American thrillers. At the less popular end of the scale, however, was the relatively slim output of a handful of writers who did engage with the nature of postwar British society, such as Gerald Kersh, Gerald Butler, Maurice Procter, John Lodwick and Julian Symons.[36] The Britain of these years was a country in which almost everything was rationed: 'In a very real sense these austerity years were a threshold to the whole first postwar era: rock-hard and grey, whitened maybe by dedication and labour. . . .' [37] There was still a strong sense of civic loyalty (to the monarchy, the police), and the period was characterised by a marked time-lag vis-à-vis the United States. Prosperity was much later in coming. Only toward the end of the fifties did people finally begin to think of Britain in terms of Galbraith's phrase, 'the affluent society'. There was still a sense of optimistic consensus and a feeling that Britain was cosily separate, with its humour, tolerance and decency. But there was also a new sense of an attack on British insularity, comfortableness, stereotypical assumptions and parochialism, and part of what these changes produced was a distinctively British version of alienation and marginality, apparent in the British thrillers of writers like Butler and Lodwick.[38] In comparison to their American contemporaries, these are writers preoccupied less with conformity than uniformity, with the 'dulling' of society and the mediocre greyness that leads protagonists to seek adventure. These are, however, writers who are little remembered today in comparison to Thompson, Goodis and others. This was unquestionably the most 'American' period of noir. It was a time during which American thriller-writing and influence on popular culture were overwhelmingly strong, with 'home grown' British noir the exception rather than the rule. The large markets both in England and France were primarily dominated by novelists who produced pastiche American hard-boiled crime fiction – and although there can clearly be important examples of noir in which a writer does not use the materials of his own society, the wholly imitative pulp novel does lose one of the most important defining characteristics of the noir thriller, that is, its responsiveness to the obsessions and anxieties of the society that produced it.

4
Fatal Men

Killer protagonists proliferate in the post-World War Two noir thriller: revenge-seekers, criminally inclined social climbers and scornfully superior psychopaths, these 'fatal men' derive from earlier noir character types, all of them being in some measure victims seeking to become active agents and taking on the qualities of the punitive investigator, the gangster or the murderer. In these later narratives, however, the focus is less on the determining force of adverse economic circumstances than on society's demands for conformity. The pressure towards conformity shapes the behaviour of some protagonists, particularly that of the upwardly mobile murderer, and is challenged by others – the revenge figure and the psychopath. In Horace McCoy's 1948 novel, *Kiss Tomorrow Goodbye,* the psychopathic gangster protagonist makes explicit the difference between the way pre- and post-World War Two narratives allocate guilt. He argues that his college education and Phi Beta Kappa key demonstrate that he should not be used, in literature or the movies, 'as a preachment' on the theme of socio-economic determinism:

> . . . it proves that I came into crime through choice and not through environment. I didn't grow up in the slums with a drunk for a father and a whore for a mother and come into crime that way. I hate society too, but I don't hate it because it mistreated me and warped my soul. Every other criminal I know – who's engaged in violent crime – is a two-bit coward who blames his career on society (235).

Ralph Cotter's speech is the ranting of a megalomaniac, but it also exemplifies a significant shift in the kind of explanatory framework to be found in the noir thrillers of this period. McCoy's protagonist is in effect rejecting one of the central themes of the author's earlier work, in which private despairs and acts of violence were viewed as the effects of a brutalising socio-economic system. Like many earlier novels, *Kiss Tomorrow Goodbye* uses the gangster as a parodic version of the American success story. But we do not follow Cotter's ascent from poverty or his efforts to reach the top of the hierarchy and become a highly visible big shot. Instead, we observe his ability to disappear into the crowd, to conceal his superiority and loathing of the multitude from all but a select few. At the same time, his self-image is built around an obsession with separateness from the conformist multitude. He is a connoisseur of his complexes who takes a perverse pride in the individuality and unreasonableness of his psychopathic responses. With his Nietzschean posturings, he is a near relation of the gangster-as-fascist, but he has a degree of self-awareness that acts both to make him a more sympathetic figure and to make his function in the novel more complex.

This psychologising of the criminal and the concomitant movement away from treating crime as the product of socio-economic deprivation is sometimes judged to weaken the capacity of the gangster narrative to act as a critique of the capitalist system.[1] There is no doubt that focusing on the psychopathology of a character can become an indulgence of horrified fascination at the sheer nastiness of the aberrant personality, combined with a reassuring sense that normative values and conventional lives are free from these evils. It would be overly simple, however, to see the critical thrust of such novels as operating only in this comparatively straightforward way. So, for example, in McCoy's novel, Cotter's sense of difference provides a perspective from which to view 'normality', and his disdain has a satiric edge: in the plain-clothes man's face, Cotter discerns 'the flowered viciousness that only many years of petty police authority can properly mature. . . . Subtlety and caution now come to you in a brand-new handy-size package – a pot-belly and twelve triple-A shoe' (72). Savouring his unspoken sarcasms, Cotter retains a chameleon-like ability to camouflage himself as ordinary, and in doing so calls into question the authenticity of those he apes, suggesting their hollowness and superficiality. As he walks along he copies the 'easy habitual manner' of the man in the street. He acts out painstakingly and 'perfectly' the performances that 'are never mirrorized for the average man' (71). As Mark Seltzer writes, analysing the serial killer's cynical conformism and 'mask-like, ironic imitation' of the 'perfect person': 'This is the madness of the sheer conformist to social forms who at the same time merely simulates those forms . . . reducing the social order to a "pretendsy" signifying game.'[2] It is this double-edged capacity that gives representations of the sociopathic personality their critical power. On the one hand, the protagonist is the mouth-piece for scathing criticisms of the society from which he inwardly holds himself apart; on the other hand, the implication is that conventional modes of behaviour must be a complete sham if they can be flawlessly imitated.

In comparison to the psychopathic killer, the revenge-seeker and the status-seeker are motivated by quite focused objectives. The obsessive mindset of someone bent on revenge acts as a comment on the tendency of others to sell out to a plausible but corrupt system and to put the demands of tame conformity above truth and justice. In McGivern's *Big Heat* (1953), for example, unreasoning anger is the starting point for an individual assault on received opinion and for revelations about the corrupt links between respectable life and criminality. The social climbers and money-grubbers (more like the legitimate gangster or the psychopath as 'perfect person') try to rise in society by their pretended normality. In doing so, they reveal the fraudulence of respectability. Unlike, say, the big-time gangster, they have no wish to be 'top dog' but simply want, like Highsmith's Ripley or Packer's Adam Blessing, to be 'ordinarily' affluent. The ironies of such narratives are often intensified by enclosing them within a small-town environment, with its self-satisfied vocabulary of decency and normalcy. The duplicity of the whole community is exposed by the representation of a murderer who is indistinguishable from the average inhabitant.

Protagonist killer narratives in urban settings tend to involve one form or another of the faceless organisation, conspiring, coercing or compelling conformity. The huge, impersonal business corporation, the crime syndicate and the Communist conspiracy can all fill the role of the system or 'outfit' that demands a collective identity. As the protagonist of Peter Rabe's *Dig My Grave Deep* (1956) says of the criminal organisation he is trying to leave, '". . . there's a deal, and a deal to match that one, . . . and you spit at one guy and tip your hat to another, because one belongs here and the other one over there, and, hell, don't upset the organisation whatever you do, because we all got to stick together . . ."' (20). The films of the period also provide many examples of the plot that opposes the small man to the big organisation. With the resurgence of gangster films in the late forties and early fifties, there is a new emphasis on syndicated crime and on the crime cartel and 'corporate gangsterism' as mirror-images of legitimate capitalist enterprise. Films like *I Walk Alone* (Byron Haskin, 1948), *Force of Evil* (Abraham

Polonsky, 1948) and *The Big Combo* (Joseph H. Lewis, 1955) all represent individuals up against corporate criminality. As Samuel Fuller's *Pickup on South Street* (1953) suggests, even the Communist conspiracy turns out to be uncomfortably similar to the economic machine of monolithic, large-scale industrial capitalism – just another big, impersonal power with hidden iniquities against which the solitary hero must battle.[3]

Revenge-seekers

Revenge-seekers can function as the most direct critics of a corrupt system, though they are not all equally outspoken. Avenging angels range from the reluctant to the overly zealous, and some are too nearly angelic to be very good at revenge. The fact that they nevertheless remain firm in their purpose is, however, a reproach to the 'silent majority'. Essentially gentle, unaggressive men who have been propelled by traumatic events into a seach for vengeance, they are kindred spirits of the ineffectual, civilised British characters of the interwar period who were unwillingly drawn into conflict by the threat of fascist violence. Fearing that their involvement will lead to the destruction of their own humanity, they are all but disqualified from their task. The quiet family man in Leigh Brackett's *The Tiger Among Us* (1957), going after the members of the juvenile gang who beat him up, reaches the point at which he comes close to shooting them, but is horrified by the extent to which he has become like his antagonists: 'Because I lusted to kill them . . . I never wanted anything so much. . . . The tiger stripes were showing on my own hide' (177). In *An Eye for an Eye*, another novel of the same year (1957, the only year in which she published crime novels),[4] Brackett portrays a mild-mannered lawyer who becomes 'possessed of a fury so sudden and wild' (95) that he is almost unrecognisable as he pursues the man who has kidnapped his wife. It is usual for the protagonist of such narratives to meet with indifference and inaction on the part of the majority of those in the wider community, people anxious not to get involved. In other versions of this basic plot pattern, instead of communal apathy there is hostility on the part of a slavishly conformist community that unites to obstruct a protagonist's quest for justice. The small town, reacting as a body and closing itself entirely against any intrusion, functions in this way to thwart an inexperienced revenge-seeker in Harry Whittington's *Hell Can Wait* (1960): 'They all seemed to be watching me. They were silent, their faces set and rigid, unblinking eyes like marbles in their sockets' (13).

Much the same conflict is to be found in urban plots involving either supposedly legitimate or manifestly criminal organisations that expect loyalty and acquiescence from all who have dealings with them. Amongst gentle avenger narratives, the best known of the fifties is perhaps McGivern's *Big Heat*, in which the humane, reasonable Bannion is driven to become a destructive force, opposing corruption that involves deep connections between the 'respectable' criminal syndicate and the whole fabric of the community: 'This was their city, their private, beautifully-rigged slot machine, and to hell with the few slobs who just happened to live in the place' (123). McGivern gives Bannion an intellectual background that defines a sane, sanguine human norm which is savagely violated during the course of the narrative. It is not that he is an innocent (he is in most respects much closer to the tough-guy image of Spade or Marlowe). But his strong family life, destroyed when his wife is blown up by those seeking to kill Bannion, gives him a 'lost centre', and he has a set of values defined by his reading of 'the gentle philosophers'. The transformation forced on Bannion is symbolised by his leaving behind the books in which man is represented as naturally good and evil as 'the aberrant course, abnormal, accidental, out of line with man's true needs and nature' (15).

The opposing type of revenge-seeker is the cold, amoral, violent outsider. The stubborn refusal of the lone wolf to buckle to social pressure and the resistance to conformity and acquiescence are also present in a character like Bannion, but in contrast to Bannion this is a figure who has no compunction about killing. He is often given an impersonal or symbolic name (just 'Parker', or Clinch or Hammer). Richard Stark [Donald E. Westlake], who represents his most disagreeable gangsters as organisation men, sets against them one of the most memorable examples of the existential loner pitted against the criminal machine. Stark's Parker has had several incarnations on screen, including Lee Marvin's powerful creation of the ruthless Walker in John Boorman's *Point Blank* (1967), Robert Duvall's humanised portrayal of the almost equally laconic and remorseless Macklin in *The Outfit* (John Flynn, 1974) and, more recently, Mel Gibson's action-hero avenger, Porter, in *Payback*, Brian Helgeland's 1999 remake of *Point Blank*.[5] What these diverse characterisations of the Parker figure have in common is their tenacious, obsessive single-mindedness: when Macklin's girl friend tries to persuade him that it need not be 'that way', he simply replies, 'It does with me.' Westlake's original intention had been to have 'the bad guy . . . get caught at the end', but his publisher (at Pocket Books) saw Parker's potential as a series character and persuaded Westlake to let him escape.

What this meant was that Parker was quite different from the usual series protagonist: 'I'd made Parker completely remorseless, completely without redeeming characteristics,' Westlake says, 'because he was going to get caught at the end. So I wound up with a truly cold leading-series character. . . .'[6] There is, however, something touching about Parker's sense of betrayal and his persistence in the face of terrible odds. In comparison to the typical Charles Williams or Jim Thompson criminal protagonist, he is in many ways a sympathetic figure. Westlake strongly stresses his uncompromising individualism and his honest acknowledgement of his own motives in pursuing what he sees as an adequate revenge.

What Parker is up against is a 'respectable' and successful criminal organisation, transformed between Prohibition and the present by their diversification of interests and the intricacies of their organisation. When Parker, in the first of the novels, *The Hunter* (1962) – the basis for *Point Blank* – decides to reclaim his money from the Outfit, he is told that it is impossible for the individual to stand up against something so pervasive: '"Coast to coast, Parker, it's all the same . . ."' (117). Except for the fact that the organisation works outside the law, it 'conforms as closely as possible to the corporate concept' (125–6). In the eyes of the Outfit, Parker is 'a heister, a hijacker'. We know that Parker is wrong in thinking that his wife was betraying him with Mal Resnick, but her acquiescence out of fear for her life makes her a foil to him. Parker's intelligent strength, psychological as well as physical, is a distinguishing trait. The first physical description of him, followed by a female response ('They knew he was a bastard, they knew his big hands were born to slap with . . .' [7–8]), fixes him in our minds as a male force, the embodiment of potent determination. His face may be changed for his own protection, as it is in *The Man with the Getaway Face* (1963), but he always retains his force and resolution, manifest in a refusal to submit that marks him out as 'a true existential'.[7] Parker is, before the start of *The Hunter*, thought to be dead. In a way Parker *is* death, a man back from the dead to revenge his betrayal and to visit death on others. This sense of a protagonist so far beyond normal life that he is 'dead to it' is central to the understanding of Boorman's *Point Blank*, in which the whole narrative can be interpreted as a fantasy of revenge passing through Walker's mind in the few moments before he dies, after having been shot at point-blank range.[8]

W. R. Burnett's *Underdog* (1957) is similarly structured around the conflict between a criminal misfit and an organisation – in this case, a partnership between gangsters and corrupt politicians that sacrifices the individual to secure a smoothly operating power structure. The protagonist, Clinch, another loner with his own kind of integrity, is drawn on a less mythic scale than Parker. A genuine 'underdog' possessing no qualities of leadership, he is sustained by his contact with a good-hearted whore and a generous political boss, Big Dan Moford. Moford, who 'runs a whole city', is too individual in his standards to fit in with the plans of 'the gang' of those who want to run things by regularising the corrupt links between crime and politics. Though Clinch bonds with Moford, he does not 'know the meaning' of words like 'pal', 'chum' or 'buddy' (27). The vocabulary of American normalcy – all words that assert a shared ethos and conventional connection – is beyond him. His very name 'hardly seems like a name at all' (52), and the integrity born of Clinch's isolation combines at the end with his reluctant affection for Moford to spur his revenge on a killer who is 'always surrounded by crawling yes-men' (75).

The period's most famous and forthright scourge of organised rackets and their 'crawling yes-men' is Mickey Spillane's Mike Hammer – a name equally calculated to imply separation from ordinarily warm human instincts. Hammer first appeared in *I, the Jury* in 1947. Spillane's protagonist, though not a criminal, is in fact a more extreme example of the brutally aggressive revenge-seeker than either Parker or Clinch. Hammer emerges from his first-person narrative as a strongly individuated centre of consciousness. He is connected to others through love (his secretary, Velda) and friendship (Pat Chambers, his police contact), but shares more with a symbolic executioner like Satan Hall than he does with a comparatively humanised and self-doubting figure like Hammett's Op, and is clearly allied to such later vigilante figures as Dirty Harry, Paul Kersey (*Death Wish*) and Steven Seagal's cop (*Out for Justice*). Hammer's origins as a comic-book character are significant, suggesting the kind of larger-than-life hero represented on Harry Sahle's cover for the unpublished 'Mike Danger' comic that formed the basis for *I, the Jury* – 'A vibrant personality . . . as ROUGH as he looks!'[9]

Spillane's early Hammer novels, published between 1947 and 1952, were by far the most popular late forties–early fifties reworkings of the revenge motif. His sales were phenomenal – over 15 million copies of his books sold by 1953.[10] One of the acknowledged masters of hard-boiled fiction, Spillane exploits the possibilities of the style in ways that make his novels very different from those of Chandler and his heirs. Spillane is described by Ed Gorman as 'the great American primitive whose real talents got lost in all the clamour over the violence of his hero. He brought energy and a street-fighter's rage to a form grown moribund with cuteness and imitation Chandler prose.'[11] Like the earlier pulp tough guys, Hammer is primarily used to expose and punish the kinds of vice associated with the evil metropolis – narcotics (*I, the Jury* and *Kiss Me, Deadly*), the prostitution racket (*My Gun Is Quick*), blackmail (*Vengeance Is Mine!*). He assails the corruption that is engendered by wealth and power and that lurks under apparently admirable surfaces. His adversaries are men like the wealthy, gracious Berin-Grotin who is actually the head of a prostitution racket (*My Gun Is Quick*) or Lee Deamer, in *One Lonely Night*, who turns out to be the evil twin, the 'head Commie' rather than 'the little man whom the public loves and trusts' (157). Confronted with such duplicitous enemies, Hammer shares the noir protagonist's alienation, his world-weary despair and his anger at urban corruption.

Hammer's vigilantism, like the intuitive, independent investigation of the private eye, implicitly expresses distrust of the 'faceless', impersonal mechanism of law enforcement.[12] He knows from first-hand experience how vicious life is, and when he says to the reader at the beginning of *My Gun Is Quick*, 'I'm not you', he is declaring a separation from bourgeois ease and illusion that has always characterised the hard-boiled investigative figure. He has an ability to understand the lawlessness of the urban jungle: 'You have to be quick, and you have to be able, or you become one of the devoured. . . .' But in contrast to many earlier hard-boiled writers, Spillane is led by his sense of life's viciousness towards right- rather than left-wing views. Mike Hammer acts out McCarthyite paranoia. It is not capitalism itself but hidden, conspiratorial organisations subverting American life that are to be feared, amongst them the Communist Party. Other thriller writers of the time expressed anxieties generated *by* McCarthyism. Even where McCarthyism is not directly mentioned, narratives in which an outsider is threatened by the accusing voice of 'normal society' are often coded references to McCarthyite persecution – to demands for conformity and for absolute loyalty, to the silencing of opposition through fear and to sacrificing the interests of the individual in the name of the collective good. Spillane, on the other hand, expresses the fears that *motivated* the McCarthyite witch-hunts. Hammer's savage one-man crusade is in some ways that of the existential loner, but he also has the views of the disgruntled moral majoritarian, directing his violence against a variety of demonised others suspected of subverting American life. What results is a macho conservatism that has, over the years, led to many criticisms.[13]

It is easy see why Spillane has alienated many with his vigorous, no-holds-barred style, his extremity of violent action and his unashamed commercialism (he is, he maintains, a 'writer' rather than an 'author', and writes only what he feels sure will sell).[14] His prose is hyperbolic, sometimes surreal and hallucinatory in its evocation of sensual or grotesque physical detail: at the end of *Kiss Me, Deadly*, for example, 'beautiful Lily', at last revealed as an appalling scarred villainess, is set alight by Hammer, 'and in the moment of time before the scream blossoms into the wild cry of terror she was a mass of flames tumbling on the floor. . . . The flames were teeth that ate, ripping and tearing, into the scars of other flames and her voice the shrill sound of death on the loose' (158). Probably the most often quoted example of Hammer's crudely violent methods is from Spillane's first novel, *I, the Jury*, which rewrites the famous conflict between desire and justice at the close of Hammett's *Maltese Falcon*. Spade's response to Brigid O'Shaughnessy's '"Sam, you can't!"' is a reasoned defence of the code of the private eye before he hands her over to the police; Hammer gives the treacherous Charlotte a lecture on the deficiencies of the jury system, declares himself to be judge and jury, shoots her and then, looking down at 'the ugly swelling in her naked belly where the bullet went in', famously answers her dying cry of '"How c-could you?"' with '"It was easy,"' (187–8). Hammer's killing of the woman he 'almost loved' haunts him in subsequent novels; it contributes to his isolation, but it is not a disabling guilt, or one which makes him question the rightness of his ethic of summary justice. Even Daly's Satan Hall, whose metaphoric qualities place him outside the bounds of human law, does not execute malefactors so cold-bloodedly.

The reader never doubts that Hammer will come out on top, and this to some extent sets him apart from the noir protagonist. Hammer asserts himself in ways that ally him closely with earlier action heroes like Race Williams and Bulldog Drummond and with more recent superheroes like Sylvester Stallone in *Cobra* (George P. Cosmatos, 1986), or *Judge Dredd* (Danny Cannon, 1995) and *RoboCop* (Paul Verhoeven, 1987), which Spillane names as one of his favourite films (the other is *The Terminator*).[15] Like these figures, Hammer possesses such prodigious endurance it approaches invulnerability and he responds with such effective violence that he is matched only by the most extreme of his predecessors. He proves his worth in surviving a series of tests, but the ferocity of his assaults and the relish with which he recounts them place him outside normal civilised humanity. His assertion that he in no way resembles his armchair-bound reader is more than just a declaration of an unillusioned knowledge of the city. It is a boast that he has the combative skills necessary for survival amidst the 'blood and terror', the 'razor-sharp claws' of the Colosseum-like city (*My Gun Is Quick*, 7). His competence is a form of superiority that is remote from the self-doubt and self-reproach of the noir protagonist.

It is in the opening pages of *One Lonely Night* that Mike Hammer comes closest to the iconic noir protagonist in reflecting on his outcast status and on the brutality that renders him indistinguishable from the criminals he pursues. Alone on the bridge in the cold, fog-like rain, suicidally depressed, he broods on the way he has been denounced by the 'little judge' who reluctantly acquitted him. He feels branded as 'a guy who had no earthly reason for existing in a decent, normal society', and goes home to dream that his gun has become 'part of me and stuck fast' (5–13). The novel in which Hammer feels most marginalised is also, however, the one in which his aggression and paranoia are most closely linked to the collective hatreds and anxieties of the American right wing in the McCarthyite early 1950s. The decision to make his villains 'the Commie bastards' who are secretly infiltrating the country is a reflection of Spillane's sense of what would appeal to the widest possible audience of the time. In tackling them, Hammer gives vent to violent impulses that would in the context of the fifties be judged as 'evil for the good'.[16] Though 'lonely' and intensely personal, his individualism is an expression of group hatreds and a rejection of the whole liberal machinery of law, restraint and civil rights. Vengeance is taken against those who affect conformity but in reality threaten the very fabric of American society.

Money-grubbers and social climbers

The revenge plot, with its central action of exposing and scourging, requires a protagonist who strips off the 'civilised' part of himself and accepts a reduction to a primitive or existential state in which he is capable of the violence required to bring down or 'reduce' the transgressor. In Gordon Williams' *The Siege of Trencher's Farm* (1969) – the basis of the film *Straw Dogs* (Sam Peckinpah, 1972), still banned on video – the protagonist sees himself poised between restraint and savagery, realising that he has so far witnessed the violent assault on his house with the eyes of 'the civilised man who stood on this side of the threshold . . .' (118). The process of crossing this metaphoric threshold, horrifyingly represented in the later chapters of Williams' book, is a central event in many thrillers. The impact of such a transition is summed up at the end of *The Executioners*, the John D. MacDonald novel on which the films of *Cape Fear* are based (J. Lee Thompson, 1961; Martin Scorsese, 1991). When Sam Bowden finally sees the dead body of Max Cady, who had even 'smelled like some kind of animal' (147), he finds only 'a sense of savage satisfaction' that he has 'turned this elemental and merciless force into clay'. In taking his revenge on a revenger, 'All the neat and careful layers of civilised instincts and behaviour were peeled back to reveal an intense exultation over the death of an enemy' (154).

A quite different kind of killer-protagonist plot is that in which the protagonist is aiming not to reduce but to augment himself. He wants to take on the substance and, often even more importantly, the trappings of a higher social status, though this may be accomplished by primitive means that are wholly at odds with what he craves, that is, civilised luxury and heightened respectability. This upwardly mobile protagonist is himself the object of satire. In some of the more interesting narratives, he is exposed by his own first-person narration as the epitome of an aggressively materialistic society: whereas, for example, Harry Whittington's more heroic protagonists would rather die fighting than 'surrender to greed, corruption and mean-heartedness',[17] a Whittington protagonist killer like Charley Brower (*Web of Murder*) reveals himself as the very embodiment of these qualities.

The ways in which these contrasting types of narrative work can be seen clearly in a novel that combines the two plot movements, *The Killer*, published in 1951 under the Wade Miller byline.[18] A narrative that seems throughout to be about a killing motivated by revenge for a dead son turns out to be as much or more motivated by the need to conceal a dodgy business deal. The protagonist is an 'uncomplicated' professional hunter hired to carry out the revenge, and his hunter's ethic has an integrity that's lacking in the life of Stennis, the man who hires him. The prosperity of Stennis is sustained, appropriately enough, by the manufacture of Stennisfab, which offers 'Standardization down to the last nail and a new kind of prefabrication' (14). The tendency for the hunter to be reduced to the level of his own prey becomes, in *The Killer*, a bond between 'throwbacks' (18) who are essentially separate from a hypocritical society upheld by those for whom 'standardised' success is the only goal. The morally debilitating effects of upper-middle-class affluence also produce the main plot turn in Burnett's *The Asphalt Jungle* (1950), in which there is a very similar counterpointing of the romantic primitive and the display-oriented social climber. Although *Asphalt Jungle* is less bound up with the sheer neediness of characters than are Burnett's earlier novels, it contains a man closely related to his thirties cast, Dix Handley. Dix's rough integrity is set against the duplicitous smoothness of Emmerich, the man who betrays the others because of his need to preserve his bourgeois respectability. The gang is destroyed by the treachery of a man who has lived 'by a system of masterly evasions, bewildering about-faces and changes of front', and, even though Dix's sentimental return home dominates John Huston's 1950 film more than it does the novel, we are equally moved by Dix as an opposing emblem of the humanity left behind in a society that values 'class' and show. Although characters like Stennis and Emmerich remain in the background of the revenge and caper plots of *The Killer* and *The Asphalt Jungle*, their catalytic roles are evident. It is ironically their aspirations to climb out of the jungle that bring them into association with a romantic primitive, a straightforward killer who seems less reprehensible in comparison to their civilised savagery.

A more common setting for the 'social climber' novel is not the city as jungle (the urban wilderness within which the main actors suffer a reduction to the primitive) but a small town or (as in MacDonald's *Soft Touch*) a 'medium-sized city'. In such a milieu we see the workings of a complex socio-economic mechanism, within which the protagonist who has violated the social codes in overreaching himself provokes an appropriate nemesis. Even gangster narratives (usually urban) can be set in small communities, for example, in Peter Rabe's *Kill the Boss Good-by* (1956).[19] Drawing on his experience as a professor of psychology, Rabe uses a power struggle within the rackets in the backwater of San Pietro as a fable in which the success drive is presented as a national manic psychosis. The self-destruction of Fell, a gangland boss who is 'resting' after a nervous breakdown, has something in common with the gangster tragedies of the thirties (for example, *Little Caesar*). What distinguishes it from its thirties counterparts is the way in which an identified mental condition is used to create an image of the sort of world Fell inhabits – in particular, of the excesses of the drive towards success in capitalistic enterprises. With San Pietro 'in the palm of his hand' (31), Fell has 'pressure left and nowhere to put it' and seems unable to stop his frenetic activity. The problem for others involved with him is to distinguish between effective entrepreneurial behaviour and incipient psychosis: Fell '"never stops"', and his behaviour is the capitalist dream gone mad (94–7).

In Rabe's third-person narrative we are able to see Fell through the eyes of those affected by his unbalanced state of mind. In several other noir thrillers of this period, first-person narratives take us inside the mind of the scheming money-grubber or social climber, using the intimacy of this approach to satirise the self-deception, greed and underlying brutality of the American success ethic. *Nothing More Than Murder* (1949), the earliest of Jim Thompson's first-person killer novels, stays with the point of view of Joe Wilmot, a small-town schemer who believes there is nothing wrong in killing for profit: it's 'just murder, nothing more than murder' (80). Thompson was a writer so disturbing and original that one wonders, with Geoffrey O'Brien, what contemporary readers made of the Lion paperback originals they picked up at news-stands, with their cover promises of 'a cheap and painless thrill'.[20] In *Nothing More Than Murder* Thompson issues the satirist's challenge to his readers to see their own faces in the mirror, inserting himself in the novel as a visiting speaker, talking to an audience that applauds because 'they didn't seem to realize that they were the kind of people this author was talking about. Well . . .' (67). When the criminally avaricious Joe protests that '"I don't want anything I'm not entitled to . . ."', an insurance investigator replies, '"Oh, sure you do. We all do."' This is at the core of the novel. Joe is a 'small fry' capitalist with his own 'ideas on making money', trying to profit by underhanded means and not reckoning with the 'big boys' (117–19). There is considerable ironic justice in Joe being 'mopped up' himself by a big-league rival, a more skilful and cunning fraudster who says to Joe as he in effect puts him out of business, '"I'm sorry, Joe. . . . It's nothing personal"' (153–4). Joe, whose mind is too slow to enable him to conceal his true character, becomes the caricatured embodiment of a culture so grasping that the 'personal' atrophies. '"It's a disappearance case"', the insurance inspector says, and what has disappeared is not just 'some dame' sacrificed to Joe's scheme but the traits of character that enable a man to 'identify himself with the human race' (142).

The dehumanised narrator handled with satiric detachment makes frequent appearances in other novels being written during this period for some of the major publishers of paperback originals: for example, in 1958–60, Harry Whittington's *Web of Murder* (Gold Medal), John D. MacDonald's *Soft Touch* (Dell), and Gil Brewer's *Nude on Thin Ice* (Avon). Whittington, who places *Web of Murder* in the tradition of James M. Cain, says of the novel's structure: 'We start the protagonist almost casually down the road to Hades and then follow him on every cruel twist and turn through increasing terror to the pit beyond hell.'[21] The description could apply to all three of these narratives, sharing as they do the characteristic noir irony of the bid for freedom that ends with worse entrapment. In each case what is involved is the entry of the protagonist into a world in which money and social position become snares that entangle him in a nightmarish parody of the success he aimed for. The status and objects pursued are transformed in sinister, surreal ways to become (as in Cain's novels) a curse and a torment. In *Web of Murder*, for example, a narrator who habitually subordinates everything to his material and professional ambitions richly deserves his fate – to be paralysed, sexually exploited and unable to extricate himself from the clutches of the woman who has all along best known how to manipulate his crass ambitions, a grotesque parody of the situation he began by trying to escape.

In MacDonald's *Soft Touch*[22] (filmed in 1961 as *Man-Trap*), the narrator, Jerry, begins as a man trapped by his own choices in a childless marriage to a drunken, unfaithful wife and in a 'meaningless job' (32). At the finish, after breaking free from being bound on a bed, he again traps himself as a result of his own greed and violence. The plot is set in motion when he succumbs to his old buddy, Vince, who shows up 'out of the past, a tiger in the night . . . offering the silky temptation of big violent money' (5). The suggestion here of boldly instinctive action is ironised by the phrase 'big violent money': the money itself is a strong physical presence and an agent of transformation, but it is also the antithesis of the animal energies of tigers in the night. These atavistic urges are a reduction entirely inappropriate to the socio-economic structure Jerry inhabits, and his sense of self disintegrates as he tries to reconcile primitive impulse with the establishment of his identity as a successful and civilised man. He catches glimpses of disorienting images of himself in the mirror and tries to shut off the deeds ('Murderer. Thief. It couldn't be me' [110–11]). MacDonald's final plot twist wipes out in Jerry's mind the whole of this experience of being 'somebody else'. Suffering from traumatic amnesia, he can only sense the events of the past two months flickering back in a bizarre and hallucinatory way, until he is drawn by an imperfect memory of the money to disinter the wife he cannot remember killing: 'And then they took me away' (152).

Gil Brewer's *Nude on Thin Ice*[23] contains an even more surreal transformation of stolen wealth into a monstrous form of fatality. His narrator, Ken McCall, exposes himself from the outset as a man entirely suited to a life of minor dishonesties. The greed and general unscrupulousness that are his undoing are failings he is always ready to identify in those he is about to betray or abandon: 'This god-damned world was populated ass over teakettle to the hilt with sparkling parasites' (57). He readily seizes any opportunity for possible gain: 'The cross-eyed gods of the universal cash register had punched the No Sale key, and the drawer was wide open – waiting' (18–19). It is an image ironically echoed by an end in which the money he has stolen (and murdered for) is locked in a steel suitcase and Ken himself is trapped 'wide open – waiting' in the doorless adobe room he has been forced to build so that the woman to whom the crime has bound him can keep her eye on him: 'I want to always be able to see you' (141).

In their self-created entrapment these murderers are men who are compelled to 'fit in' if they are not to arouse suspicion. Other protagonist killers set a higher value on conformity for its own sake, particularly in two female-authored novels of the time, Patricia Highsmith's *The Talented Mr. Ripley* (1955) and Vin Packer's *The Damnation of Adam Blessing* (1961), both of which move the crime novel closer to the novel of manners and in doing so bring the guilt of the community more sharply into satiric focus. In contrast to protagonists who need to conform in order not to arouse suspicion, Tom Ripley and Adam Blessing crave approval and integration. In dealing with the social world, Highsmith's Ripley is the more successful and the more sophisticated in his judgements. Adam Blessing, as his name suggests, is more innocent, more victimised and, because of his innocence, less successful. Both Highsmith and Packer explore the indeterminacy of guilt, invoking official standards of guilt and innocence only to subvert them. There is in their novels a much greater sense of complicity and sympathy than there is in the male-authored narratives – with Packer's Adam Blessing because of his gauchely unattractive innocence and even more so with Tom Ripley, whose actions have a disturbing appeal and, in the context of the novel, make an odd kind of sense.

As Tom Ripley sets out on his mission, supposedly aimed at persuading Dickie Greenleaf to return from Europe, it is possible to read his journey as an inversion of the great American voyage of discovery. Released from the pressures of conformity and from the snare of poverty, Tom acquires on board ship a 'versatile', magical cap, capable of transforming his character and personality. Having killed 'good-natured, naive Dickie' and having assumed his identity, Tom's reflections echo the American myth of a new-found land – the 'clean state' and 'the real annihilation of his past' (98–9). Although he is travelling east rather than west, this is his rebirth as a 'true American', another parodic version of the American success ethic. Tom is determined, like the immigrants to America, to make good, moving 'Upward and onward!' (32). His extraordinary success is dependent on exactly imitating the class (or at least one particular member of the class) to which he aspires. He is careful, in his impersonation, not to improve on Dickie too much (for example, not learning the subjunctive). A comic version of American adaptability, he develops a new sense of self. His other-directedness, oversensitivity and diffidence all make it easier for him to transform himself. Murder, too, serves this fantasy of upward mobility, disposing of the inconvenient facts of a subservient past. Ripley's ability to be another self brings into focus the falsity and superficiality of the social judgements that confer status and respectability, and our tendency as readers is to hope that the rest of society will fail to detect Ripley's deception. Asked by a German interviewer whether Ripley would ever lose out, Highsmith declared, 'Nein, nein! Nicht bevor ich sterbe.'[24] The suspense of the novel is built on tension between the exposure he risks and his success in evading detection, with Tom vacillating between confidence in his luck and fear of nemesis. The open-endedness of his fate both overcomes the 'fatality' of noir and signifies the continuance of his subversive principle in the world.[25]

Patricia Highsmith, who published her novels as hardbacks with firms such as Harper and Doubleday, tried to avoid generic categorisations, observing that a writer was better treated and more seriously reviewed if he or she was not, say, 'a suspense novelist' but 'just a novelist'.[26] Vin Packer (the pen-name of Marijane Meaker) was, on the other hand, a regular writer of Gold Medal paperback originals, an exception amongst the generally male contributors to the fifties paperback boom.[27] She wrote both crime novels and lesbian 'shockers' (like the hugely popular *Spring Fire*), though she, too, was eventually packaged as 'a mainstream writer whose books just happened to include crime'.[28] *The Damnation of Adam Blessing* shares some of the characteristics of the Ripley novels. Adam is a less attractive and rather less complex character than Tom Ripley, but there is a similar use of close third-person narration to create sympathy for the protagonist and understanding of his feeling of sensual longing for the good things in life. Both characters can be seen to function as a means of social satire, and in both cases we forgive their crimes because of the crassness and cruelty of those who have wealth and power. Like Highsmith, Packer creates her protagonist as an orphan seeking a toehold in a treacherous society, using the tensions generated as a way of exploring the American class structure and the myth of self-transformation and upward mobility. The crimes of both protagonists consist in devising ways to alter their identities, adopting methods just enough beyond the normally acceptable to put them (if the truth were known) even further beyond the pale than accidents of birth have placed them. From the very beginning, when the orphaned Adam hero-worships the wealthy man who extends condescending kindnesses to him, he works at concealing his origins (or rather, lack of origins) and pretends to strangers that he is the son of 'that rich man'. What we see throughout is Adam's own impotence, actual and metaphoric, his failure, his 'immense loneliness' (96) and his increasing desperation. He is a Candide figure, an innocent adrift in an unfriendly world, equipped with none of the social graces, hypocritical charm or guile of those who are well adapted to life. He repeatedly thinks far better of people than they deserve and wants only to confer 'blessings' on them so that they will repay him with kindness and fellow-feeling. Like Candide, he is on the receiving end of a series of misfortunes so great that a normal person would be driven to extreme misanthropy, but for the irretrievably innocent Adam there is nothing that can make him stop living in hope. The final irony is the murder he commits, killing the beastly wife of another of his father figures in the hope that this will demonstrate his gentlemanly commitment to settling his debts. As with his present-giving, he is attempting in his own way to become a benefactor. It is, of course, a misguided effort, but Adam nevertheless acts as a foil to the rich and powerful, whose actions and motives are far less generous.

Psychopaths

In creating Ripley, Highsmith leaves open the possibility of interpreting his behaviour as schizophrenic: for example, he is able, once he has returned to his identity as Tom Ripley, to free himself from guilt for a murder committed whilst impersonating Dickie. The emphasis, however, is strongly on his typicality, his American versatility and blankness of character. Viewed in this light, his ability to reinvent himself as the occasion demands and to feel as 'free of guilt as his old suitcase' (154) is symptomatic of the widespread tendency to evade feelings of guilt and responsibility. He has the optimistic American belief in fresh starts, the standard delusion of noir protagonists. Our dominant impression of Ripley is not of psychological imbalance but of rational self-interest, and in fact part of his insidious appeal lies in his sheer pragmatism. It lies in the fact that he does not resort to murder except when it presents itself as the only reasonable means of securing his goal or preserving his freedom.

A number of other protagonist killer narratives of the time, however, are so extreme in their behaviour that the label of 'psychopath' is more obviously appropriate. By the fifties, the pop-psychology clichés of the psychopath were firmly entrenched and frequently deployed in both the fiction and the films of the period. This is a trend that has continued; over the last three or four decades audiences have been agreeably terrified at the cinema by many memorable incarnations of the psychopath as alien and monstrous, a darkly irrational threat to normal society whose death brings closure, allaying our fears of otherness. In much fiction of the fifties and sixties, even where the psychopath is presented as a superficially affable figure who tricks people into thinking of him as normal, he is also readily identified and eliminated. The novels of John D. MacDonald, for example, frequently centre on the opposition between normative and psychopathic (or 'sociopathic') characters. Travis McGee is given the task of defeating such opponents as the amoral predator Junior Allen in *The Deep Blue Good-by* (1964) and, in *The Girl in the Plain Brown Wrapper* (1968), Tom Pike, a magnetic, shrewd, entrepreneurial type who likes 'killing folks' (78, 302). In MacDonald's non-Travis McGee novels, such characters are sometimes given their own sections of narrative, bringing them much more to the fore, as in *April Evil* and *The Neon Jungle* (1953), though here again they are by the end isolated and destroyed. The use of the psychopath as narrator was well enough established by the late fifties for it to be readily available at the slick and quick end of the paperback market, for example in British gangster novellas like Hank Janson's *Kill This Man*, the narrator of which is a psychotic hit man whose sadism has been provoked by female submissiveness (his mother, caricatured as a grotesque old hag grovelling before him) and who likes 'to see folk running around doing what I tell them . . .' (11).

Less routine, more disturbing representations of the psychopath, however, use the figure not as an alien evil but in the double role of parodic representation and embittered satirist, like Travis Bickle in *Taxi Driver* (Scorsese, 1976), 'the only character who possesses a moral vision'.[29] As in *Kiss Tomorrow Goodbye*, our perspective on events may be controlled by the psychopath's own point of view. Such narratives often blur the contrast between conventional and aberrant behaviour. This is an effect also familiar, for example, in the films of Hitchcock, whose psychopaths, though easily subjected to pop-psychological diagnosis, are disturbing precisely because of their apparent normality: films like *Shadow of a Doubt* (1943), *Rope* (1948), *Strangers on a Train* (1951) and *Psycho* (1960) implicate the audience by hinting at the criminal potential in everyone. In *Strangers on a Train*, Hitchcock's adaptation of Highsmith's first novel, we are led to share the wish of Guy (Farley Granger) to get rid of his troublesome wife and we feel the insidious appeal of Bruno (Robert Walker).[30] In *Shadow of a Doubt*, Uncle Charlie, a man indistinguishable from respectable people (honoured by the townsfolk at his funeral), functions as a scourge of small-town hypocrisy, excoriating the 'swine' you would see if you ripped the fronts off the houses: 'He is a killer with a mission, bent on the destruction of what he sees as ugly. . . .'[31]

The idea of killing as social criticism is developed in both Jim Thompson and Patricia Highsmith novels. In Thompson's *Nothing More Than Murder* (1949), for example, there is a summary of the news of the time, with random deaths and people being 'blown up, drowned, smothered, starved, lynched. Mercy killings, hangings, electrocutions, suicides. People who didn't want to live. People who deserved killing. People who were better off dead' (27–8). Thompson was one of the most remarkable of the fifties successors to writers like James M. Cain and Horace McCoy and, like them, he gained greater recognition in France than in America.[32] He is, however, more self-consciously modernist than either and, in his best-known novels, far more radically unsettling. The French proclaimed him to be 'le plus noir', the most American and the most pessimistic of the noir thriller writers.[33] Highsmith, who lived for most of her adult life in France, was in fact another writer better known and more highly respected in Europe than America. Thompson is obviously in many respects a very different writer from Highsmith, who would, for a start, never be grouped with the hard-boiled school. But in their representations of psychopathic personalities there are some striking similarities. Both writers specialise in narratives that play on the 'abnormally normal'[34] appearance and behaviour of the psychopathically unbalanced killer. Neither is aiming simply for the shock value of violence emerging where it is least expected. In their novels, the 'average-looking', 'everyone's next-door neighbour' identity of the killer is used as a means of implying that psychosis is in some ways a representative condition. Their killers' minds are split between conformity and violation. They are divergent enough to provide a cynically detached commentary on the society through which they move, but nevertheless simulate normality in an utterly plausible way. The effect is that, in looking at them, we both feel complicity and see, reflected in their states of mind, the suppressed violence of the whole community, whether the affluent suburbia of Highsmith or Thompson's typical American small town.

Highsmith's *Deep Water* (1957) is, like the earlier *Strangers on a Train*, the portrait of a blandly appealing psychopath, a man who does not see himself at all in this light, though 'diagnosed' within the text as borderline psychopath. The entirely civilised Vic van Allen, with his pleasant, 'ambiguous' face (9), scrupulously retains a demeanour that conforms to the rules of society. But he is different enough and intelligent enough to see through the pretences and petty vanities of others, and on most social occasions we are party to the acerbic running commentary in Vic's internal reflections – his sarcastic observations, his caricatured images and the surreal insights that liberate him from a stifling environment. When told '"He thinks you're cracked"', Vic replies '"And the cracks shall make you free"' (163). He also commits three perfectly understandable murders. Since, in Highsmith's third-person narration, we stay very close to Vic's mind, we are led to see his killings as his ultimate expression of the contempt he feels for his neighbours. In his farewell reflections on Wilson, who seems to him to represent 'perhaps half the people on earth', he smiles 'at Wilson's grim, resentful, the-world-owes-me-a-living face, which was the reflection of the small, dull mind behind it. . . . Vic cursed it and all it stood for. Silently, and with a smile . . . he cursed it' (259–60).

From 1949 on, with *Nothing More Than Murder*, Jim Thompson created a succession of offbeat and subversive portraits of psychologically disturbed protagonist-murderers. *Nothing More than Murder* was followed by *The Killer Inside Me* (1952), *Savage Night* (1953), *A Hell of a Woman* (1954), *The Nothing Man* (1954), *A Swell-Looking Babe* (1954) and *Pop. 1280* (1964). All but *A Swell-Looking Babe* are written in the first person, and all use the form for savage satiric exposure. The most remarkable and ambitious of these are the first novel Thompson wrote for Lion, *The Killer Inside Me*, and a companion piece written a dozen years later, also for Lion, *Pop. 1280*.[35] In both novels, the alienated position of the psychopath creates a perspective from which he looks down on his small-town society as a scathing observer, stripping off illusory surfaces and denouncing what he sees. Robert Elliott, in *The Power of Satire*, quotes Ben Jonson's lines on Archilochus, who according to tradition could 'Rime 'hem to death'. This 'curious legend', as Elliott observes, captures something of the 'malefic power' of the satirist to wound his enemies: 'The word could kill; and in popular belief it *did* kill.'[36] For Lou Ford and Nick Corey, the killer-protagonists of *The Killer Inside Me* and *Pop. 1280*, there is also a strong connection between the 'malefic power' of words and the act of murder. The satirist's curse is a substitute for killing: 'I wanted . . . [to] do something worse' (*Killer Inside Me*, 51). When Lou and Nick do kill, they represent themselves as simply taking to a logical conclusion their critiques of small-town American society, and as putting into practice the secret wishes harboured by others. Both are 'typical' not just in the sense that they have the chameleon-like ability to impersonate 'normality' but also in that they do 'what other people merely think'.[37] They are shown as conforming scrupulously to the conventional social forms that, as lawmen, they officially uphold, but as cynically recognising the hollowness of these forms and of the 'pretendsy' (*Killer Inside Me*, 187) nature of most people's apparent adherence to them. Lou Ford's role as denouncer of a corrupt and morally bankrupt society is most to the fore in his speech to Johnnie Pappas, whom he is readying himself to kill: '"Yeah, Johnnie . . . it's a screwed up, bitched up world, and I'm afraid it's going to stay that way. . . . Because no one, almost no one, sees anything wrong with it"' (118). Much of the surreal, blackly comic force of *The Killer Inside Me* comes from the tension between the two sides of Lou's personality, a tension that manifests itself in his straight-faced parodies of cliché and in ironies that only he can fully understand. Conveying the real anger felt by those at the bottom of the heap who are terrorised into obedience, Lou represents his own schizophrenia as an internalisation of society's hypocrisy: '"I guess I kind of got a foot on both fences. . . . All I can do is wait until I split"' (119).

Pop. 1280 has another small-town sheriff who acts as both the expression and the self-appointed scourge of a sick society. Nick Corey presents himself as someone who will not 'think bad' of people 'until I absolutely have to'. But when he does make up his mind he knows what to do: 'I always know' (21). A trickster figure, moving behind a facade of genial ineffectuality ('"Me? Me kill someone? Aw, now!"' [80]), he satirically exposes and punishes the latent aggressions and iniquities of small-town life. Like Lou Ford, Nick justifies his actions on the grounds that he is just honestly admitting and acting out the self-interest that motivates the entire community: 'What I loved was myself, and I was willing to do anything I god-danged had to to go on lying and cheating and drinking whiskey and screwing women and going to church on Sunday with all the other respectable people' (119–20). He delivers diatribes on communal hatred, hypocrisy and self-deception, and the ironies of his declarations get more savage as the end of the narrative nears. Nick declares that he is going to start cracking down on anyone who breaks a law, '"Providing, o' course, that he's either colored or some poor white trash that can't pay his poll tax"' (155). Much more explicitly than Lou, Nick represents himself as a Christ figure, a final aberration that embodies a pitying and frustrated sense of the awful realities of human life:

> Not homes. . . . Just pine-board walls locking in emptiness. . . . And suddenly the emptiness was filled with . . . all the sad terrible things

> that the emptiness had brought the people to . . . the stink and the terror, the weepin' and wailin', the torture, the starvation, the shame of your deadness. . . . I shuddered, thinking how wonderful was our Creator to create such downright hideous things in the world, so that something like murder didn't seem at all bad by comparison (197–8).

Nick's role, under the circumstances, is just 'followin' the holy precepts laid down in the Bible. . . . To coax [people] into revealin' theirselves, an' then kick the crap out of 'em' (206).

In two of the other paperbacks Thompson wrote for Lion in the fifties, *The Criminal* (1953) and *The Kill-Off* (1957), the central murder is not finally 'solved', nor the murderer known for certain: Thompson has further varied the form of the thriller by providing no answers, no fixing of guilt on one person. Through the device of multiple narrators, he captures the scandal-mongering and ill nature that set the tone of small-town life and establishes the shared guilt of a whole community. As Nick Corey says – getting to the heart of Thompson's own satiric methods – '"there can't be no personal hell because there ain't no personal sins. They're all public, George, we all share in the other fellas' and the other fellas all share in ours"' (98).

5
Fatal Women

On the pulp fiction covers of the 1950s the most familiar figure is the femme fatale. She is repeated with countless minor variations, the immodest icon for a period during which sex became one of the major ingredients in the paperback boom. This is the decade that saw the beginning, both in film and pulp literature, of a great outpouring of femme fatale plots.[1] The changes taking place in the representation of women in crime fiction could also be observed in the pulp magazines of the era. *Black Mask* covers which in the 1930s had depicted women as helpless victims were by the 1940s picturing aggressive dames shooting .45 s or even sub-machine guns, or stamping with spiked heels on a man's hand.[2] In the fifties, this iconography was made still more provocative in the cover art of the host of new paperback originals being published by Gold Medal, Lion and others.

A handful of the paperback covers is reproduced here (Figures 4–7): Miss Otis, reclining in a flimsy gown and red bracelet, with extravagant blonde curls and lips parted seductively on the cover of a British gangster paperback of the early 1950s; with the same Veronica Lake hair, wearing a tight sweater and thrusting her hip out in a provocative pose, David Goodis' 'blonde on the street corner' (1954); the sultry, scantily clad redhead who lies back holding a motel key in one hand and a cigarette in the other on the 1961 cover of Charles Williams' *Stain of Suspicion* (1957); and Hal Ellson's *Tomboy* (1957), represented on the cover as a Lolita-like street urchin, posed in much the same way as any street-corner blonde, leaning back, tight-sweatered, cigarette in hand, wearing an expression that is unmistakably sexual in its appeal. The grown-up version of the look had been amply established in the *films noirs* of the mid-1940s: Barbara Stanwyck in *Double Indemnity* (1944), Veronica Lake in *The Blue Dahlia*, Ava Gardner in *The Killers*, Rita Hayworth in *Gilda*,

Figure 4 Ben Sarto, *Miss Otis Blows Town* (1953)

Figure 5 David Goodis, *The Blonde on the Street Corner* (1954)

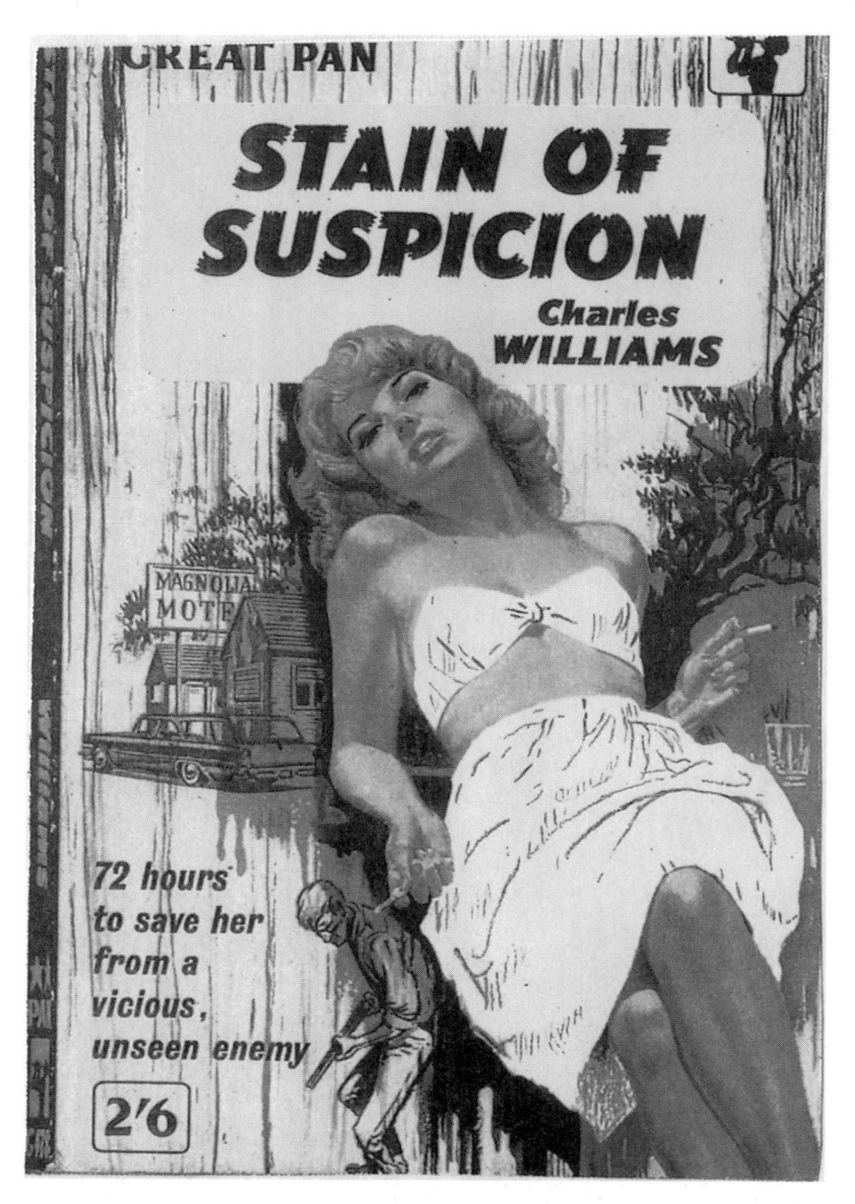

Figure 6 Charles Williams, *The Stain of Suspicion* (Pan, 1959)

Figure 7 Hal Ellson, *Tomboy* (Bantam, 1957)

Jane Greer in *Out of the Past* (all 1946–7).[3] One of the defining characteristics of the noir cycle has been seen as the increased centrality of the female figure, with the woman becoming crucial to the hero's struggles and perhaps constituting his central problem, contributing to his sense of an unstable world and of the failure of masculine desire.[4]

The power of such roles and the reproduction of such images have ensured that the femme fatale is (with the exception of Bogart's Philip Marlowe or Sam Spade) the most immediately recognisable of noir's iconic figures. The elements of the image constitute a kind of visual shorthand for dangerous attraction and steamy corruption. It is an explicitly sexual iconography, and the threat represented by the dangerous woman is sometimes simply that of the sexual predator drawing in a male protagonist who suffers loss of control and destabilisation of identity. Such anxieties are also, however, generated by the much more direct imitation of male aggression and appropriation of male power. In addition to holding a cocktail glass or a smouldering cigarette, the femme fatale often holds a gun on the cover and has by the end of the narrative pulled the trigger.

But if you look beyond the boldly clichéd cover art you see that many of the noir thrillers of the 1950s not only reproduce but rewrite and challenge the stereotype of the sexual, aggressive, independent woman. Even within *film noir* the audience can be brought to look critically at the male compulsion to control women sexually and at the way in which male society itself is culpable. It can be distanced from the male perspective, or can be brought to witness something of the inner struggles of the femme fatale.[5] The underlying 'message' of dangerous woman films is often that 'the male ideal of self-sufficiency is not only impossible to achieve but in many ways self-destructive': women are 'merely catalysts, and in the end it is often the men who are destructive to themselves'.[6] Hollywood, however, constrained not only by the Hays Code but by conventional expectations about the ultimate repression of the sexual, aggressive woman, tended to package the femme fatale narrative in ways that limited the 'progressiveness' of the cycle and confirmed popular prejudices by figuring the defeat of the independent female and the reassertion of male control.[7] Novelists were free to play much more extensively *against* stereotype, often setting up plots that initially lead us to judge according to stereotype and then reversing our expectations, or complicating our judgements and in the process establishing strong female figures who, though sexual, are admirable and/or indomitable. The literary as opposed to the Hollywood femme fatale is less likely to be repressed, killed or otherwise punished for her strength and transgression.

All four of the covers illustrated here helped to sell novels that subvert the expectations that they would have aroused in their readers. Ben Sarto's Miss Otis is true to type in her qualities. She is brashly sexual, 'daintily cruel' (75–6) and manipulative, but unlike the standard Hollywood femme fatale she is not doomed to destruction by these qualities. She is in fact a series character, both tough and sympathetic, a hard-headed business woman who is as much a survivor as, say, Defoe's Moll Flanders. The blonde in the David Goodis novel is seen by the protagonist in conventional terms, but brings death and destruction to no one and has by the end of the novel been allowed to speak quite fully of her own sense of Depression-induced frustration and deprivation. Her primary role on the cover, in fact, is to abet Goodis in establishing formulaic expectations which he will undercut, thus drawing his readers into a sense of how completely immobilising the Depression years were. The cover of Charles Williams' *Stain of Suspicion* deliberately fosters confusion about the identity of the femme fatale and so contributes to the novel's assault on small-town prejudice. The motel and the cover blurb refer to the woman who seems, to the narrow-minded local community, to be the very image of a tramp and a murderess, but her red hair (we eventually realise) identifies her as another woman, the actual killer, unsuspected by any of her townsfolk because she appears to everyone to be 'the generic young suburban housewife' (154). Hal Ellson's Tomboy, a character whose inner life we come to understand even more fully, is revealed as a frightened young girl who has assumed a role – knowing and aggressive – which helps her to survive in a tough urban world. This chapter looks at some of the pulp fiction in which femme fatale stereotypes are deployed in an obvious and straightforward way, but mainly considers the wide variety of ways in which these stereotypes are challenged and undermined.

Tramps and tomboys

The repression of the 'dangerous female' in conventional *film noir* is much discussed. Janey Place, for example, categorises *film noir* as a male fantasy that first allows the expression of female power and then destroys it, and argues that if cinema audiences remember *film noir*'s 'potent stylistic presentation of the sexual strength of women which man fears', they will also remember the defeat of this transgressive strength.[8] Whilst the more sophisticated examples of literary noir play knowingly with and ironically expose this male fantasy, there is also, of course, a large body of pulp fiction that exploits stereotypical expectations just as unashamedly. In Harry Whittington's *Hell Can Wait*, for example, Angie, the femme fatale, is introduced to us as the very embodiment of the tramp who drives men to raging jealousy, using sex to acquire wealth, inconstant and opportunistic in her attachments. On the opening page she is sprawled provocatively in a bikini, taunting the adoring young man who stands over her with a look that establishes her effortless ascendancy: 'From the way she regarded him, you got the faint sensation that she was looking down on him' (5).

The reversal implied by Angie's challenge to the male gaze is one of the greatest inherent dangers associated with the fatal woman. She appropriates masculine powers, creating a persona that both attracts and threatens the noir male. Whittington's narrator is insulated from Angie's charms by the fact that he is still grieving for his dead wife, but noir plotting generally requires the protagonist himself to succumb. This is a pattern often found in a strikingly overstated form in British gangster paperbacks of the 1950s, which provide not just a wide selection of femme fatale plots but a lively diversity of images containing the paradoxical combination of 'masculine' and 'feminine' traits that conventionally characterise the 'potent' woman. The murderous woman, uniting exaggerated feminine attributes with a 'male' potential for violence and aggression, is explosively embodied by Clara in Duke Linton's *Crazy to Kill* (1950). She is a woman whose softly feminine attractions are themselves a deadly weapon: 'Clara with two ivory-hued mounds of feminine dynamite exposed . . . to an inch above the hard, detonating nipples' (24). Alternatively cross-dressing can be the correlative of this contradiction, as it is, for example, in *Dainty Was a Jane* (1948), by Darcy Glinto (Harold Ernest Kelly), a novel that is in many ways, as Glinto says, just 'the old, old stuff' about gangland violence, but with something that 'added up different' because one of the main gang members is actually 'a top class dame masquerading as a guy' (126). 'Dainty' Sabina, though doomed to death in the end, carries a knife and is violent and ambitious enough to aspire to gang leadership.

The 'unnaturally' sexual, aggressive, death-dealing woman is also separated from the human norm by her association with images of animality and madness. The connection between unclean female sexuality and mental instability is epitomised in the scene in Charles Willeford's *Wild Wives* (1956) in which the protagonist tries to interpret the dying words of the husband he has helped to kill: 'Something about sanitation – sanity?' (70–1). In British crime novels of the time, protagonists encounter 'completely screwy' women transformed by drugs and female hysteria into crazed animals 'that clawed and shrieked'; they see 'lovely lips' revealing a maniacal nature by being 'curled back in a snarl'.[9] The equation of female aggression and sexuality with perverse moral madness and mental sickness is one of the commonplaces of the time, the strongest implication being that certain kinds of sexual behaviour in women itself undermines 'sane' social arrangements. Just as sexual recklessness is there for all to see on the average pulp cover, the signs of underlying psychological imbalance are so standardised as to be easily recognisable. In a run-of-the-mill American thriller of the late fifties, Day Keene's *Dead Dolls Don't Talk* (1959), the murderess ('a sort of slob's Jayne Mansfield') is presented as the very image of her psychosis, her 'sins and excesses . . . beginning to show in her face. . . . The girl couldn't be really sane' (7–16). In Bruno Fischer's *The Lady Kills* (1951) the clues to an unbalanced character are to be discovered in childhood aberrations, such as her willingness to shoot an old dog ('King') that had to be put down (48). When this 'king-killer' appears to have killed again (69–70), she presents it as self-defence against male violence. What she is constructing, however, is a duplicitous female narrative, which is in due course discredited by male probity. As the father says 'sardonically', '"Women make pretty noble creatures of us men . . ."' (31).

One way of partially altering the representation of the femme fatale is to make it 'the truth of the matter' that female violence is only a response to the violence of the 'noble creatures' themselves. Combined with the kind of slick plot reversal more characteristic of the traditional detective story, this strategy can be found in Fredric Brown's *The Screaming Mimi* (1949), which creates narrative suspense by revealing the 'ripper' to be a woman rather than a man, but which compensates the woman by its pop psychological explanation that she herself was the victim of an earlier (male) ripper. A more serious exploration of male culpability is John Franklin Bardin's *Devil Take the Blue-Tail Fly*, published in England in 1948 but (though Bardin was American) without an American publisher until nearly 20 years later.[10] It is a novel that has strong affinities with the psychological focus and oneiric quality of much classic *film noir*. Although it lacks the wider social resonance of many male killer narratives, it develops the theme of patriarchal oppression through a haunting and sympathetic study of a mind unable to escape from the prison of a male-dominated past. Her father was 'a strong man' who 'enclosed his family, locked them within the bounds of his own personality' (77–9), and the male world has continued to be imprisoning for Ellen, a musician whose music signifies her own being, the inner, expressive self that is sacrificed in the effort to bring her into conformity with a 'sane' role. Repressive male power is also wielded by her husband, Basil, who has locked her harpsichord and hidden the key, making her believe eventually that the key was in the harpsichord all along – that is, that she herself 'held the key' instead of the patriarchy. Ellen is encouraged by her psychiatrist to 'stand aside . . . and inspect herself' (67), in effect to abandon her own perspective and see herself with the eyes of others. Ironically, it is her second self, 'Nelle', that presides over her madness, separating itself from the adjusted, social self of Ellen and dictating the violent adjustments she makes to her world.

An environmental explanation of the action of the femme fatale can work in an analogous way, shifting responsibility to a male-dominated society that has (just as in the thirties gangster saga) inadvertently formed an aggressor as a by-product of victimisation. Even a novel with as clichéd a title as Wade Miller's *Kitten with a Whip* (1959) can diverge from the expectations encouraged by presenting the 'kitten' as 'just a pitiful kid, born with two strikes against her and a broken bat in her hands' (12), doomed by her background to 'end up lousy' (15). In contrast to the femme fatale in, say, *The Lady Kills* (a spoiled rich girl whose female evil is clearly inherent rather than socially conditioned), the 'kitten', though almost equally close to the type of the slut (entrapping, scheming and playing on her childlike appearance), is explained as a product of a world that is itself 'childishly muddled' (36).

Whether naturally mad and bad or driven to aggression by a bad male world, the femmes fatales considered so far have all been fated themselves to 'end up lousy', and this kind of containment of their disruptive aggression and sexuality is fairly standard in the fiction as well as the films of the time. Literary noir does not, however, require 'a reassertion of control on the part of the male subject'[11] and in fact offers ample opportunities for the survival and even the prospering of the tough, independent, sexual woman. In a canonical *film noir* like *Out of the Past* (aka *Build My Gallows High*, directed by Jacques Tourneur, 1947), Kathie Moffett (Jane Greer), the seductive and coolly calculating femme fatale, must in the end meet her death. In the novel *Build My Gallows High*, however, the Geoffrey Homes (Daniel Mainwaring) book on which the film is based, 'Mumsie', as she is in the novel, is not killed. She is throughout the true spider woman, 'collecting' men and willing to do whatever it takes to acquire and hang on to money, a 'realist' who establishes for herself 'a good life, all the dough she wanted. . . . No illusions' (109). In the end, the taciturn private eye – Red in the book (Jeff Bailey, the Robert Mitchum character in the film) – dies knowing that Mumsie, in spite of her utter cold-heartedness, will survive as part of a set of relationships that always operates.

The tough tart who seems able to survive in a male world better than most men in fact becomes a familiar figure in both American and British pulps of the time. She can be seen in her most caricatured form, for example, in a British gangster novel of the fifties, *Yellow Babe*, by 'Ace Capelli', one of the pseudonyms of Stephen Frances, who also wrote the Hank Janson novels. The narrative centres on Lotus, a Chinese singer, a 'reigning moll-in-chief' who is dismissed as a dumb broad, 'just a little yellow babe without all her buttons' (10). Perfectly feminine but actually a manipulative survivor, she is not to be blamed for her treatment of men because '"She learned in a tough school"' (86). She has lived 'with one gangster lover after another and always the minks that go with them and the emotion growing cold inside her . . .' (81–6). When she and her lover are caught by the gang boss ('Johnny was in a pair of shorts. . . . She wasn't dressed as formally as Johnny' [84]), Johnny is emasculated, but, tough as ever (and with no more use for the unfortunate Johnny), Lotus emerges in one piece, eventually becoming 'a famous girl in her own light' (88–90).

It is a relatively short step from allowing the survival of the powerful woman to the more thoroughgoing enjoyment of her toughness and allure. One of the most entertaining examples of such a figure is to be found in another fifties series of British gangster paperbacks, featuring the character of Miss Otis, who happily indulges her proclivities and seems to regret very little. Ben Sarto's (Fawcett's) Miss Otis novels started with *Miss Otis Comes to Piccadilly* in 1946. From a male point of view, they can perhaps be seen as an over-the-top and therefore fear-free indulgence in the 'forbidden' fantasy of the powerful and indestructible female with all her erotic allure intact. In American sensationalist and erotic paperbacks of the same period, there was a distinct market in lesbian fiction[12] and it seems clear that Miss Otis had something of the attraction of a leather-clad dominatrix, the same kind of 'strong woman' appeal to be found in the pulp erotica of the time. The opening description in *Miss Otis Throws a Come-Back* (1949) captures Mabie Otis in all her glory: nearly six feet tall in her high heels, full-bosomed, posing with a 'cat-like voluptuousness . . . with an underlying suggestion of strength and cruelty', the silk of her dress stretched tightly over her thigh, 'making the limb look as if tautened for a spring. An experienced dame, you would say' (3). 'The Otis' is a kind of Thatcherite gangster's moll, running her own business and more than a match for the men who try to take her on. This tough broad is the femme fatale given 'hero status', unashamedly sexual, dominant, hard-headed, smart and calculating, manipulative – and hugely popular.[13] In *Miss Otis Throws a Come-Back,* she is in business with an ex-FBI officer who has become an entrepreneur with 'the many bucks any clever cop can get on the side', but who is not man enough to satisfy the Otis, who longs for a man who can 'ride up rough with her on occasion'. In *Miss Otis Blows Town* (1953), when her current man is shot dead by a rival gang, she has to decide which of the available men she will use to help and sexually entertain her. Well able to remain cool and magnificent in a crisis, she manages at the end to see off the hit man sent to kill her by taking his gun away, slipping 'the little gat from under her mink' to disarm Swell Jacky (109, 127).

A much younger and far less assured version of the strong woman is created in *Tomboy* (1950), by Hal Ellson, who wrote (out of his personal experience of working with violent teenagers in New York) over a dozen juvenile delinquent novels, starting with *Duke* (1949), the story of a black Harlem gang leader.[14] *Tomboy,* Ellson's second novel, is a reversal of the more usual divided woman image. Rather than being a character who conceals aggression under a softly feminine exterior, the protagonist must, to survive in a street gang, conceal her soft side. Even more than Miss Otis, she acquires toughness in order to survive by the rules of the male world. Tomboy, the sadistic bitch of the juvenile gang, is also Kerry, a 'lost soul', a frightened child living a life of precarious poverty, with a drunken father and an absent mother. As with the male victim/transgressor protagonist, we see the ironic gap between public self (tough, competent) and inner self, alienated, adrift, disguising fear as bravado and cruelty. In a world in which only men are regarded as capable of competent agency, Tomboy has deliberately and successfully modelled herself on male behaviour. When she says she wishes she were a boy, Mick replies, 'Well, I don't blame you for wishing that. It's kind of lousy to be a girl, I guess. A boy can do everything. Girls can hardly do anything. . . . Except you, Kerry (40, 24). In initiating new members into the gang, she is even more savage than the boys, in a willed reversal of the active-male passive-female duality: 'Tomboy struck savagely and was the last to stop. . . . "I don't have to take it," Tomboy said. "I hand it out"' (25, 38). But the scenes in which she behaves in a violent and sadistic way are interspersed with frequent reminders of her terrified private self ('there was nothing, nothing anywhere except the sound of her sobbing' [67]). It is only as part of the gang, that she can briefly forget 'that dark, bleak world outside' (71). The sense of her own dispossession surfaces repeatedly, leading to an end in which she goes on the run with Lucky: '"Okay, we made it, kid. . . . We're off for somewhere. How do you feel?" "Scared," Tomboy answered. "Scared as hell!"' (150).

Seeing double

Ellson uses an internally divided female protagonist to challenge the conventional judgement of conformity and violation of conformity. He creates, in *Tomboy*, sympathy for a character who, superficially viewed, seems sadistic and who apparently is completely separate from 'decent' society, turning instead to the juvenile gang for support and for her sense of self. This fragmenting of identity, giving us access to a hidden side of a character's subjectivity, can also be an important element in *film noir*, if, for example, directors find ways of giving the audience a more complex image of the woman as someone who is herself involved in performance and in the manipulation of her image, perhaps trapped by the role she performs[15] just as Tomboy is by her tough public image. The written text provides more obvious opportunities for giving space to competing narrative voices, and literary noir of the period accordingly offers many more instances than does *film noir* of this self-division.

Cornell Woolrich, for example, pays close attention to the subjective experience of his women and to their ability to create different selves as the occasion demands, a process dramatised in such novels as *The Bride Wore Black* (1940) and *I Married a Dead Man* (1948, written as William Irish.) [16] In *Waltz into Darkness* (1947, also written as William Irish), Woolrich creates an archetypal destructive and seductive femme fatale who is also ultimately a sympathetic character because of the space provided for a counter-image of inner struggle to emerge. By setting the story in the nineteenth century, Woolrich foregrounds the 'modern woman' iconography that marks Julia out as a femme fatale, for example, the 'slips' she makes by smoking or by displaying her more sexual side. Woolrich's tendency to represent a woman's apparent nature not as a product of inherent traits but as something constructed carries the implication that a 'bad' or 'good' role can be assumed by any woman (the bad, of course, corresponding to the dark seductress at home in 'the world of cheap dives', the good to the innocent, redemptive woman capable of faithfulness and self-sacrifice).[17] There is also, however, a suggestion in *Waltz* that the 'good wife' image of 'Julia' is constructed out of some inherently childlike quality in her other self, 'Bonny', that has been destroyed by her experiences. At the end of the novel, 'another face, never born' peers through her mask, strengthening our impression of a woman trapped by the roles she plays (302).

Writers of the time often handle the dark/domestic contrast with a lightness which suggests how laughably stereotypical it was. Harry Whittington, in *You'll Die Next* (1954), for example, plays with the idea of a protagonist who is anxiously uncertain about how the opposing traits might be combined in his own wife, in the past a beautiful singer who might really be a femme fatale. Can he trust her or does her past contain secrets that have now surfaced to destroy him? Does her domestic 'performance' hide a femme fatale who would betray him? The domestic woman/sexual woman dichotomy dominates the opening pages of the novel. Lila making Henry popovers for breakfast is juxtaposed with her past in the Kit-Kat Club and with her skills in bed, raising the question of whether the latter necessarily indicate a louche past, or whether they are (as Lila implies) just a part of their 'ordinary' domesticity, to be rounded off by a good breakfast.[18]

Opposing female types represented by the creation of pairs of women are a recurrent element in both cinematic and literary noir. In *film noir*, *Dark Mirror* (Robert Siodmak, 1946), with Olivia de Havilland in a sane twin–mad twin plot, is one of the most discussed examples of a convention-confirming double-woman plot, in which the mad twin is the embodiment of aggressive sexuality, female violence and duplicity. An equally schematic literary treatment of the theme is James M. Cain's *Sinful Woman* (1948), in which contrasted twins are similarly used to characterise female sexuality. Sylvia Shoreham is an actress who plays both 'good' female roles (Edith Cavell) and 'bad' roles (' I Took the Low Road'). Her sister, the deranged Hazel, acts as a kind of parodic version of the femme fatale roles of Sylvia, imitating her gestures and expressions while she engages in a series of casual liaisons that would 'make a hooker in the Red Mill at Tijuana look like a Minnesota schoolteacher' (78).

Some of Margaret Millar's psychological melodramas are also built around this kind of pairing, using the coupling to mystify the reader, as it does in *Dark Mirror*, but also to explore the subjective experience of women trapped within socially constructed female roles. *The Iron Gates* (1945), for example, creates two maternal perspectives, that of a naive/angelic biological mother and that of a treacherous/phallic step-mother haunted by her murder of the biological mother. Characteristically of Millar, the guilt is shared and sympathies divided: the 'good mother' has been culpably passive and naive, and the suffering of the murderess is fully represented as she experiences a terrifying rift between her inner turmoil and the conventional social self that she 'makes up' when she looks in the mirror (34). In Millar's *Beast in View* (1955) the supposed female victim is actually the predator, a woman compensating for childhood humiliation by becoming her own version of the 'good girl' to whom she was always compared, and on whom the guilt for her crimes appears to fall. There are similarities with *Dark Mirror*, in which the bad twin, jealous of the favoured twin, accomplishes such a reversal, though in the Millar novel it is the non-sexual woman, 'the prude' (179), who is bad. Shamed by her realisation that her parents think her incapable of fulfilling the 'desired' female role, she abandons her real self and in revenge transforms herself into the stereotype of the bad girl who is attractive to men, becoming her rival not as she is but as Helen constructs her, the harpie, a 'deformed twin' (158).

Like her husband, Ross Macdonald (Kenneth Millar), Margaret Millar deals recurrently with the psychology of crime. Her novels are complicated psychological puzzles that keep her readers in suspense as well as working to dismantle the whore/angel duality. Other writers of the time found a variety of ways, generally less convoluted than Millar's, of building their plots around two women whose fates are intertwined and whose story in some sense acts to counter conventional expectations about female guilt and innocence. The most well-worn ploy is simply the representation of the 'bad' woman as inherently good or the conventionally virtuous woman as in reality culpable: so, for example, the familiar figure of the whore with the heart of gold shocks bourgeois assumptions in novels like William McGivern's *The Big Heat* (1953); the independent woman who has been misrepresented as a tramp because of small-town prejudice is central to Charles Williams' *Stain of Suspicion* (1958) and Day Keene's *Notorious* (1954).

One of the best-known *film noir* examples of the whore redeemed is the Gloria Grahame character, Debby Marsh, in Fritz Lang's adaptation of McGivern's *The Big Heat* (also 1953). The inner conflict she feels is symbolised by the angelic and the disfigured sides of her face. The disfigured side, scalded by the coffee her gangster lover has thrown at her, is hidden from view as she lies dying, asking Bannion how she would have got on with his dead wife and in the process resurrecting her for Bannion (she was 'an Irish blow-top'). With great pathos, Debby asserts an attachment to normal life. Mrs Deery, on the other hand, appears at the outset as a suspiciously polished example of the perfect wife and grieving widow. In McGivern's novel (which Lang follows fairly closely), Mrs Deery lives in a 'clean, orderly little world' in which she has 'everything about her . . . meticulously arranged' (9), whereas Debby,with her 'tall, spectacular body' (94), is the very image of the high-class prostitute. It is Mrs Deery, however, who is corrupt to the core. Before she shoots Mrs Deery, Debby tells her (in Lang's film version) that they – the respectable wife and the gangster's moll – are 'sisters under the mink', but the comparison, of course, is just the crossing point en route to the final reversal. In shooting Mrs Deery (so that her husband's suicide note, documenting the city's corruption, will be made public) Debby turns the femme fatale into someone who has acted violently with our full approval. Through her usurpation of 'male' power, she has actually made herself a more complete woman: '"I'm a tough guy. I did what you couldn't do, Bannion. I did it for both of us"' (166). Drawn to Bannion because he stood up to her gangster lover, she has finally had the courage to resist her own objectification ('he left me there like an overcoat or something he forgot' [109]), and in learning self-respect has acquired the power to accomplish something wider, ultimately acting not just for Bannion but for '"everybody . . . who lives in the city"' (171).

In one of the more common versions of the two-woman structure, the protagonist is given the task of distinguishing between the two, as, for example, in *Blow Hot, Blow Cold* (1951), by Gerald Butler, a British writer who published half a dozen novels between 1940 and 1951. Butler confronts his protagonist with the dilemma encapsulated in the novel's alternative title, *Choice of Two Women*. A weak-willed drifter and adventurer is driven to choose between an apparently respectable, rich woman and a French barmaid. Although he knows the former to be a 'silly, spoiled child' (68) and the latter to be true to him, he chooses badly, joining in the shady activities of the real fatal woman and leaving the devoted barmaid to reflect ruefully that she has not made him 'any better, any steadier' (191). The more insight the protagonist is given in telling innocence from guilt, of course, the less noir the narrative is likely to be, and the closer to a 'male defence of beleaguered virtue' form, however seemingly unconventional the virtue is. This is most transparent in a simple and only marginally noir novel like *Hell's Angel*, written by Stephen Frances under his Hank Janson pseudonym.[19] An ill-assorted group sheltering from an approaching hurricane in a coastal hotel in Florida includes two women: 'the Blonde', Paula, who is 'all woman. All sex . . .', and Muriel, 'a young expensively dressed woman who acted too superior to deign to notice that anyone existed outside of herself' (31). When we first meet them, neither woman is given a name, which accentuates the typing, and the contrast is underlined by their conflicts. Muriel, charging that Paula is no different from '"a professional"', is told by Janson that 'respectable' women only differ from her because '"their price included a wedding ring"' (90). It is, of course, the blonde's own fortitude and cunning that actually resolve the danger, in a situation in which the 'good woman' is worse than useless.

The confined space of the hotel in *Hell's Angel* is used to establish a social microcosm, containing a representative collection of prejudices and misperceptions. In American noir of this period, it is again very often the small town that serves as this kind of microcosm, within which negative judgements of the apparent femme fatale are used as a measure of bigotry and of the limitations of a conformist ethos. In Charles Williams' *Stain of Suspicion*, the hostility of a small town is turned against a woman, Mrs Langston, who appears to fit the stereotype of the femme fatale, and, in town gossip, is widely assumed to have killed her husband in collaboration with her lover. The very respectable-looking wife of the sheriff, Mrs Redfield, is, however, the actual murderess, whom we eventually realise must be the femme fatale on the novel's 1961 cover. She has killed her previous husband as well for a small insurance policy, but has not been found out because 'she's not the type' (129): 'I was positive she'd killed a man, and maybe she'd killed two, but you couldn't really believe it. I looked at the modest cotton dress, the flat slippers, the pony tail . . . this was the generic young suburban housewife . . .' (154). Day Keene's *Notorious* is similarly plotted to reverse a town's 'accepted' assessments of two female characters: Marva, a nightclub singer, who is typed as a loose woman from the moment she returns to the town she had left in disgrace, and her opposite number, the apparently regular and virtuous postmistress, Hannah Merry, 'one of the nicest girls in town' (153). The latter not only kills but uses her position to throw suspicion on Marva. By foregrounding the real killer's methods of manipulating local opinion, *Notorious* implicitly suggests the *type* of the femme fatale (nightclub singer, suspected call girl) is a construct of the small-town mentality, a ready-made image easily summoned up by a cunning rival.

In the above examples, it will be clear that what such novels often do is to exonerate one strong woman (the supposed 'scarlet woman') whilst identifying another kind of strong woman (the covert tramp and killer) as the source of evil. The tough woman remains suspect and dangerous, even though female independence seems to be endorsed, as when

Marva stands up to her accusers, showing that there is 'nothing weak or helpless about her' (64). Several writers of the time, however, by focusing on the culpability of female passivity, much more completely overturn the bad/active versus good/passive dichotomy. Although there is a sense in which these are also 'woman-blaming' narratives, they implicitly support female self-assertion. John D. MacDonald, for example, who often conveys a sense of admiration for tough-minded women, also includes in his novels numerous examples of female characters who make the mistake of passivity and whose willingness to submit to male violence serves to encourage it. Betty Mooney in *The Damned* (1952) lets go of her 'hard core of independence' (139) in her relationship with Del Bennicke, not only becoming dependent on a brutal man but allowing 'pain and humiliation' to make her his property. Sylvia Drovek in *The Crossroads* (1961), a masochist who responds to being dominated and frightened, is used and victimised by the men in the novel. Lois Atkinson, in *The Deep Blue Good-by* (1964), acknowledges in her self-diagnosis that she is a natural victim who too readily acts on a 'concealed desire' to accept the kind of domination inflicted on her by Junior Allen, under whose sway she feels a kind of 'terrorised lethargy' (42–4).

The point is made even more strongly in novels that pair the passive woman with a more assertive and active counterpart, in the process forcing us to see female aggression as a healthy contrast to obliging weakness. Dolores Hitchens, for example, in *Stairway to an Empty Room* (1951), juxtaposes the soft and compliant victim/villain Biddy, whose crime has consisted of effacing herself (by pretending to be a murder victim), with her sister, Monica, a resourceful detective figure and self-declared 'old maid', fastidious and 'picky' (11). Controlled by a manipulative scoundrel, Biddy has gone along with a plot to murder another exploited woman, whose body is taken for hers – a crime for which her own husband is wrongly imprisoned. The rightness of the more forceful sister is confirmed through Biddy's abandoned child, whom Monica first calls 'Biddy', but then reflects, 'She's not soft and sweet like Biddy. She's – savage' (17). It is a savagery that is ultimately vindicated, since the child's fierce proclamation of her father's innocence is proven right.

The reassessment of the apparently blameless, passive, victimised female can also be seen in *Prelude to a Certain Midnight* (1947), by Gerald Kersh, who was one of the most individual writers of British noir during this period. Kersh's novel, which centres on the murder of a child by a sadistic killer, much more explicitly places the blame for male violence on masochistic submission in women. Female abjectness is embodied in Catchy, a woman who is so sweet-natured that 'she gave everything, took nothing, and forgave those who ill-treated her . . .' (8–9). The opening glimpse of an older Catchy creates her as a tearful, still masochistic woman who becomes grotesquely drunk in order to forget ('I'd do anything for you, I'd lie down and let you walk on me. I'd be your slave. . . . You're so strong, so ruthless, so powerful . . .' [13–14]). Ironically, given that the murdered child Sonia 'thought the world of her', it is the masochism of Catchy that stirs the sadistic impulses in the murderer who kills Sonia. The investigating detective sets out in some detail the theory of the 'willing victim': 'any woman who gets a thrill out of suffering and submission will . . . stimulate some man . . . to feel he's compelling her to suffer and submit' (51–3). Although Kersh gives only qualified approval to her main foil (Asta Thundersley, the 'sympathetic . . . Battleaxe' [29]), he leaves no question as to Catchy's guilt, and the brutal last paragraph of the novel is given over to her 'maudlin grief, stale liquor and decay', making the narrator long for a high wind 'to blow her and her kind from . . . the fly-blown face of the exhausted earth' (191).

One of those who most consistently works by revising stereotypes of opposed female types is David Goodis, who was amongst the most original and compelling of American paperback crime novelists in the fifties and sixties. Critics have often observed that Goodis repeatedly creates two types of woman, the fragile, waif-like woman, and the fat, aggressive woman (an 'obese, muscular caricature of female dominance, that he really desires', but who seems to the protagonist to block his true happiness with his 'true love').[20] There is an element of truth in this, but it is also the case that the repeated pattern is transformed into a source of narrative and thematic interest by the ways in which Goodis uses the central contrast to consider the femme fatale/good woman duality.

In *Cassidy's Girl* (1951), for example, the play with this dichotomy is signalled by the title itself: is 'Cassidy's Girl' going to turn out to be Mildred (the sexually aggressive woman) or Doris (the waif)? The Doris relationship is linked to a romanticised vision of a dream-escape to South Africa; the Mildred relationship, on the other hand, is associated with what seems throughout most of the novel to be a dead-end environment. Having established the contrast, however, Goodis then overturns it. The 'nightmare' milieu is in fact inhabited by people capable of taking control and asserting their own power, whereas Doris, a princess-in-the-tower figure, does not want to be freed. One of the strengths of the novel lies in its movement towards a refutation of the more conventional noir association of urban sordidness with fatality, and the irony centres not just on Cassidy's delusion about the nature of the choices available to him but on his misreading of the women who define his options. The reader at first tends to accept Cassidy's view of Mildred as a powerful female luring him to destruction, an imprisoning force who seems to have 'put a curse' on him (136–7); in his representation of Doris, Goodis again uses metaphors that are deliberately misleading, suggesting in the early scenes, for example, that she and Cassidy can rise up together like 'battered, choked animals' (41). He also, however, issues warnings about Doris which Cassidy himself refuses to see, describing the 'lost dead look far beyond caring' (48). In a redemptive final showdown, Doris sits oblivious to the scene while Mildred and Shealy (a cynic who insists on recognising the extent of their entrapment but who is also capable of purposeful action) demonstrate a human strength that Cassidy has previously failed to recognise in them because of his own self-contempt for being so 'fallen'.

Goodis' tendency is always to use his pairs of women to tease out conflicts within the protagonist himself, gradually revealing self-deception and self-division, representing the crises faced in terms of choices posed by contrasting relationships. In *The Burglar* (1953) both key women – Gladden and Della – are sympathetic victims as well as fatal women, and Goodis foregrounds from the beginning the inclination of the male world to blame women alone for its failures. The plot hinges on the choices that the protagonist has to make with regard to these relationships, and we ultimately realise that this depends mainly on an unrealised and unresolved tension in his own mind, largely centred on the 'child-woman', Gladden: once again the sexually active female, the 'typed' femme fatale, turns out not to be the destructive force within the novel. *Street of No Return* (1954) similarly uses contrasting women to figure the protagonist's own weakness. Female aggression is located in the sadistic Bertha, a grotesque caricature of a woman who takes pleasure in beating a man into submission; female allure in the loved woman, Celia, a contradictory combination of prostitute and childlike purity. Although she is in thrall to the brutal Sharkey, Celia herself is a sustaining force. It is only when Whitey finally gives up his hopes of her that he loses his male purposefulness altogether and descends to Skid Row ('he could feel his spinal column turning to jelly' [86]), and it is only his final glimpse of her some years later that briefly gives him back his ability to act with some integrity and courage. Celia, then, obviously forms part of a very familiar sexual triangle (the woman of a powerful male whose possession of her is challenged by a weaker male), but in comparison to the traditional femme fatale, she is in herself a woman who strengthens rather than weakens the protagonist.

Seeing through men

In the same year as *Street of No Return*, Goodis published *The Blonde on the Street Corner*, in which he more explicitly establishes his paired women not just as the embodiments of male self-division but as constructions of the protagonist. Each woman is in her own way disturbing to the male sense of self. The poor pale Edna is too good for 'a no-good bum'; the blonde on the street corner threatens to trap him with her 'bargain-counter merchandise' (79–85, 1–2). In many of the best noir thrillers of the period, the figure of the femme fatale in particular is seen through the eyes of a protagonist whose own views are presented as warped, possibly even deranged, and the effect is to undermine the stereotype, revealing it to be the product of male fantasy, desire and the will to dominate. This satiric exposure of male perceptions can be an important element in novels with multiple points of view. John D. MacDonald, for example, in his non-Travis McGee novels, uses multiple perspectives as a means of challenging stereotypes: in *The Damned* (1952), when we are allowed access to the thoughts of the mama's boy, John Carter Gerrold, we see that his disturbed view of his new wife as a murderess explains his capacity for violence towards her; in *The Neon Jungle* (1953) we see women misperceived through the eyes of such characters as Walter Varaki (who likes imagining that he is Mike Hammer) and Vern Lockter (a psychopath who satisfies his power drive by controlling women). In novels which focus our own perceptions through a single protagonist, some of the most effective writers – especially Charles Williams, Charles Willeford and Jim Thompson – structure entire narratives around the satiric presentation of the male point of view, implicitly reassessing the role of the tough and triumphant femme fatale.

The destabilising of point of view is, of course, a crucial element in *film noir* as well as literary noir, though it is not generally possible to handle this as flexibly in film as in novels. Christine Gledhill, for example, analyses the significance of the fact that the images of women projected in *film noir* are produced in the course of male investigations. Female sexuality is contained and rendered less progressive, though voice-over and flashback structures can to some extent serve to undermine the male perspective, suggesting that the story a male narrator tells is wrong, or at least part of a 'complex web of stories'.[21] In literary noir there is often a much stronger emphasis on the distance between the narrating voice, with its expressions of male judgements, and the woman who is being observed and judged. This leaves room not only for an ambiguous response on the part of the reader but for a more radical reversal. It might permit a complete ironising of the male perspective, creating both a subversive representation of male stereotypes and a space within which the strong, independent woman can get and even sometimes keep the upper hand. The noir thrillers of this period, in representing the male need to control women's sexuality in order not to be overwhelmed by it, are often looking critically at this male need. They are in this respect comparable to the neo-noir films of more recent decades (for example, *Vertigo, Chinatown, The Grifters*), in which the threats posed to a man's welfare or psychological stability are represented as the projection of male anxieties. Perceived threats reflect male fears related to uncontrollable drives, the loss of will, subjectivity and conscious agency.[22]

An early example is *Eve* (1945), by James Hadley Chase, in which a first-person narrative is used to ironise the narrator's sense of 'knowing himself'. Both Eve and the narrator, Clive Thurston, are characters who live many lies. His resentment of her duplicity is put into perspective by our recognition of his own more serious deceptions. He leads a 'secret' life as an 'exceedingly unpleasant person', not only dishonest but unethical and 'worthless' (21–2). Clive is ironically planning to write a 'satire on men' when he himself is the figure in the novel ripest for satiric exposure, inhabiting a spiritual–intellectual wasteland summed up in the title of a work by a genuinely talented rival author: *The Land is Barren*. Although Eve's role is to tempt men and disorder their lives (being both literally a whore and the mythic Eve), there is, in contrast to most cinematic versions of the temptress, a strongly sympathetic explanation of her nature, and she remains at the end a kind of eternal principle of tough female self-assertion, whereas the narrator, who has assembled his male persona out of the qualities of others, is punished by damning self-revelation: 'I have . . . stripped myself' (9).

As with other strategies for subverting gender stereotypes, it does not necessarily follow in such texts that the representation of female characters is itself positive. Even if chief blame is shifted to male weakness, the woman can still be duplicitous (like Eve) or as brutal as the men with whom she is involved. This can be seen, for example, in *Hurry the Darkness* (1951), by Maurice Procter, a British ex-cop who was mainly known for a series of police procedurals written in the fifties and sixties, such as *Hell Is a City* (1954).[23] In *Hurry the Darkness*, Procter creates a femme fatale, 'Bud', who seems at first to have all the conventional traits of the man-devouring spider woman. Although she does not, during the course of the narrative, rise markedly in our estimation, a shift in perspective puts her at the end in the position of sympathetic transgressor in flight from the inevitable consequences of her action. She has (justifiably, we feel) shot the male protagonist, Jeff, whose perspective has dominated the rest of the novel and whose views of her are explicitly identified as a product of his own failings: 'Because Jeff knew that he had treated Bud unfairly he drowned a spark of regret – which he did not understand – in a flood of abusive retrospection. . . . She would lie down in the heather with any man who asked her. She was promiscuous, irresponsible, dishonest . . .' (150).

Many American novels of the fifties expose in more thoroughgoing ways self-serving male valuations of women. Wenzell Brown's *The Naked Hours* (1956) begins as a 'lost weekend' novel, with Jack Cowan, presented through close third-person narration, waking up next to 'jailbait'. His first thoughts are murderous ones: 'Cut it out, he warned himself. You were thinking the same thing about Agnes only last night. You got killing on your mind . . .' (7). Cowan has a suppressed past (prison and dishonourable discharge, followed by a mercenary marriage to Agnes, 'hitched to some old bitch that's heavy with dough' [15]). Although he draws back from murder, the real violence of Cowan's nature is imaged in his twinning with a dark double, Bassie, who looks so remarkably like him that he seems 'an extension of his own being' (75). Cowan reflects that 'if he were Bassie' it would be easy to silence Lily by strangling her, and this suppressed violence conditions all of his judgements. Having already agreed to the murder of his own wife, he wishes he had 'choked the life out of [Lily]' earlier (149). When Cowan is brought to trial for his wife's death, readers are able to see clearly how his actions appear to someone other than himself, and they are given no reason to accept his own rationalisations. In the end, only his panic and drunkenness seem to stand as extenuating circumstances. Gil Brewer's *Wild to Possess* (1959) is another close third-person narrative that reveals the protagonist's own character through his assessment of the women with whom he has actual or potential sexual relationships. Four women in all are presented through the eyes of this deeply flawed and aggressively male character: one (the wife he has killed) was 'like a wanton. Greedy and insatiable' (18); another is 'a bitch . . . a lay. To anybody who comes along' (150); a third, 'a knock-out in jet and cream', reminds him of his dead wife (64–5); and even Rita, who is in a small way the heroine, is judged with male scorn ('She was going to be the helpful type. That was all he needed' [62]). As he sums up his position, he reflects, '". . . you can't trust any woman, so what the hell?"' (150).

It is in first-person crime novels, however, that the possibilities for ironising male stereotyping of women can be most fully exploited. Published in the year following *Wild to Possess*, *Nude on Thin Ice* (1960) shows Brewer sharpening his satirical focus by creating a heavily ironised first-person narrator. Callously abandoning one woman, the narrator speeds off in pursuit of another woman perceived in terms of his own sexual fantasies. It is entirely appropriate that his punishment at the end is entrapment with a woman who has ceased to maintain herself as an imitation of male fantasy, instead reverting to the antithesis of the blonde, sylph-like ideal – 'that short fat girl with the oily black hair' (142). Charles Willeford also plays entertainingly with the figure of the self-deceived narrator who alternately desires and fulminates against the fatal women in his life. Willeford, writing paperback originals from the mid-fifties on, seems to have intended publishing with Gold Medal, but as Lee Server says, his eccentricity, his 'Nabokovian sense of humour' and his 'generally insane' protagonists interfered with sales to the more established paperback houses.[24] In *High Priest of California* (1953) Willeford presents one such protagonist, the cold and manipulative Russell Haxby, whose point of view is repeatedly undermined by the ironising of his cynical judgements: Alyce's concealment of the fact that she has a syphilitic husband is particularly unacceptable to him because it is 'the kind of deal that men pulled on women – not women on men' (43). This is juxtaposed with patently insincere moralising. He avers, for example, that marriage is a sacred trust and develops his complaint about the way in which Alyce has treated 'an upstanding fellow who had the best intentions' (43). Even in Willeford's *Wild Wives*, a more conventional treatment of sexual triangles, the narrator's assessments of Florence (the woman with whom he becomes involved) are undermined by his characterisation as a contemptuous user who is himself as guilty as Florence is of trading sex for money (74–5).

As will be apparent from these examples, there was, well established by the mid-fifties, a varied and lively noir practice of ironising male self-deception and the distortions of masculine conceptions of women. Unquestionably, however, the two writers most fully identified with this type of satirised protagonist (generally though not invariably a first-person narrator) were Charles Williams and Jim Thompson. Contributing paperback originals to imprints like Gold Medal and Dell, Williams showed himself to be one of the period's most subtle crime writers, demonstrating, especially in his novels of the mid-fifties, what Geoffrey O'Brien calls a capacity for 'relentless exploration of male character'.[25] Though he is not as savagely eccentric and original a writer as Thompson, he convincingly adopts the personas of narrators whose shoddy morality, unscrupulousness and lack of self-knowledge are part of the substance of the narrative. One of Williams' most gripping pieces of male self-exposure is *Hell Hath No Fury* (1953), probably better known as *Hot Spot*, the title chosen for Dennis Hopper's quite faithful 1990 film adaptation. The descriptions of the femme fatale, Dolores Harshaw, all suggest overripe sexuality. With her 'bos'n's vocabulary', her drinking and her vacillation between being kittenish and belligerent, she is a caricature of woman as sexual predator: 'God knows I've always had some sort of affinity for gamey babes, but she was beginning to be a little rough even for me' (35). Although Dolores, like Victoria Haines in Whittington's *Web of Murder*, can objectively be said to possess many of the attributes of the spider woman, Harry's judgements of her are put into perspective by the fact that he so readily categorises her with the other women he thinks of as having bedevilled his life ('What was my batting average so far in staying out of trouble when it was baited with that much tramp?' [37]). His own complete amorality and self-interest are revealed throughout to be the actual cause of his troubles, and are abundantly apparent before he has anything to do with Dolores. Like the protagonists of *Nude on Thin Ice* and *Web of Murder*, he happens upon the femme fatale he deserves: '"We belong together. . . . We need each other. You said I was a tramp; well, did you ever stop to think you're one too?"' (113). Her 'snare' is her knowledge of his guilt, and Williams devises a nicely ironic reworking of the eternal devotion theme: '"You said nobody could ever take my place, and you'd never be able to leave me. I thought that was awful sweet. Don't you?"' (109). It is crucial to the plot both that she is triumphant and that she is, for Harry, a dreadful fate – and it is arguably a weakness in Hopper's film that for Harry to drive away at the end with a Dolores played by Virginia Madsen seems too little like a punishment. In the novel, the grim ironies of the end are made painfully clear: 'I've found my own level again, and I'm living with it' (184–5).

In *A Touch of Death* (1953) Williams creates a narrator who, like the protagonist of *Hot Spot*, claims a certain amount of sympathy. Again, though, we become very aware both of his own uncertainties in judging the femme fatale and of his corrupt and entirely mercenary motives. He not only loses the contest with the femme fatale but ends confined in a lunatic asylum, her schemes having so entirely discredited his narrative of events that he is deemed crazy. The woman, Mrs Madelon Butler, is the classic spider woman. She is also, however, allowed enough latitude, within the narrative of Lee Scarborough, to establish a conceivably sympathetic explanation for her conduct, and, like the femmes fatales in such neo-noir films as *Body Heat* (Lawrence Kasdan, 1981) and *Last Seduction* (John Dahl, 1994), 'ruthless and amoral' though she is, she has some admirable strengths – intelligence, sophistication, cool determination – and uses these to safeguard her own interests. The narrator's attitudes towards women are established from the outset as blithely exploitative. She asks, '"You take women pretty casually, don't you?"' and he replies, '"There's another way?"' (14). His obsession with the money becomes overwhelming, ultimately itself arousing sexual passion, as when Madelon 'stirred the loosened bundle with a caressing slowness . . .' (167). The effect of her poise and skilful self-fashioning is that the narrator never knows whether she is acting or not, whether she is teasing and mocking him. He feels he has the upper hand and will literally and metaphorically screw her, but she turns the tables by simply walking away with money that he ultimately realises she has been carrying all along. What finally unhinges him and makes him 'wake up screaming' is his uncertainty to the end about what her real intentions were, and we, as readers, are left equally in the dark.

Another Williams femme fatale who resembles the potent women of neo-noir movies is Mrs Cannon in *The Big Bite* (1957). Like *Touch of Death,* this is a novel with a mercenary hard man as narrator, himself satirised as he judges the femme fatale, displaying even more obvious male prejudice than Harry Madox and Lee Scarborough. Mrs Cannon, represented as much the more intelligent of the two, not only is able to outmanoeuvre the protagonist but is capable of seeing through to the real implications of the position she is in. It is she who is given the bleak insights of the noir vision of the world:

> I wonder how long that veneer of toughness would have lasted if you'd ever had the intelligence to see, just once, how many ways there are in this world you can be utterly destroyed by random little sequences of events. . . . We're all destroyed . . . for wanting too many things and not caring how we get them (150).

Although she is doomed at the end, she takes ample revenge. With considerable poetic justice she leaves the narrator, John Harlan, trapped by his own arrogance and scheming. From their early conversations we see the narrator's judgements as over-confident and dangerously mistaken. Williams drives the point home by having Mrs Cannon match his macho comments with little parodies of male sexism, as when she puts him down by returning his own insult, telling him, '"Just don't be an egg-head. You're stacked all wrong"' (106). When she turns the tables on him, her appraisal is devastatingly accurate: 'subtlety is not his dish of tea' and 'psychological fine points' are not his forte (137–40). In the end, she sees to it that he receives both the money and an exactly appropriate revenge, rectifying his emotionally barren life by bequeathing him '"the only emotion – besides greed – that I believe you capable of feeling. Fear."' It is a sophisticated torment, allowing him to '"savour [his] emotion to the fullest"' (183). As in *Hot Spot* and *Touch of Death*, Williams leaves his protagonist tortured with ironic appropriateness for his greed and stupidity, outmanoeuvred by a woman he has underrated and treated with condescension.

Jim Thompson often exposes the self-deluded ways in which even quite ordinary men (like Roy Dillon in *The Grifters*) judge the mothers, wives and girl friends in their lives. When he pushes the characterisation of his protagonists further towards the psychopathic, he creates a sense that stereotypical representations of women are not just reflections of male greed and self-satisfaction but projections of disturbed minds. Dusty, the narrator of *A Swell-Looking Babe* (1954), is, as his name implies, someone who suffers from an inability ever to see things with complete clarity. Afflicted by the illusion that he can return to a womb in which everything will be solved and all desires satisfied, he kills both of his father figures and tangles himself in a web of criminality. Without one of his paradisal women, Dusty feels completely devoid of motive power. The 'babe' of the title is a Utopian vision of womanhood, 'not just one but *all* women' (6), a personification and refinement, ageless, suggestive of manatees or goddesses. Dusty thinks of his entrapment as financial when in reality it is psychological, and his construction of the eternal woman is symptomatic of his inability to move beyond his own traumas.

In the same year, Thompson published his most disturbing portrait of an unhinged male mind, *A Hell of a Woman* (1954), in which the narrator is the door-to-door salesman, Frank 'Dolly' Dillon, whose nickname captures something of the inadequacy of a man who is forever failing to assert himself in the male world. Thompson gives Dolly, who is very evidently responsible for his own failures, free rein to rant against the women in his life, creating with cumulative force the image of a mind possessed by hatred. As the novel progressively distances the reader from his self-pitying, self-justifying voice, it becomes clear that to Dolly *every* woman is 'a hell of a woman', an emasculating tramp he can blame for his troubles in the world. So, for example, when he hits his wife, he adopts what to him is a reassuring manner: 'I leaned against the door, laughing . . . I hadn't really hurt her, you know. Why hell, if I'd wanted to give her a full hook I'd taken her head off' (28). After she throws him out, Dolly begins to tell us about how he got married to Joyce:

> No, now wait a minute! I think I'm getting this thing all fouled up. I believe it was Doris who acted that way, the gal I was married to before Joyce. Yeah, it must have been Doris – or was it Ellen? Well, it doesn't make much difference; they were all alike. They all turned out the same way (31).

It is characteristic of Thompson's darker novels that, towards the end, almost every view Dolly expresses has acquired ironic force. In the sections written by 'Knarf Nollid', Frank Dillon reveals still more about himself than he does in the other narrative, composing 'Through thick and thin: the true story of a man's fight against high odds and low women . . .' (95). As the narrative becomes increasingly surreal, and Dolly's murders do not enable him to 'depart this scene of many tragic disappointments' (103), he drifts on to an even more symbolic woman, 'the lovely Helene, my princess charming', at which point narrative coherence breaks down altogether:

> And right at the start it made me a little uneasy; I got to wondering what was real and what wasn't: And maybe if I saw her as she really
> *one more bag like all the rest*
> was, I wouldn't be able to take it. But that was just at first . . . I mean she had to be
> *a bag in a fleabag, for Christ's sake, and I couldn't go any*
> beautiful and classy and all that a man desires in a woman . . . (179–80)

One line of narrative recounts Helene's (the emasculating harpy's) castration of Dolly, another (which we take to be reality) his self-mutilation and suicide, the culmination of Dolly's self-destruction – '*. . . and she didn't want it, all I had to give . . .*' (184–5).

6
Strangers and Outcasts

The lonely protagonist of mid-century noir is often left running blindly or wandering aimlessly, as isolated at the end of his narrative as he was at the beginning:

> He ran on . . . plunging into the wastes of endless land and sky, stretching forever. . . . Blindly he stumbled on.
>
> Dorothy Hughes, *Ride the Pink Horse* (1946)

> And later, turning the street corners, he didn't bother to look at the street signs. He had no idea where he was going and he didn't care.
>
> David Goodis, *Black Friday* (1954)

> . . . I left the shelter of the awning and walked up the hill in the rain.
> Just a tall, lonely Negro.
> Walking in the rain.
>
> Charles Willeford, *Pick-up* (1967)[1]

Transients, drifters, escapees from a past of fear and guilt – these are protagonists living at the margins, outside of respectable society or unable to return to a home that is as they left it. The places in which these characters find refuge are themselves marginal, unstable and threatening. In the *film noir* of the period, this pervasive feeling of rootlessness is often linked to the post-World War Two problems faced by returning soldiers, who struggled to achieve readjustment and reintegration into family and society.[2] This specifically postwar sense of alienation merges with a wider sense, strengthened in the McCarthyite fifties, of a society that punishes failures to conform and suspects those who do not 'belong'. In the novels discussed in this chapter, most of the protagonists are not veterans. Even Hughes' 'Sailor' is a man who, through political influence, avoided the war. But they are all, for one reason or another, 'displaced persons', fugitives, casualties of a past that has left them scarred and has cut them off from a stable domestic existence and from a society they seem unable to rejoin. Like Nelson Algren's Frankie Machine in *The Man with the Golden Arm* (1949), they suffer from the 'American disease of isolation'.[3]

In contrast to the marginalisation represented in interwar victim narratives, their plight is less to do with a desperate search for some way out of an economic impasse than with an irremediable sense of exclusion. The movement of their narratives is almost always away from something. If positive goals glimmer, they soon disappear. The 'wrong man' pursued in so many plots of the time is frequently a victim of misperception and prejudice, unable to get along in a society that regards him with suspicion and hostility. He is a scapegoat figure who functions to expose corruptions either because he is made to carry communal guilt or because he is driven by wrongful persecution to investigate the secrets of the antagonistic community. He is also often driven to explore his own guilt, given that even the 'wrong man' tends to be guilty at some level. Within a European context, the best-known 'stranger and outcast' narratives of this period are those which express the existentialist consciousness of life's absurdity experienced by the man who stands alone in an inhospitable world, without any of the props of habit, routine or social convention. Meursault in Camus' *L'Étranger* (1957) moves through his involvement in the violent death of an Arab to his confrontation with the reality of his own death. This 'fall into consciousness' is an essential feature of man's experience of the absurd. Film critics often see this kind of existential awareness, loneliness and dread – Camus' assertion that 'at any corner the absurd may strike a man in the face' – as one of the defining features of *film noir*.[4]

In postwar America, amongst the most interesting adaptations of such motifs are those in which alienation and marginality are associated with racial exclusion. As Chester Himes said, given the characteristics of the tough thriller (its depiction of character as a product of social conditions and its use of the viewpoint of the outsider as a way of exposing the failures of the dominant society) it was surprising that there were not more black detective stories.[5] The second two sections of this chapter will focus on the coupling of noir themes and conventions with a strong element of protest against racial injustices. It has been said that race displaced class as 'the great unsolved problem in American life' during the forties, when civil rights activism began gathering force, culminating in the protests and racial conflicts of the fifties and sixties.[6]

It has been suggested that *film noir* responded to this upsurge in racial tension and activism by subsuming 'untoward aspects of white selves' in racial imagery, often through the 'casual exploitation of racial tropes'. Even though this was a time of left-liberal strength in Hollywood and 'good racial intentions abounded' (for example, in *Crossfire*), the witch-hunts of the House Committee on Un-American Activities (HUAC) in the late 1940s led to some diminishment of leftist enthusiasm, and studios retreated from liberal race pictures. The *film noir* of this period, it has been argued, uses racial others as equivalents to white corruption.[7] There is something to this, though even within canonical *film noir* the emphasis on breaking down moral categories and conventional distinctions calls into question the whole nature of borders, whether social or racial. One of the abiding themes of noir is the impossibility of sustaining a black/white moral dichotomy, and, although whiteness can obviously constitute an invisible norm, in the world of noir it stands equally for the whited sepulchre of a hypocritical society. Our sympathies are with the characters victimised by such a society, rendered 'placeless' by their exclusion from it. When the noir theme of displacement, instead of having just familial or geographical implications, relates to 'getting out of your place' in the sense of transgressing against racial prohibitions, these violations are also viewed sympathetically.[8] In the novels of the fifties and sixties, there is a much more explicit exploration of racial and ethnic otherness than there is in *film noir*. Just as they make fewer concessions to conventional images in their handling of female characters, the writers who focus on a racially derived sense of alienation are not generally stigmatising the transgressor but are satirising a society that thinks in terms of racial boundaries.

It is a natural step for noir to use, say, a black protagonist to exacerbate the outcast status of a marginalised man. One of the most important developments in the literary noir of this period is a movement in this direction, both in white-authored 'civil-rights noir'[9] (by William McGivern, David Goodis, Dorothy Hughes, Charles Willeford and others) and in the substantial body of African-American writing in which noir conventions are joined to a racial theme. The record of publishing houses is far from good, and the outstanding black crime writer of the period, Chester Himes, faced difficulties with publishing his work in the United States as well as with trying to work in film: 'I don't want no niggers on this lot', Jack Warner proclaimed when Himes was in

Hollywood in the early forties.[10] Nevertheless, Himes and other black writers, such as Charles Perry, Herbert Simmons and Iceberg Slim (Robert Beck), continued to write and publish, though not always in America, novels that made powerful use of the noir sense of otherness and marginality as an equivalent for racial exclusion.

Displaced persons

'Wronged man' plots, which are often also 'wrong man' plots, are a staple of *film noir*. One of the earliest examples is *I Wake Up Screaming* (H. Bruce Humberstone, 1942), adapting the 1941 Steve Fisher novel in which a psychotic policeman frames and pursues an unnamed narrator (Frankie Christopher in the film, played by Victor Mature). There are many other classic *films noirs*[11] in which the protagonist is wrongly accused, hounded or victimised by a society that misjudges and despises him. He is unlikely to be entirely innocent. Several of the protagonists of the literary noir discussed here, for example in *Brother Death* and *Nightmare Alley*, are guilty even though they must also be seen as having been wronged. Others will have committed a murder by the end of the narrative (*Wary Transgressor, Ride the Pink Horse, Dreadful Summit*). An 'innocent eye' perspective is less usual in post-World War Two fiction and film than it is in the literary noir of the thirties and early forties, and the effect of the narrative is less likely to be a sense of shocked disillusionment than of weary recognition. The narrative tends to be structured around an opposition between 'home' and 'wandering'. Home may well be completely inaccessible to 'the man with no place'[12] (*Ride the Pink Horse, Nightmare Alley*). In less darkly noir versions of the pattern, a small possibility may remain of a redemptive repositioning of the protagonist with respect to home, though probably not a return to home as it once was (*Blue City, Detour to Death*). The damaged, displaced protagonist sees society from an unfamiliar angle, without any of the conventional props for preserving peace of mind, and, in contrast to the outsider hero of adventure stories, he is unlikely to accomplish a restoration of order.

The British version of the 'wronged man' plot is in many respects an extension of the prewar novels of Greene and Ambler. A 'lost' British male or ill-equipped adventurer finds that he is out of his depth in a world more devious and brutal than his own. In the British gangster pulps of the 1950s, the figure of the tarnished innocent or doomed loner often surfaces – for example, 'Johnny the Kid' in Darcy Glinto's *Protection Pay-Off*, or the protagonist who gets caught up in a heist gone wrong in Hank Janson's *Flight from Fear*. Within the confines of these hurried narratives social context exists only as part of the stylised imitation of the power struggles of American gangland. But alongside the formulaic gangster pulps there were novelists like Robin Cook (who later took the name Derek Raymond), John Lodwick and James Hadley Chase (René Raymond), and these are writers who do locate their narratives within a distinctively British or European postwar world. Cook (old Etonian and one-time bagman for the Krays),[13] in his first novel, *The Crust on Its Uppers* (1962), wrote as British a version of the gangster saga as one could hope to find. Drawing on enough rhyming slang to require a glossary ('Ice-cream = ice-cream freezer = geezer' [12]), Cook created a vivid narrative of crime and betrayal, with protagonists desperately attempting to escape their lot in life by deliberately choosing an outcast status: 'This is no blag, then, morrie. It's a tale of someone who . . . was sick of the dead-on-its-feet upper crust he was born into, that he didn't believe in, didn't want, whose values were meaningless . . .' (15).

Though René Raymond's Chase novels were often imitative ('speed, violence, women and America'),[14] he did also write novels that were less conventional and that were set closer to home. Both he and John Lodwick create characters who are the recognisable descendants of Greene's and Ambler's struggling, unheroic protagonists and bored 'ordinary citizens'. Just as Cook's protagonist leaves behind the exhausted world of the English upper crust for the alluring dangers available to the criminal classes, the protagonists of Lodwick and René Raymond dream of freeing themselves from the humdrum routines of domesticity and dull austerity that depress the spirits of more ordinary citizens. These postwar drifters, however, find the world of 'adventure' to be a trap like any other. Lodwick's *Something in the Heart* (1948) and *Brother Death* (1948) and Raymond's *More Deadly Than the Male* (1946) and *Wary Transgressor* (1952) – the first written as Ambrose Grant, the second as Raymond Marshall – all belong to this 'home grown' tradition. Greene himself, whilst he was working at Eyre and Spottiswoode, is thought to have contributed (at least by 'very strong line editing') to *More Deadly Than the Male*.[15] In all four of these novels, the prewar figuring of England as innocent and of the continent as corrupt and violent has been broken down, replaced by a sense of characters in transition between equally tainted and demoralised scenes. Postwar England is afflicted by boredom and depression; violence is near at hand; the continent is rife with intrigues from which it seems impossible to escape, in spite of the fact that the war has ended. The movement of the narrative is often between the continent and England, with the protagonist unable to extricate himself from all of the machinations that prevent a return to 'normality'.

More Deadly Than the Male has 'American' elements, as does *Wary Transgressor*, but in contrast to, say, *No Orchids for Miss Blandish*, it has a great deal that establishes the essentially British character of the narrative, from scarcity of guns to soothing cups of tea, with a London setting that provides a kind of low-key, sleazy counterpoint to the romanticised violence of American big cities. George, the protagonist of *More Deadly Than the Male*, a timid, dispirited book salesman, indulges in Walter Mittyish daydreams that parody the style and straight shooting of the American gangster novel, a wry parallel, perhaps, to Chase's own writing life, spent borrowing so much from an alien genre. It is fantasy that prompts his decision to exchange his ordinary, ineffectual self for a life of criminality, an idea of adventure that is ironised throughout. George's accidental possession of a pistol (pointedly, a German pistol and a relic of war) helps to ensnare him in the seedy affairs of small-time criminality and confers on him the kind of masculine authority he normally lacks, but in the end his life is dominated by tedium and freedom is as elusive as ever: '" . . . they loaded the gun without telling me. You see, they were determined to make me a murderer"' (216). Raymond's *Wary Transgressor* also involves a legacy of past violence and the bemusement of an inadequate drifter who does not really belong anywhere. He feels himself briefly free to choose but, like George, finds that the acts he commits are less 'his own' than he thought them to be, leaving him even more trapped than he was to begin with. The narrator, David Chisholm, is American rather than British, and a veteran who has seen more than his share of brutality. But he is essentially a victim of the events of a European war, a fugitive wanted for a 'blood bath' he witnessed (101), unable to return home. It is, again, weariness of violence and of flight that dominates the conclusion of the novel. Too tired to go on the run again, Chisholm, like George, passively awaits his destined end, 'feeling more alone than I had ever felt before in my life' (158).

Another weak, gentle English George vainly hoping for freedom is the protagonist of John Lodwick's *Something in the Heart*. He is 'a gentleman . . . on the down-run, with speed gathering' (96) in a world so inured 'to horror, torture, and the rest' that people's sensibilities are no longer touched by tales of exclusion and persecution (114). George's escape from soul-destroying domesticity takes him outside the conventions of the English class structure into a world where smuggling and other crimes are concealed under the cover of a circus, which is (like carnival atmospheres, for example, in American noir) a form of marginalised performance, a display of 'safe' danger enacted outside the bounds of respectable society as well as an extension of the disreputable moneymaking schemes that flourished in wartime. The irony is that this life at the margins leaves George feeling just as unfree as he felt at the outset. In due course he takes on the roles of wrestler, bear tamer, smuggler and murderer, but his life is as routinised and inauthentic as it has ever been. Also in 1948, Lodwick published *Brother Death*, which reverses the movement of his protagonist, bringing him back to Britain after a 'murky background' (70) of wartime activities that both brutalised and compromised him. Rumbold's involvement in the treacheries of wartime underground work have helped to make him a man with 'no political scruples', hoping 'to remain aloof' and not be 'driven, cornered, the victim of chance and circumstance and the whims of others financially more powerful than myself' (35, 53–5). He wants to return to England rather than being caught up in 'the toils of a previous existence', and is under the illusion that once he is demobilised he will be free (93). Like the other British protagonists of this period, though more 'naturally' amoral and violent, Rumbold is shown primarily as a man who is weak and adrift, 'Possessing neither point of departure nor lines of resistance prepared in advance; no bearings . . . no established rule of conduct . . .' (76). Returning home, he finds that in the metaphoric house of England he is united with those he meets only through his capacity for murder: ' "We're all murderers in this household, you know . . ." ' (156).

Lodwick's Rumbold travels across Europe from Marseilles to Madrid and the length of England, from Devon, where he murders, to Scotland, where he himself dies. Although he briefly visits his parents, he never reaches a point of rest, even at home feeling ill at ease and out of place: his only reliable companion is 'brother Death'. Many American crime novels of the period – though their protagonists are far from the disruptions, the lingering distrusts and animosities of postwar Europe – embark on similarly rootless wanderings within their own country, experiencing the same radical homelessness and isolation. In the 1947 film of Dorothy Hughes' *Ride the Pink Horse*, the central figure, Gagin (Robert Montgomery, who also directs), says of himself, 'I'm nobody's friend.' We do not know his first name, and he is described by the villagers of San Pablo as 'the man with no place'. In Hughes' novel (1946), the nameless, 'place-less' condition of the protagonist is even more extreme. The 'God-forsaken town' is more alien. In the midst of Fiesta, a 'run-down carnival' is taking place. The town is reached by travelling through miles of nothingness, 'across the wasteland' (8), and the traveller himself is more anonymous, known only as Sailor. The archetypal Sailor has journeyed away from the familiar city to a town in which he is 'alone, separate': he is 'the dream figure wandering in this dreadful nightmare', feeling 'trapped by the unknown' (95, 124). Much of the blame for his plight rests with Sailor, but he is also a 'wronged man', damaged by a more powerful and devious sometime ally whose power he has mistakenly dreamt of sharing. The final choice that Sailor makes severs him completely from his former life on the periphery of power. Balancing the regularity of being 'a sucker' against the freedom 'beyond the mountains', he escapes to 'open country . . . the wastes of endless land and sky', his final choices having placed him beyond even the human community of the oppressed and outcast (200).

Published in the same year as *Ride the Pink Horse*, William Gresham's *Nightmare Alley* was adapted to become another of the classic *films noirs* of the late forties, an intense evocation of fear directed by Edmund Goulding (1947). Gresham, who was fascinated by carnivals and circuses and 'the darker side of the entertainment world',[16] uses the travelling carnival to create a disorienting, distorted reflection of the larger society. Like Sailor's Fiesta town, it is a place 'out of this world', and the carnivalesque atmosphere creates a marginalised reality that comes to stand for life stripped of all consoling illusions. In Hughes, the most horrifying spectacle of the Fiesta is Zozobra, a 'giant grotesquery' embodying 'a fantastic awfulness of reality'; in Gresham, the 'awfulness of reality' is symbolised by the carnival geek. The myth is that the geek is 'one of the unexplained mysteries', neither man nor beast; the reality is that he is simply a drunk who, worn down by hardship and ill fortune, has been reduced to a sideshow attraction (like Zozobra, in fact, really 'man-made'). The myth is ironically echoed in the closing paragraphs, when the protagonist himself is reduced to the status of the geek. The motif of the fall into darkness, as in the geek's descent into the carnival pit, is the image that we know from the outset must govern the movement of the narrative. The 'nightmare alley' is an indeterminate, dark, transitional location from which there seems to be no escape for a man pursued by fear, with a light of hope that keeps receding. At the most general level it is an image of existential despair ('"Man comes into the world a blind, groping mite. He knows hunger and the fear of noise and of falling. His life is spent in flight . . ."' [197]). The protagonist, Stanton Carlisle, both plays upon and suffers from this fear, manipulating crowds reminiscent of the London Bridge crowd of *The Waste Land* ('The crowd flowed over and stood waiting . . .'), made up of people who are easily exploited because of the vacancy and impoverishment of ordinary lives. The conman's secret is that '"Fear is the key to human nature"' (56). At the root of the fear is the estrangement that haunts Stan throughout the narrative. The end of the novel charts his decline into total isolation, drunkenness and squalor. His final effort to work as a 'pitchman' is a surreal caricature of his former activities: distorted faces laugh at him, footsteps pursue him, until in desperation he kills the policeman who has run after him: 'any time he starts after me I can keep killing him. He's mine. My own personal corpse' (208).

Part of the power of the Hughes and Gresham novels comes from the fact that the symbolic sweep of their narratives suggests a society wholly given over to unconstrained greed, corruption and universal fear. Though each novel has, within its carnival atmosphere, redemptive glimpses of a restorative community (Pancho and his carousel in *Ride the Pink Horse*, the alternative family of carnival folk in *Nightmare Alley*), both are expressions of a more general and unrelieved pessimism than is to be found in most of the other 'wandering stranger' novels of the period. Particularly in narratives that are closer to the investigative tradition of literary noir, the protagonist's confrontation with alienation is mitigated by the fact that flight can be supplanted by some kind of active agency. Whether encountering a new place (*Detour to Death*), observing their own town or city from an unaccustomed perspective (*Blue City*, *Dreadful Summit*) or simply being forced out of a routine (*The Big Clock*), protagonists see life's viciousness more clearly. Also, however, if their own moral characters are somewhat more robust than those of Sailor and Stanton Carlisle, they see their way to taking some kind of action. There is a 'rites of passage' element in these novels, centring on men, generally young, who are in transit from one stage of life to another, compelled to grow up and let go of accustomed routines and so to perceive an otherwise familiar place with a stranger's eye.

The 'stranger in town' pattern is a tenacious theme in both film and literature. It can use a far from innocent stranger as the catalyst, on the model, say, of Hitchcock's *Shadow of a Doubt* (1943), a narrative in which a decidedly bad man (in the case of Hitchcock's Uncle Charlie, a serial killer) enters an apparently idyllic town and brings to the surface the repressed knowledge of what you would find if, as Uncle Charlie says, 'you ripped the fronts off the houses'. In literary noir, something of this sort happens in, for example, *Dead Beat* (1960), the novel Robert Bloch published the year after *Psycho*. A young man, representing a generation damaged by Cold War neuroses, is used by Bloch to expose the underside of seeming reputability in the town as it reacts to his presence. In another of his recurrent incarnations, the stranger who intrudes into small-town family life is an innocent man who happens into a town and, like the misperceived femme fatale, has to cope with the prejudices of a community that only superficially exemplifies traditional values and contentments – as in Helen Nielsen's *Detour to Death* (1953).[17] Nielsen's protagonist on the run, Danny, is like 'all the people in the world who were strangers on earth' (5–6, 13, 64). When he arrives in Coopertown, it seems to be inhabited entirely by dauntingly superior-looking citizens – 'Did they all have to be so tall?' (14). Soon suspected of murder, Danny is (see Figure 8) the very type of the isolated man persecuted by a conformist community. The townsfolk are 'stone deaf' to his protestations of innocence (53), but Danny's persistence ultimately uncovers the horrors that are ironically concealed in 'Peace Canyon', the real nightmare that resides in the silence at the heart of the American dream, 'a world without sound' hiding its 'curse of blood' until Danny finally succeeds in making his narrative heard. Although he has his own small secret, this is only draft dodging rather than the 'dark past' that usually forces the noir protagonist to take flight. He is thus in essence a good character for whom the status of the outsider is only a 'detour' and not something irrevocable.

The home–wanderer dichotomy also structures a number of crime novels in which the protagonist sees his own home from an unfamiliar angle, having undergone changes that bring him back to once familiar territory with a permanently altered perspective. Three of the best late forties examples of this kind of narrative are *The Big Clock* (1946), *Blue City* (1947) and *Dreadful Summit* (1948). Ross Macdonald's early novel, *Blue City* (written under his actual name, Kenneth Millar), figures the return home as a transition from childhood to adulthood. A young war veteran, Johnny Weather, comes back to a home town that seems to have changed out of recognition, and to a series of shocks concerning the father with whom he has lost contact. Almost every chapter begins with an image of how things seem to have changed, echoed in Johnny's dreams of rooms empty or full of 'unfriendly faces' (85–6). The corruption of the town is akin to that of Hammett's Poisonville, the police having brought in strike-breakers who have 'been here ever since', and the town is under the sway of strong anti-labour forces who uphold their views in the name of 'the American way' (94–5). Johnny's overwhelming feeling is one of loneliness and of exclusion from normal domestic life, both craving and resenting the togetherness glimpsed through lighted windows. It at first seems to him that the strangeness of the town must be the consequence of a radical change, but his crucial

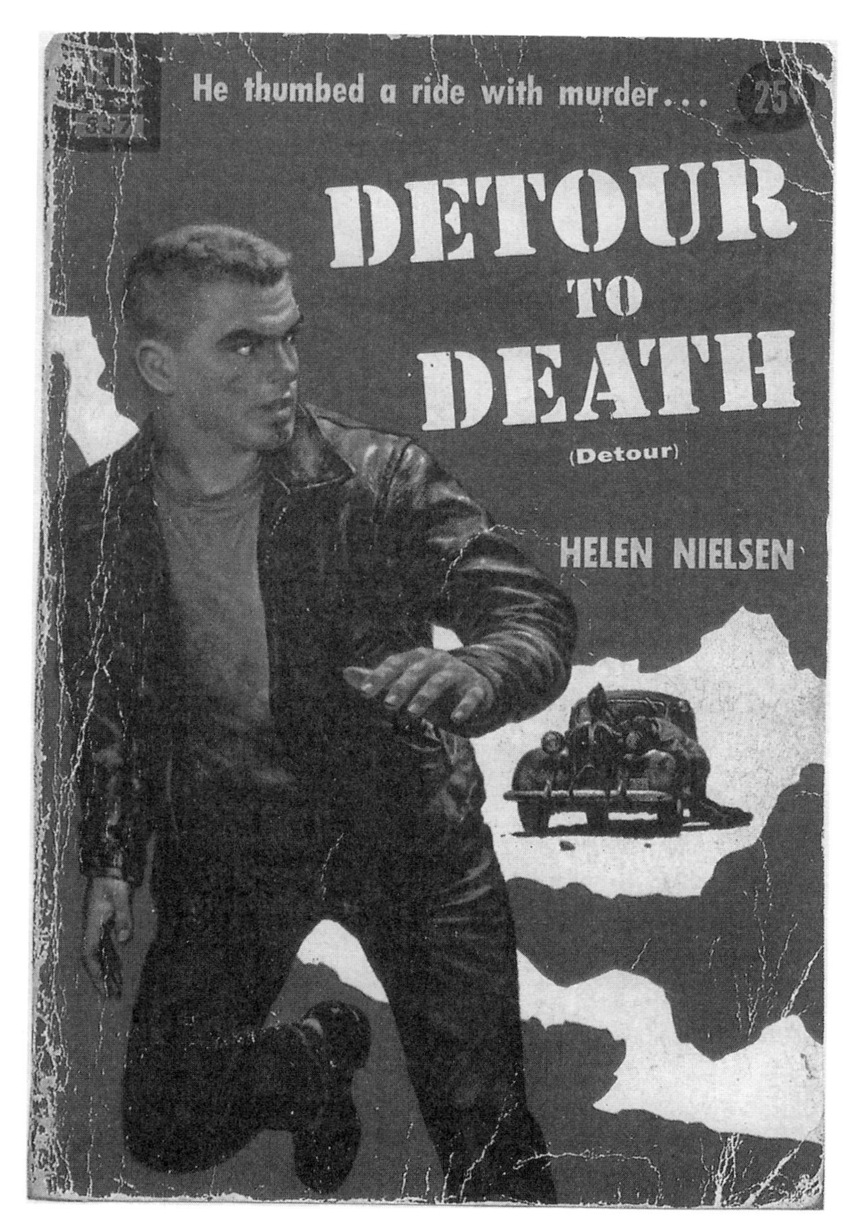

Figure 8 Helen Nielsen's *Detour to Death* (Dell, 1953)

realisation is that what he is seeing is simply a development of the town as it was when his father held sway. As Johnny himself gets drawn into the conflicts and cover-ups and as he persists in trying to get to the bottom of things, he himself becomes a suspect, feeling 'outlawed' even to himself (136). Like George in *The Big Clock*, he experiences a self-estrangement increased by hearing strangers cast him in the role of murderer and speculate on his motives. The end holds open the possibility that he will choose to stay in the town and work to better it, but, having become part of 'marginal life' (149), he seems unlikely to rejoin a normative community.

The same is true of George LaMain, the teenage narrator of Stanley Ellin's first novel, *Dreadful Summit*. Filmed by Joseph Losey in 1951 as *The Big Night*, the book, like the film, is a symbolic coming of age narrative, with a protagonist who has just celebrated his sixteenth birthday undertaking a nightmarish odyssey through a strange and hostile society. He views its sins with the semi-innocent eye of someone who himself has a capacity for violence and whose familial past is (like that of Macdonald's Johnny) more implicated in wrongdoing than he realises. During the course of the narrative what he discovers is his connection to other individuals, particularly to the guilts of his father and mother. He never deviates from his goal ('I think I liked Al Judge a lot before I knew I had to kill him' [8]), though the phallic gun he carries is an embarrassing token of manhood (it keeps threatening to tumble out in public), and though the adults who seem potentially helpful turn out to be incapacitated by bourgeois anxieties ('"If I didn't have my lousy job to think about, George, I'd be in there with you all the way"' [63]). George takes on an increasingly grown-up appearance ('I made a face like a tough guy' [40]), and his initiation into adult society has something of the old-fashioned tough-guy ethos about it, bringing painful knowledge but also an acceptance of guilt and responsibility, when the boy decides to take the blame for the crime he has committed. This redemptive choice diminishes the pessimism of *Dreadful Summit*. It remains dark, however, in comparison to Losey's film, which removes a significant element of George's family guilt (the truth that his mother is a murderess) and also of George's own guilt, since in the film he does not actually kill Al Judge.

Kenneth Fearing's *The Big Clock* (the basis for one of the best-known wrong man *films noirs*, directed by John Farrow in 1948) is an urban rather than small-town novel, but by using the restrictive community of a highly structured organisation it brings to the fore similar tensions between conformity and estrangement. Fearing's poetry and novels had from the thirties on spoken for people who felt themselves to be controlled by forces they could not comprehend. He was, as Julian Symons says, 'a poet whose rolling lines of despair, protest and Whitmanesque optimism remain underrated'.[18] *The Big Clock* begins with the protagonist as part of what appears to be an exceptionally unified family, all of whom are named George (George, Georgette and Georgia), living what looks to be the ideally harmonious American family life. In the course of the novel, however, it becomes plain that this appearance is constructed over actual betrayal (George habitually womanises), and even George's stories for the six-year-old Georgia have by the end become fables of split identity and self-estrangement. George is a notable example of the overlapping roles of the noir protagonist, assigned the task of chief investigator of 'the stranger' (75 – George himself) who is suspected of being the murderer, and also the intended victim of the actual murderer. In this self-divided state, he has to confront a system symbolised by the big clock, 'a fatal machine' that is a trope for the whole modern industrial organisation: 'I told myself it was just a tool. . . . But I had not fully realised its crushing weight and power' (114–15, 145). In the film, after George outwits Janoth, who falls to his death, the mood of the end is established by George's reunion with his wife. In the novel, on the other hand, the tone of the end is dominated by George's conviction that he has only delayed his fate. What George has learned by the destabilisation of his role in life is how easy it is to become the outsider who has to be excluded and destroyed if prosperous, conventional society is to survive. In the cover-story concocted to explain the search for George-as-stranger, he is transformed into an emblem of the dangerous alien threatening to undermine a whole way of life. As he hunts himself, he becomes aware as never before of the gap between his internal sense of self and his self as constructed by others. The experience transforms him from 'a smug, self-satisfied, smart-alecky bastard just like ten million other rubber-stamp executives' (121–2) into someone who recognises the destructiveness of the system and the precariousness of the individual life.

No crime writer of the period created more hopelessly marginalised men than David Goodis. He represented with obsessive intensity isolated, displaced protagonists, in hiding from others or from themselves, travellers unable to go home. For French readers and critics, Goodis seemed to share something of the 'existential melancholy' of McCoy and James M. Cain.[19] Amongst his most characteristic protagonists is the frightened, friendless man who has felt compelled to abandon a secure, often successful life and who finds himself spiralling downwards.

As we have seen, in some of the novels discussed in this section (*Detour to Death, Blue City*), the lonely man who manages to master certain investigative skills can move the plot towards more positive closure; in others (most notably *Dreadful Summit*, but also *The Big Clock*) the protagonist who discovers within himself a kind of toughness and integrity can add a redemptive element to an otherwise bleak story. Goodis readers, however, learn not to expect such respite. He is one of the most reliably pessimistic of noir writers. At the end of *The Moon in the Gutter* (1953), for example, Kerrigan gives up his search for the man responsible for his sister's death and returns to live with the woman who paid for his murder: 'He moved along with a deliberate stride that told each stone it was there to be stepped on, and he damn well knew how to walk this street, how to handle every bump and rut and hole in the gutter' (513). Kerrigan and other Goodis protagonists endlessly walk the streets, but this repetitive motion is combined with inherent immobility or paralysis. There are sometimes visions of a place 'elsewhere' (South Africa, South America, Florida), holding open the romanticised possibility of escape for the hunted man. At the end of *Dark Passage* (1946), for example, there is the dream of a reunion in Peru, though hedged about with 'all these ifs' (399) and a much more remote fantasy in the novel than in the film. For the man engaged in a quest, there are occasional opportunities for retribution (for example, in *Nightfall* [1947] and *Cassidy's Girl* [1951]). But the closing of a trap is more likely than the qualified optimism of the 'general idea' of Peru (*Moon in the Gutter*, 399).

In spite of an ending in which doubt is supplanted by 'the knowledge' that promises to dispel Vanning's fears (137), *Nightfall*, filmed by Jacques Tourneur in 1957, is a novel dominated (as is the film) by the terror and paranoia of a man on the run. This is a specifically postwar narrative, with Vanning's difficulties explained as a common effect of the war. Men have returned with 'the wrong outlook' and get themselves in trouble, which, given Vanning's actual innocence, becomes an edged comment on the readiness of American society to read 'the past' of the war into every veteran's life. The surreal atmosphere of *Nightfall* is established on the first page, with Vanning 'afraid to go out', haunted by a premonition which is itself a phantom created by the past, both paranoid and pursued. He is suffering from 'regressive amnesia' (136–7) and it is only by struggling to recover the past that he can defy what strikes him as an ill fate so arbitrary and accidental that it is 'almost comical' (69).

Vanning is a man tortured by his homelessness, his 'hollow', 'grotesque' feeling juxtaposed with his longing for family life and children. In *Cassidy's Girl* (1951), the first of his Gold Medal 'skid row' novels, Goodis emphasises even more strongly this despairing exclusion from normal domestic life. Like many other Goodis characters, Cassidy has been a solidly successful middle-class type who is now on the skids because of accidents of fate that seem not to be his fault but which actually raise the question of whether he simply lacks the ability to take charge of his own life – a weakness perhaps 'corrected' when he leaps through the window at the end to defend Mildred. The issue of whether a character who fails to assert himself deserves 'getting kicked around' (161) is one of Goodis' most persistent preoccupations. He almost invariably establishes a powerfully realised sense of economic deprivation, dispiriting city streets and characters whose daily round is confined to 'a narrow, dust-covered twisting path bordered with the leaning, decayed walls of tenements' (*Cassidy's Girl*, 56). In comparison to the proletarian tough-guy novelists of the thirties, however, his stress falls more heavily on the possibility of choice, allowing (like Ellin) some degree of dignity to be reclaimed by the recognition of one's own burden of individual responsibility.

The novel in which the pressure of economic circumstance weighs most heavily, and in which characters' capacity for choosing a different life seems most circumscribed, is *The Blonde on the Street Corner*. Though written in the fifties (1954), it is a powerful representation of Depression America, adapting the conventions of the noir thriller to capture a mood of crippling despair. In *Cassidy's Girl*, violent action achieves at least some kind of partial resolution (the defeat of Haney Kenrick), even though Cassidy still feels a great 'heaviness' of spirit (173). *The Blonde on the Street Corner*, by its violation of convention, juxtaposes the possibility of sudden, violent, transgressive events (the stuff of the thriller) with the hopelessly mundane, intolerably drab ordinary lives of men and women during the Depression. These are lives of such quiet desperation and such passivity that even sex and violence exist in only routine and diminished forms. The novel is a lament for wasted years – 'just standing on the corner and waiting, waiting' (5) – extended to a generalised image of the Depression, which has left 'Millions of guys on the corners in the big cities. Standing around . . .' (36–7). The jobs intermittently available are 'slow death' (31), and the effect of Goodis' novel is to persuade its readers that this process of attrition is in its way worse than the eruption of random violence. There are only two violent episodes in the novel, both characterised by the pointlessness of the whole Depression world. In the first, the protagonist comes to the aid of a man goaded by one of the 'bastards from upstairs' (115–23); in the second, he is cornered by the blonde, who realises with satisfaction that she has finally found 'someone who gave it like a beast' (139–40). Neither incident changes in any way the conditions of life for those who spend their days having to 'walk up and down' in the cold, grey streets of Philadelphia, which is impossibly far from the idyll of Florida, where 'everybody's happy. . . . It's warm, it's nice' (75–6, 15).

Goodis recurrently uses the freezing city streets of his home town as a setting that contributes to the immobilisation of his protagonists, whose narratives tell of their failed attempts to escape from the past by withdrawing from society. *Black Friday*, published in the same year as *Blonde on the Street Corner* (1954), begins with the desperately cold Hart walking alone in Philadelphia, cheering himself up by contemplating suicide. The winter weather of a northern American city not only emphasises Hart's sense of being locked in wretchedness but images his essential isolation (when you're alone, as Charley muses, '"it's a cold world"' [60]). Goodis' most widely known novel, *Down There* (1956), filmed by Truffaut as *Shoot the Piano Player* (1962), is similarly dominated by cold and snow and wind – which, in the opening paragraph, 'stabbed at the eyes of the fallen man in the street' (3). The hostility of the elements is only one of the destructive forces assailing a protagonist, Eddie, whose aim is to stay safely in hiding and to remain detached, to look 'as if he can't feel anything' (48). Pursued, however, he is forced to repeat the process of loss that made him withdraw in the first place, forcing on him the traditionally noir recognition that the past will not stay in 'another city, another world' (104) and that 'the sum of everything was a circle, and the circle was labelled Zero' (82).

Civil wrongs

An old black man, a strongly positive character in Goodis' *Street of No Return* (1954), urges the protagonist, Whitey, to avoid the despair to which Goodis characters are always tempted to succumb. The answer, he says, 'is never zero . . . while you're able to breathe' (51). Goodis confronts his marginalised protagonist with the black and Puerto Rican characters he encounters when he crosses the border that separates Skid Row from 'the Hellhole'. It is a symbolic journey that makes explicit the racial basis of marginalisation and that contrasts the standard Goodis character (who is where he is because of inner weaknesses) with characters whose fate is determined not by inner weaknesses but by skin colour. The naming of 'Whitey' in itself suggests a stereotype that is broken down in various ways. Suspected by both blacks and Puerto Ricans of being a potentially hostile and dangerous white man, his mildness and lack of prejudice mean that he is accepted and befriended. He learns from characters who have been marginalised on the grounds of race but who have not allowed their experiences to deprive them completely of backbone. The gentle and timid Whitey, having settled into Skid Row, simply does nothing, 'lost in the emptiness of a drained bottle' (2). The present-time part of the narrative is set in motion when Whitey crosses 'the boundary line', moving from the security of Skid Row and entering a territory that, like Chester Himes' Harlem, is surreal in its chaos and violence, 'a madhouse' with maze-like alleys and circular stairways (52–3, 149). Wrongfully arrested on suspicion of murder when he tries to help a dying policeman, Whitey is thrown into the world of injustice and fear that most inhabitants of the Hellhole experience. He is rescued and sheltered by Jones Jarvis, an old black man who has a stronger belief in his own proud identity than the protagonist. Whitey has not used his real name for seven years, in contrast to Jones Jarvis, who insists on people recognising that Jones is actually his first name. Like Whitey, Jones has a past that a man might want to escape (wrongfully charged with raping a white girl), but unlike Whitey he has retained his defiant sense of who he is ('and I said, "How'd you like to kiss my black ass?"' [45]).

Goodis was only one of a number of white writers of this period to use the generic focus on marginality to address seriously the issue of race from a white liberal perspective at the time of the civil rights movement. In earlier popular fiction, members of racial minorities had often been depicted as villains. Post-World War Two, however, this began to change. Pronzini and Adrian, in *Hard-Boiled*, cite Hal Ellson's stories of Harlem teenagers, *Duke* (1949) and *The Golden Spike* (1952), and Evan Hunter's *Runaway Black* (1954, written as Richard Marsten). They also reprint Gil Brewer's 1956 'Home', a brief and harrowing story in which a black protagonist has come home to a Southern town where he is wrongly accused of molesting a white woman: 'how could he have been so dumb as to forget? . . . He was home!'[20] In other crime fiction of the period as well, Mexicans, Puerto Ricans and African-Americans are given key roles. Sometimes, as in Goodis, characters whose marginality is racially determined act as a comment on the plight of the protagonist. Other novels, such as McGivern's *Odds Against Tomorrow*, Hughes' *Expendable Man*, Willeford's *Pick-up* and, rather later, Jim Thompson's *Child of Rage* (1972) use racially marginalised characters as protagonists. In either case, these are novels that represent some of the ways in which the otherness of a different skin colour is akin to noir fatality, determining a character's destiny.

So, for example, both Gresham, in *Nightmare Alley*, and Hughes, in *Ride the Pink Horse*, use racial otherness as a key element in their narratives. In *Nightmare Alley*, as Stan flees, he has an encounter with a black fugitive that adds an additional dimension to Gresham's representation of the society in which Stan has tried to rise. Named after one of the most eminent nineteenth-century human rights leaders, Frederick Douglass Scott, the grandson of a slave and the son of a Baptist minister, is a man who is both racially and politically in opposition to the dominant society ('a goddamned nigger Red', the *real* 'specter' haunting Grindle, that of an organised labour opposition). A tenuous connection is established as Stan and Scott talk their way towards an agreement about the state of the world, but Scott puts Stan's own self-serving position into perspective by arguing that someday 'people going to get smart *and* mad', and change things (200).[21] In *Ride the Pink Horse*, Sailor's chief friend and ally is the half-Indian, half-Spanish 'brigand' who runs the merry-go-round. The whole setting is built around a Fiesta which is explicitly symbolic of the meeting and merging of different races, a brief period when bloody repression and exclusion are put aside in an illusion of unity: '. . . But under the celebration was evil . . . a memory of death and destruction . . . Indian, Spaniard, Gringo; the outsider, the paler face' (18). Centuries of conflict in which the once powerful can easily become the outcast and downtrodden have generated the need for the Fiesta, and Sailor, who is himself dispossessed, forms a natural bond with the Indians, both with their temporary illusions of dreams fulfilled and with their outcast status, as he himself is forced to abandon his hopes of making good in the world of the Gringos who achieve conquest by 'the buying and selling of money' (51–2).

Several other novelists of the fifties and sixties – for example, John D. MacDonald, Fredric Brown, Margaret Millar – make strong thematic use of racially marginalised characters. MacDonald, in *The Damned* (1952), makes his Mexican characters part of a mythic structure in which a ferryman carries people across a river that confronts travellers with what has been there from ancient times – mortality disrupting life's journey. The novel opens and closes with the Mexican ferryman, slyly referred to a god (170), who provides a detached judgement of the hurrying people of modern civilisation – seeming to him 'like those bright toys for children. . . . The expensive ones with the painted faces and the key in the back' (167). More usually, black and Mexican characters are judged by a prejudiced white society, and readers in turn judge the faulty values of that society. From the fifties on, the white male hold on the investigative role in crime novels begins to loosen. The shift is evident, for example, in the film adaptations of John D. Ball's Virgil Tibbs novels, most notably *In the Heat of the Night* (published in 1965, filmed by Norman Jewison in 1967). In some novels, an investigative figure who is himself a victim of discrimination functions to establish a sympathetic connection with the victim/perpetrator. This kind of doubling, or kinship of men living at the margins, can be seen in Fredric Brown's *Lenient Beast* (1957), in which Ramos, Mexican in origin, is an outsider on the police force; he is not representative of 'solid citizen'-type society (105–6), but instead is a victim capable of making a connection with a murderer who is himself a victim. In other novels, investigators belonging to ethnic minorities function to dissect the ways in which the dominant society fears and represses 'the other'. One of the most interesting of such novels is Margaret Millar's *Stranger in My Grave* (1960), in which Pinata, a bail bondsman and investigator, looks Spanish or Mexican but, as an orphan, does not actually know his ancestry: '"I know who I am . . . I just don't know who [my parents] were"' (40). His own sense of exclusion is so strong that he identifies himself with 'the stranger' in the grave, a Mexican father whose identity has been concealed and whose 'blood', it has been feared, will taint the offspring of the heroine: '"In this blood of hers are certain genes which will be transmitted to her children and make monsters of them. Like her father. Right?"' (247).

In Millar's noir melodrama, suspense is generated by unanswered questions about the identity of the 'stranger in my grave', his much earlier death being the result of his isolation and of the suppression of his narrative. Only at the end does he speak through a letter that his daughter is finally able to read. The noir preoccupation with the undermining of identity and with the communication of a marginalised character's narrative is central to some of the most striking thrillers of the fifties and sixties. These are novels in which the 'marginal man' theme is turned into an even more explicit examination of prejudice and exclusion. In Dorothy Hughes' *The Expendable Man* (1963), William P. McGivern's *Odds Against Tomorrow* (1957) and Charles Willeford's *Pick-up* (1967) white writers, by casting black characters as noir protagonists, make very effective use of genre fiction as a means of addressing one of the most pressing social issues of the time.

McGivern's liberal message is spelled out clearly. His tactic is to use shifting close third-person narration to bring us into contact with the consciousness of both his white and his black protagonist as they play out a heist-gone-wrong plot. The novel opens with chapters written from the perspective of Earl 'Tex' Slater, not overly bright (in fact, 'dumb as hell') and a very small-time crook: '"A hillbilly full of temperament. To give the job a little tone"' (11). McGivern organises the narrative so that before readers see Earl's prejudice they see his inadequacy, fears and uncertainties. The focus is on his own poor white trash background, growing up in a shack where 'we lived like niggers', beaten and shamed by his father for playing with black children (30), and we are drawn into sympathetic awareness of his 'half-understood need to be something' in other people's eyes (65). Ironically, in the course of the narrative, Earl recovers his dignity by forming a bond with John Ingram, an intelligent, articulate black gambler. It is not an 'Uncle Tomish' accommodation,[22] but rather, for both of them, the desperate reaching-out of the noir protagonist for contact with someone who might be an ally and assuage his feeling of dread and alienation. Racial tensions constantly surface in their exchanges, but as they talk about how they became involved in the robbery Earl actually 'sees' Ingram and recognises how both of them alike are victims of a power structure that treats them with contempt: '"Well, Novak fixed you up fine, didn't he? . . . He fixed us both up fine"' (153). In their conversations about their poor backgrounds and the way the rich treat them, Earl's life begins to acquire the narrative shape it had always lacked – a narrative reaching its inevitable conclusion in the fatal decision to help Ingram that allows him to reclaim his own integrity.

Dorothy B. Hughes' *The Expendable Man* (1963) places her black protagonist at the centre of a wrong man plot, using colour as part of the noir protagonist's alienation. It is the main factor determining his status as a persecuted outsider. The impact of the protagonist's blackness is all the greater in *The Expendable Man* because in other respects Hugh Densmore is part of a life that is the antithesis of noir marginality and isolation. He is a successful doctor, part of a warm, loving and affluent family, possessing none of the psychological flaws which usually undermine the identity and security of noir protagonists. Ironically, he is chosen as 'the expendable man' because he is a doctor (and hence could carry out an abortion), and it is a combination of compassion and caution that leads him to make some unfortunate decisions. Densmore's colour is concealed from the reader in the early part of the narrative. It is only at the point at which the law steps in to begin persecuting him that his colour is mentioned: '"This guy says a nigger doc driving a big white Cadillac brought Bonnie Lee to

Phoenix"' (58). The effect is to enable readers to identify with him before they know he is black, and also, as in Willeford's *Pick-up*, the deferral of information about his colour makes us more aware of the determining force of his blackness: the eyes of the police officers, 'as if they were iron bars, moved to contain Hugh' (90). The resolution, in which Hugh's 'detective work' uncovers the truth and justice looks like it will in some measure be done, is in essential respects non-noir, but the 'wrong man' plot and the changes wrought in him do have strong affinities with noir. As he leaves Phoenix Hugh reflects 'He had been light-hearted then; he wondered if he would ever again know the same careless happiness. He wondered if he would ever be cleansed of his innocent guilt' (236).

In Charles Willeford's *Pick-up* (1967) our knowledge that the protagonist is black is deferred until the last lines of the novel. Willeford is a writer who often provides an end that forces you to reread the rest of the novel in a different light, and in *Pick-up* the twist introduced in the last few lines ('Just a tall, lonely Negro . . .') radically alters our understanding of the whole novel. Like Goodis' *Blonde on the Street Corner*, *Pick-up* both plays on and undercuts the generic characteristics of the noir thriller. It opens with a meeting between the protagonist and a femme fatale. Helen lures Harry Jordan even further into a precarious and marginal existence, and their suicidally depressed relationship appears to culminate in murder. Harry's arrest seems to be another means of fulfilling his death wish, since he is sure that 'Blind justice' (118) will ultimately get him. Ironically, the fact that he is denied the end he foresees for himself only strengthens our sense of his pathos and isolation, as do the novel's closing lines. Once we have read them, we are compelled to look again at the ways in which other characters have judged Harry and helped him along his downwards path: the working men's comments on Helen and Harry, his ferocity in response, his fight with the marines over Helen, the doctor's questions about Helen's race, the reaction of people in the prison to him and the views of Helen's mother (who rages against his 'depravity') are all more comprehensible in the context of prejudice. By delaying until the end our recognition of what lies behind such scenes, Willeford has also avoided the overly explicit message to be found in some of the other white-authored crime novels representing black experience. It is we as readers who must, by reconsidering the text, answer for ourselves the question of how far the fate of the noir protagonist has been forced upon him by the fact that he is black.

Rage in Harlem

Anger and fear are a part of white-authored representations of black experience, but there is, as we have seen, a tendency to soften the impact of these emotions by sentimentally optimistic resolutions (*Stranger in My Grave*, *Expendable Man*) or by representing the emergence of character traits that seem to offer some hope of healing reconciliation (most obviously in *Odds Against Tomorrow*). In the African-American fiction of this period, on the other hand, rage and fear are less contained. The pain of the outcast is much closer to the surface. The narratives, more darkly noir, move towards a form of closure that is bitter, angry or grimly comic rather than potentially affirmative and reassuring. The contributions of black writers to crime fiction have been much more fully analysed in recent years, and in Britain the Payback Press in particular has made available a wide range of African-American crime-writing, including novels, for example, by Charles Perry, Robert Deane Pharr, Clarence Cooper, Iceberg Slim and the complete 'Harlem Cycle' of Chester Himes, who was the most prolific and important African-American crime writer of the fifties and sixties.

Some of the notable early examples of black crime-writing are most strongly linked to classic detective fiction. There were, for example, the novels and stories published in the thirties by the Harlem Renaissance writer George S. Schuyler, such as *The Ethiopian Murder Mystery*,[23] and much recent critical attention has been given to Rudolph Fisher's *The Conjure-Man Dies* (1932), a novel that for the first time creates a black detective duo and centres the narrative on black characters and themes.[24] But while *Conjure-Man* remains what is essentially a locked-room mystery, from the mid-thirties on black writers also began to produce novels and stories much more closely allied to the noir thriller. That is, they wrote narratives in which the focus is often on the criminals rather than the detectives and in which there is a much more direct treatment of prejudice and racism. Even in the Harlem Cycle of Chester Himes, which features the famous detective partnership of Coffin Ed Johnson and Grave Digger Jones, the novels are equally concerned with the creation of a wide assortment of criminals and other outcasts, and with the elaboration of the teeming life of Harlem, an 'outcast location' so intensely realised that the setting itself can be seen to have the same kind of grotesque reality as Himes' characters. It is an enclosed, carnival-like milieu from which no one can escape, a cause of maiming and deformity that, like blackness itself, serves to mark and isolate those who are fated to live there.

One of the striking things during this period is how many African-American non-genre writers (for example, Ann Petry, Richard Wright,[25] Herbert Simmons, John A. Williams) wrote fiction which, like the noir thriller, used characters' involvement in violent crime to create bleak, often savage representations of ghettoised black life. So, for example, Ann Petry's short story, 'On Saturday the Siren Sounds at Noon' (1943), is a moving, compressed version of the noir narrative of the victim who becomes an aggressor – of a good and loving man driven to kill his wife by knowledge that is unbearably horrifying. John A. Williams, in 'The Man Who Killed a Shadow' (1946), uses the same victim-turned-perpetrator pattern to make a more direct assault on the mutual incomprehension that is inescapably part of a segregated society: 'Saul, looking timidly out from his black world, saw the shadowy outlines of a white world that was unreal to him and not his own.'[26] The adaptation by mainstream black writers of the situations, plot constructions and character types of the noir thriller provides a disturbing means of representing the effects of a harsh environment and of giving dramatic form to the kinds of injustice that arise from the misperception of 'the other'.

Herbert Simmons' first novel, *Corner Boy* (1957), for example, very effectively employs the elements of genre fiction to represent a fundamentally unjust society. He makes the doomed career of a young hoodlum into a study in racial marginalisation and isolation. The ironically named haunts of the black teenagers, throwing dice at Club Paradise, suggest aspirations never to be fulfilled. The novel centres on the fates of characters who long for something above ghetto poverty. For Jake, the 'bad boy' protagonist, the way out is drug dealing, and he briefly feels he has attained the American dream at the wheel of his Cadillac, confident that 'It was a good world as long as you had money to buy it . . .' (162–3). But a white girl's accidental death, and the complete misconstruction of their relationship by the white community, leads to Jake's ultimate isolation in prison and a belated recognition of how fully his race has excluded him from the real power structure of society.

In the same year that Simmons' *Corner Boy* was published, Chester Himes brought out *For the Love of Imabelle* (*Rage in Harlem*), published by Gold Medal in 1957. It was initially written for the French paperback publisher Gallimard after Marcel Duhamel suggested to Himes that he write a detective story in the American style for his *Série Noire*. Himes had begun writing crime fiction in the 1930s, by his own account under the influence of Hammett's *Black Mask* stories, when he was serving seven and a half years for armed robbery in the Ohio State Penitentiary.[27] He developed from the start a savagely comic style that was to become his hallmark in the ten novels of the Harlem Cycle (1957–69). There has in recent years been a substantial reappraisal of Himes' work, which was at the time most highly valued in Europe, particularly in France, to which he had moved in 1953, where the absurdity and dark laughter of his books met with a more sophisticated critical response. Some American critics of the time responded favourably to Himes' work, but the market for work by black writers was relatively small at this time. Himes' books did not sell especially well, and he was under attack from various quarters – not only from white critics who objected to his anger and ferocity, but also from black and Communist critics. As Melvin Van Peebles says, 'Chester saw America unflinchingly . . . hilarious, violent, absurd and unequal, especially unequal.'[28] But the expression of these views through the surreal extremity of Himes' crime novels was a strategy that was little understood. Having already accepted hard-boiled crime fiction as literature worthy of serious attention, European audiences, on the other hand, much more readily recognised Himes' attempts 'to communicate sociological protest within the confines of a literary genre'.[29]

A decade before he began the Harlem Cycle, Himes published his first novel, *If He Hollers Let Him Go* (1945), which drew on his own experience as a wartime worker in the segregated Los Angeles defence plants.[30] The fundamentally serious themes of Himes' thrillers are abundantly apparent in this mainstream novel, in which black estrangement, fear and disillusionment are powerfully represented. The narrator, Bob Jones, who says that race had 'never really gotten me down', encounters prejudice in California of the early forties that makes him see the entire society around him from a different perspective – 'All that tight, crazy feeling of race as thick in the streets as gas fumes' (7). The atmosphere of violence and the sense of absurdity that dominate Himes' crime novels are intensely present in *If He Hollers,* as the ordinary life of Bob Jones spirals out of control: 'I was looking for my white boy again. . . . I was going to walk up and beat out his brains. . . . After that I could go up and sit in the gas chamber at San Quentin and laugh. Because it was the funniest goddamned thing that had ever happened . . .' (119). Jones increasingly feels that '"I don't have anything at all to say about what's happening to me"' (156). His fear is ultimately not just of persecution and mob violence but of America itself. He has tried to conform, but after the events of the novel, he is 'cornered . . . small and weak and helpless . . . without soul, without mind . . .' (182 – see Figure 9). Like

Figure 9 James Avati's cover illustration for the 1949 Signet edition of Chester Himes' *If He Hollers Let Him Go*

Goodis' *Blonde on the Street Corner*, Himes' novel moves towards a conclusion in which the protagonist cannot commit any act decisive enough to alter his circumstances. Finally unable to shoot the white boy or to make a break from the police, Jones in the end acquiesces in a system which only allows him to go on living on the most debasing of terms.

Himes wrote a handful of other non-genre novels, including *Lonely Crusade* (1947) and *Pinktoes* (1965). The last complete novel of his Harlem Cycle, *Blind Man with a Pistol* (1969), was also in a sense placed in a different category when it was elevated from the *Série Noire* and published instead in the more prestigious 'Du monde entier' series. This reflects a process of moving beyond generic boundaries that begins with *Blind Man* and goes considerably further in the unfinished *Plan B*, in which the trajectory of the plot is towards civil war with apocalyptic slaughter, towards violence escalating on such a scale that it is sometimes suggested that Himes left the novel unfinished because he could see no 'logical answer' to the problems he was writing about.[31] Within the main body of the Harlem Cycle, Himes uses a range of the devices of the noir thriller that function to fragment any secure perspective, to destabilise identity and to challenge conventional judgements. He uses, for example, investigative figures who are themselves excessively violent, unstable and ambiguous in the roles they occupy. Multiple points of view and departures from a linear time frame undermine all sense of orderly progress. Several analyses of Himes' work have represented him as breaking decisively with the existing forms of American hard-boiled writing, but this kind of contrast is grounded in much too narrow a definition of the tradition of which Himes is a part.[32] Hammett's Op is perhaps the nearest to the 'black badman'[33] figures of Grave Digger and Coffin Ed, but the macabre humour and surreal violence of Himes' novels also have much in common with the noir thrillers of his own period, particularly with the fiction of Jim Thompson.[34] His ironising of the American dream, the creation of protagonists excluded and haunted by unattainable desires, is a central part of the noir tradition, from James M. Cain and Horace McCoy to Thompson, Goodis and beyond.

Another argument sometimes advanced is that Himes is not really a 'protest' writer 'because his work lacks a sense of redemptive change', offering instead only a 'vast pall of futility',[35] but here again, it is the resistance to optimistic resolutions that allies Himes most obviously with the long-standing noir tendency towards pessimistic satiric expressions of rage and disgust. As in Gresham's *Nightmare Alley*, the delusive fantasy of escape is either nostalgic or an amalgam of bogus economic and religious hopes for salvation. The naive characters, the 'squares', Himes creates (Jackson in *Rage in Harlem*, Roman in *All Shot Up* [1960], Sonny in *The Real Cool Killers* [1959]) are preyed upon by trickster figures (Casper Holmes in *All Shot Up* and the Reverend Deke O'Malley in *Cotton Comes to Harlem* are two of the most memorable). Recurrently in the Harlem Cycle, gambling and religion seem to offer characters a way out of this entrapment. 'Hitting the number', in particular, becomes a symbol of economic salvation, paralleled by the more conventional salvation that appears to be offered by religious prophets and sometimes helped along by looking 'straight up into heaven [to] find the number' (*Rage in Harlem*, 86). Religion, as a self-serving financial enterprise, knows its place in the hierarchy of human hopes: '"Nothing takes the place of God," Doctor Mubuta said in his singsong voice . . . then added as an afterthought, as though he might have gone too far, "but money"' (*Blind Man*, 228–9).

The sense of inescapable entrapment is reinforced in the world of Himes' novels by the imprisoning boundaries of race, symbolised by the hellishness of the Harlem ghetto. This is a world in which purposeful action is impeded by extreme heat or (in *All Shot Up*) extreme cold and in which many of the inhabitants look 'like people from another world' (213). In *Blind Man with a Pistol*, when asked what is inciting people to 'senseless anarchy', Digger replies, '"Skin"'. The culprit can be identified as lack of respect for law, lack of opportunity, irreligion, poverty, ignorance or rebellion, but the real 'mother-raper at the bottom of it' is the fatality of racial injustice (*Blind Man*, 323, 342). The people's hopes for riches (*Rage in Harlem, All Shot Up*) or salvation in the form of escape to Africa (*Cotton Comes to Harlem* [1965]; *The Heat's On* [1966]) are routinely betrayed. The inhabitants of Harlem are imaged by Himes as physically and psychologically damaged, 'forced to live there, in all the filth and degradation, until their lives had been warped to fit' (375). What Himes retains of his early naturalism is a strong element of determinism, which stands behind his fantasies of deformation.[36] He embodies the absurdity of the black man's life (he called one of his autobiographical volumes *My Life of Absurdity* [1976]) in an extraordinary variety of freakish characters trapped within a carnival-like milieu that is cut off from the rest of society.

As in the novels of Goodis, for example, the disabling of characters by the dominant society isolates them and propels them towards transgressive acts. Coffin Ed, with his acid-scarred face, is so severely traumatised that, though he continues to function positively as a detective, he is no longer entirely sane. In *The Heat's On* (1966), when Ed knocks out Red Johnny's teeth, he looks like a 'homicidal maniac', 'dazed as though he had just emerged from a shock treatment for insanity' (434). On his 'junkie's tour' of Harlem, he moves with Madame Cushy 'like a monstrous Siamese twin' and tortures Ginny, knowing that he has 'gone outside of human restraint' (465–7). Coffin Ed's brutality is simply one manifestation of the bizarre and random violence that characterises Harlem as a whole, the inevitable consequence of its exclusion from the dominant society. In *The Heat's On*, the albino giant, Pinky, is an abused and bemused innocent, too freakish to be accepted by his own race, effectively homeless and fatherless, and too simple-minded to understand the realities of the society that exploits him. As, for example, in Iceberg Slim's *Trick Baby* (1967) the 'otherness' of a different colour is driven home by placing an incongruously white character in a black context. Pinky's desperation leads him into increasingly surreal disguises, as he tries to find an appearance that will be less outlandish than his own. He is still absurdly covered by a disintegrating disguise at the end of the novel, having gone on a journey that is pointless and circular, that takes him not to the 'heaven' of Africa but only to Sister Heavenly, to death and destruction.

The violence of Himes' novels is, like his characterisation, surreal in its extremity. *All Shot Up* opens with an old lady 'flying through the air, arms and legs spread out, black garments spread out in the wind . . .' (165). It includes the decapitating of a motorcyclist, his 'taut headless body' spurting blood until the motorcycle crashes into a jewellery store, 'knocking down a sign that read: *We Will Give Credit to the Dead*' (244). 'Big Six' shuffles along with the knife stuck through his head ('"It's a joke," the man said knowingly. . . . The woman shuddered. "It ain't funny," she said' [287]). Blackly comic violence is a constant feature of Himes' Harlem novels, but from the mid-sixties on the elements of social protest and the whole issue of violence as a means of bringing about change came more to the fore. Himes himself considered *Blind Man with a Pistol* to be 'his most important work', containing 'much of his feeling about what is happening here in America'.[37] The most violent of Himes' completed novels, *Blind Man* represents various visions of a possible solution to the racial conflicts of the sixties, ranging from brotherhood and the Black Jesus movement to the radicalism of the Black Muslims. There has been considerable critical controversy over Himes' own attitude towards violence. In his Preface to *Blind Man*, he writes, 'I thought of some of our loudmouthed leaders urging our vulnerable soul brothers on to getting themselves killed, and thought further that all unorganised violence is like a blind man with a pistol.'[38] This clearly implies a contrast between unorganised and organised violence, and at least some critics[39] have argued that he had by this stage in his life become an advocate of organised, bloody revolutionary acts, though at the same time implying that he had reached an 'ideological impasse' that prevented him finishing *Plan B*. In the inset story of the blind man, he is a figure who *is* different (not only black but blind) but who tries to proceed as though he is normal. In consequence he and the world radically misjudge one another. A chaos of misunderstandings on a subway journey leads him to shoot at a belligerent 'big white man' but instead to hit a 'fat yellow preacher'. During the ensuing pandemonium, in which 'Some thought the world was coming to an end', the black man shoots again at the white man, this time killing a policeman and being shot down himself. It is a miniature of senseless violence, based on misperception and correspondingly random in its effects, achieving nothing by way of improvement of conditions or resolution of problems.

In his earlier novels, Himes' tone of edgy comedy enables him to round off in a positive way without sentimentalism. Even at the end of *Cotton Comes to Harlem*, although the violence has claimed so many lives that the undertaker 'was kept busy all week burying the dead', the compensation is such profitable business that Jackson finally is able to marry Imabelle, and Cotton Headed Bud gets back to Africa after all, with the money from the bale of cotton buying 100 wives. But the energy of Himes' grotesquely farcical plots is readily channelled into something altogether darker, as is apparent, for example, in the comic cat fight in *Cotton Comes to Harlem*, when the tussle between Iris and Mabel suddenly changes from an anarchic brawl to a shooting. Iris snatches the pistol from Deke's hand and empties it into Mabel's body, 'so fast it didn't register on Deke's brain' (92). Harlem is 'a carnival harem' (*All Shot Up*, 165–6), characterised by its 'grotesque realism': that is, it is not an essentially positive carnivalesque vision, but one based on degradation and debasement, in which 'all suddenly becomes meaningless, dubious and hostile', a vision of an 'alien world' of 'terror, hostility, and the loss of meaning'.[40] Himes' street scenes have a nightmarish intensity. The vitality of the people can have a positive celebratory element: 'Half-naked people cursed, muttered, shouted, laughed, drank strong whiskey, ate greasy food, breathed rotten air, sweated, stank and celebrated' (*Blind Man*, 261). But his human grotesques are living in a place that is dilapidated and dangerous, cut off from the outside world and ill-suited to human life.

In *Blind Man*, the conditions of a Harlem ripe for apocalyptic violence are embodied in Reverend Sam's house: 'No one knew what it looked like inside, and no one cared' (195). A 'horde of naked black children' swill 'like pigs' out of troughs, and the bogus Reverend Sam points out to the bemused policemen that it is simply an expedient way to live for a family separated completely from economic sufficiency (197). Himes' savagely lyrical, almost Swiftian lists of the 'contents' of the ghetto reinforce his view of Harlem as a dwelling that has become unfit for human habitation. The eyes of Grave Digger and Coffin Ed sweep over the scars and graffiti on the walls of an apartment block, all testifying to the violence and sordidness of the place: '"And people live here," Grave Digger said, his eyes sad. "That's what it was made for"' (251). In such an atmosphere, it is perhaps not surprising that in *Plan B*, pushing the pessimism of his underlying vision to its conclusion, Himes added the deaths of his two detectives to the toll of escalating violence and civil war. As one of the novel's French reviewers wrote when the unfinished *Plan B* was published, it was Himes' 'bloody farewell to literature and his legacy of despair'.[41]

Part III
1970–2000

A voyeuristic private eye who faithfully follows a mass murderess, surreptitiously guarding her; a transsexual Mancunian hit woman; a Chicago psychopath who takes on the identity of the woman he kills; a pornographic film-maker who gets caught up in the Profumo affair; a commodity fetishist and modern cannibal; a detective searching for the man whose identity he has usurped and whose heart he has eaten; an addict in a hi-tech scramble suit that turns him into a blur who is given the job of hunting himself; a 12-year-old girl learning to survive and kill on the savage streets of a near-future New York:[1] in the last three decades, noir protagonists have appeared in many different guises, and their very diversity testifies to the vitality and contemporaneity of this form of crime fiction. But however aberrant, bizarre or grotesque his (or, increasingly, her) incarnations may be, these are still recognisably near relations of the hard-boiled investigators, victim-protagonists and killer-protagonists of earlier noir thrillers. In this final section, my aim is to explore both the links between post-1970s and traditional literary noir and to illustrate something of the energy and variety of contemporary noir and of the growing body of mainstream fiction that has assimilated characteristic themes and techniques of the noir thriller.

Although literary noir has never altogether disappeared from the bookstands nor *film noir* from the screen,[2] there was arguably a period in the early sixties when the appeal of noirish fiction and films was somewhat diminished. The 'spirit of the times' tended towards optimism. In America, as we have seen, there was the continued growth of white suburban affluence and the mood of expectancy associated with the 'brave new rhetoric' of Kennedy's presidency.[3] In Britain there was a sense of moving towards the advanced economic and technological society that America already had, and the upbeat, 'joyful irreverence'[4] of the Swinging Sixties – a time more in tune with James Bond[5] than with the noir anti-hero. In both countries, however, there were at the same time many tensions, doubts, failures and signs of dissent that gathered force as the events of the sixties, from the assassination of Kennedy on, undermined confidence and strengthened the spirit of protest. As Mailer implies in *An American Dream*, after the trauma of the assassination the 'dream' turns to a vision of violence and murder.[6] At the end of the sixties and in the early seventies, American society was being shaken by riots in the black ghettos, the assassinations of Robert Kennedy and Martin Luther King, the growing opposition to the Vietnam War, higher crime and unemployment rates, Watergate and increasingly vociferous demonstrations of counter-culture discontent. Though the changes in British society were less dramatic, there was nevertheless a comparable movement away from the mood of the sixties. The early seventies saw bitter confrontations between government and unions, the collapse of the boom in the stock market and the property market, rising unemployment and inflation and worsening conflict with the IRA. 'Outbursts of militancy, violence, and terrorism, the revelations of corruption in high places, and the break-up of the optimistic consensus' led many to see the British seventies as a return to the gloom of the 'devil's decade' of the 1930s.[7]

Both America and Britain, then, were experiencing the kind of political and social malaise that made the cynicism and satiric edge of noir seem all too appropriate. Even during the sixties there were a number of films – some of which Silver and Ward group with canonical *film noir*, some with neo-noir[8] – that drew on the films and novels of earlier decades, and by the early seventies the phenomenon was attracting considerable critical attention. As Naremore writes, 'Whether classic noir ever existed, by 1974 a great many people believed in it.'[9] There was increased use of the 'noir' label by film critics and more 'consciously neo-noir' films began to appear (Walter Hill's 1978 film, *The Driver*, is singled out by Silver and Ward as one of the 'earliest and most stylised' examples).[10] Adaptations of literary noir were becoming more numerous: J. Lee Thompson's 1962 film of John D. MacDonald's *The Executioners* (*Cape Fear*); three adaptations of Chandler novels – Paul Bogart's 1969 *Marlowe* (an adaptation of *Little Sister*), Robert Altman's 1973 film of *The Long Goodbye* and the Dick Richards' remake of *Farewell, My Lovely* (1975); Altman's 1974 film of Anderson's *Thieves Like Us*; the adaptations of Ross Macdonald's early Lew Archer novels, *Harper* (Jack Smight, 1966) and *Drowning Pool* (Stuart Rosenberg, 1975 – 'the last vestiges of the classic gumshoe');[11] Burt Kennedy's 1976 adaptation of Thompson's *The Killer Inside Me*; and three separate American adaptations of the more nearly contemporary but equally noir Parker novels of Richard Stark (Donald Westlake): *Point Blank* (John Boorman, 1967), *The Split* (Gordon Flemyng, 1968) and *The Outfit* (John Flynn, 1973).

There were bound to be some changes in literary noir as the 'lurid era' of the 25-cent paperback originals drew to a close in the sixties. There was, however, no real watershed, and one's sense of continuity is strengthened by the fact that some of the most notable noir crime novelists of the fifties and sixties were still publishing in the seventies: amongst others, Stanley Ellin, John D. MacDonald, Ross Macdonald, Margaret Millar, Patricia Highsmith, Charles Willeford, Donald Westlake (under his own name and as Richard Stark) and James Hadley Chase. The influence of such mid-century novelists as Thompson, Goodis and

Himes on contemporary writing was made possible by the reissue of their work from the 1980s on in Black Lizard and Vintage Crime editions in the United States, and, in late-eighties Britain, in Maxim Jakubowski's Black Box Thrillers and Blue Murder editions. Many of the new voices of the period offer striking revivifications of the traditional patterns of literary noir. Edward Bunker, for example, drawing on his own experiences, writes from the criminal's point of view about the effects of imprisonment, deprivation and exclusion in novels like *No Beast So Fierce* (1973) and *Little Boy Blue* (1981). The staple fare of gangland revenge and betrayal is given freshness and immediacy by the dialogue of George V. Higgins' first novel, *The Friends of Eddie Coyle* (1970), the film adaptation of which (directed by Peter Yates, 1973) is judged by Silver and Ward to be 'closer to the true noir cycle than the homage offered by such films as *Chinatown* and *Farewell, My Lovely*'.[12] A tough British version of these themes is developed in Ted Lewis' Carter novels of the seventies. Long-established noir themes have continued to exert their hold in more recent fiction. Craig Holden, in his first novel, *The River Sorrow* (1995), provides a distinctly modern (or postmodern) reworking of sexual obsession and wrong man plots. James Ellroy, writing in the eighties and nineties, uses the more extreme possibilities of the crime novel to recreate the violence and corruption of post-World War Two Los Angeles, imaging the beginnings of 'half a century of tumult and change in America'.[13]

Other recent writers, particularly in Britain, have used basic noir plots for even more explicitly political purposes than those of Ellroy. As at the time of Greene and Ambler, British writers in particular have effectively assimilated thriller conventions with the serious treatment of wider historical conflicts. Philip Kerr, in his *Berlin Noir Trilogy*, locates the investigations of Bernie Gunther in a very fully realised European context, *March Violets* (1989) and *The Pale Criminal* (1990) being set in Berlin in the years immediately preceding World War Two and *A German Requiem* (1991) moving from Berlin to Vienna and the beginnings of the Cold War. Also set in Germany, Ian McEwan's *The Innocent* (1990) uses the murder committed as a result of an obsessive love triangle as a metaphor for the divisions and conflicts in Berlin during the 1950s. Colin Bateman, in *Cycle of Violence* (1995), makes similarly metaphoric use of a traditionally noir 'inescapable burden of the past' theme, weaving it together with the public tragedy of an Ireland in which it is equally true that '"What goes around comes around, eh?"' (241). As these examples might suggest, British literary noir has in recent years emerged as a much more distinctive phenomenon, with successive 'new waves' of writers creating novels that address contemporary issues and that are capable of appealing to a much wider audience.[14]

The last three decades have also seen the creation of a large number of new investigative series, some more noirish than others. The hard-boiled style was developed in an identifiably British way during the eighties by writers like Julian Barnes (writing as Dan Kavanagh, in a four-novel series relating the seedy but generally humorous and upbeat adventures of a bisexual private eye called Duffy), Mark Timlin (in his long-running Nick Sharman series) and Robin Cook (Derek Raymond, whose Factory novels are amongst the darker investigative series). In the United States the formula has been given a variety of strong regional identities.[15] Several series protagonists have contended with the crimes of northern cities: Lawrence Block, for example (who started in the sixties by writing paperback originals for Gold Medal), began, in the seventies, a series of novels featuring an ex-cop, Matt Scudder, a guilt-ridden, gloomy alcoholic (eventually ex-alcoholic) investigator of a New York in which it seems that 'people could adjust to one reality after another if they put their minds to it' (*A Stab in the Dark*, 137). In the eighties, Loren Estleman started to write his rather less noir series of Detroit-based Amos Walker novels, which tend to move towards detective-story resolutions, complete with penetrations of disguise and revelations of identity (for example, in *The Midnight Man* and *Downriver*). In the nineties, Sam Reaves introduced his cab-driving Vietnam veteran Cooper MacLeish, who first appears in *A Long Cold Fall* (1991), in which sentiment, human warmth and hearts of gold effectively counteract the noir potential of the pitiless Chicago cold and the 'blind universe' that grants Cooper 'the grace of survival' (14). Louisiana has been another location well served by tough investigators. At the more noir end of the scale, there is James Sallis' New Orleans detective, Lew Griffin, who, like many another investigator, is guilt-ridden and ex-alcoholic, but also a university teacher and a writer, postmodern and self-reflexive – and black (Sallis, who is white, says he was '20 or 30 pages in before I realised he was black').[16] Working nearby is James Lee Burke's Cajun detective, Dave Robicheaux, the protagonist of narratives in which the defeat of villainy is set against reminders not to accept 'the age-old presumption that the origins of social evil can be traced to villainous individuals' who can simply be locked away (*A Stained White Radiance*, 302) – a dark awareness that is in turn moderated by life-affirming contacts with a loved child (*A Stained White Radiance*) or an earthy dance (*Dixie City Jam*). Strongly positive elements, particularly the affirmative presence of family, also counterbalance the sense of a 'whole nother side of

[American] life, a darker, semilawless, hillbilly side' (*Give Us a Kiss*, 6), in the 'country noir' novels of Daniel Woodrell, some of which (like *Under the Bright Lights*) feature another Cajun investigator, Rene Shade.

In series such as these the honourable ghost of Marlowe is often near at hand, encouraging the nobler possibilities within the hard-boiled tradition, bringing to the fore the moral integrity, the compassion and the tough–sentimental view of life that infuse the investigative narrative with a redemptive potential and make it less darkly noir. Contemporary writers both acknowledge Chandler's influence and try to differentiate themselves from him, as Ross Macdonald did in the late fifties, when he modified his 'heir to Chandler' role, declaring that *The Doomsters* (1958) marked 'a fairly clean break with the Chandler tradition'.[17] One way in which more recent crime writers have made the break has been to distance their protagonists from the identity and ethos of the lone white male, the crusader-knight of the mean streets. They have done this either by creating an investigator who is himself black, as in Sallis and Mosley, or by making the protagonist homosexual (as in Joseph Hansen's Dave Brandstetter novels) or part of a close-knit group of mixed race and gender. James Crumley, who introduced two hard-drinking, tough-talking protagonists – Milodragovitch and Sughrue – in the 1970s, is a self-declared heir to the Chandler tradition (describing himself as 'a bastard child of Raymond Chandler'),[18] but emphasises that his is a much less traditional morality. He defines his own sensibility as conditioned by the disillusionments of the Vietnam War and his 'vision of justice' as in consequence less clear-cut. His protagonists are 'reverent towards the earth and its creatures'[19] and sustained by eccentric alliances with criminals and other misfits. In addition to male bonding, there are the beginnings of surrogate families – Sughrue, for example, holding 'Baby Lester laughing in my arms' at the end of *Mexican Tree Duck* (1993).

Like many other recent investigators, Crumley's protagonists, though retaining some of the romanticised qualities of the lone male, are no longer solitary defenders of macho values. What we see in novels of this kind is a 'softening' of the protagonist by allying him with others, often with a larger surrogate family that represents those marginalised by the dominant society (non-white characters, strong women, outcasts of all kinds). This is a widespread tendency, evident in the little family collected together by Easy Rawlins, in the bond between the white, straight Hap Collins and the black, gay Leonard Pine (in the comic noir novels of Joe Lansdale, such as *Savage Season* and *Two-Bear Mambo*) and in the representative sampling of minorities and misfits allied with Andrew Vachss' 'outlaw' private detective, Burke.[20] Even in the decidedly Chandleresque novels of Robert B. Parker (who wrote his Ph.D. thesis on Hammett, Chandler and Ross Macdonald), the protagonist, Spenser, develops strong ties both with an impressive black sidekick, Hawk, and with his Jewish psychiatrist-girlfriend, Susan Silverman.

With a few exceptions, most obviously Chandler himself, this study does not include detailed examinations of crime novels that develop series investigators. As the above discussion perhaps suggests, this is primarily because, whether traditional or contemporary, series characters tend to have 'non-noir' traits like integrity, loyalty and compassion – qualities that make them more positive and resilient figures than other types of noir protagonist, often sentimentalising them and allowing them to attain more reassuring narrative resolutions and redemptive human attachments. The changing nature of private eyes and other investigative series characters is, however, closely related to developments that can also be seen in the more obviously noir narratives of recent decades. The alternative family offers the investigative protagonist a real human connection, a hedge against what Ballard, in *High-Rise* (1975), calls 'a new kind of late twentieth-century life' that thrives on 'the rapid turnover of acquaintances, the lack of involvement with others' (36). It provides a way of belonging that does not involve acquiescence in a wider society which, whatever its underlying disorders, has an almost irresistible surface allure. As will be seen in Chapter 7, it has been increasingly the case in the noir thriller that various kinds of 'belonging' – assimilation, complicity, dependency – have become nightmares as disturbing as deprivation and exclusion. In post-eighties noir, as America and Britain moved into the Thatcher–Reagan years, there is a marked emphasis on tedious homogeneity and on the threat posed by the erasure of difference consequent on an addiction to the pleasures and games of a consumer society. In novels in which this kind of dependency is a source of anxiety, what often distinguishes the more positive characters is an ability to form individual bonds in a society that seems to be losing its capacity for genuine social relationships. Particularly in American noir, there are fewer of the isolated figures who withstood the conformist pressures of a small community in the literary noir of the fifties and sixties; instead of existential loners, there are protagonists who demonstrate that communal ties need not mean loss of individual identity.

In recent critical debate, one question frequently raised is whether the fashionable trappings of neo-noir are themselves symptomatic of an acquiescence in slickly commercial postmodern nostalgia. The sense that 'noir' created in the seventies and eighties was a 'retro' and nostalgic avoidance of contemporary experience has been encouraged by the often cited essay, 'Postmodernism and Consumer Society', in which Jameson gives *film noir* 'a central role in the vocabulary of ludic commercialized postmodernism'.[21] Referring to *Body Heat* (Lawrence Kasdan, 1981), Jameson notes the film's 'faintly archaic feel' and its small-town setting, which 'has a crucial strategic function: it allows the film to do without most of the signals and references which we might associate with the contemporary world, with consumer society – the appliances and artefacts, the high rises, the object world of late capitalism'.[22] Leaving aside for the moment the matter of nostalgic pastiche, the most important question is whether self-consciously 'noir' contemporary narratives are to be seen as escaping from or as engaging with contemporary issues. One of my central arguments in Part III of this study is that the literary noir of recent decades, even when its settings are retro, has been as concerned with exposing the nature of contemporary consumer society as earlier noir was with satirising, for example, the conformist ethos of small-town America in the fifties.

Whether it is 'reality' or just our perception of it that has changed, contemporary debate has been dominated by the writings of 'cultural specialists' (academic critics, for example) who produce models and interpretations of consumer culture,[23] thereby modifying the rhetoric and themes of social–political analysis. The view of contemporary society as a culture of consumption, consuming not just commodities but performances and spectacles – and consuming the consumer – has come to the fore, increasingly in the eighties and nineties, as one of the dominant themes of literary noir, shaping the representation of protagonists as well as the content and structure of narratives. In America, consumerism was clearly well established in the years following World War Two. As John Updike recalls the fifties in 'When Everyone Was Pregnant', 'Romance of consumption at its height. . . . Purchasing power: young, newly powerful, born to consume.'[24] Reagan's presidency, however, was even more closely associated with encouragement of a commodity culture and the entrepreneurial spirit, with the promotion of selfishness, greed, a get-rich-quick mentality and the rise of the yuppie.[25] In Britain, the Thatcherite eighties, during which personal wealth rose 'by 80 per cent in real terms',[26] were similarly a time of rapidly expanding personal consumption. Although 'all the totems of an advanced consumerist society' had been present in the seventies, it was really only in the eighties that the consumer paradise arrived. As Peter York says,

> . . . the eighties effect took quite a lot of things coming together; the right time, right place, right people, right feelings, right fistfuls of cash. This wasn't *just* a consumer boom. Yes, we did go out and buy more – more TVs, more VCRs, state-of-the-art hi-fis, etc. – but it was really a new generation of consumerism with changes in advertising, retailing, financing, attitudes and expectations. And it's *still with us*: it set the pattern for the next ten or fifteen years.[27]

Britain, then, was 'all getting a bit . . . yes, *American*, really'[28], and this applied not only to the consumer boom but to all the attendant emphasis on presentation, performance, the celebrity culture and 'personal projection'. There was a huge expansion in the amount of electronic space available for the projection of images: 'We were starting to sell ourselves, now, in a way we'd never even dreamt of before.'[29]

Just as thirties thrillers took deprivation as their theme, the noir films and novels of more recent decades have turned their attention to the excesses and dependencies of the society of the media, the spectacle, the consumer. Consumerism is obviously not an element new to noir. The thirties gangsters, characterised by stylish consumption, 'swell clothes', penthouses, high-powered cars, expensive restaurants, were used as a means of exploring the growth of American consumerism, often with an anti-consumerist subtext that equated vulgar display with moral disorder.[30] Close attention to fetishistic detail (hats, guns, shoes and other accessories) and a general fascination with fashion (for example, the 'to-be-looked-at-ness' signified by the clothing of fashionably dressed women) were part and parcel of classic noir.[31] In neo-noir films with a retro look, the incorporation of such things can be seen as a consumer society indulgence, 'a kind of window-shopping through the past'.[32] And there are unquestionably neo-noir films of which this is a fair enough criticism – *Mulholland Falls* (Lee Tamahori, 1996), for example, in which 'the chief function of these four tough guys is to light cigarettes with Zippos and model a peacock collection of suits and accessories'.[33]

Even retro noir, however, often engages seriously not only with the historical period it represents but with issues that are of contemporary relevance, and the detailed observation of consumption, style and decor can be part of the critical thrust of the film. In Ulu Grosbard's 1981 film, *True Confessions*, for example, a thoroughly noir tale of two brothers set in mid-forties LA,[34] the whole style of life of the priest (Robert De Niro) – his surroundings, his dining out, his golf clothes and clubs – is used to establish him in opposition to his brother, a detective (Robert Duvall). The detective's single brown suit and modest apartment help to confirm his status as a figure who will pursue the corrupt regardless of the consequences. They are also, however, no guarantee of his own incorruptibility, and his conspicuous non-consumption is in part an ironic reference back to the integrity of the shabby private eye. This is a detective who has been a bagman and who does not 'give a shit' that Jack Amsterdam did not kill the 'virgin tramp'. He will go after him anyway. *True Confessions* is not, then, an exercise in nostalgic reincarnation, but instead uses retro evocation of the forties private eye films both to demythologise the traditional genre and to raise complex questions about moral responsibility and complicity in a corrupt society.[35]

In films and novels not aiming to evoke the styles of the forties and fifties, fashions and commodities even more obviously constitute part of what is being satirised. In literary noir, this is apparent in the work of writers like James Hall, James Ellroy and Bret Easton Ellis in the United States and the left-wing nineties noir of, for example, Christopher Brookmyre and Iain Banks in the United Kingdom – amongst several others who have contributed to the development of genuinely British forms of noir. In a large body of contemporary noir, the representation of consumerism does much more than simply establish the 'texture of life' that constitutes the background to the narrative. Characters are (as in *True Confessions*) defined in relation to consumerism. The attack on those who 'consume' the natural world emerges strongly, for example, in Ross Macdonald's 1971 novel, *The Underground Man*, in which the greed of the destructive rich, careless of the land on which they build their extravagant houses, is juxtaposed with the simple integrity of Lew Archer, identified from the opening scene with the natural simplicity implied by feeding peanuts to his 'scrub jays' (1–2). In a nineties novel like Hall's *Buzz Cut* (1996), there is a similar opposition between simplicity and rampant consumerism, epitomised in the contrast between Thorn, with his 'trial and error' handmade fishing canoe on the one hand and, on the other, Morton Sampson, with a cruise ship that is the ultimate in consumerist luxury. In the comic 'noir grotesque'[36] of Carl Hiaasen, which takes the commercial exploitation of South Florida as a recurrent theme, the good guys are the reclusive drop-outs from the consumer society, like 'the guy at the lake' who lives in a cabin that 'looks like a glorified outhouse' (Skink, in *Double Whammy* [1988]) or Stranahan, in *Skin Tight* (1989), who lives in solitude in a 'dirt cheap' stilt house, 'delighted to be the only soul living in Stiltsville' (713–14). Plots follow the rise and fall of Thatcherite yuppies in pursuit of the 'fistfuls of cash' that will buy them state-of-the-art commodities (Huggins, Brookmyre), consumer greed acts as a metaphor for moral bankruptcy (Leonard, Willeford), cannibalism acts as a metaphor for ungovernable and dehumanising consumer urges (Ellis). In addition to elaborating the image of the consumer, many contemporary noir thrillers have explored the closely related images of the player and the voyeur, adding new dimensions to character types (victim turned gambler, gangster, investigator) familiar from more traditional narratives.

The concept of the player has become prominent in discourse ranging from street argot (the player as, for example, pimp and pusher) to sober academic theorising (the player as any participant in the many conflicts of interest that can be modelled as games).[37] In all of these uses of the term, the underlying assumption is that players can influence events and that, whatever their environment, people must be players in order to be part of the games that determine pleasure and profit. Acting as a player has become a prime metaphor for moving from the status of victim to that of an active agent of domination and change. As in much earlier noir,[38] one of the prominent themes is the hidden connection between criminality and supposed respectability, and the lies and false narratives that contrive to conceal the fact that politicians are just gangsters in positions of power. But whereas this connection was, in earlier decades, linked to a quite specific nexus of crime, business and politics, to an interrelated control structure with crooks running the show, the metaphor of the player and the game is generally used to suggest that everyone is playing their own game and that, in contrast to the gamblers of earlier narratives, they stand at least some chance of influencing their fates.

The figure of the voyeur has similarly been given an increasingly pivotal role in both film and fiction. In *film noir*, as has often been observed, 'the male prerogative of the look' is much in evidence, though there are examples of films in which a woman appropriates this prerogative, as Carol does, say, in Siodmak's *Phantom Lady* (1944) when she unnerves a barman by staring at him until he finally cracks.[39] In more recent films and novels, 'looking' is complicated in ways that act to disrupt the traditionally male activity of voyeurism[40] by representing the female appropriation of the power of the look, by questioning the extent to which the role of the voyeur can be equated with masculine dominance and by exploring the ways in which a woman in the role of 'passive actor' (the one seen) can simultaneously be an active agent. Contemporary novels have also, of course, paid increasing attention to the implications of a highly developed technology of voyeurism, with its wider network of seeing, controlling and commodifying. What we find here, then, is the breakdown of dichotomies between user/used, active/passive, actor/acted upon, watcher/watched, both because of role reversals and because of the network of relationships in which, for example, the watcher is watched by others who are observing and perhaps manipulating his (or her) reactions.

In the cinema this has become, naturally enough, a recurrent theme. As a male activity it is epitomised in a film like *The Osterman Weekend* (Sam Peckinpah, 1983), in which the devious surveillance associated with political scheming and paranoia becomes indistinguishable from sexual voyeurism. The watcher is watched, and each watcher observes the sexual activities of the other, including the snuff-movie-like scene of the wife of one being killed whilst naked in bed. The whole activity is so pervasive a part of the television-centred life being led that it passes unnoticed even when one 'watcher' is accidentally stranded on the kitchen television screen. The cinema of the eighties and nineties also provides many examples of the appropriation and reversal of male voyeurism: for example, there is the placing of a man as a sexual object, as when Dorothy makes Jeffrey undress in David Lynch's *Blue Velvet* (1986), or the casting of Gina Gershon in the sort of role that would once have gone, say, to Robert Mitchum, admiring the physical charms of Jennifer Tilly in *Bound* (Larry and Andy Wachowski, 1997). In crime novels, this kind of appropriation is frequently found in the (non-noir) lesbian–feminist crime novels that began appearing in the late 1970s and early 1980s, for example, M. F. Beal's *Angel Dance* (1977) and Vicki P. McConnell's *Mrs Porter's Letter* (1982),[41] and, more recently, in decidedly noirish novels by writers like Stella Duffy, Susanna Moore, Helen Zahavi and Vicki Hendricks.

Game-playing, voyeurism and consumption have not supplanted more traditional themes, but have become increasingly predominant in a range of noir narratives, including the Gothic and future noir variants discussed in the final chapter. This contemporary refashioning of noir themes is a manifestation of the flexibility and responsiveness to social change that have characterised noir from its inception and of the continued vitality of the form. There has been considerable cross-fertilisation between the noir thriller and related genres. Crime writers have written for a more broadly based audience and mainstream writers have adapted noir characters, plots and motifs. There have also been changes in the way books are promoted and marketed. In Britain, for example, there has been a 'deliberate and commendable move by many publishers to promote good fiction with a criminal element outside the straightjacket of a fixed crime "list" or imprint. . . .'[42] Arguably the various remodellings indicate that the idea of noir has spread so widely that it has become difficult to pin down. At the same time, however, transformations help to clarify some of the constant, recognisable elements of 'the noir vision': the unsettling subjectivity of the point of view, the unstable role and moral ambivalence of the protagonist, and the ill-fated relationship between the protagonist and a wider society that itself is guilty of corruption and criminality. In the mid-fifties, Borde and Chaumeton drew the conclusion that the 'moral ambiguity, the criminal violence, and the contradictory complexity of events and motives' worked together in *film noir* 'to give the spectator the same feeling of anxiety and insecurity', and that this was 'the distinguishing feature of *film noir* in our time'.[43] Their summary captures some of the identifying traits of noir, but the persistence of this 'network of ideas'[44] from the 1920s through to the end of the 1990s suggests the necessity of revising the Borde and Chaumeton argument regarding the historical specificity of noir: 'The noir of dark film is dark *for us*,' they wrote, 'that is, for European and American viewers in the 1950s.'[45] What is true of *film noir* (as studies such as Naremore's have demonstrated) is true to an even greater extent of literary noir. If noir is 'the reflex of a particular kind of sensibility . . . unique in time as in space',[46] then the historical limits set must correspond to the greater part of the twentieth century – and extend, perhaps, to 'the near future'.

7
Players, Voyeurs and Consumers

> 'We walk in,' Robbie said, 'I open up with the MAC and you open up with the Hitachi.'
> 'The *camera*? You're kidding me.'
> 'I told you that, didn't I? I want to see it, I want to study it . . .'
>
> Elmore Leonard, *Split Images* (228)

When it's 'showtime', millionaire murderer Robbie Daniels lovingly assembles some of his favourite consumer durables, a $4000 video camera and a 'compact little submachine gun', a MAC-ten 'painted with free-form shapes in rose and dark blue on a light blue background' (27–8); he gives careful thought to what he is going to wear (a dark cashmere and a light canvas shooting coat), gets into his silver Rolls Royce and sets out to film the death of a rich acquaintance whose main offence is that he 'never remembers Robbie's name' (184). In its preoccupation with consumerism and the creation of spectacle Elmore Leonard's *Split Images* (1981) is characteristic of many of the noir thrillers written during the last three decades.

The motifs of players, voyeurs and consumers are obviously present as well in the thrillers of earlier periods. We have looked, for example, at the themes of game-playing and showmanship in Paul Cain stories, at the voyeurs of James M. Cain novels (who want to possess the women on whom they have gazed), at the pleasure in consumption that motivates Highsmith's Ripley, at the display and performance required of the successful gangster and at the pathos of the small-time crook's failure to attain even ordinary material well-being in a greedy society. In Anderson's *Thieves Like Us* (1937) the protagonist, Bowie, having entered into his way of life in a spirit of play, travelling with 'some fellows on the carnival' (242), feels absolutely bound by his gang's code of loyalty. The economic deprivation that has produced Anderson's thieves is underscored by a touchingly peaceful interlude during which Bowie soaks in the 'richness' of their temporary living room, its radio, its chairs with brocaded coverings and lights shaped like candlesticks. As events close in on them, Bowie and Keechie, longing only for economic sufficiency, are turned into a spectacle. They are absurdly misrepresented by the newspapermen who report the exploits of 'the Southwest's phantom desperado' and his gun-toting companion (376).

In comparison to contemporary noir, however, the earlier uses of these motifs are less central, in terms of both theme and structure. This can be seen, for example, if one considers Anderson's novel alongside Tarantino's *Natural Born Killers* (1995),[1] a lovers-on-the-run fable of our own decade. The Tarantino story is contained almost completely within the preparation of a documentary, part of a series that profiles serial killers. His protagonists are very conscious of themselves as game-players and performers, as a spectacle to be consumed by a huge television audience. In Anderson's story, the consumer durables are fleeting reminders of a longed-for domestic life and the young outlaws would scarcely recognise themselves in the lurid newspaper accounts of their crimes. In *Natural Born Killers*, on the other hand, the entire narrative is structured around the creation and consumption of the 'saga' of Mickey and Mallory. 'Movie Mickey', in the inset 'romantic' movie *Thrill Killers*, rants against the 'minimum wage train' and shouts of wanting cash and fast cars: 'And I want it now!' (43). But the main theme of Tarantino's own film script is not the causal connection between economic deprivation and violent crime but the possibility of a mutually reinforcing relationship between violence and its mass-public representation – 'stylized, serialized and specularized'.[2] Mickey and Mallory are a product to be marketed by the media, created in part by a journalist who seizes upon the chance to interview Mickey as 'one of those golden moments that happens maybe only four times in a lucky journalist's career' (25). They are also, however, self-created. As inventors of spectacle, they are ultimately the protagonists of their own movie: 'OK, Wayne, your little movie just underwent a title change . . .' (98).

Some of the recent crime novels discussed here, in particular, the black gangster novels of Goines, Headley and Smith, more closely resemble novels of the thirties in their focus on economic causation. It is deprivation that necessitates 'performances' of quite a high order from those trying to rise out of poverty. Frequently, however, performance is more an end in itself, and the fates towards which characters move are not simply the product of necessity but of sheer engagement with and enjoyment of the activity, the creation and consumption of spectacles. As in earlier noir, passivity is often represented as the attitude that is most dangerous and culpable (not to enter the game, to be an object, to be consumed), but at the same time the noir protagonist faces the dilemma that the more active options (playing, performing, controlling the gaze, consuming) are all forms of complicity with a corrupt society. These are not, however, fixed oppositions, since a common characteristic of these various roles is their invertibility: characters are represented as simultaneously acting and acted upon; the consumer is consumed, the player combating a rival is also the rival combated, the watcher is watched, the performer has the status of both subject and object. The instability of identity tends in earlier noir to be a matter of chronological sequence, for example, in the sort of plot in which a victim becomes the aggressor. More recently, on the other hand, divergent possibilities tend to coexist and the both/and nature of this characterisation[3] heightens the sense of complicity that is at the core of the contemporary noir thriller. Whereas in earlier decades fatality is linked to difference, deprivation and exclusion from the normal human community, contemporary noir is less likely to involve an alienated protagonist than someone altogether too 'like us', their complicity evidenced by their participation in the most commonplace activities of modern society – performing, viewing, consuming.

The figure of the player is closely analogous to the gangster or small-time crook as the embodiment of capitalistic self-interest and ambition, but as a term it is value-neutral, suggesting an approach to life based on rational self-interest, the calculation of advantage, the understanding of one's opponents. The 'gangster-capitalist' is invariably associated with corruption; the player is simply a man or woman who follows the rules appropriate to any given game rather than appealing to some ultimate moral code. There has been increasing attention given since the 1970s to exploring the common elements in 'games' as diverse political contests, armed conflict, crime and punishment, sport, poker. Game theorists analyse successful strategies where there are conflicting interests. They look at the ways in which participants take account of the reactions of rivals to any given strategy, and at the extent to which they show themselves willing to co-operate, form coalitions, retaliate, make threats, stubbornly resist, lie and cheat. The role of reputation is of central importance in game theory, which provides a non-judgemental way of looking at the necessity of carrying through whatever threats are made. This wider interest in analysing and theorising games is reflected in the metaphors, characterisation and structure of many contemporary thrillers. There is a general implication that it is the player's choice of game that determines the rules he follows, and also that this choice separates him from the players in other games. A recurrent motif is agency acquired at the expense of community. That is, the player's involvement in one kind of game separates him from others, such as close friends and family. The game is a serious business, most often with an economic motive behind the play, but this is combined with enjoyment, which is to say that the game can become an end in itself. Role-playing becomes a vital activity, generating a preoccupation with performance and spectatorship.

The voyeur has obvious affinities both with the private eye and with the man trapped by obsession, like the protagonists of *Double Indemnity* or *The Postman Always Rings Twice*. In more recent novels, however, acts of investigative and obsessed looking are often assimilated to the modern technology of voyeurism – taping, photography, film – and are much less closely associated with the specifically male gaze. The increased fascination with acts of voyeurism is linked both to a post-Watergate/Vietnam concern about surveillance and to a more general sense that we live in a culture of spectacle and spectators. From the late sixties on, discussions of media culture and the society of the spectacle have proliferated. The often quoted opening sentences of Guy Debord's *Society of the Spectacle* (1967) sum up one influential line of argument: 'In societies where modern conditions of production prevail, all of life presents itself as an immense accumulation of *spectacles*. Everything that was directly lived has moved away into a representation.'[4] It is not necessary to accept the more extreme implications of this and other postmodern ruminations on 'sensory overload' and 'saturation' to see that such analyses are symptomatic of a widespread concern with the nature of spectatorship – with questions about the effects of a constant flow of images and sounds and about the ways in which spectators themselves influence and select the spectacles they watch (like the crowd at a Roman circus, giving the thumbs up or thumbs down). There are obvious implications for fiction that centres on violence, which has increasingly represented the act of violence as the creation of spectacle in a world in which everyone consumes and produces images and spectacles.[5] As a central element in the noir narrative structure, the 'consumer' has always been there, but consumption in all its forms is a more dominant theme in the contemporary thriller, often accompanied by more explicit attention to the commodification of people, the irony of the 'consumer consumed' and the postmodern city, 'saturated with signs and images', as a centre of play, performance and consumption.[6]

Players and their games

In noir narratives of the 1930s and 1940s, the figure of the game-player or gambler is most often seen committing himself to a doomed enterprise. He is a man who has placed a losing bet against fate. The protagonist of *You Play the Black and the Red Comes Up*, for example, who only wins when he is playing to lose, says despairingly, 'I figured the wheel was hoodooed and the black would come up forever' (31). When Harry Fabian, in *Night and the City*, gambles all on his big fight venture we know he is inviting the fate that befalls him. The gambles themselves signify desperation. The game is played in the vain hope of breaking free from a grim cycle of defeat and degradation. In such texts, the only character for whom gambling carries different connotations is the boss, the head of the gambling and other rackets, like Crotti in Paul Cain's *Fast One*, who is himself presented as analogous to an inexorable fate ('When you buck Crotti you're bucking a machine' [119]). As Dana Polan points out in his discussion of such figures as Corrigan in *The Lady Vanishes* and the casino owner Armand in *The Great Sinner* (both 1949), these are men 'outside of time . . . for whom life is a safe repetition'.[7] They never actually gamble in the sense of taking risks, since it is they who control the system and they can rely on the law of large numbers to safeguard their success. They are the human gods presiding over a game in which the ordinary player stands no chance of winning, and can indeed often be assimilated to a more general sense of noir fatality.

In more recent noir the dominant game-playing narrative that emerges is one which associates the player with more potential control and confident agency.[8] Whereas the roll of the dice or the spin of the roulette wheel are perhaps the most commonly recurring images of gambling in the pre-World War Two thriller (signifying a gamble the player cannot control), in recent noir thrillers the plot more often turns on games in which the outcome depends upon the tactics, the cunning and duplicity, the bluffing and counter-bluffing of skilled players. The 'gambling against inexorable fate' narrative does not, of course, disappear, and these contrasting types of narrative can in fact be seen encapsulated in two recent neo-noir films, *The Winner* (Alex Cox, 1996) and *Rounders* (John Dahl, 1998), the first involving dice and roulette wheels, the second poker. In *The Winner* the god-like character of Kingman looks down on the casino and pulls the plug when the protagonist threatens to defy probability: if anyone does 'get lucky', the gods will destroy him. *Rounders*, on the other hand, locates fatality in the choice of which game to play: one's course in life is only apparently chosen but in reality determined by 'destiny'. The game itself, however, is represented as something not to be won by luck but by skill in understanding the other players, by application and tenacity. The latter approach is summed up by Burke in Vachss's *Blue Belle* (1988) when he forcefully advocates approaching life as an active player, determinedly making choices rather than believing that 'your life is a damn dice game' (217).

Game theorists take note of the fact that the word 'game' might be seen as having somewhat misleading connotations, that is, as implying 'amusement, light-heartedness, and a recreational contest',[9] whereas in truth the activities that can be modelled as games (economic and business problems, the tactics of warfare or politics) involve serious and fundamental conflicts of interest. In the world of the thriller as well, the trope of the game and the player is generally located in the wider context of economic and political activities. At the same time, even in the serious analyses of game theorists, the element of fun remains.[10] This combination of entertainment and serious purpose very often emerges in thriller narratives. Exploring the borderline between 'serious' necessity and playful indulgence or fantasy fulfilment is sometimes self-reflexive: the thriller itself represents the difficulties of the real world but at the same time absorbs readers into the world of play. But such novels also bring to the fore, as one of the issues at stake in the moral world of the thriller, the question of what prompts characters to cross the line from necessity to indulgence in games for their own sake. This sheer indulgence in game-playing and the diversity of intersecting games are central elements, for example, in Robert B. Parker's *Chance* (1996), in which 'the players in the Boston mob scene' (230) carry on with their 'games' in Las Vegas, or in George V. Higgins, *Trust* (1989), a sly, allusive fable of crooked players set in 1968, in the run-up to Nixon's election as President. Higgins' main character, Earl, the kind of anti-hero the era deserves, is a sportsman who was in earlier years responsible for fixing college basketball games – a crooked player for whom dishonest used car-selling and blackmailing are just extensions of his earlier career. Higgins gradually exposes a series of tangentially related forms of sport, ranging from the low-level sleazy deals of Earl up to local political manoeuvrings and, a little higher in the scale, to characters involved in the Washington political scene, where Neil Cooke feels he's '"a *player* ... You can say what you want about Richard M. Nixon. ... But there's a lot of us out there that know why Dick wants it, and by God, we'll see that he gets it . . ."' (231).

Part of the player's skill, then, is represented as his ability to choose the right game and the right venue, and the narratives of such novels often move forward by juxtaposing perspectives from within different games. Higgins does this largely by the creation of revealing conversations amongst the various players. The more usual method is to use the multiple viewpoints produced by shifting first- or close third-person narration, as in a recent British thriller, Greg Williams' *Diamond Geezers* (1997), which is structured around four separate game plans, each with its own rules and goals: Asian-rights activists trying to gain political leverage; Ron, a small-time criminal, wanting to stay on top of things; a protagonist who pretends to play on Ron's team as a move in his own game (running off with Ron's wife); and Councillor Goodge, manipulating the other players to enhance his public image. What Ron and Goodge have in common is a recognition that 'maintaining a positive image in a competitive world is of the utmost importance' (126). Although Goodge is, in the end, the main player who benefits from the 'show' created, his triumph is accidental and he is in no sense the god-like controller of the game. He is, however, a tenacious player, and is ready at the end, as a prospective Member of Parliament, to take another step in the hierarchy of the game – to 'leap into another league' (41).

The implication in *Diamond Geezers* is that everyone who is a fully functioning member of society is a player. In Williams' novel, the action is mainly male-dominated, but many writers of the eighties and nineties include women amongst their key competitors. In Eugene Izzi's *Players*, an American thriller of the mid-1990s, it is only the simpleton, Mute, who thinks in a fatalistic way that any success must bring punishment ('God must be planning something seriously bad for him tomorrow' [350]). Throughout, Izzi juxtaposes the gambles everyone takes with the different ways in which they all try to control their fates, expanding his cast of players and allowing us to follow all of the intersecting paths of many characters who would be marginalised in other types of thriller. The emphasis is on choice and refusal to surrender passively to fate, and Izzi pointedly gives women equal status as players, whether they are unscrupulously sampling the exhilaration of coming out on top ('This, she knew, was something she could get used to' [133–5]) or justifiably rejecting a passive domestic role to pursue success in a game of their own choosing. In Charles Willeford's *Kiss Your Ass Good-bye* (1987) the protagonist prides himself on his skill in the battle of the sexes, always winning until he meets 'Jannaire', who completely misleads him about the nature of the game being played. Similarly, in Andrew Coburn's *Goldilocks* (1989), role reversals make women much more active competitors, breaking free from domesticity. One of the few Coburn characters to emerge at the end in a stronger position is an ageing widow who, after a lifetime of repression, discovers that she, too, can take part in the game, ultimately bidding farewell to the last man, 'Goldilocks', who is ever likely to try taking over her house with '"When you get to hell . . . tell Harold [her dead husband] everything"' (242–3). Yet another kind of empowered woman is at the centre of Nicholas Blincoe's *Acid Casuals* (1995), in which the reversal of expectations involves casting Estela, who used to be Paul, as a transsexual hit woman, a 'modern woman' (22) who has taken control of her life by changing her gender – 'reborn as a killer tart' (209).

Many of the players so far considered are represented as motivated by economic need, but the satisfactions of selecting a game, learning the winning moves and shaping the story of one's own victory ('"tell Harold everything"') often assume much greater importance. The degree of choice and narrative control associated with being a successful player by and large runs counter to any strain of economic determinism. Even where a novel begins from an ascent out of economic deprivation, play is both a response to financial need and an activity that is an end in itself. In *No Beast so Fierce* (1973), Edward Bunker, who has converted his own experience of crime and imprisonment into compellingly direct thrillers (and who also became a familiar face when he played Tarantino's Mr Blue in *Reservoir Dogs*), represents his narrator as determined to challenge his fate by defining his own rules of the game: 'I declared myself free from all rules except those I wanted to accept – and I'd change those as I felt the whim.' Crime is where he belongs, his 'free choice' and also 'destiny': 'Fuck society! Fuck their game!' (107–8). His grim resolution originates in deprivation and a deep-seated sense of grievance, but soon develops into something more than the urge 'to strike back' (143–4). By the end of the novel, we see clearly how much it is the activity itself rather than need that drives him. He has a craving to gamble and, having escaped to an idyllic 'faraway place in the sun', he grows 'tired of peace'. It is much more than dwindling resources that lures him back to his old life: 'My stomach is nervous with anticipation of playing the game again' (300–1).

In many contemporary black crime novels, there is a similar combination of harsh necessity and pleasure in being a successful player, with playing the game signifying an assertion of the ability to choose and a rejection of blind chance. The early seventies novels of Robert Dean Pharr, representing characters who 'just happen to be in the numbers racket',[11] suggest a world governed by fate. In *The Book of Numbers* (1970) and *S.R.O.* (1971), the numbers racket, like dice and the roulette wheel, is the kind of gamble that images a doomed appeal to fortune in the face of hopeless odds. On the other hand, however, Pharr creates representations of the kind of gamble that depends not on luck but on skill, resolution and, a key aptitude for the games-player, the ability to bluff. These are talents also much in evidence, for example, in such conman novels as *Trick Baby* (1967) and *The Long White Con* (1977), by Iceberg Slim (Robert Beck), himself an experienced player who spent his younger days as a pimp and hustler. In the darkly comic fantasy of Pharr's *Giveadamn Brown* (1978), an unpromising, 'unhandsome' young southern boy proves himself a worthy heir to a drug empire by hitting on a bluff, a kind of philosopher's stone of heroin production, the 'one ingredient' needed to produce 'the finest synthetic dynamite in the world . . .' (133). Though Giveadamn is an innocent who works by untutored intuition alone, his grasp of the power of the dream enables him to come up with a piece of inspired trickery and so to take control of his destiny.

Most of the players in the black street novels of this period are considerably less innocent than Giveadamn. Like the gangster anti-heroes of Burnett and Trail, they come from an impoverished ethnic minority seeking upward mobility,[12] men shaped by harsh circumstance, behaving brutally, full of delusions of grandeur. Though sympathetically created, their characters are explained not by the impaired masculinity of many noir protagonists but by a kind of macho self-assertion which, viewed from a female perspective, can be seen as disabling in terms of community. For the players themselves, however, it is what empowers them as agents, and is an essential element in the games in which they are engaged, not least because their reputations on the street depend upon toughness in enforcing agreements and policing the behaviour of other players. Some of the most striking examples of this sort of narrative are Donald Goines' novels, such as *Whoreson: the Story of a Ghetto Pimp* (1972) and *Street Players* (1973). For the pimp-protagonist of the latter, all that counts is being known as 'one of the big players' rather than as some 'chili-bowl pimp' (125): '"Whatever I did, Duke, you can bet I did it like a player"' (10). His arrogance and violence are fully in view, but are seen as rational elements in the game he is playing, establishing the credibility of his threats and the substance of his reputation.[13]

Britain has also, in the 1990s, seen the publication of several black street novels, most notably the Yardie novels of Victor Headley. Headley's *Yardie* (1992), like Goines' novels, centres on characters who are players in the rough games of drug dealing and prostitution. The protagonist, 'D.', 'the Front Line's newest Don', like Whoreson or Earl, learns his game at an early age. Headley puts more explicit emphasis on adverse economic circumstances than does Goines, writing in his Preface to *Excess* (1993) that 'the worst in anyone' is brought out by 'deprivation, lack of opportunity and general sense of frustration' (viii). But if necessity is the original spur, male pride in being a player is also a powerful inducement: D. 'was the ruling king, and all the hustlers and players were his subjects and acting as such' (103). Inspiring both love and fear, he gains the constant flattery of an 'army of sycophants', adding to 'the inflated view he had of himself' (103). As in Goines' novel, we are asked to side more with the male protagonist than with the woman whose testimony gets him arrested for rape and murder. His sympathetic role is confirmed by female devotion, the end of the novel (like that of *Players*) being dominated by a loving woman's shock at his fate. The self-determining power of such characters is evident, and remains even when a stronger female point of view is added to reinforce our sense of the cost of the game, of agency achieved at the expense of community by a male player who is a 'rogue' rather than a 'homebody'.[14] Karline Smith's *Moss Side Massive* (1994), for example, tells a very similar kind of story, but one in which female perspectives are more fully represented, and in which the mother is a powerful figure, though not a sufficient force to stop mayhem amongst her sons, particularly given that she is denied the truth about the street life that supports them. Just as in, say, Trail's *Scarface*, there is a split in the male self between family identity and the role of the street player (the mother in *Moss Side Massive* is 'happy to see her son, Clifton', but would not be happy to see him if she knew he was also a 'bad bwai called Storm' [63–4]).

In other novels in which the pressure of economic necessity is less to the fore, the metaphor of the player implies devising and playing games for their own sake, independent of any rational end, such as reputation or financial gain. Instead, the game involves entry into a world of fantasy, more individualistic, less co-operative. All such games to some extent isolate the player, not only separating him from his own family group but, at the extreme, dividing him from most of his fellow men. Elmore Leonard, for example, constructs the plot of *City Primeval* (1980) around the competing sets of rules dividing his diverse groups of players. At critical junctures there is doubt about which code will prevail: do the 'rules, like a game', prohibit, say, killing a man who is unarmed or can one coolly and deliberately choose this way of executing someone? Is a 'good' player like Raymond Cruz actually playing the same kind of game as the psychotic Clement? Raymond sets him up for a final shooting match, and, in refusing to play, Clement insists on how much he and Raymond are actually alike, even though '"We got our own rules and words we use"' (101). Leonard often explores the attraction and potency of the role of the cowboy for men engaged in any form of armed combat, as well as the moral ambiguities that such an image conceals. As also, for example, in *Riding the Rap* (1995), there is a distinct Wild West element in Raymond Cruz's vision of how he will deal with Clement: '"Mano a mano. No – more like High Noon. Gunfight at the O.K. Corral . . ."' (139).[15] This is not, however, the world of 'Hang 'em High' (*Riding the Rap*, 249) and Raymond's victory is accomplished by playing a game which he would, at the outset, have rejected for the barbarity of its rules of play.

The end of *City Primeval* remains ambiguous (and noir) primarily because Raymond cannot actually think of a reply to the baffled Clement's dying 'What did you kill me for?' (274). There is no answer to the question of what motivated him to compel Clement to play his game. If 'civilised' rules of engagement are abandoned, it is only a short step to the psychotic whose games are entirely his own. Amongst these wholly 'non-co-operative game players', there is, for example, the unhinged Terry, a hard man preparing for the apocalypse, in Charles Higson's *The Full Whack* (1995). Terry announces (as he beats a man to death), '"Let me tell you about the rules. Rule one, I am the ref. See? . . . Rule number three, there are no rules, everything is allowed. . . . Good game. Good game"' (161–2). Psychosis, in game-player narratives, is imaged as the playing of a game so detached from usual norms that there is no element of rationality or co-operative behaviour or enlightened self-interest in the player's conduct. In its extreme form, such psychosis produces characters like the killer in Julian Symons' *The Players and the Game* (1972), Mr Darling, a mild-mannered estate agent who writes a journal in which he expounds his 'Theory of Behaviour as Games' (10). Like Terry, he sets himself up as creator and referee of his own rules of play and is determined to make others play in his game: '"Consider this as a game, and yourself as one of the players,"' he says to a girl he is about to kill (142–3). In contrast to, say, the psychopaths of Jim Thompson's novels, Terry and Mr Darling are not used to reflect on or to reflect the psychological malaise of the society they live in, but to act as limit points of individualistic preference. They are extreme examples, unjustified by economic necessity, of 'making your own rules' and saying to conventional society, in violation of all 'stable social convention', '"Fuck their game!"' The rules they play by are so far removed from 'common knowledge of rationality and the game's structure' that there can be no 'reasonable conjecture' about their next moves.[16]

The eyes of the beholders

> 'It's not necessarily whether you win or lose, darling,' she once said. 'It's how you look while you're playing the game.'[17]

For most of the players discussed above, performance is a central element in the games they are playing. In the black gangster street novels, for example, all of the players are, in one way or another, putting themselves on show. Reminiscent of the thirties gangster, with his extravagant style and ostentatious consumption, Earl has his jewellery and perfect clothes, D. his green Mercedes and 'soft-leather' shoes' (*Moss Side Massive*, 44), Clifton his designer sunglasses, leather jacket and Timberland boots. For them, as for earlier gangsters, the role assumed is what ensures their upward mobility. This heightened awareness of making an appearance, of the creation of an image and of observing eyes, is even stronger in contemporary than in traditional noir, in which, of course, tension was frequently created by the ways in which men looked at women. What we see in more recent novels is a greater mutuality, that is, of men and women looking at one another. So, for example, in the straightforward and unsubtle games of Goines' 'street players', mutual appraisal is a constant element in the power struggles taking place. Charles tries to take the play out of Earl's hands with some young girls he is staring at contemptuously, but is put down by the boldest of them, who returns his attention by staring 'straight into his eyes' (*Street Players*, 22–3). Earl, whose 'looking' is much more successful (he studies, appraises and chooses his whores), very consciously makes himself the object of feminine admiration, taking 'just as much trouble dressing as a woman would' (45). Both watcher and watched have power. Earl, in both capacities, has most power, but female characters also deliberately exploit both roles and, although one could not pretend that in Goines' novel the power of the gaze is equal for men and women, there is clearly a degree of reciprocity.

Female-authored novels of the nineties, like those of Duffy, Moore, Zahavi and Hendricks, represent many women who 'appropriate the male gaze', taking on an aggressive role in other ways as well. The control or manipulation of the gaze, whether by using one's role as object (Duffy) or by being the one who gazes (Moore, Zahavi and Hendricks), is seen as involving entry into a dangerous game. As with the games considered above, and as with the voyeuristic activities represented in traditional *film noir* (for example, *Double Indemnity*), participation may be empowering but also carries the risk of a loss of control. Stella Duffy's *Calendar Girl* (1994), one of Duffy's series of dyke detective novels featuring Saz Martin, creates a 'woman-as-enigma' who remains inscrutable in spite of the desire of other characters to know and possess her. The novel's title summons up one of the most clichéd images of woman-as-sex-object, though in the end we feel sure that she has not been a passive object. She instead seems to have been someone who has used her creation of roles as a choice that allows her to function in a society in which 'face value' is all, as an assertion of independence and even, paradoxically, of integrity. In a New York club, 'Calendar Girls' (65–8), which resembles the classic *film noir* site of female display, the casino that looks like a brothel, she is one of the identically 'designed' girls (given the same hair and eye colour) who tempt men to part with their money. The idea of a constructed identity, created for display and consumption, runs all through the novel, with the 'calendar girl' as someone in search of excitement, playing other roles in which she tempts both men and women into risk and danger. A duplicitous yet also an intensely sympathetic figure whose death is mourned as the novel closes, she has affinities with Karen DiCilia in Elmore Leonard's *Split Images* (1981), who plays a role that makes her 'like a movie star' (81) and is willingly trapped by her enjoyment of a world in which her flamboyance attracts looks.

In feminist crime fiction we often see the formation of identity through the solution to a crime.[18] Duffy's novel, which is to some extent a piece of conventional detective fiction, with alternate chapters providing an investigative narrative, is brought closer to noir by the loss of community and the sense of unknowability (that is, we cannot finally know whether the woman at the centre has a core of integrity or has simply been 'fragmented'). A more unequivocally noir vision informs Moore's *In the Cut* (1995), in which the dangers of both gazing at others and displaying oneself are made more insistently evident. As in much traditional noir, the narrator's insecure identity finds self-preservation impossible. Moore's protagonist, Frannie, in many respects occupies the role of the femme fatale, independent, sexually defined, courting danger, anything but domestic. The male protagonist of earlier noir often misjudges the motives and character of the woman at whom he gazes and is entangled by desire, as Jeff Bailey is in *Out of the Past*, from the moment he sees Kathie Moffett coming into the bar out of the sunlight. Frannie meets her end as a result of sundry such misjudgements. *In the Cut* begins with an act of voyeurism. Frannie happens on a man who is being given a blow job by a red-headed woman who is later found murdered and 'disarticulated'. Frannie's voyeurism is a complex act of looking in which she reflects on her own difference from the girl ('oh, I don't do it that way, with a hitch of the chin like a dog nuzzling his master's hand' [9]) but also wants to come closer to the girl's own perspective. In the course of a narrative during which she takes much pleasure in looking – 'curious to see if the performance of his dressing would make me want him again . . .' (88) – she traverses the distance between herself and the girl. In the end, in spite of her boldness and resource, she is as helpless as the redhead.[19] Like the male noir protagonist, she commits errors of perception, 'looking' without really seeing until it is too late, and finds herself unable to remain a detached, safe observer. She cannot remain 'in the cut' – 'A word used by gamblers for when you be peepin'. . . . From vagina. A place to hide' (178–9).

Whereas Frannie's obsessive looking forces her out of her secure female place into victimisation, other female voyeurs are led to abandon their female locations and roles in more radical ways. In assuming control of the gaze they also move towards male violence, creating revenge fantasies that much more directly constitute an assault on male-centred narratives. Both Zahavi's *Dirty Weekend* and Hendrick's *Miami Purity* have the kind of extremity associated with satiric inversion. Zahavi's novel begins with Bella 'in the cut', peeping out from her safe basement, only to realise that she herself is being observed by 'A man in black. Looking out of his window and down into hers' (16). Once she decides that she has 'had enough' of being in this sort of position, her story 'really starts' (21–2). She takes control of the whole dynamic of seeing and being seen, presenting herself as a sexual object, re-inventing herself until she becomes their most 'fertile fantasy', looking back at and evaluating the male gaze: 'She turned to look at him. . . . His piggy eyes were watching her' (94–5). In returning the gaze, she judges the men she encounters as grotesquely unappetising physical objects. Having also appropriated male violence, Bella survives in the end as a mythic figure. The victim has emerged as a triumphant aggressor, both a caricature (the exaggerated embodiment of sexual violence) and a warning to the male aggressor and the male voyeur: 'If you see a woman walking . . . Just let her pass you by' (185).

Vicki Hendricks' *Miami Purity*, another female rewriting of male thriller conventions, gives a much more positive role to the female gaze. Hendricks creates more interesting ambiguities, in that her novel does not depend so much for its effect simply on a heightening of either the victim or the aggressor roles. Her protagonist is neither satirically reduced to simple-mindedness (like Bella) nor knowingly introspective (like Frannie) but intermittently perceptive, often wayward and mistaken, admirable mainly for her temporary determination to lift herself out of a life which has no real narrative (since she can remember nothing of it). 'Sherri' is both victim and aggressor, wholeheartedly sexual, capable of redefining herself, as suggested by her changes of name. She is inclined to succumb to 'fate' but also willing to work very hard at controlling her destiny. We are ultimately left unsure about the way in which to apportion blame, since her sexuality, like that of the male noir protagonist, has a strong element of fatality about it ('Sexual heat was always permanent in me, no escaping it' [29]) and her erotic choice is the all too aptly named Payne. Hendricks' recent *Iguana Love* (1999), set in a world of scuba diving, body building and numerous naked bodies, is even more centred on ultimately empty and self-destructive acts of voyeurism. "I have to look,"' the narrator, Ramona, tells one Greek sculpture in tights, '"You've created yourself for looking"' (134). In the same scene, Ramona begins her own development towards a very male kind of muscular perfection, becoming like the men who are the objects of her voyeuristic fascination, 'a solid construction' (185) that is both a remarkable spectacle and a killing machine: 'My arms were steel, my tits were rock . . . I was the stronger brute' (179). In her struggle to achieve the reversal, however, Ramona has become not only a cold aggressor but her own victim, her 'solid construction' metaphorically linked to a cage, 'the way I built myself' (185).

Several male writers of the eighties and nineties, for example Jim Nisbet, Marc Behm and Paul Theroux, have also developed markedly voyeuristic themes. In their work, however, the focus is more likely to remain on the mind of the male voyeur and his complicity in a wider system that trades in voyeuristic experiences – the market place, regimes of representation, the network for the production and distribution of pornography, the use of such images in both blackmail and surveillance. One of the most sympathetic representations of male voyeurism is Marc Behm's *Eye of the Beholder* (1980), in which we are led from the start to identify with 'the Eye', entering his perceptual space, and feeling uneasily complicit in his compulsive 'Peeping-Tom-ism', but also coming to understand his lack of control. His voyeuristic position does not give him 'masculine dominance'. Although the woman on whom he spies is not co-operating deliberately with him, there is no sense of her victimisation.[20] Behm resembles writers like Goodis, Willeford and Thompson in the way that he takes genre conventions and makes of them something quite original. *Eye of the Beholder* is an intense and compelling reworking of the private eye as voyeur. The 'Eye', like earlier noir investigators, is distinguished from the classical detective by his own involvement in the crimes he records, prowling outside windows, compulsively following Joanna Eris, witnessing many of her murders and even tidying up after her, dabbing blood from a wall or burying a body more deeply. In our judgements of Joanna herself, though her murders are legion, we are influenced by the bizarre and touching voyeurism of the 'loving eye' that records them. Each has experienced loss and victimisation, and as he tracks her through more rapid changes of identity than even he can keep track of, he records flirtations and brief liaisons that parody the mercenary couplings of the world that has victimised them. The Eye not only gazes himself but observes the gaze of *other* men, occasionally men who seem capable of offering Joanna love and security, but more often sexual predators, at best shallow and crass, at worst brutal.

Despite the scale of the bloodshed, *Eye of the Beholder* is characterised by a mood of gentle sadness, especially with the inexorable approach of the death of its ageing protagonists. This elegiac quality, reminiscent in a way of Burnett's later novels, makes it unusual, however, amongst voyeuristic crime novels, which more commonly move towards resolutions in which a violent end is precipitated by a loss of the control sought (whether by the watcher or the one watched). So, for example, Nisbet's 1981 novel, *The Damned Don't Die*, represents the violent breakdown of the sense of immunity felt by the voyeuristic audience. Originally published as *The Gourmet*, this is a narrative in which there are layers of voyeurism, of watching and listening and of the fetishistic consumption of others that was suggested by the original title. The novel begins with a character listening to a murder, an act that gives us a queasy insight into the voyeuristic relationship of the audience to the perpetrator of psychotic violence. The protagonist is ex-cop, now private eye Martin Windrow, whose name seems a reminder of the false security felt during acts of voyeurism, of a protective window separating audience from act. Windrow's search comes to centre on a photograph album (itself is a fetishistic object, kept by the murderer), documenting the lives he is investigating from early conventional married days to sado-masochistic excess and death, recorded by photographers who become more professional as the voyeuristic activities become a more public display. Much is revealed by looking at the victims as they look back from the photos, and the key lies in the interpretation of response: are the victims abject? masochistic? willing?

In Nisbet, both men and women allow themselves to move into the role of the passive, victimised female. Paul Theroux's *Chicago Loop* (1990) is a mainstream novel that uses the movement across gender lines to explore the nature of guilt, aggression and violence. One of the central questions in the analysis of voyeurism, as of sadism, is to do with the complicity of the victim – the acquiescence of the passive person. Choice is something that Theroux's psychopathic protagonist, Parker Jagoda, feels he gives to his victim, Sharon. He has only unlocked a door and told her it is unlocked ('He had not forced her. . . . And so she would have to take the consequences . . .' [15–17]). Her compliance traps both of them in a sado-masochistic game that ends in death: as at a Mapplethorpe exhibition he attends, the issue for Parker is whether 'he's using them and they don't know it' or whether 'they want to be used' (45–6). The narrative charts Parker's transition from aggressor to victim, a search for atonement that leads him to become Sharon. In transforming himself into a woman he ceases to be, like the other men, a spectator. Taking on Sharon's identity cannot ultimately rid him of remorse but makes him better understand Sharon, enabling him to experience her invisibility and also to understand her complicity, 'her share of the violence' in her offer of herself as 'a submissive lover' (176).

The photographs taken by Behm's Eye, the photo album in the Nisbet novel and the Mapplethorpe exhibition in Theroux all involve the transformation of the voyeuristic object into a picture, but none of these novels is primarily concerned with regimes of representation. In many noir thrillers, however, attention is much more directed to voyeuristic desire not just as an aspect of individual power relations but, transformed into pictures (particularly moving pictures), as part of the whole structure of commercial activity in a society that is increasingly dominated by photoelectronic images.[21] The issue in such novels is not just *whose* gaze it is but who creates and uses and profits from the representations, and what function they have within the socio-political order. The exploration of filmed performance and voyeuristic participation has been a natural preoccupation of film-makers. The cinema, with its 'scopic regime' is, of course, particularly well suited to the exploration of the voyeuristic satisfactions of both film-makers and audiences,[22] forcing us to see ourselves in the role of voyeur and to think through the distinctions between observer and observed, inside and outside. A self-reflexive cinematic treatment of voyeurism has not always been easy for audiences to accept. This was very evident in the response to the 1960 Powell and Pressburger film, *Peeping Tom,* which so outraged critics that the reaction virtually ended Powell's career. The film, following a serial killer/film-maker who records the deaths of his victims, forces the audience to share the murderer's morbid urge to gaze and attacks the hypocrisy of a society that feeds off faces and bodies. In more recent decades, voyeurism in relation to the technologies of reproduction has been much more widely treated. Both films and fiction have explored the binding of identities to 'machines of perception and representation' – 'to the public reproduction, and reproducibility, of private, torn, and opened persons'.[23] Our mass-media witnessing of scenes of public violence and our identification with others '*by way of* the witnessing of public violence and its simulations'[24] is at issue in such films as *Blow Out* (Brian DePalma, 1981), *Videodrome* (David Cronenberg, 1983), *Mute Witness* (Anthony Waller, 1995) and *8mm* (Joel Schumacher, 1999), and also in the noir fiction of writers like Andrew Vachss, Robert Ferrigno, James Ellroy, Anthony Frewin and Ted Lewis.

One of the most extended explorations of Hollywood image-making in relation to the commercial development of American society is in the novels of James Ellroy's *L.A. Quartet,* which repeatedly return to the theme of the bond between the money-makers and the myth-makers. In *L.A. Confidential* (1990), for example, Raymond Dieterling is one of those who bears greatest responsibility for the brutal events of the novel. Father of modern animation and founder of a very thinly disguised Disneyland empire, he is portrayed as someone who, under the sway of an ambitious moneylender, produces pornographic cartoons, 'erotic, horrific' films (466) intended to finance other business schemes. Such films having shaped the obsessions of his deeply disturbed son, Dieterling feels responsible for the macabre murders the son commits. The stylised and explicit psychopathic murders of *L.A. Confidential* acquire the status of perverted artistry created to express the psychological damage sustained by the murderer. A gruesome counterpart to the animated films of Raymond Dieterling, the murders are transmuted into pornographic art work, 'artful desecrations' with 'embossed red streaming from disembodied limbs' (440, 344). Ellroy recurrently writes about lives that have been warped by voyeuristic participation in films produced by those in pursuit of wealth and power. The dominance of Hollywood storytelling combined with the addiction to spectacle spurs the disaffected to narrative acts of their own, although it often also means that characters can only conceive of themselves in terms of the conventional roles of the cinema. In *The Black Dahlia* (1987), for example, the title character has sought to create herself in a Hollywood image. The endless lies she tells are all assimilations of her own life to Hollywood stories, but stardom ironically only comes to her after she has been murdered, when every turn of the plot brings 'another instalment of the Black Dahlia Show'. Identity is bound to public reproduction, and the standardised looks and stories of American cinema are shadowed by the dark mockery of death and perversion.

The combination of commerce and voyeurism is not, of course, confined to Hollywood. Several other noir thrillers, for example by Vachss and Ferrigno, have traversed the seedy, marginalised world of pornography. Vachss' *Blue Belle* deals with sexual violence as spectacle, one of the addictive products sold in a market place in which everything has a commercial value, including flesh. The owner of Sin City, the depraved Sally Lou, has made his living out of the worst kind of porno videos and is the centre of a coalition of 'sex-death freaks', whose 'killer shark' ghost van, one of his 'money machines' (278–80), is a purveyor of killing spectacles. In Ferrigno's *Dead Silent* (1996), set in southern California, both visual and auditory drives are being catered for by sundry sleazy and clandestine recording activities, with secret watching and listening. The novel opens with a doubly voyeuristic scene, the overhearing through bedroom walls of telephone sex which is itself being recorded for voyeuristic consumption; it moves swiftly to a double murder recorded on a video camera. The entry into strangers' lives, 'that whole forbidden-zone thing' (76), is inextricably bound up with commercial deals, not just in the selling of the tapes but in performance on them as a career route. The whole of society seems dominated by voyeurism and prone to confusion about the relationship between image and reality. Elliot, who lives in a house protected by a vast camera and speaker system, is an archetypal voyeur who speaks for a postmodern take on fiction and reality, pronouncing, for example, on the quaint and irrelevant question of whether the murder heard on the tape is 'real'. The macabre fate he meets is that of the voyeur whose spectatorship draws him into the danger of a real world from which he has physically and intellectually tried as far as possible to distance himself.

In British thrillers, it is the blue film market of the late 1950s and the

1960s that has been the historical context for two of the best treatments of the business of voyeurism: Ted Lewis' *Jack's Return Home* (1970) and Anthony Frewin's *London Blues* (1997). Lewis was one of the key figures in the 1970s revival of British noir. Between 1970 and 1980 he published seven novels, including two other novels, *Plender* and *GBH*, in which pornography is an important element.[25] *Jack's Return Home* is a harder, meaner version of the 'can't return home' plot recurrently found in post-World War Two American thrillers. What gives Lewis' novel its power is its terse, unflinching style (unlike many earlier British thrillers, it is hard-boiled as well as noir), its tight plot and its gritty northern settings, effectively translated to the screen in the 1971 Mike Hodges film, *Get Carter!* When Jack returns home and sees his brother Frank in his coffin, the past presents itself as flashbacks and 'bits of a film', and it is in the context of this sort of image that we see his eventual discovery of an actual film. The town itself, as the rich get richer, is designed to be looked at, with affluent life styles displaying themselves for envious inspection (80). But behind the display of wealth there are less acceptable kinds of display, centrally a blue film in which Carter is shaken to recognise his niece (or daughter – he cannot be sure) and which irretrievably alters Jack's own 'film' of a past that he looks back on, as both voyeur and participant.

In *London Blues*, which takes the film *Get Carter!* as its starting point, Frewin creates one of the most subtle contemporary representations of the economic and political interests of which pornography is a part – though it is only one (and far from the most damaging) of the forms of watching that goes on. As Ellroy does in *L.A. Quartet* and *American Tabloid* (1995), Frewin mixes historical with fictional events and characters, though in contrast to Ellroy his intent is not to shock by the extremity of his fictions but, by weaving his story around a trade branded as 'shocking' (59–60) in sixties tabloid exposés, to tease out the real corruptions under the surface of a hypocritical society. The novel starts with a complicated voyeuristic act, its present-day framing narrative opening with the sudden appearance of one of Tim Purdom's black-and-white sixties porno films, interrupting a bootleg video tape of *Get Carter!* The narrator discovers it 'as I'm watching Michael Caine watching the film . . .' (11). The character of Carter himself is seen by Frewin's narrator to possess a kind of self-respect and integrity that make him a player to be reckoned with, a 'tough guy' worthy of comparison with the American hard-boiled investigators of earlier generations. One of the questions we are left to ponder at the end is whether the main protagonist possesses any of the qualities that the framing narrative attributes to Carter. Young and 'Peter Pan-ish' (50), he drifts into the late fifties pornography business, supplying blue movies and finding himself on the periphery of the Profumo Affair without really having any clear knowledge of what is going on. Purdom is in some measure fascinated by the sleazy world into which he is drawn ('It brings out the voyeur in me' [68]), but he is essentially detached, not even involved as a voyeur in comparison to Stephen Ward. 'Just another guy on the make, that's all' (123). As 'a living, breathing part of the decline of the British Empire' (135) he is a joke, though nonetheless inescapably part of the 'eerie' atmosphere of the *demi-monde* in sixties Britain – 'a spectator. A passive member of the audience wondering what is going to happen next' (284). The central irony is that the real question is: 'who are we not supposed to be looking at?' (264). By the end, if Tim has indeed survived, then he has gone into hiding and has himself become a 'lacuna', one of the secrets we are not supposed to be looking at. The curtain 'seems to come down' on him, and he becomes the unseen, part of a suppressed history that emerges only piecemeal (289).

All-consuming quests

Voyeuristic activities are themselves amongst the most obvious forms of consumption in late twentieth-century society, but 'consumer lust' in a broader sense (the power of consumerist society to direct lust to commodities and the commodification of people) has become an increasingly central theme in literary noir. By and large, instead of the fabulous objects (the Maltese falcon or the 'green ice') of earlier noir quest narratives, it is ordinary consumer goods that assume symbolic status. Their function can, of course, be very traditional: like the falcon and the emeralds they can be emblems of the falsity or emptiness or treacherousness of the commodities that are prized and pursued. In George Pelecanos' *A Firing Offense* (1992), addiction is presented as the driving force behind the whole of the commercial enterprise, a theme developed through the image of state-of-the-art hi-fis emptied of their capacity to feed one addiction (to spectacle) but instead filled with substances (drugs) designed to feed another. In Ed Gorman's *Night Kills* (1990), portraying a society in which the presidents of advertising agencies would 'hand over' young women (namely their own daughters) to win lucrative accounts (12), the plot turns on the sale of advertising space which is in reality the sale of an undertaking *not* to advertise the indiscretions of men who have opened themselves to blackmail by buying the services of young women. In the Pelecanos and also the Gorman novel, the selling of these 'false commodities' is part of a very fully established socio-economic context within which advertising, selling and buying are the principal activities. Their entrepreneurs are represented as being involved in creating space within legitimate businesses to operate scams that use the skills of the commercial mind.

Elaborations of the relationship between crime, commercialism and consumption can focus on characters' resistance to the power of the consumer society to 'consume' people or on characters whose psychopathic and satirically presented excesses embody the all-devouring nature of consumerism. Both Charles Willeford and Elmore Leonard, for example, use consumerism as part of the background to their fictions, functioning to establish the moral perspective within which we judge their assorted criminals. Leonard's novels often follow the old-fashioned private eye precedent in using indifference to material goods as an index of human worth: uncontrolled consumer urges can signify psychopathic imbalance; indifference to consumption is an indicator of warm, amiable humanity. *Swag* (1976), for instance, introduces Stick, a petty crook who is inclined to bemused scepticism about the pleasures of consumerism. In *Stick* (1983), he acts as a foil to Chucky and Barry. The former is entirely willing, as 'part of doing business', to 'give the Cuban somebody to kill . . .' (249), a caricature of acquisitive energy, wheeling and dealing in a crude imitation of Barry, who is himself a crude imitation. Both live in a 'spoiled for choice' way, Barry with his choice of colour-co-ordinated cars and chauffeur's uniforms, Chucky with his proliferating hats and phones: '"Anyway, what's my goal, the American dream," Chucky said. "What else? . . ."' (249). Ordell, in *Rum Punch*, 'working his ass off being cool', gives equal attention to his 'four-hundred-dollar oxblood-colored alligator loafers with tassles' and to the attractive range of slickly advertised Berettas, MAC-10s, Uzis and Styer AUGs he is trying to sell (143, 149). Leonard's *Split Images* (1981) again identifies the psychopath with the pointless consumer choice of his gun collection, establishing the nexus of violence and sophisticated consumerism by detailing Robbie's showcase display of handguns.

In Charles Willeford's Hoke Mosley novels, on the other hand, both his series detective and his psychopaths tend to function as innocents outside the customary round of American acquisitiveness. In *The Way We Die Now* (1988), for example, the guilt revealed is that of a commercial society. The novel is introduced with a quote from Burroughs – 'No one owns life. But anyone with a frying pan owns death' – and weaves together various subplots involving the 'owning', controlling and destruction of human life. Hoke, going under cover, descends to the level of a tramp and, having joined the marginal people that America tries to conceal, recognises that anyone sufficiently less successful to have become invisible can (like the missing Haitian workers) be dumped with impunity. In other novels in the series, Willeford's psychopathic characters are used to provide an outsider's perspective on the consumer society. 'Junior' Frenger, in *Miami Blues* (1984), is released from prison only to find that there nothing 'outside' that he really wants. Neither milk shakes nor powder-blue Caddy convertibles turn out, after all, to be desirable (104). In *Sideswipe* (1987), the caricatured embodiments of the American dream of contented consumerism are Stanley and Maya, and their 'ideal family' is thrown into relief by the psychopathic Troy, who presents himself in terms of a different kind of American dream, a dying breed of tough outsiders: there are not many like him left, '"And it's a good thing for the world that there isn't"' (115). Troy allies himself with 'a few men of style, my style', as opposed to men living in cities who are like rocks in a leather bag – like Stanley, 'round and smooth as marbles . . . the perfect specimen of American male', in 'glorious retirement in sunny Florida', polishing his new Escort every Sunday (116). Willeford is not romanticising Troy, any more than Thompson romanticises his psychopathic malcontents, but he does use the perspective of alienated male violence to bring out the limitations of bland consumerism.

The crises of identity faced by the contemporary noir protagonist are very often to do with the guilt and anxiety of the insider rather than with the alienation of the outsider. All firm sense of identity is eroded by complicity, by a willingness to pursue standardised goals or even to make a commodity of oneself in order to secure a place in consumer society. If you compare Walter Mosley's Easy Rawlins to the traditional private eye, for example, you see that one important strand Mosley has added to the tradition is related to Easy's ownership of property. His 'secret life' is his business success, his complicity with the American success ethic: 'All of what I had and all I had done was had and done in secret. Nobody knew the real me. Maybe Mouse and Mofass knew something but they weren't friends that you could kick back and jaw with' (*White Butterfly* [1992], 169). Most centrally in *Red Death* (1991), Mosley explores Easy's sense of being trapped by this fact into a compromised position that involves in effect selling himself to the most dubious of political masters. Like Himes, Mosley uses the role of his black protagonist to focus attention on the marginalisation of his novel's black characters and to bring the novel into areas of Los Angeles which in Chandler, say, were treated as alien. The main theme, however, is less to do with Easy's otherness than with his fears about being assimilated on immoral terms. What bothers him is his complicity in the society within which he seeks to secure a prosperous life for himself. The presence of McCarthyism in the novel is used primarily for exploring the nature of this complicity, with personal relationships undermined less by political suspicions than by the urge to survive and prosper in an 'American' way. His shady property ownership has put him in a position that is vulnerable to corrupt pressure from a man who appears to be an upright official but is in fact far worse than any of the supposed enemies of the state. Easy becomes 'a flunky for the FBI' rather than risk losing his property and his freedom, and in consequence is tormented by the knowledge that he 'wasn't, and hadn't been, my own man' (235–6). Mofass, whose betrayal of Easy is at the root of his troubles, forces Easy to concede that his own betrayal of friendships and collaboration with the FBI is no better than the behaviour of Mofass: '"What was you gonna do fo' that FBI, man? . . . He said he'd save yo' money if you do somebody else dirt, ain't that right? How come you any different than me?"' (266).

In novels in which the act of consumption is much more integral to the structure, commodity fetishism and unrestrained consumerism are sometimes figured as the vices of serial killers. As Seltzer argues, 'the general forms of seriality, collection, and counting conspicuous in consumer society . . . and the forms of fetishism' can all be seen in connection to serial killing.[26] In James Hall's *Buzz Cut* (1996), for example, a narrative focusing on the activities of a psychopathic killer is given point by extended metaphoric play with the idea of consumption. We witness the perpetual feast of a cruise ship and ultimately see as well the willingness of its owner, in order to keep the ship's feast going, to sacrifice passengers to feed a psychopath's metaphoric hunger. The ship and its 'anniversary cruise' are a floating embodiment of American consumerist display: 'An endless stream of food and liquor rolling up the gangway . . .' (108–9). The 'glittery facades' and 'false allure' of the *Eclipse* are no defence against Butler Jack, a psychopath whose own mother has made a commodity of herself in her marriage to Morton Sampson, president of the Fiesta Cruise Lines. Jack takes the whole ship hostage while its privileged guests 'celebrate Morton Sampson's unceasing success' ('you name it, if they had ten million in the bank, they were invited to the party' [109]). His endeavour is a parallel to the fanaticism and the 'unfathomable hunger' of the men who built skyscrapers, except that his hunger drives him to wield power over the extravagant, gluttonous people whose indulgence on the cruise ship is perceived by him in fevered, hyperbolic terms. As in earlier killer protagonist novels, the psychopath is both a reflection of his society and a savage satirist. Hall gives Butler Jack his own sections of the narrative to express his revulsion at the society he seeks to revenge himself on, committing revolutionary violence on the rich world's 'safe and happy arrangements' (224–5).

Going beyond genre fiction but nevertheless closely linked to the techniques, materials and metaphors of the consumer society thriller, Bret Easton Ellis' *American Psycho* (1991) is the ultimate consumption novel, carrying to Swiftian satiric extremity the imagery of devouring, commodification and objectification – the equation of uncontrolled consumer urges with the psychopathic imbalance of a modern cannibal. The huge furore over *American Psycho* has been plausibly attributed to its mainstream status, its publication not as a piece of genre fiction but by Alfred A. Knopf as one of its Vintage Contemporary paperbacks.[27] The eighties had seen the publication of many novels notable for their depiction of gruesome killings, both noir thrillers (Ellroy's *L.A. Quartet* novels, for example, are never short on bloody details of grotesquely brutal serial killings) and horror novels (like the best-selling 'splatterpunk' novels of Clive Barker). As Robert Skal writes, both Ellis and Stephen King depict, from radically different perspectives, 'the monstrous spectacle of the consumer consumed. Ellis' world of blood-soaked designer labels recognisably upgrades the voracious mall zombies in *Dawn of the Dead*: they shop till they drop, eat your brains, then shop some more.'[28] Skal's explanation of the outrage over Ellis' novel is that this sort of excess can perhaps be tolerated in popular film and fiction but that if the 'hideous progeny' of the genre writers is allowed to 'start tracking blood up the staircase of the Manhattan castle' it is quite another matter. Although the critical response to *American Psycho* may seem the reverse of Orwell's patronising argument that modernist moral confusions were unsuitable for the literature of the 'common people', there is a fundamental similarity: one literary preserve should not be contaminated by another; every genre should know its place.

Amongst contemporary cross-generic novels, *American Psycho* is one of the most disturbing and unforgettable, though it might be argued that to call this novel 'unforgettable' is not necessarily a recommendation. Its appalling images are not easily dismissed from the mind. Since part of Ellis' point is excess, Patrick Bateman's monstrous acts are described in so excessive a way that as we read on we ultimately feel numbed by them – which is also, of course, part of Ellis' point. The novel's opening details establish a world of commercial oversaturation in which the most common reaction is one of 'total and sheer acceptance' (5–6). The omnipresent bums and beggars, viewed with brutally comic callousness by Price, Bateman and their like, define the lowest social boundaries of the society, and are used by Ellis as a heavily stressed reminder throughout the novel of those who are in effect non-existent, the nobodies in a world where '*Everybody's* rich. . . . *Everybody's* good-looking' (23). The failure to see anything other than pleasing, saleable surfaces is abundantly (perhaps over-abundantly) established by the dense texture of product description and methods of beautification, with whole passages of meticulously detailed, heavily ironised consumerism creating an elaborate context within which the later lists can operate effectively – lists into which increasingly shocking items are inserted, with the same banal tone recording corpse-disposals and cannibalism, Ralph Lauren dress shirts, Toshiba portable compact disc players and Mitsubishi rechargeable electric shavers.

Patrick Bateman is the psycho as normal all-American boy, the embodiment of insipid niceness, 'the boy next door' (11). He has affinities with Thompson's folksy psychopaths in *The Killer Inside Me* and *Pop. 1280*, but his metaphoric function as the ultimate consumer creates tensions that are far more extreme. As the facade progressively disintegrates ('I'm having a difficult time containing my disordered self' [301]), there are ever more damning failures, on the part of the rest of society, to see the beast under the blandness: '"You're not really comprehending any of this. . . . *I* chopped Owen's fucking head off. *I* tortured dozens of girls. . . ." "Excuse me," he says, trying to ignore my outburst. "I really *must* be going"' (388). The killing can be seen as an expression of Bateman's inability to cope, but more fundamentally it is an expression of the nature of the society to which he wants to belong (and into which his sickness and inhumanity do actually 'fit') – of a depersonalisation 'so intense' that 'There wasn't a clear, identifiable emotion within me, except for greed and, possibly, total disgust' (282). Bateman records his growing sense of the meaninglessness of all higher ideals and emotions, creating an inner 'desert landscape . . . devoid of reason and light and spirit. . . . Surface, surface, surface was all that anyone found meaning in . . .' (374–5). This is a society in which the ideas of both decency and indecency are defined in terms of tastes. Stash cannot be '*perfectly* decent and nice' if he asks for '*chocolate chip sorbet*'; 'evil' is just a casually used endearment; 'insane' is a description of someone wearing tasselled loafers; you are 'crazy' if you fail to join a tanning salon (20, 24, 31, 48). Bateman's glib contextualising of his atrocities is also a statement of Ellis' wide-ranging condemnation of American society, as he curses principles and moral distinctions, all of which seem to him to come down to nothing more than 'die or adapt. I imagine my own vacant face, the disembodied voice coming from its mouth: *These are terrible times*' (345–6).

Although they are not aiming to convey the terror of 'terrible times' in the way that Ellis does, several British thriller writers of the nineties have centred their plots on the atrocities of a society in which everything is subordinated to consumption. By the mid-1990s, after 15 years of Conservative hegemony, British thriller writers were increasingly constructing narratives that aimed to expose what Will Hutton, in his best-selling 1995 critique, called 'the state we're in', the result of failed Thatcherite efforts to bring Britain closer to the market-oriented financial system of the United States, with its economic deregulation and promotion of consumption. This was, Hutton argues, an 'abandonment of society to the market' that instead brought inequality, social distress, delegitimation of the British political system and deterioration of the underlying economy.[29] The New Wave British crime novelists of the nineties have been strongly influenced by American writers (by Jim Thompson, Chester Himes and Charles Willeford, but also by more recent writers like Elmore Leonard and Carl Hiaasen[30]), and they share many of the themes of their American counterparts of the eighties and nineties.

These are novels, however, that are distinctively British in tone, style and setting. There are still British thrillers set in the United States (and written in an appropriate style) but, in contrast to the gangster pulps of the fifties, they are very far from being rapid mass-market imitations. There is, for example, the powerful series of noir novels by Tim Willocks, including *Bad City Blues* (1991), with its exploration of addiction, obsession and revenge in an archetypal Southern town;[31] and there is the mainstream noir of Martin Amis' *Night Train* (1997), a tale of suicidal despair amidst the futuristic commercial glow of a cyberpunk American cityscape. More commonly, however, contemporary British thrillers have been set in Walthamstow (Jeremy Cameron), Manchester (Nicholas Blincoe) or Meadow Road near the Oval Cricket Ground (Ken Bruen) and written in styles recognisably regional: '"Vinnie my son," I goes, "you come off second best mate . . ."' (Cameron, *Vinnie Got Blown Away*, 1). They are generally, as Ken Bruen's narrator says of one of his favourite words, 'Hip, Contemporary. Sassy' (*Her Last Call*, 32). In contrast to the 'Brit grit' writing of earlier decades (Ted Lewis, Maurice Procter, Gerald Kersh) they offer a much greater admixture of surreal and comic elements, whether they are writing stories of 'London's new outlaw underclass'[32] or of company take-overs played out in London's yuppie flats and wine bars. But in spite of their lightness of tone, they offer serious criticism of British society and politics. Even writers who do not link their plotting to actual political goings-on provide some sharply satiric pictures of a society in which material success, desirable goods and attractive surfaces are all founded on crime of one sort or another.

Attacks on rampant consumerism can be launched from deprived areas. So, for example, within the council-estate world of Cameron's *Vinnie Got Blown Away* (1995) and its sequel, *It Was an Accident...* (1996), we meet the almost innocent figure of the narrator, Nicky Burkett, a car thief with a happy-go-lucky commitment to the consumer society and a prudent respect for the rules that (by implication) structure the whole of this society: 'Lean on someone smaller, don't get involved with someone bigger and better...' (*Vinnie*, 19). The most obvious milieu within which to satirise consumerism, however, is one in which consumption is notably conspicuous, amongst those most evidently enjoying the consumer boom of the eighties – the 'fun, greed and money', 'the hot credit and the Good Things'.[33] As David Huggins' narrator says in *The Big Kiss* (1996), 'It was the high-water mark of the Thatcher revolution and, except for the Red Wedge, everyone was at it' (28). Some of the most entertaining of the New Wave crime writers, such as Huggins, Ken Bruen, Christopher Brookmyre and Iain Banks, choose their main cast of characters from social groups that were cashing in on eighties consumerism. Huggins' narrator, Steve Cork, who built up his business in the mid-eighties, at the height of the Thatcher revolution, has created the kind of life defined by a detached Tudor-style house in Roehampton, a Fiat Punto for his wife and a Mitsubishi Shogun. His nemesis is a man who represents such a lifestyle carried to extremes – the unacceptable face of upward mobility, and significantly not a creator (as Steve has been) but a taker-over. Like Elmore Leonard, Huggins links over-the-top, uncreative greed with a latent psychotic and sadistic streak. Mental imbalance ultimately explains the obsessive progress up the business ladder of the rapacious entrepreneur, who conceals his psychosis under a surface so conventionally smooth that there is 'something of the replicant' about him: looking as though he has been 'cast in plastic from a mould', he uses an electric razor twice a day to patrol 'the frontier between himself and the rest of the world' (14).

The criminally inclined yuppie gets more sympathetic treatment in Ken Bruen's blackly comic *Her Last Call to Louis MacNeice* (1998), which, rather like American gangster sagas, uses the point of view of a protagonist, Cooper, for whom crime is a business. His enterprising criminality mirrors yuppie ambitions and his fate, neatly noir, is entirely appropriate. Cooper narrates in a laconic, laid-back style that makes no distinctions between hard-boiled violence and loving consumerism – the turbocharged car ('A Subaru Impreza, its cousin won the Monte Carlo rally. Yeah, like that' [9]), the 'flash' flat and the possessions by means of which he identifies himself. The Louis MacNeice lines he is told to memorise ('an addict to oblivion' and 'no intention') capture something of his hollow, rootless life, which has no deeper thought or intention than the maintenance of surfaces: 'I did not look for the sneer beneath the surface . . .' (14). Cooper's career as a robber and even the repossession business he set up as a front have prospered as though it is divinely ordained destiny: 'fuck me, ain't it rich, the business took off', since God Himself probably 'enjoys a bit of villainy. . . . Else how to account for the Tory party' (29–30). It is a decade in which there seem to be boundless opportunities for those with some skills in 'the art of deception' (56), until they inevitably encounter someone 'bigger and better' – as Cooper, of course, does, leaving him in a state of paranoid apprehension and with 'Zilch' from his latest robbery: 'What is it – the bank robbers' prayer: "Lemme get away CLEAN." I was dirty to my soul . . .' (123).

Both Brookmyre and Banks chronicle the dirtiness of the British eighties from north of the border, as does Irvine Welsh, who in 1998, with *Filth*, combined the 'bad day in Bedlam' qualities of *Trainspotting* (1993) with elements of the noir crime novel. Welsh's novel opens with a brutal murder and has a psychopathic, unreliable narrator, Bruce Robertson, 'a bad bastard who happens to be a cop'.[34] Although Thatcherite politics are only briefly mentioned in *Filth*, it is a much more overtly political novel than *Trainspotting*. Welsh's 1994 play *Headstate* had aimed 'to capture the essence of Britain after 15 years of Tory rule',[35] and *Filth*, through the narrative of Robertson's tapeworm, covers much the same period of time ('You idolise Thatcher over the Falklands . . .' [389]), creating a surreal satire in which a voracious consumer of drugs, women and police canteen culture is in turn consumed by a tapeworm that speaks for his nagging conscience – an infestation of which he finally rids himself.

Brookmyre, though he lives in Edinburgh, is in origin, like Banks, a Glasgow writer. Said to have his Glaswegian birthplace 'inscribed all over his face: tough with attitude',[36] he creates violent crime narratives, of less bizarre extremity than *Filth* but similarly conceived as 'post-Thatcherite nightmares'. His first two novels, *Quite Ugly One Morning* (1996) and *Country of the Blind* (1997), are set in nineties Scotland, where the entrepreneurial activities and shoddy morality of the eighties continue to flourish in the underhanded schemes, gruesome murders and establishment cover-ups around which he develops his plots. Jack Parblane, Brookmyre's hard-boiled journalist, investigates conspiracies and dirty deals that have their origins in the Thatcherite eighties. Parblane's proof of 'whodunnit' at the end of *Country of the Blind* involves Swan, 'that self-made Eighties-Thatcherite-Revolution success story', and Dalgleish, one-time junior minister at the DTI and now High Tory Secretary of State for Scotland. Both have been financially 'propped up' by a thoroughly corrupt Tory tabloid owner in return for such favours as 'massaging reports' about his business revenues, helping to conceal his dealings in pornography and aiding him behind the scenes in his 'weaponry transactions' (359–60). In *Quite Ugly One Morning* the nauseating, xenophobic, frighteningly right-wing Stephen Lime has hatched a scheme to kill off long-stay geriatric patients to facilitate the closure of a hospital, thus making room for '"Hotel. Conference facilities. That sort of thing. Multimillion-pound development"' (200). The parable of spectacularly greedy consumption sustained by large-scale human sacrifice is supported by satiric vignettes of the massive Lime in his luxurious bath (thinking of his 'wider rings of girth' as 'evidence of health, strength and vitality') and of his 'hideous' house with its 'green, savannah-like shag-pile carpet' and its 'monstrous glass chandelier'. Fittingly, Lime's undoing begins with an exceptionally messy murder and the trashing of the victim's flat by a grotesquely caricatured hit man who imagined that he was acting in an entrepreneurial spirit: '. . . he had managed to kid himself for a while that Lime might even be impressed. He had "thought on his feet to protect the investment" . . . Lime liked words like that' (40).

Iain Banks, whose *Complicity* (1993) is a more 'mainstream' post-Thatcher-era thriller, has been described as 'an old-fashioned socialist, forced by distaste for the former Conservative administration into nationalism'. 'After Thatcher came to power,' he says, 'I felt alienated and a lot more Scottish.'[37] Set in the early nineties, *Complicity* is more overtly moral and political than most genre fiction attempts to be, reinforcing its attacks on moral bankruptcy, commercial selfishness and corruption in high places with passages of explicit discussion of the law, democracy and political allegiances: "We have chosen to put profits before people, money before morality, dividends before decency, fanaticism before fairness, and our own trivial comforts before the unspeakable agonies of others . . ."' (301). This is the murderer's justification for his acts. In the manner of much traditional noir, Banks is using the psychopath both as a metaphor for and a critic of a sick society, quite explicitly putting the argument that in a 'climate of culpability' with such widespread 'perversion of moral values', nothing that the killer has done has been out of place (301). He represents himself as a product of the system, 'a businessman' (299–301), settling accounts for the exploited, tipping the balance against those who can afford to live in houses with views over golf courses, can own Range Rovers and foxhounds, and enjoy richly carpeted floors, black leather furniture, chrome-and-glass tables and all the hi-tech luxuries that money can buy (34, 56–7, 85–6). The murders described during the course of the novel (of the prominently corrupt, appropriately dispatched) have an element of Ellroy's theme of grievances 'written on the body'. They constitute a diatribe against those in power conducted by means of grotesque physical violations, each symbolising the exact nature of the corruption attacked. The friendship between the main narrator, Cameron Colley, and the murderer raises very directly the whole issue of how we judge the murders committed. The making of such judgements is part of a complex treatment of the question of complicity in an immoral society. As the murderer says, '"Don't you see? I'm agreeing with you; I listened to all your arguments over the years, and you're right: the twentieth century *is* our greatest work of art and we *are* what we've done . . . and *look at it*"' (301).

8
Pasts and Futures

In Gibson's *Neuromancer* (1984), the protagonist, Case, exiled from cyberspace, sleeps in 'the cheapest coffins' and roams the streets of Night City, a place that is 'like a deranged experiment in social Darwinism': 'Stop hustling and you sink without a trace.' Isolated and self-destructive, worn down until 'the street itself [has come] to seem an externalisation of some death wish' (13–15), Case is hired to go on a virtual reality quest, 'the Straylight run'. His goal, Villa Straylight, belongs to a family that controls the world's two most powerful artificial intelligences; it is also, however, the highly wrought product of minds that in many ways seem remote from the era of hypertech and cyberspace. '"The Villa Straylight," said a jewelled thing on the pedestal, in a voice like music, "is a body grown in upon itself, a Gothic folly."' Its proliferating structures rise towards 'a solid core of microcircuitry', but are at the same time the emblems of an old family that has grown rich by exploiting others, 'growing inward' into a 'ragged tangle of fears' (242). As Ratz, the Chatsubo bartender, says, 'what grotesque props . . . castles hermetically sealed, the rarest rots of old Europe . . .' (278).

Gibson's novel, 'the quintessential cyberpunk novel',[1] is a fusion of the noir thriller, science fiction and the Gothic. Its computerised data matrix, Gothic castle and crazed aristocratic family merge entertainingly with its hard-boiled protagonist living precariously and immorally on the seedy margins of a corrupt world. A debt to Chandler is often suggested, though Case is in fact closer to Kells, the protagonist of Paul Cain's *Fast One*, an utterly cynical convicted criminal with a history of rash behaviour and drug addiction. In recent decades, particularly in the eighties and nineties, the label 'noir' has been applied to texts and films that combine elements of the noir thriller with future world and

Gothic fantasies. Arguably this development is a return to origins. The hard-boiled tradition so inextricably bound up with noir is in part defined by the gritty realism of its style, its faithful representation of contemporary life and its hard-bitten response to socio-political corruption. In many respects, however, both literary and cinematic noir also have strong affinities with the literature of fantasy and romance, blending realistic representation with non-realistic and expressionist elements that are heightened, distorted, stylised and excessive – the knight of romance in Chandler, the mythic dimensions of Hammett's Poisonville, the supernatural suggestiveness of Woolrich's prose,[2] the monstrous satiric grotesques of Thompson's psychopath-narrator novels.[3] Indeed, it is often this pull towards excess which gives noir its unsettling power, its savage intensity and its haunting sense of irreversible fate, and, in novels that centre on a protagonist like Chandler's knight of the mean streets, it is the essentially romantic figure of the tarnished hero who is the 'last man standing' against this mood of fatality.

'One can imagine', James Naremore says, 'a large video store where examples of [*film noir*] would be shelved somewhere between gothic horror and dystopian science fiction: in the center would be *Double Indemnity*, and at either extreme *Cat People* and *Invasion of the Body Snatchers*.'[4] The family resemblances to be found amongst noir, Gothic and science fiction are rooted in their shared history. The origins of science fiction are often seen to lie in later romance genres such as the Gothic novel.[5] Old terrors are newly imagined, and, in cyberpunk, an old vocabulary (castles, romancers, ghosts, gods, voodoo) is coupled with a vocabulary of AIs (artificial intelligences), cranial jacks, the deck and the matrix. Gibson's fiction, especially *Count Zero* (1986) and *Mona Lisa Overdrive* (1988), repeatedly moves between technological 'magic' and the supernatural.[6] The questing cyberpunk hacker is routinely haunted by past evils, by age-old forms of exploitation, superstitious horrors and decadent aristocratic cruelty. The cyberpunk text is as likely to be analysed in a critical study called *Gothic* as it is in one called *Cyberia*,[7] and the same is true for such recent films as *Terminator*, *Alien* and *Blade Runner*. It is not only recent texts, of course, that can be located and discussed within both genres: *Frankenstein* (1818) can be credited with creating one of the most powerful and enduring Gothic 'terror-symbols' but is also widely accepted as 'the first real science fiction novel'; *Jekyll and Hyde* (1886) occupies a central place in the Gothic tradition and is at the same time one of the most important early examples of 'science fantasy'.[8]

The noir thriller is very often, like both *Frankenstein* and *Jekyll and Hyde*, a fantasy of duality, and *Jekyll and Hyde*, in particular, is a form of doppelgänger narrative rewritten countless times in the literary noir of the twentieth century. An apparently respectable protagonist's dark side surfaces, cannot be controlled, commits murder and brings ruin and destruction. Other elements in *Jekyll and Hyde* – sinister locations, darkness and decay, the fragmentary narrative, the suggestions of psychological monstrosity and regression to barbarity – are also familiar ingredients of the noir thriller. What sets Stevenson's novel apart from traditional noir, of course, is the admixture of fantasy. In recent decades, however, the stylistic and iconic aspects of non-fantastic literary noir (the tough style, the hard-boiled investigator, the gangster and the small-time crook, the femme fatale) have been reunited with literary forms in which there is a higher level of permissible fantasy, whether that fantasy is given a plausible scientific basis or involves blurring the distinctions between natural and supernatural. This kind of cross-breeding is to be seen in cyberpunk from Gibson's *Neuromancer* trilogy in the eighties to such recent novels as K. W. Jeter's *Noir* (1998), as well as in other near-future narratives, such as the Ballard and Womack novels analysed at the end of this chapter. It is also seen in modern Gothic novels like those of Hjortsberg, Ackroyd and O'Connell.

If we think in terms of the defining features of literary noir, what we see in 'fantastic noir' is the intensification of two centrally important noir themes, the destabilising of identity and the inescapable presence of the past. As the comparison with *Jekyll and Hyde* suggests, divided identity is one of the shared preoccupations of the noir thriller and the Gothic novel. It is also frequently one of the underlying themes in the strand of science fiction which explores the interrelationship between the human and the technological. In non-fantastic noir, alienation from self can be evident in the fragmented narrative of a psychotic mind and in the confused or fearful responses of characters who encounter symptoms of this psychosis. In Gothic noir self-division can be literalised. So, for example, in Hjortsberg's *Falling Angel* (1978), Johnny Faithful has actually devoured the heart of Harry Angel. In Ackroyd's *Hawksmoor* (1985), the twentieth-century detective figure is haunted by his ghostly double, a late seventeenth- early eighteenth-century murderer.

Science fiction, too, has its dark doubles from *Frankenstein* on, but the distinctive science fictional means of destabilising our sense of unified character and human identity is by combining man with machine, or by challenging our perception of a human–mechanical divide. Man–machine symbiosis or brain–computer interfaces, the creation of artificial intelligences and biological engineering all disrupt our sense of the unity and integrity of individual bodies and minds. Bruce Sterling, for example in *Schismatrix* (1985), populates his future world with divergent species, the 'Mechs', enhanced by such things as brain–computer interfaces, and the 'Shapers', produced by the methods of bioengineering. In Rudy Rucker's *Software* (1982), giant artificial intelligences, 'boppers', extract the protagonist's 'software' (the information in his brain) and put it into a robot body. The sources of anxiety in fantasies of this kind are most often to do with external control (socio-political fatality) rather than inescapable inner demons (psychological fatality). The boundaries between inner and outer worlds are breached, producing fragmentation and the dissolution of a coherent self and raising radical questions about the nature of being (what is the essence of the human?). The intersection with the noir thriller, however, is more evident in the way this metamorphosis into the 'posthuman' foregrounds the issue of agency, bringing protagonists to wonder, not without cause, whether they retain free will and individual autonomy. For Gibson's Case, when he is trapped in the matrix by Neuromancer, the question is whether he has simply become a second-order electronic construct manipulated as an image by more powerful entities. Cobb Anderson, in Rucker's *Software*, asks himself what built-in programs are now a part of him: 'Were the boppers in a position to control him on a real-time basis? Would he notice the difference?' (120).

This apprehension about loss of control is closely analogous to the noir sense of fatality found in those novels which associate fate with the machinations of determinedly corrupt, possibly conspiratorial political and economic powers. A familiar figure in traditional noir is the man who does not realise that his actions are being externally controlled. In Hammett's *Glass Key*, for example, Ned Beaumont is unwittingly used by Paul Madvig, who is in turn under the sway of Senator Henry and his daughter, to whom Paul is a lower form of life, 'fair game for any kind of treatment' (780). The manipulating forces in the world of cyberpunk are generally less modest in their ambitions than the local if representative power brokers of traditional noir. Cyberspace transcends all local and national boundaries, and paranoia is on a correspondingly large scale, involving gigantic multinationals and omniscient intelligence organisations. This future-world projection, however, is not perceived as a fundamental departure from the more local forms of political and socio-economic control. Rather, it is the continuation of an old struggle by other means. Cyberpunk fiction moves away from the speculative dominant of 1960s science fiction, with its dramatic temporal and spatial dislocations, and turns instead to extrapolative world-building.[9] Its 'near-future' narratives imply inextricable connections between the past (our present) and a future in which both the streets and cyberspace replicate and satirically distort the structures and corruptions of contemporary corporate capitalism.

This diminution of temporal distance is also a characteristic of the Gothic noir narratives of Hjortsberg, Ackroyd and O'Connell. One of the distinguishing features of the Gothic is a 'fearful sense of inheritance in time', combining with a claustrophobic sense of enclosure in space to produce 'an impression of sickening descent into disintegration'.[10] The infernal cities of these writers are New York, London and the imaginary New England factory town of Quinsigasmond. They are all repositories of shadowy, ancient forces, but these dark powers are symbolically linked to the mechanisms, the buildings and the inescapable boundaries of the modern city. In the almost present futures of Ballard and Womack, the past is equally determinate, leaving the characters of the narrative with buried fears, hatreds and desires, begetters of a future that is in essence a reversion to the past – an encounter with the Conradian 'heart of darkness' that no noir protagonist ever manages to leave wholly behind.

A hell of a city

The themes of self-division and the inescapable past dominate William Hjortsberg's *Falling Angel*, which was filmed by Alan Parker as *Angel Heart* in 1987. The Faustian story of a satanic pact is grafted on to what at first appears to be a hard-boiled detective story, beginning with a phone call to the Crossroads Detective Agency, 'satisfaction guaranteed' at reasonable rates. It is possible to see the surprises of the narrative as the result of a generic switch from crime fiction to the Gothic novel. In a sense, however, the Gothic is heavily present from the opening sentence: 'It was Friday the thirteenth and yesterday's snowstorm lingered in the streets like a leftover curse' (1). Hjortsberg's skill lies in using throughout the language of superstition, curses, diabolic forces and evil incarnate to intensify and give horrifying substance to a noir narrative that centres on the investigation of dark secrets. It is a potent combination because we know that at bottom these narratives are the same. The hunter is indistinguishable from the hunted, and damnation is never negotiable.

'Harry Angel the famous shaman' (45) falls into a city in which there seems to be no way to evade the omnipresent Louis Cyphre. Ranging the city from its heights to its depths, Angel sees diabolical happenings at every level, though the real movement of the narrative is towards a recognition that evil is inescapable because it belongs to Harry's inner as well as his outer world. This is not just a matter of 'another bunch of crooks' in both high and demonic places (253). Harry's deficient self-knowledge is, of course, traditionally noir. Many a noir protagonist feels himself, like the amnesiac protagonist of John D. MacDonald's *Man-Trap*, to be plunging through a long tunnel in which lights whip by 'illuminating fragments I could not understand' (152). When he finally recognises his true self he sees how deeply implicated he is and understands his fate. Like Angel, the noir investigator often finds that he has been somewhat careless in his choice of employer and fails to grasp why people keep dying around him. The noir amnesiac may all too effectively repress the memories that surface to give him nightmares – in Angel's case, of pursuer and pursued changing places and an evil twin embracing him with a savage kiss. What Angel adds to the noir thriller's scepticism about the possibility of goodness and innocence is a literalisation of devouring ambition ('Poor old Harry Angel . . . I killed him and ate his heart') and of the hidden self, Johnny Favourite, who has already earned damnation. The detective narrative's 'de-ciphering' has ironically revealed only a different sort of cipher, the true inner emptiness of Johnny Favourite. 'Where do you search for a guy who was never there to begin with?' (51). And alongside the satirically edged representation of the hollowness of the ambitious man is the final stress on the inevitability of death itself, the cipher as the 'zero' point that Louis Cyphre says is '"a portal through which every man must eventually pass"' (212).

Like Hjortsberg's novel, Peter Ackroyd's *Hawksmoor* subverts the rational confidence of classic Holmesian detection by imagining a connection that is only supernaturally explicable between pursuer and pursued, detective and murderer. However, where Hjortsberg provides a neatly dark resolution (the terrible truth of self-recognition), Ackroyd is more concerned with retaining a sense of ultimate, irresolvable mysteries, and thus moves towards a conclusion that is much more ambiguous than Johnny Favourite's incontrovertible failure to cheat the devil of his due. In Ackroyd's novel, this carefully preserved ambiguity serves the mainstream ambitiousness of metaphysical themes that are not fused with the kind of satirical observation to be found in *Falling Angel*. What Ackroyd presents in *Hawksmoor* are two mysteriously connected series of murders separated, in historical time, by about 250 years, the modern murders coinciding in almost every detail with the sacrificial murders long ago committed or 'willed' by Nicholas Dyer, who has been given the approximate historical niche of the architect, Nicholas Hawksmoor. The twentieth-century investigator has only baffling, haunting glimpses of the past that has created his present. His name, Nicholas Hawksmoor, suggests something of the doppelgänger relationship between investigator and murderer: as characters move through the novel, they repeatedly encounter their own inexplicable union with other human beings and experience the loss or dissolution of their own identities. The whole novel is structured in such a way that we as readers experience the viewpoints of several different characters – the minds of the murderer, the victims and the detective. The main murderer in *Hawksmoor* has been given a name which suggests a victim (a 'dyer') rather than a murderer; he begins life during the years of Plague and Fire as an orphaned child, outcast, terrified, drawn in amongst others who live on the margins of society. The detective is denied his traditional role of explaining a comprehensible crime and achieving neat closure. Ackroyd plays with the idea of the detective story that as a form moves towards an end which is really a discovery of the beginning (that is, of the origin of the crime), driving home the point that as metaphysical questions our speculations about origins and ends are unending and 'unbeginning', leading us back into an infinite regress of questions about where we came from and towards the equally unresolvable question of where we are going. We would like to think of ourselves as progressing, but instead only repeat the patterns of past ages. The crimes in *Hawksmoor* are part of a cycle, not specific acts pertaining to and resolvable at a particular time, but part of an endless repetition, and the investigator is himself constituted by the past, not detached from it.

Hawksmoor uses what seem to be supernatural events to undermine confidence that the evidence will be susceptible to empirical enquiry. Ackroyd's *Dan Leno and the Limehouse Golem* (1994) develops a similar theme, the power of the irrational within the human mind, by creating a narrative in which superstition, prejudice and terror lead people to identify the Gothic monster, the golem, as the perpetrator of horrific crimes, but in which the actual source is something equally dark, mysterious and unknowable within the mind of a murderess (who is herself a victim). As in *Hawksmoor*, there is a 'gothic' rapport between characters and the places they inhabit, with London providing a topography of dark spaces and fear-laden enclosures. Both books echo De Quincey's 'On Murder Considered as One of the Fine Arts', with its account of the Ratcliffe Highway slaughter.[11] In *Dan Leno*, these murders are central to a plot which involves both performance and repetition of past crimes – the 'fine art' of re-enacting 'the immortal Ratcliffe Highway murders of 1812 . . . silently dispatched into eternity by an artist whose exploits will be preserved for ever in the pages of Thomas De Quincey' (25).

Like O'Connell's novels, *Dan Leno* is dominated by the themes of performance and spectatorship which are central to many contemporary noir thrillers. The Gothic, associated as it is with excess, the violation of taboos and the expression of violent emotion, lends itself to an exploration of the acting out and witnessing of transgressive performances in which players and spectators alike exceed the boundaries of the permissible. What Ackroyd builds on in *Dan Leno* is the association between Gothic heightening and our equivocal enjoyment, as audience, of the gruesome spectacle of murder. Like the post-seventies noir thriller generally, this is written to appeal to our appetite for sensational crime and then to make us reflect on the nature of that appetite, on our uncertainty about the relationship of fantasy to act and on violence which is 'inseparable from its reproduction as spectacle'.[12] *Dan Leno* is closer than *Hawksmoor* to the structure of the generic thriller. Much of the fragmented and deceptive narrative is seen through the eyes of a murderer whose identity we do not know until the very end. The combination of concealment and spectacle leads us to focus on the tension between secret deeds and a compulsion to display, to assert oneself publicly through dramatically violent acts.

The final revelation of the murderer's identity adds to *Dan Leno* a preoccupation that is more commonly present in the work of contemporary female crime writers. That is, Ackroyd emphasises the need felt by a woman both to author her own story and to be able to act and perform as a man can. For Elizabeth Cree, who is on stage with Dan Leno, the theatre offers the means of transforming herself from a repressed and powerless girl: 'My old self was dead and the new Lizzie . . . had been born at last' (106). Lizzie feels that she attains the status of the Romantic male outlaw hero made famous by De Quincey, 'an outcast who enjoys a secret power . . . transformed into an avenger whose bright yellow hair and chalk-white countenance afforded him the significance of some primeval deity' (37). Although her genius for performance, her imaginative and mimetic powers, are perverted into the 'fine art' of murder, she is nevertheless remarkable for her inventiveness. She escapes herself by triumphantly taking on other roles, cross-dressing, developing a male 'slanguage' and writing an incriminating diary for her husband John Cree, on his 'tyro' aspirations to the artistry of the

Ratcliffe Highway murders: 'I must admit that I applauded my own work' (24–30, 62).

The popular invention of the Limehouse Golem, widely supposed to be the perpetrator of Lizzie's crimes, raises other questions about the way the human imagination works. Rather than structuring the novel around the supernatural connections established in *Hawksmoor,* Ackroyd uses *Dan Leno* to explore people's need for supernatural explanations. The golem is a Gothic conceptualising of the persistence of evil, 'as if some primeval force had erupted in Limehouse . . . Some dark spirit' for which London itself is responsible (83, 162). By incorporating George Gissing and Babbage's Analytical Engine in his narrative, Ackroyd suggests, as he does in *Hawksmoor,* that basic fears and needs will inevitably connect the human future with the past. Technology will not eradicate evil and indeed, ironically, will itself be blamed for ancient forces within man himself. The golem, like the computer, invokes 'the horror of an artificial life and a form without spirit', an 'automaton' (88, 269).

In exploring the need for explanatory myths, Ackroyd captures the atmosphere of avid bloodthirstiness and voyeurism that prevails as the public gossip about the murders. He is not, however, equally concerned with analysing the nature of such spectatorship or the implications of being the audience of violence. Jack O'Connell, on the other hand, responding in an oblique fashion to a society in which there is growing pressure for censorship, is much more intent on understanding the act of viewing transgressive behaviour than he is with the performance of the acts themselves. Novels like *The Skin Palace* (1996) and *Word Made Flesh* (1999) are an idiosyncratic mixture of thriller plots, Gothic atmosphere and the science fiction topos of the alternative or parallel world. Within Quinsigamond many of the more disturbing aspects of twentieth-century life are replicated in heightened, grotesque, often surreal ways and reflected in the fun-house mirror of satire. The invention of Quinsigamond removes recent history to a fantasy world. O'Connell is also, however, the most directly satirical of all the writers discussed in this chapter and he brings his novels very close to the climate of contemporary debate about the representation of sex and violence (pornography is a central issue in *The Skin Palace,* violence in *Word Made Flesh*). The Gothic scene-setting functions to make strange a very familiar set of conflicting views on the justification of such representation and on 'the Preservation of Dangerous Art' (286). Quinsigamond itself is like a stage. The streets, O'Connell says, 'seem to exist to be pure spectacle'. Sex and violence alike are filmed and fictionalised by the inhabitants, the images stored in subway tunnels and labyrinthine underground libraries and killed for by powerful individuals.

The Skin Palace centres on the clash between different myths of America. It is a land of criminal opportunity on the one hand, a land of free artistic expression on the other. Jakob Kinsky, the son of a powerful gangster, nurses his ambition to become a director of 'hyperreal' *films noirs*: '"Give me some crime, cynicism, claustrophobia. . . . City grime. As much shadow as you can manage . . ."' (196–7). The novel is dominated by images of screens – from drive-in cinema screens and gigantic projections of multiple images to the television next to the couch. Characters define themselves in relation to the roles of creator, actor or spectator. Both of the main characters (Jakob and an aspiring photographer, Sylvia Krafft) are obsessed by the cinematic image, and, through their experiences, O'Connell poses the questions of risks and benefits. O'Connell suggests the excessiveness of the pornographic and voyeuristic compulsion, especially in his descriptions of Herzog's Erotic Palace, which is like a 'textbook example' authored by 'a visionary egomaniac living on hallucinogens and gothic novels . . . theatrical to the point of self-parody . . .' (67–8). Nevertheless he insists on the relationship between this compulsion and an appetite for understanding which is denied only by the dense (Sylvia's unsatisfactory mate Perry), the criminal (the gangster Kinsky) or the mindlessly censorious crusader (the Women's American Resistance and Families United for Decency).

The most recent of the Quinsigamond novels, *Word Made Flesh*, is another extended meditation on the themes of voyeurism, violence and bearing witness. Here, it is violence rather than eroticism that is mainly at issue. The novel confronts readers with the question of what it means to be spectators of violent acts, and how you differentiate voyeurism from 'witnessing' in a fully human and responsible way. The first horrifying spectacle, a man being flayed alive, draws us in as audience, buttonholed by the conspiratorial, queasy patter of a narrator who only wishes that we could hold the blades ourselves; he sees us flinch, but we do not close our eyes, 'and that will make all the difference'; he encourages us to view the victim 'as more object than person. This has worked for others in the past' (11–17). The narrative contains both spectators and players, and the most pressing issue is whether you can try to understand the world of the players without yourself being corrupted, and without anaesthetising your sensibilities.

As in *The Skin Palace*, O'Connell's narrative sustains the idea that image and story have transforming power. The object on which the plot turns is a book that contains the story written by a teenage girl who has made 'a weapon of her epiphany' after witnessing the July Sweep, a pogrom in which her whole world 'was summarily destroyed and, literally, shredded into pulp' (179f.). The power of her words in evoking a horrifying spectacle can be read as a demonstration of the sinister fascination of violence: the man responsible for the July Sweep wants to possess the book because in it he finds his deeds elevated to a legend. But the book is also a testament, a proof that words can transmute events into something that could convey the meaning of the 'Erasure' across 'space and time and culture' (310). *Word Made Flesh*, like *The Maltese Falcon* or Gibson's *Virtual Light*, is a quest narrative, but the object sought is more important than the falcon (an empty signifier of commodity fetishism) or the glasses of *Virtual Light* (offering a template of a future world that corrupt commercial forces aim to create). The fabulous manuscript of O'Connell's novel embodies the power of fiction itself to represent the past and shape the future.

The mean streets of the Metaverse

As the aspiring noir director in O'Connell's *Skin Palace* scouts for locations 'that agree with the images already screened in the skull-camera', he points an actual camera at scenes very like those in Ridley Scott's *Blade Runner* (1982), looking down on Gompers Station, with its 'indiscriminate tangles' of 'recombinant junk' (367). For O'Connell this sort of scene signifies a European past of pogroms and dictators, the violence of which continues to haunt the New World. In *Blade Runner* the urban decay and detritus of the late twentieth century, dominating the look of the film's cityscape, are a visual reminder of the determining force of present corruptions (the evolving present-as-past) in a dystopian future world. Although neither *Blade Runner* nor the novel on which it was based – Philip K. Dick's *Do Androids Dream of Electric Sheep?* (1968) – open into a parallel world of cyberspace, Scott's visual reminders of the mean streets of the classic noir cycle have become an identifying feature of the aesthetic of cyberpunk. The inner-city spaces of *Blade Runner* merge past and future. Images of urban alienation and corporate power structures in a sleazy, threatening metropolis are combined with modern 'add-ons'. In the making of the film, a 1920s set used for gangster films and *films noirs* was 'retrofitted' with 'a variety of mechanical stuff'; ducts, rewirings, video monitors; matte-paintings were used to incorporate looming towers, so that the city resembled 'a vast, boundless refinery'. The remorseless pressures of consumerism were embodied in flying billboards and loudspeakers blaring commercials.[13]

In Philip K. Dick's novel, dust and 'kipple' (junk) rather than vertiginous darkness characterise the future-world cityscape, suggesting ghost towns more than *films noirs*. But the sense of estrangement and dislocation, of loss of bearings, is equally strong. This is reinforced in the novel by the creation of a parallel world (not dissimilar to cyberspace in its disorienting effects), when Deckard is taken by a patrolman to a complicated modern building that he has never seen before. He is accused of being an android himself and told that he comes from a phantom police department. In fact, he has been arrested by an android-dominated police department which inhabits a 'closed loop' cut off from the rest of San Francisco – an alter-world interlude that, like cyberspace, acts to bring different levels of reality together in disquieting ways and to loosen the protagonist's belief in his ability to distinguish real worlds from false ones. Deckard's crisis of confidence deepens when Phil Resch, whom he associates with android 'inhumanity', passes the Voigt-Kampff test: '"Do you have your ideology formed,"' Resch asks, '"that would explain me as part of the human race?"' (108). This is at bottom a very traditional moral question, and one that has repeatedly been raised in the noir thriller: that is, at what point does one cross the line that separates humanity from inhumanity? Deckard admits to himself at the end, having killed the androids, that what he has done has 'become alien to me' (172).

As cyberpunk develops the ideas of manufactured or augmented selves and invasive technology, the more pessimistic implications are readily apparent. The protagonist, by coming into a closer relationship with the non-human, sacrifices a coherent sense of self, of human values and confident agency; or, in other plot patterns, humans themselves are programmable and thus susceptible to the control of external powers. It is not necessarily characteristic of cyberpunk, however, to give expression to such doubts. Writers like Mark Laidlaw and Rudy Rucker, for example, celebrate the competence of the surfers and hackers who adventure through cyberspace, like Rucker's Jerzy Rugby, who walks away from *The Hackers and the Ants* (1994) as 'a free man with a dynamite story' (305). Many recent films that share something of the 'future noir' look of *Blade Runner* are similarly upbeat, in the sense that individual action defeats those who abuse technological powers. So, for example, in *Total Recall* (Paul Verhoeven, 1990), which is also based on a Philip K. Dick story ('We Can Remember It for You Wholesale'), there are many noirish features, not just visually but in the theme of split identity and 'a really sophisticated mind-fuck'. In noir, however, the crucial discovery that Quaid is the 'bad' Hauser would be of decisive importance, and Quaid would exist only, as Cohaagen says, as 'just a stupid dream'. In fact, however, by the exertion of the sheer physical strength generally associated with Schwarzenegger action-hero roles, the protagonist is able to break away to become Quaid. The noir possibility hovers behind the 'open' end ('Kiss me before we wake up'), but it is the kiss and the 'dream' Quaid that carry conviction, and the end of the film functions to confirm the romantic possibility of action and of a clean break with an old, bad self. This pressure towards achieving mastery, whether by traditional heroic resolve (analogous to the masculine competence of action-oriented hard-boiled fiction) or by technological virtuosity, is strongly present in much cyberpunk, modifying the 'future noir' mood, bringing it closer to 'cyberian' optimism than to dystopian pessimism.[14]

The filming of *Blade Runner* itself might be taken to demonstrate the tension within future noir between optimistic and pessimistic forms of closure. Dogged as it was by production and post-production disagreements, *Blade Runner* emerged in its well-known variant forms. The version that was first screened in 1982, though characterised neither by technophilia nor by the romantic sweep of, say, the *Star Wars* trilogy, did move towards reasonably positive closure, with the voice-over and the last scene, moving out of the grimy city towards togetherness without a termination date, bringing the film nearer to the upbeat ending of *Total Recall*. The Director's Cut, on the other hand, released in 1992, approaches the ambivalence of the more disturbing noir visions, not only resisting romantic closure but implying that Deckard himself may, after all, be a replicant. To open the film to the possibility of such a reading is to suggest comparison with those bleakly ironic noir narratives in which a protagonist finds that he is hunting himself or (here) his own kind. Although Dick's *Electric Sheep* does not reinforce its moral ambiguities with this kind of doubling, some of his other fiction shares this destabilising ambiguity, particularly *A Scanner Darkly* (1977). This is a novel that develops in an uncompromising way a narrative pattern that implies the existence of a dark, unrecognised inner self. The consequent disabling of the individual's capacity for independent action creates a closed loop from which there is no escape.

One of Dick's most compelling near-future novels, *A Scanner Darkly* is also the most despairingly personal. His painful experience of drug abuse in the sixties becomes the basis for a science fiction world in which other forms of control combine with addiction to produce a nightmare of noir entrapment. In his 'Author's Note' at the end, Dick argues that he is representing nemesis rather than fate, since any potential addict has the power to choose, but the punishment is conceived in terms of deterministic cause and effect: that is, once addiction has taken place, fatality takes over. Within the narrative choice is only really present in a Flitcraft-like episode in which Dick's protagonist, Bob Arctor, suffers a blow to the head that jars him into a rejection of bourgeois stability and tedium. Ironically, like many protagonists in the traditional noir thriller, Arctor finds not freedom but a worse-than-bourgeois entrapment. Within the context of a high-surveillance science fiction world, forms of entrapment are, of course, sufficiently thoroughgoing to make ordinary paranoia pale into insignificance. Like *Blade Runner, A Scanner Darkly* creates a hunter character reminiscent of the private eye, but here with a much stronger sense that he is a victim. He 'didn't volunteer' and 'never did know' (234). Those in control of the splitting of personality are entirely willing to sacrifice Arctor to get the information they need about the illegal growing of the plants that produce Substance D, 'the flower of the future', the substance that affects users by bringing 'death of the spirit, the identity' (250–1, 233). *A Scanner Darkly* is the narrative of an assault on the protagonist's sense of self, with name changes (he is Bob and Fred and Bruce), his transformation by a hi-tech scramble suit into a 'blur', his splitting into hunter and hunted (when Fred is assigned the job of observing Bob Arctor), and his final loss of all grasp of who he is. Arctor is 'repeating doomed patterns', going through the same thing over and over like 'a closed loop of tape' (62–3). There is a stage in the narrative at which Arctor, giving a speech, deviates from his script, and he seems at this point capable both of ironising his role as 'the vague blur' and of a coherent critique of life in southern California – a commercial for itself, endlessly replayed, as if 'the automatic factory' cranks out indistinguishable objects (31–2). This lucidity, however, is short-lived. The anxiety underlying *Blade Runner* is the humanistic fear of dehumanisation through violence. In *A Scanner Darkly*, the anxiety is centred on becoming another sort of replicant, simply a manufactured object incapable of breaking away from the master script of his society – 'Actor, Arctor . . . Bob the Actor who is being hunted . . .' (125).

The cyberpunk writers influenced by *Blade Runner* and Philip K. Dick are seldom so enclosed within doomed patterns, even when the protagonist (as in Jeter's *Noir*) is named 'McNihil'. The technology which can close the circle of fatality – mechanisms of total control and omniscient surveillance – can also be pressed into the service of the action hero, and in so far as it envisages effective action cyberpunk moves closer to the traditions of male romance. Given its strong links with tough-guy fiction, traditional noir has, of course, often crossed over into action heroics, retaining a distinctly noir character only if the action hero is ultimately unsuccessful or if, in victory, he is thoroughly tainted by the world of violence and corruption with which he is involved (Paul Cain's Gerry Kells rather than Daly's Race Williams; Hammett's Continental Op rather than Chandler's Marlowe). However noir the future world he traverses, the cyberpunk 'cowboy' tends to have something in common with the two-fisted (anti-)hero. High technology, like the Colt .45, can serve any ends, whether repressive or rebellious. William Gibson and Bruce Sterling are regarded as amongst the more pessimistic of cyberpunk writers. Their 'doomed vision' is characterised as a 'dark and hopeless' refusal to see 'technology as inherently liberating'; they harbour a belief in human programmability and create protagonists who allow themselves to be exploited by higher powers.[15] Even Gibson's Case, however, shows himself capable of appropriating effective technologies and stepping outside of the closed loop of the addict's dependency, the consumer's passivity or the subservience of the player who is confined to one game board.

At the end of *A Scanner Darkly*, the corpse-like protagonist can no longer act. He can 'react' (233), but his reflex programmed reaction in secreting one of the 'flowers of the future' leaves us with only a glimmer of hope in the final paragraph. Gibson's anti-heroes, on the other hand, are not totally in the power of the anachronistic rich or of the interdimensional corporations, or even of the giant artificial intelligences. They are tinged with the rebellious glamour of Burroughs' wild boys, '. . . glider boys with bows and laser guns, roller-skate boys, . . . slingshot boys, knife throwers, . . . bare-hand fighters, shaman boys who ride the wind . . .' (*The Wild Boys*, 147). Case, at the end of *Neuromancer*, fuelled by suicidal impulse and self-loathing, has no clear knowledge of what he is trying to achieve and no way of guessing the outcome. He is, however, capable of choice: '"Give us the fucking code. . . . If you don't, what'll change?"' (307). Exhilarating action is still a possibility, as it often is in the hard-boiled strand of the noir thriller, even if the change effected in *Neuromancer* is left open to question and the 'posthumanist' bias of cyberpunk is evident in the fact that the main result of Case's endeavours takes place on a wholly non-human level, with Wintermute having 'meshed somehow' with Neuromancer, thus freeing itself to talk to its own kind. In *Count Zero* and *Mona Lisa Overdrive*, however, there are elements of a more traditionally humanistic closure, with nature playing a redemptive role (Turner and the squirrel wood) and some positive human, or at least modified human, connections. Gibson's move away from the 'posthuman' perspectives of *Neuromancer* can also be seen in *Virtual Light* (1993), in which the central contrast is between an attempt to achieve a closed, coercive system and the opposing force of 'play' and unpredictable desire.

Michael Hutchinson, speaking of the dependence of authoritarian systems on citizens who can be counted on to act predictably, quotes George Bush's dictum, 'The only enemy we have is unpredictability.'[16] It is precisely this unpredictability in the exploitation of high tech that typifies the key players in *Virtual Light*. The computer becomes less of a character in its own right and more an instrument which can be used either to oppress ('fate' in the hands of the mega-corps) or to liberate, the means to realise desire. One of Gibson's most prominent themes here is an immobilising, paranoid sense of fatality. The presence of the Death Star, an all-seeing techno-equivalent to fate, and the interconnected mega-corporation leave no question about the sheer size of what the individual is up against: '"You don't know shit about shit. . . . It's just too *big* for someone like you to understand"' (229). But there is also the possibility of tricking fate. Help comes from the Republic of Desire, an organisation (or disorganisation) demonstrating that the interconnectedness of computers may facilitate mega-corporational control, but that it can also be empowering, preserving space for anarchic desires. The plot turns on the revelation of the fact that the corporate powers intend to 'do' San Francisco 'like they're doing Tokyo' (270), with the Republic of Desire aiding the protagonist, Rydell, because they hate the idea of a rebuilt San Francisco and a controlled, designed future. The existing San Francisco, full of hidden depths, forbidden zones and hard-to-grasp interactions, stands for the mystery, randomness and unknowability that act as some kind of guarantee of old-fashioned human warmth and connection. The bridge, central to this world, is an emblem of the carnivalised city. Gibson's hard-boiled protagonist is appropriately disorderly and unpredictable. Rydell fits the noir pattern of the wandering adventurer, questing across boundaries in pursuit of the woman carrying a fabulous object (the virtual light glasses, containing the plans for the new San Francisco) that signifies greed and the unscrupulous pursuit of wealth. Gibson has a nicely ironic way of achieving closure, with Rydell in such deep trouble that he is ideally suited to a programme called Cops in Trouble ('in deep, spectacular, and . . . clearly *heroic* shit' [290]). But the emphasis on 'heroic' is real as well as comically incongruous. The values that Rydell has helped to preserve are as positive as those defended by Marlowe, but, as in much other contemporary noir, his strength is less a matter of lonely integrity in mean streets than of energy sustained by spontaneous communal street life.

A 'Gibson for the 1990s',[17] Neal Stephenson, in *Snow Crash* (1992), invented the word 'Metaverse', and, like Gibson, he uses proliferating realities to satirise consumerism and the addiction to spectacle as well as to celebrate possibilities for the anarchic expression of desire. The 'heroic shit' model of the player-narrative is immediately established in *Snow Crash* by the naming of the central figure: Hiro Protagonist. In a contemporary version of the noir ethic, Hiro uses the weapons of corruption against the corrupt – advertising (when he defeats the scrolls), programming, violence. He shares with the hard-boiled detective an alienated, counter-culture persona, being someone who 'needs to work harder on his co-operation skills' (3). He is half-black and half-Asian and lacks a firm class orientation; intelligent and tough, a resourceful outsider, he is his own man, willing and able to kill if necessary. As his name suggests, however, he is less developed, less vulnerable and less beaten down than the true noir protagonist. When we learn of his spectacular competence as the last of the freelance hackers and the greatest swordfighter, we begin to suspect him of having more of an action-hero lineage. He is a resourceful player who is ultimately successful, defeating with a hacker's ingenuity a plot for world domination.

'Snow crash' is a drug/computer virus premised on the mind/machine interface: '"Does it fuck up your brain? . . . Or your computer?" "Both. Neither. What's the difference?"' (41). Like other standard cyberpunk dangers, it evokes such dystopian fears as totalitarian control, loss of identity and loss of personal autonomy. The virus is metaphorically linked with the franchise. That is, what thrives in one place will thrive in another, and both are associated with an ethos of 'no surprises', comforting uniformity and an end to adventure. As in *Virtual Light*, the central theme hinges on the traditional humanistic opposition between individual randomness and the metaphysical and ideological certainties of religion and politics; also as in *Virtual Light*, without deploying any techniques that are strikingly Gothic, the narrative suggests the interpenetration of past and future, confronting Hiro Protagonist with a threat that is at once very ancient and very up-to-the-minute. Snow crash produces a culture-wide version of the kind of assault on individual identity that, in traditional noir, destabilises an effective individual sense of self. An underlying myth of language formation carries the argument that the tendency of languages to diverge (post-'Infocalypse') acts as a kind of guarantee of independence, conferring immunity to 'viral infections' that bypass 'higher language functions' and tie into 'the deep structures', thus enabling 'viral ideas', from Nazism to 'crackpot religions', to establish themselves (369–76). The generally sympathetic criminality of the various factions in the novel (including the Mafia and a mutant member of the Aleuts) is set against the apparent normality and virtue of tele-evangelists, consumerist society and mass culture.

Again, then, this is the characteristic cyberpunk mix of the archaic with the hi-tech, blending pasts (ancient forces, age-old iniquities, buried evils) with futures (whether of technological empowerment or dystopian repression). This mixture has become a staple element of youth culture, whether in manga (the legendary Akira kept long dormant under Neo-Tokyo, 'a city in the wild grip of technology gone mad'), video games, virtual nightclubs and virtual reality (VR) theme parks.[18] Recent future noir includes the 'cyber noir' or 'cybershock' novels, *neoAddix* (1997) and *Lucifer's Dragon* (1998), by the British writer Jon Courtenay Grimwood, a freelance journalist who writes regularly, amongst other things, for the Japanese film magazine *Manga Mania*. As in the cyberpunk of Gibson and Stephenson, dark forces are met by technological efforts to defy fatality. In *neoAddix*, for example, biotech resurrection is one answer to an old order that seemed to have a monopoly of special powers: their trope is vampirism, that of the protagonists is technological enhancement. Grimwood's plot brings together the world of ancient aristocratic degeneracy (a sinister vampiric 800-year-old Prince) with the modern world of corporate corruption. The heir to the psychopathic Prince will be drawn from competing and thoroughly corrupt tycoons, and battle is waged by means both supernatural and technological. 'Tek', magic, the subconscious, the ghost world, dream time and astral travel are all just a difference of perspective on powers of the mind that have evolved only in terms of the way in which information is accessed. Grimwood's protagonists, Alex and the cyber-jockey, Johnnie T., appear to die and are resurrected by techno-wizardry: '"Do you remember who you are? . . . Doesn't matter. You'll be someone else when you wake up anyway"' (220). More than anything, it is this destabilisation of identity that justifies the label 'cyber noir', along with Grimwood's creation of dark doubles. Alex becomes that which he fights. Darker than Gibson or Stephenson, Grimwood ends *neoAddix* with an ultimate contest in which Alex must call on and accept 'the help of the Prince, and every other Grand Master who howled and gibbered in the wasteland of his brain', after which he recognises that he is 'no longer remotely human', and in the aftermath is more damaged and isolated than are most cyberpunk protagonists. Believing himself hideously scarred, with scars no one else can see, he lives in almost total isolation, 'the anchorite of San Lorenzo' (357).

The science fiction/Gothic/noir combination is by no means confined to novels that use cyberspace as the parallel dimension in which alternative identities can be created. The balance easily shifts towards the Gothic/supernatural, with the more dreamlike and grotesque elements coming to the fore. Michael Marshall Smith, whose subsequent novels, *Spares* (1996) and *One of Us* (1998) also involve cloning and memory implantation, published his first novel, entitled *Only Forward*, in 1994 – a whimsical, funny and often macabre form of future noir in which the fantastic dimension is located in dream time, or dream accessed waking. The narrator, Stark, is a 'strong dreamer' who, like the hacker or cyberspace jockey, is a guide to a future world, a troubleshooter, a fixer and finder, and the epitome of hard-boiled cool. He is able to go into a tough neighbourhood, for example, because 'I look like the kind of guy who pimps for his sister not just for the money, but because he hates her. I can look like a guy who belongs' (18). At the same time, he always feels he has to play the hero and works less for the money than for what interests him or what is right. This private-eye-like integrity, however, is broken down by the exposure of his own dark side: he is himself the source of the evil he is tracking, and must confess both his unreliability as a narrator and his current sense of disorientation ('I'm not myself. Or maybe I am. It's been so long I can't remember' [254]). The nightmare that initiates the troubles of the narrative turns out to have been his own, and at the macabre, horror-novel climax, Stark recognises his guilt. The truth, finally, is not just 'more stark' but 'more Stark' (289). As this punning revelation suggests, Smith's tone mixes the blackly comic with the lightly jokey, and his playfulness extends as well to the noir sense of fatality: 'If there's anything I really hate, it's things going better than I expected. . . . Things turning out well fills me with nameless dread . . .' (62). *Only Forward* is throughout a tongue-in-cheek narrative of a postmodern tough guy brooding on the persistence of his modernist anxieties: 'The rough beast doesn't just visit me occasionally: there's a regular fucking bus route' (67).

Invitations to the underworld

Future noir has also developed in directions quite different from the elaborately fantastic world of cyberpunk. Two of the most genuinely and disturbingly noir near-future visions, both published in the mid-nineties, are Jack Womack's *Random Acts of Senseless Violence* (1993) and

J. G. Ballard's *Cocaine Nights* (1996), the first American, the second British. These are novels that have a clear place in mainstream fiction, though bookstores also shelve them with genre fiction, either with science fiction (Ballard on the strength of his niche as a science fiction writer) or with crime fiction. Both are first-person narratives of guilt and violence, patterned in ways very familiar from the noir thrillers we have examined. Ballard's is a story of the narrator's investigation of a horrific crime in an effort to clear his brother. It is an investigation that ends not only with a recognition that there is a sense in which his brother is guilty, but with him taking guilt upon himself (the investigator thereby being transformed into a man seen at the end as a malefactor). The Womack novel is in the tradition of narratives that involve an innocent narrator drawn into a world of deprivation and violence and crossing the line by committing an act of murder which leads irrevocably to utter isolation in savage surroundings. But the use of a young girl in the narrator's role makes *Random Acts* a striking departure from the tradition. Ballard and Womack are both imagining a semi-contemporary future, with the present sliding almost imperceptibly into near future. Ballard sets his novel in a leisured, privileged retirement community, Womack sets his in a desperately poor urban environment, but both use traditional elements of the thriller to explore the movement of a society towards violence. Womack's explanations have more in common with those of much earlier noir thrillers. Deprivation and casual injustice are shown to be irrevocably shaping the life of a girl who is not dissimilar to Ellson's *Tomboy* – young, tough and doomed to take her place in a disintegrating urban environment. Ballard's novel, on the other hand, imagines a world without economic deprivation, sheltered from all of the destructive forces abroad in Womack's New York, and asks whether under such conditions violence would in fact disappear. Each is in a way an Edenic fable. In *Random Acts*, the former life of the nuclear family is the innocent, sheltered childhood world of an intelligent middle-class family living apart from the encroaching darkness. *Cocaine Nights* presents us with a Johnsonian Happy Valley in which all is supplied, but in which the spectacle of violence is required (though this, too, might be said to have an element of social determinism, with changes caused by economic satiation rather than economic need). What the deprivation and the boredom release is, in each case, something within – Conradian hearts of darkness revealed at the end of symbolic journeys.

Ballard's science fiction novels, from *The Drowned World* (1961) on, made him the 'idolised role model' for cyberpunk writers, admired for pushing to the limits 'the bizarre, the surreal, the formerly unthinkable

. . .'[19] *Cocaine Nights*, which seems at first glance to be a realistic novel of Mediterranean retirement, is in fact very closely related to the bizarre and surreal body of his science fiction, its deceptive surface so strongly reinforcing our sense of the conventional and mundane that the emerging 'future' is all the more disturbing in its coupling of banality and violence. As in much contemporary noir, crime is conceived as a combination of spectacle and game, fascinating, addictive and more dangerous than the participants realise. Conrad's *Heart of Darkness* is an unmistakable presence behind Ballard's evocations of savage joy and frenzy that are, like the 'certain midnight dances', inextricably bound up with a savage violence not that far removed from the cannibalism, heads on stakes and 'unspeakable rites' with which Kurtz's midnight dances end. In his earlier novels (*The Drowned World*, *The Crystal World*) Ballard often created narrative patterns that led critics to think, in spite of his denials, in terms of Conradian journeys into the interior, though with the Conradian theme modified (for example in *The Crystal World*) by imagining a journey towards the inner self, the core of the unconscious that contains brightness as well as darkness, a zone of transformation in which imaginative free play flourishes in opposition to the symbolic order, the world outside where the return of unconscious desire is suppressed.

In *Cocaine Nights*, Ballard uses a different structure: Dionysus on tour, rather than a journey to a forbidden zone, contained within an investigative framework that ends by revealing shared guilt. Ballard's Bobby Crawford parallels the 'mysterious stranger' in *The Bacchae* – 'the god himself', the spirit of the instinctive group-personality and 'the ambiguous master-magician of pleasure and pain, beauty and cruelty'.[20] When the protagonist, Charles, comes to the Costa del Sol it is because his brother Frank is accused of the murder of five people. He begins by thinking that Frank must be pleading guilty as 'part of some bizarre game he was playing against himself', but the 'game' is quite other than he imagines, and he is drawn into staying by an attempt on his life, which is not so much a warning as an attempt to integrate him into the inner life of Estrella de Mar, '"a kind of invitation. Almost an invitation to . . ." "The underworld? The real Estrella de Mar?"' (174). It is for Charles, as it clearly also was for his brother, a liminal experience. On the face of it, all he does is fly to the present-day Costa del Sol, but even in the opening paragraph there is a sly insinuation of his affinities with Ballard's future-world protagonists, an implication both that he is crossing into an alien zone and that he is carrying with him his own repressed, forbidden repository of guilts and desires:

> Crossing frontiers is my profession. Those strips of no-man's land between the checkpoints always seem such zones of promise. . . . At the same time they set off a reflex of unease that I have never been able to repress. As the customs officials rummage through my suitcases I sense them trying to unpack my mind and reveal a contraband of forbidden dreams and memories. And even then there are the special pleasures of being exposed. . . . (9)

The phrases here establish the most important terms of the following narrative: crossing frontiers, zones of promise, able to repress, forbidden dreams and guilty memories. The Costa del Sol, like other strange zones of Ballard's science fiction, is both a realm of the imagination (a place that 'doesn't really exist. That's why I like the coast . . .' [17]) and a preview of the future: 'It's Europe's future. Everywhere will be like this soon'; '. . . It's the *fourth* world. . . . The one waiting to take over everything . . .' (23, 215–16).

Until it is touched by the Dionysiac spirit of Bobby Crawford, the Costa del Sol is completely null. This is more than just a picture of a world of moneyed leisure. Ballard heightens the descriptions enough so that they become surreal and dystopian: the 'memory-erasing' cubist architecture of the houses and apartments with white facades 'like blocks of time that had crystallised beside the road'; the residents, preternaturally still, holding unread books and watching television with the sound off (34–5, 75, 215–16). Into this 'walled limbo' (34), Bobby Crawford brings his youthful good looks (looking like 'a handsome and affable gangster' [68]) and, above all, his extraordinary fluidity and energy. He is capable of changing everyone's lives but also full of 'dark, lurking violence' (205). Having stumbled on to the truth that crime and creativity go together, Crawford puts people in touch with 'dormant areas' of their minds, making them fascinated by the 'other world' of crime 'where everything is possible', where they can break the rules and sidestep the taboos (245), 'leaving behind a treasure of incitement and desire' (263). Fires, speedboat chases, explosions, rapes all become communal spectacles: 'Crime at Estrella de Mar had become one of the performance arts. . . . Brutal, but great fun' (146). This, then, becomes an alternative vision of the future. Communal life is energised by transgressive behaviour: 'One of the modern world's pagan rites was taking place, the torching of the automobile, witnessed by the young women from the disco, their sequinned dresses trembling in the flames . . . a premonition of the carnival blaze that would one day consume Estrella de Mar' (158–60).

Estrella de Mar is first seen as 'a place without shadow', secure on its handsome peninsula, the 'private paradise' of 'a happier twentieth century' (65–6). Jack Womack's New York, on the other hand, is a place close to the world of urban noir. *Random Acts*[21] depicts a savage cityscape, the future of an America in which all urban centres are disintegrating into rioting, destitution and gang warfare. As their circumstances decline, the family of Womack's young narrator, Lola, is forced to move to the more marginal and dangerous parts of the city, journeying away from civilised security to live on the margins of West Harlem. Lola endures a Conradian journey not just to the 'worst' that the city contains but to a forced reassessment of her own identity, a reduction to a primitive level of being: 'I can't remember what I used to be like . . . it fears me' (231). She, is, like Marlow, shocked by how rapidly one accommodates oneself to appalling things: 'It was weird though that you could adjust to something so quick' (125). Feeling that all that is left to her is her 'rack and rage' (241), she at last beats to death her father's cruel employer, in what seems to her 'dreamtime': 'There's no denying I was mindlost' (251–2). Her capacity for murder is only one of the horrors discovered by Lola, who in the end commits herself to the world beyond all that is familiar, 'with the DCons' (256), the emblem of everything savage.

Random Acts is science fiction as extrapolation. The element of fantasy consists entirely of an extension of all the worst possibilities of urban American life. The jacket claims 'cyberpunk intensity' for the style, and the novel has in common with cyberpunk a strong sense of countercultural aggression. It is, however, far more genuinely noir than most cyberpunk, in part because it does not open up the possible alter-worlds of virtual space and imagined cityscapes, but instead presents the remorseless pressure of events which seem all too real, and which Lola increasingly finds herself unequipped to express: 'There's no wording proper what downed last night. The world brutalises however you live it whatever you do' (221). As everything, including her own language, breaks down, Lola's questions about the future echo the anxiety, fear and overwhelming sense of fatality that have recurrently been at the core of the noir narrative: '"How'll we endtime Iz?" I asked. "What's meant?" "Unknown" Iz said. "Spilling tomorrow into today's suited sometime but not once it darkens. Nada's changeable come nightside . . ."' (233).

Notes

Introduction

1. Martin Rowson, *The Waste Land* (Harmondsworth, Middx.: Penguin, 1990), jacket copy.
2. Raymond Chandler, 'The Simple Art of Murder', *Atlantic Monthly*, December 1944, quoted by Tom Hiney, *Raymond Chandler: a Biography* (London: Vintage, 1997), p. 101.
3. Malcolm Bradbury and James McFarlane (eds), *Modernism 1890–1930* (Harmondsworth, Middx.: Penguin, 1976, 1985), p. 26; Scott R. Christianson, 'A Heap of Broken Images . . .', in Ronald G. Walker and June M. Frazer (eds), *The Cunning Craft: Original Essays on Detective Fiction and Contemporary Literary Theory* (Macomb: Western Illinois University Press, 1990), pp. 141–7, considers affinities between hard-boiled detective novels and Eliot's *Waste Land*, emphasising setting, narrative fragmentation, the representation of the meaninglessness of modern life and the subjective, oppositional nature of hard-boiled popular modernism.
4. Ginette Vincendeau, 'Noir is Also a French Word', in Ian Cameron (ed.), *The Movie Book of Film Noir* (London: Studio Vista, 1992), p. 52, quoting Raymond Borde and Etienne Chaumeton, *Panorama du Film Noir Américain* (Paris: Éditions de Minuit, 1955).
5. James Naremore, *More Than Night: Film Noir in its Contexts* (Berkeley: University of California Press, 1998), pp. 38 and 48.
6. Malcolm Bradbury and Howard Temperley, *Introduction to American Studies* (London: Longman, 1981, 1998), p. 46. See also Jon Tuska, *Dark Cinema: American Film Noir in Cultural Perspective* (Westport: Greenwood Press, 1984), p. 152. Tuska argues that noir is in effect an anti-generic movement, that is, implicitly a critique of the escapist fare offered by more traditional Hollywood genres. This contrast between more traditional genres and noir is neatly captured in the two Muse figures at the end of the Coen brothers' 1991 film, *Barton Fink* – the picture-postcard girl of romance on the one hand and, on the other, the severed head of Audrey, noir victim and inspiration.
7. Christine Gledhill, 'Klute 1: a Contemporary Film Noir and Feminist Criticism', in E. Ann Kaplan (ed.), *Women in Film Noir* (London: British Film Institute, 1972), p. 14.
8. Bradbury and McFarlane, pp. 41 and 47.
9. Michael Shelden, *Graham Greene: the Man Within* (London: Heinemann, 1994), p. 99; Naremore, pp. 48 and 53; Lillian Hellman, 'Introduction' to Hammett's *The Big Knockover and Other Stories* (Harmondsworth, Middx.: Penguin, 1969), p. 9.
10. Naremore, p. 43.
11. Even though critics like Silver and Ward take account of European influences, they have remained committed to a view of *film noir* as essentially

American in character – 'the unique example of a wholly American film style'. Alain Silver and Elizabeth Ward (eds), *Film Noir: an Encyclopedic Reference to the American Style* (Woodstock, NY: Overlook Press, 1992), p. 1. Others, like Robin Buss, in *French Film Noir* (London and New York: Marion Boyars, 1994), have more strongly stressed the influence of, for example, European directors working in America after the war, German Expressionism and the Gothic.

12. Naremore, p. 237.
13. Reprinted in R. Barton Palmer (ed.), *Perspectives on Film Noir* (New York: G. K. Hall and Co., 1996) and in Alain Silver and James Ursini (eds), *Film Noir Reader* (New York: Limelight Editions, 1996, 1999).
14. Revised and expanded third edition. The Silver and Ward *Encyclopedic Reference*, which was first published in 1979, is one of the essential *film noir* reference books.
15. Raymond Borde and Étienne Chaumeton, 'Towards a Definition of *Film Noir*' (1955), and Todd Erickson, 'Kill Me Again: Movement becomes Genre' (1990), in Silver and Ursini, pp. 17–26 and 307–30; Naremore, pp. 220 and 38.
16. Naremore, pp. 276–7 and 10.
17. There have, in addition, been another 400-plus noir-influenced films distributed directly into home video, cable and so on. Erickson, in Silver and Ursini, pp. 307 and 323–4. 'Tech Noir' is the name of the nightclub in *The Terminator* (James Cameron, 1984); 'Digital Noir' is a website that concentrates on cyber noir.
18. J. P. Telotte, *Voices in the Dark: the Narrative Patterns of Film Noir* (Urbana and Chicago: University of Illinois Press, 1989), p. 5.
19. That is, a definition appropriate to literary noir must go beyond things like low-key lighting, chiaroscuro effects, deep focus photography, extreme camera angles and expressionist distortion.
20. Julian Symons, *Bloody Murder, From the Detective Story to the Crime Novel: a History* (London: Pan, 1972, 1992), pp. 201–3.
21. Martin Rubin, *Thrillers* (Cambridge: Cambridge University Press, 1999), pp. 5–7 and 17–32. As Rubin observes, the label 'thriller' has been contentious, and in formulating his own definition he rightly jettisons, for example, the widely applied definition offered by Jerry Palmer in *Thrillers: Genesis and Structure of a Popular Genre* (London: Edward Arnold, 1978), viz., that a thriller requires just two ingredients, a hero and a conspiracy – which is, as Rubin argues, both too wide (including, for example, the classic detective story) and too narrow (excluding many texts and films that would generally be counted as 'classic thrillers', such as Greene's *Confidential Agent*, Highsmith's Ripley novels and Hitchcock's *Psycho*).
22. Silver and Ward, p. 3.
23. Fritz Lang, quoted in Peter Bogdanovich, *Fritz Lang in America* (New York: Praeger, 1967), pp. 86–7.
24. Examples of Thompson narratives that function in this way are discussed at the end of Chapter 4. Telotte, p. 35, and see Gledhill, 'Klute 1', in Kaplan (ed.), *Women in Film Noir* on ways in which conflicting interpretations can be brought to the fore in *film noir*.

25. James Sallis, *Difficult Lives: Jim Thompson, David Goodis, Chester Himes* (New York: Gryphon Books, 1993), p. 5.
26. The similarities to Hammett have been noted by Jon Thompson, 'Dashiell Hammett's Hard-Boiled Modernism', in Christopher Metress (ed.), *The Critical Response to Dashiell Hammett* (Westport, Conn.: Greenwood Press, 1994), p. 119: 'the principle of equivalence between the underworld and the bourgeois society proper that produces an essentially anarchistic vision of society in *The Secret Agent* finds resonances in the violent, mayhem-filled cities described in Hammett's fiction . . .'.
27. Robert McKee, *Story: Substance, Structure, Style, and the Principles of Screenwriting* (London: Methuen, 1999), p. 82.
28. Noir is also distinguished from certain kinds of hard-boiled fiction by the fact that the 'tough guy' investigator, heir to the action adventure hero, can, like the Holmesian detective, emerge as a scourge of wrongdoing, defeating a villain by decisive physical action as the detective defeats him by effective intellectual endeavour.
29. Erickson, in Silver and Ursini, p. 319, quoting Eugenio Zaretti, art director of *Slam Dance*.
30. Erickson, in Silver and Ursini, p. 308; Naremore, p. 10.
31. Tuska, pp. 150–1, suggests that a film which is 'noir' only at times but not in its resolution is perhaps better classified as a 'film gris' or melodrama, rather than as 'a truly *black* film'. Comedy can also, if it becomes dominant, make a film or text 'less noir': a noir atmosphere can combine with black humour but is deflated by certain kinds of comedy. Silver and Ward, p. 331, discuss the difference between *films noirs* that contain elements of comic relief (a common ingredient) and films in which the 'tonal divergence' is greater, producing, say, a comedy thriller. In films of the nineties, the point can be illustrated with reference to the tendency towards broad comedy to be found in such noir-related films as the *Lethal Weapon* series (Richard Donner, 1987–98), which goes too far in the direction of emphasising the humorous aspects of the relationships to be truly noir, in contrast, for example, to a darker version of the buddy-cop film like *Colors* (Dennis Hopper, 1988). See Erickson, in Silver and Ursini, p. 324.
32. Telotte, pp. 4–5.
33. Alfred Appel, *Nabokov's Dark Cinema*, quoted by Robert Porfirio, 'No Way Out: Existential Motifs in the Film Noir', in Palmer (ed.), *Perspectives*, p. 117.

Part I: 1920–45

1. Introduction to *Fingerman* ([1950], London: Ace, 1960), p. 6.
2. *Fingerman*, p. 5.
3. David Madden (ed.), *Tough Guy Writers of the Thirties* (Carbondale, Ill., 1968), pp. xxv–xxvi.
4. George Orwell, 'Raffles and Miss Blandish', in *Collected Essays* (London: Secker & Warburg, 1961, 1975), pp. 249–63.
5. John Houseman, 'Today's Hero: a Review', *Hollywood Quarterly*, 2, No. 2 (1947), p. 163, and John Houseman, *Vogue*, 15 January 1947, quoted by

Richard Maltby, 'The Politics of the Maladjusted Text', in Ian Cameron (ed.), *The Movie Book of Film Noir* (London: Studio Vista, 1992), p. 41.

6. Joseph T. Shaw, quoted by Bill Pronzini and Jack Adrian (eds), *Hard-Boiled: an Anthology of American Crime Stories* (Oxford: Oxford University Press, 1995), p. 9.
7. Herbert Ruhm (ed.), *The Hard-Boiled Detective: Stories from 'Black Mask' Magazine, 1920–1951* (New York: Random House, 1977), p. xiv.
8. Rick A. Eden, 'Detective Fiction as Satire', *Genre*, 16 (Fall 1983), pp. 279–95, argues that the hard-boiled detective is akin to the Juvenalian satirist, in contrast to the Horatian tone of formal detective fiction.
9. George Orwell, 'Wells, Hitler and the World State' (1941), in *Collected Essays*, p. 161. For a fuller discussion of these pre-World War Two English dilemmas, see Lee Horsley, *Fictions of Power in English Literature: 1900–1950* (London: Longman, 1995), pp. 155–61.

1 Hard-boiled Investigators

1. For example, in the Introduction to Bill Pronzini and Jack Adrian (eds), *Hard-Boiled: an Anthology of American Crime Stories* (Oxford: Oxford University Press, 1995), p. 6, and in Geoffrey O'Brien, *Hardboiled America: Lurid Paperbacks and the Masters of Noir* (New York: Da Capo Press, 1997).
2. Dana Polan, *Power and Paranoia: History, Narrative and the American Cinema, 1940–1950* (New York: Columbia University Press, 1986), p. 238.
3. Chandler, *The Big Sleep* (1939), p. 105. Foster Hirsch, *Film Noir: the Dark Side of the Screen* (San Diego: A. S. Barnes, 1981), p. 170, argues that this sharper distinction between hunter and hunted makes the private eye investigative framework thematically the least rewarding of the various noir story types.
4. Anne Cranny-Francis, 'Gender and Genre: Feminist Rewritings of Detective Fiction', *Women's Studies International Forum*, 11 (1988), p. 69.
5. For further discussion of Nebel, see: David Geherin, *The American Private Eye: the Image in Fiction* (New York: Ungar, 1985), pp. 36–42; John M. Reilly (ed.), *Twentieth-Century Crime and Mystery Writers* (New York: St Martin's Press, 1980, 1985), pp. 666–7; Lee Server, *Danger is My Business: an Illustrated History of the Fabulous Pulp Magazines: 1896–1953* (San Francisco, 1993), pp. 67–9; Pronzini and Adrian, pp. 83–4.
6. 'Backwash' (*Black Mask*, May 1932), reprinted in Pronzini and Adrian, p. 93.
7. Alain Silver and Elizabeth Ward (eds), *Film Noir* (London: Secker & Warburg, 1979, 1992), p. 43.
8. Nebel, 'Death's Not Enough', in *Six Deadly Dames* ([1930s; 1950] Boston: Gregg Press, 1980), p. 159.
9. 'Backwash', p. 88.
10. *The Adventures of Cardigan* ([1933–5], New York: Mysterious Press, 1988), p. 127.
11. See Reilly, pp. 234–7, Geherin, pp. 8–16, and Philip Durham, 'The "Black Mask" School', in David Madden (ed.), *Tough Guy Writers of the Thirties* (Carbondale, Ill.: Southern Illinois University Press, 1968), pp. 67–8.
12. Durham, in Madden, pp. 54–5: Daly was 'short on style' but created 'the

type' of the hard-boiled hero and, in many of his stories, established the moral ambiguity of this central figure.

13. 'The False Burton Combs', in Herbert Ruhm (ed.), *The Hard-Boiled Detective: Stories from 'Black Mask' Magazine, 1920–1951* (New York: Random House, 1977), p. 4.
14. 'False Burton Combs', in Ruhm, p. 17.
15. 'False Burton Combs', in Ruhm, pp. 29–30.
16. Geherin, p. 10.
17. Daly, *The Third Murderer* (New York: Farrar and Rinehart, 1931), quoted by Geherin, p. 12.
18. See Richard Gid Powers, *G-Men: Hoover's FBI in American Popular Culture* (Carbondale, Ill.: Southern Illinois University Press, 1983), p. 77, whose analysis makes it clear how far Race Williams was part of a very strongly established nineteenth-century tradition of action heroes; see also Ron Goulart, *Cheap Thrills: an Informal History of the Pulp Magazines* (New Rochelle, NY: Arlington House, 1972), pp. 118–19.
19. Published in *Black Mask* in June–September 1927.
20. All of the Satan Hall stories mentioned here are collected in *The Adventures of Satan Hall* (New York: Mysterious Press, 1988): page references for individual pieces are to this edition.
21. There are often unmistakable echoes of the Wild West. Indeed, the basic plot of Hammett's first novel, *Red Harvest* (1929), has served as the basis both for Sergio Leone's spaghetti western, *A Fistful of Dollars* (1964), and more recently for the gangster western, *Last Man Standing* (Walter Hill, 1996). The shift to a western setting is facilitated by the fable-like quality of Hammett's tale of a representative town, metaphoric of national corruption.
22. *Blood Money* is Hammett's first novel (not published as a novel until 1943), which couples two stories – 'The Big Knock-Over' and '$106,000 Blood Money' (1927) – now most readily available as the concluding stories in *The Big Knockover and Other Stories*.
23. See, for example, William F. Nolan, *Hammett: a Life at the Edge* (Congdon and Weed, 1983), pp. 77–8, excerpted in Christopher Metress (ed.), *The Critical Response to Dashiell Hammett* (Westport, Conn.: Greenwood Press, 1994), p. 5.
24. For various other interpretations of the symbol of the glass key (for example, as emblematic of impotence and guilt-ridden sexuality and as signifying Ned himself as a 'hollow man' and moral failure) see the extracts from reviews and articles in Mettress, pp. 109–31.
25. See Annette Kuhn's discussion of *The Big Sleep* in Kuhn, *The Power of the Image: Essays on Representation and Sexuality* (London: Routledge, 1985), pp. 74–95.
26. It is telling that Chandler himself wanted Cary Grant for the role of Marlowe in *Murder, My Sweet*. See Ian Ousby, *The Crime and Mystery Book: a Reader's Companion* (London: Thames and Hudson, 1997), p. 115.
27. See Silver and Ward, p. 192.
28. Reprinted in *Fingerman*, p. 50.
29. Reprinted in *Trouble is My Business*, pp. 134–7.
30. Reprinted in *Trouble is My Business*, p. 22.

31. Stephen Knight, *Form and Ideology in Crime Fiction* (London: Macmillan, 1980), p. 148.
32. Brian Docherty (ed.), *American Crime Fiction: Studies in the Genre* (Houndmills: Macmillan, 1988), p. 77; Chandler, 'The Simple Art of Murder', *Atlantic Monthly* (December 1944), quoted in Tom Hiney, *Raymond Chandler: a Biography* (London: Vintage, 1997), pp. 101–2.
33. See Knight, pp. 142–3.
34. Frank Krutnik, *In a Lonely Street: Film, Genre, Masculinity* (London: Routledge, 1991), p. 128; Silver and Ward, p. 192; Knight, pp. 142–3 and 158.
35. William F. Nolan, of Paul Cain, Introduction (July 1987) to *Seven Slayers* (Los Angeles: Blood and Guts Press, 1987).
36. Ted Malvern, for example, in 'Guns at Cyrano's', is connected to the criminal world by his parentage and (predictably, since this is Chandler) feels guilty about being 'a guy who lives on crooked dough and doesn't even do his own stealing'. *Fingerman*, pp. 247–8.
37. Paul Cain (who also wrote as Peter Ruric for his film and television work) wrote for *Black Mask* in the period 1932–6. Some of his short stories were republished in 1946 in a collection entitled *Seven Slayers*. Whitfield wrote for *Black Mask* between 1930 and 1933; his first novel, *Green Ice*, was published by Knopf in 1930. See Reilly, pp. 135–6 and 898–900.
38. Knight, pp. 145–6.
39. Joseph T. Shaw, 'A Letter to the Editor of *Writer's Digest*' (September 1930), in Metress, pp. 111–12.

2 Big-shot Gangsters and Small-time Crooks

1. See Jonathan Munby's discussion of the popularisation of Dillinger during the Depression (in comparison to his postwar representation): *Public Enemies, Public Heroes: Screening the Gangster from Little Caesar to Touch of Evil* (Chicago: University of Chicago Press, 1999), pp. 151–6.
2. Richard Gid Powers, *G-Men: Hoover's FBI in American Popular Culture* (Carbondale, Ill.: Southern Illinois University Press, 1983), pp. 19–25, analyses the anti-crime mythology of vigilante and G-Men films. The fullest and best recent discussion of the representation of the gangster in Hollywood films is in Munby's *Public Enemies*.
3. 'Public enemy' is a phrase that entered popular rhetoric after the April 1930 release of a Crime Commission list of Chicago's 28 most dangerous 'public enemies'. See David E. Ruth, *Inventing the Public Enemy: the Gangster in American Culture* (Chicago: The University of Chicago Press, 1996), p. 2.
4. Powers, pp. 3–32 and 68.
5. *Kiss Tomorrow Goodbye* was directed by Gordon Douglas. Another notable Cagney performance as a psychopathic gangster was in *White Heat* (Raoul Walsh, 1949). See Munby, *Public Enemies*, pp. 115–16, on the contrasts between these roles and Cagney's earlier portrayal of Tommy Powers in *Public Enemy* (William A. Wellman, 1931).
6. Ruth, p. 25, referring to S. Tee Bee, 'With the Gangsters', *Saturday Evening Post*, 198 (26 June 1926), p. 54.
7. Munby, *Public Enemies*, pp. 4–5.

8. Powers, pp. 90–1; Jack Shadoian, *Dreams and Dead Ends: the American Gangster/Crime Film* (Cambridge, Mass.: MIT Press, 1977), pp. 59–60.
9. Burnett in Pat McGilligan, *Backstory* (Berkeley: University of California Press, 1986), p. 57, quoted by Munby, *Public Enemies*, p. 46.
10. Alain Silver and Elizabeth Ward (eds), *Film Noir* (London: Secker and Warburg, 1979, 1992), pp. 17 and 324–5.
11. Munby, *Public Enemies*, pp. 84–5. In supporting his argument that *film noir* is simply a more overtly modernist mutation of 'older formulas', Munby also notes that many films previously categorised as gangster films have been reclassified as *films noirs* – for example, *The Killers*, *Kiss of Death* and *Ride the Pink Horse* (Munby, *Public Enemies*, pp. 7 and 115–43). See also Jonathan Munby, 'The "Un-American" Film Art: Robert Siodmak and the Political Significance of Film Noir's German Connection', *iris*, 21 (Spring, 1996), pp. 74–88.
12. Ruth, p. 48.
13. For example, Foster Hirsch, *Film Noir: the Dark Side of the Screen* (San Diego: A. S. Barnes, 1981), pp. 170–2, argues that in comparison to the weaker noir anti-hero the gangster is lacking a psychological dimension. Many gangster novels, like those by Burnett and Trail, do, however, explore the motivations and neuroses that drive the gangster and do give him the ability to confront and understand his problems (see discussion in this chapter of Trail's *Scarface*). See also Munby, *Public Enemies*, pp. 47–9: 'Little Caesar's desires for the signs of official society signify his yearning for cultural inclusion and acceptance.'
14. Appel's first novel, *Brain Guy*, was published in 1934. *Brain Guy* and several of his short stories (collected as *Hell's Kitchen* and *Dock Walloper*) were reissued by Lion paperbacks in the 1950s. Appel also wrote some paperback originals, such as *Sweet Money Girl* (1954) and *The Raw Edge* (1958).
15. That is, the 1934–9 stories published by Lion in 1952 as *Hell's Kitchen*. The reissue cited here is: New York: Berkley Books, 1958.
16. Ruth, p. 62.
17. George Grella, in John M. Reilly (ed.), *Twentieth-Century Crime and Mystery Writers* (New York: St Martin's Press, 1980, 1985), p. 129. Once paperback originals began to be published in the fifties, Burnett wrote some of his novels (*Underdog* and *Big Stan*, for example) for Gold Medal. His novels of the forties and early fifties, however, were all published in hardcover with Knopf. Blanche and Alfred Knopf were also responsible for furthering the careers of other hard-boiled writers, such as James M. Cain, Chandler and Hammett. See James Naremore, *More Than Night: Film Noir in its Contexts* (Berkeley: University of California Press, 1998), p. 52.
18. Burnett, in McGilligan, *Backstory*, p. 58, quoted by Munby, *Public Enemies*, p. 47.
19. Powers, p. 13.
20. Burnett, in McGilligan, *Backstory*, p. 57, quoted by Munby, *Public Enemies*, p. 45.
21. Powers, pp. 4–6.
22. This approach brings Trail closer than Burnett to the tendency of Hollywood studios (under pressure to acquiesce in censorship) to add 'crime doesn't pay' riders to gangster films, see Munby, *Public Enemies*, pp. 51 and *passim*.

The censors demanded, for example, that the film of *Scarface* be subtitled 'the Shame of a Nation'.

23. That is, the 1934–5 stories published by Lion in 1953 as *Dock Walloper*. This is the edition cited here. It includes a story, 'Dock Walloper', written in 1953 for this edition: this story is reprinted by Bill Pronzini and Jack Adrian (eds), *Hard-Boiled: an Anthology of American Crime Stories* (Oxford: Oxford University Press, 1995), pp. 230–56.
24. See, for example, *Thieves Like Us*, pp. 284–5 (in *Crime Novels: American Noir of the 1930s and 40s*, No. 94, The Library of America, 1997), on popular support for robbing banks on the part of 'Real People'.
25. In the film, there is a stronger stress on the irony of things looking good just when they get bad (with Marie and Pard ironically precipitating Roy's death by their devotion); in the book the real force of the irony is much more to do with Roy, an essentially humane, generous, honourable man, perceived as the menace to society 'Mad Dog Earle' (161), and the function of Marie and Pard is mainly to provide confirmation of his humanity. Powers, p. 7, notes that the real-life gangster called 'Mad Dog' was (in contrast to the non-violent Roy) actually tried for killing one child and wounding four others.
26. Steve Chibnall and Robert Murphy (eds), *British Crime Cinema* (London: Routledge, 1999), pp. 5–7.
27. There is, for example, in *Love's Lovely Counterfeit*, pp. 134–5, a passing comparison of an ex-gangster boss to Hitler.
28. 'Fritz Lang', *New York World Telegram*, 11 June 1941, quoted by Siegfried Kracauer, *From Caligari to Hitler: a Psychological History of the German Film* (Princeton University Press, 1947, 1974), pp. 248–9.
29. *Monthly Film Bulletin* (April 1948), 47, quoted by Chibnall and Murphy, pp. 38, 8–9.
30. Brian McFarlane, 'Outrage: *No Orchids for Miss Blandish*', in Chibnall and Murphy, pp. 37–50.
31. Borde and Chaumeton credit Greene with playing a role 'in the birth of film noir (*This Gun For Hire*), in the acclimatization of noir in England (*Brighton Rock*), and in its international development'. Quoted by Naremore, p. 48.
32. Greene, *Ways of Escape* (Harmondsworth, Middx.: Penguin, 1981), pp. 56–7.
33. Paul Duncan, 'It's Raining Violence: a Brief History of British Noir', *Crime Time*, 2, No. 3 (1999), p. 81.
34. *They Drive by Night* was made into a film, directed by Arthur Woods, in 1938. It was influenced by Expressionism and was visually akin to later *films noirs*: 'its rainy roads, glittering dance halls, dismal lodgings and degenerate murderer seem to prefigure American film noir'. Steve Chibnall and Robert Murphy, 'Parole Overdue: Releasing the British Crime Film into the Critical Community', in Chibnall and Murphy, pp. 4–5.
35. Ibid.
36. Silver and Ward, p. 201. The playing down of Fabian's unsympathetic character is carried much further in Irwin Winkler's 1992 remake of *Night and the City*, in which Robert De Niro's warmer, more likeable Harry Fabian contributes to a less 'noirish' film.

3 Victims of Circumstance

1. Norman Mailer, *An American Dream* ([1965], London: Flamingo, 1994), p. 15.
2. Frank Krutnik, *In a Lonely Street: Film, Genre, Masculinity* (London: Routledge, 1991), in his analysis of male figures in *film noir*, offers many insights into the noir victim, particularly in his chapters on 'the "tough" suspense thriller' and 'the criminal-adventure thriller' (125–63); Foster Hirsch, *Film Noir: the Dark Side of the Screen* (San Diego: A. S. Barnes, 1981), pp. 175–90, also provides a useful account, taking in a range of films that illustrate different patterns of victim noir.
3. Kevin Starr, 'It's Chinatown', *The New Republic*, 26 July 1975, p. 31, quoted in David Fine, 'Beginning in the Thirties: the Los Angeles Fiction of James M. Cain and Horace McCoy', in David Fine (ed.), *Los Angeles in Fiction* (Albuquerque: University of New Mexico Press, 1984), p. 43; and *Louis Adamic*, quoted in Mike Davis, *City of Quartz: Excavating the Future in Los Angeles* (London: Vintage, 1990), pp. 36–7.
4. Fine, 'Beginning in the Thirties', in Fine (ed.), pp. 43–4 and 62.
5. Edmund Wilson, 'The Boys in the Back Room', in *A Literary Chronicle, 1920–1950* (Garden City, NY: Doubleday Anchor Books, 1952), p. 217; Thomas Sturak, 'Horace McCoy's Objective Lyricism', in David Madden (ed.), *Tough Guy Writers of the Thirties* (Carbondale, Ill., 1968), pp. 142 and 146.
6. Chandler's view of Cain ('Faugh. Everything he touches smells like a billy-goat.') is summarised in Richard Schickel, *Double Indemnity* (London: British Film Institute, 1992), pp. 33–4.
7. McCoy persuaded his publisher not to use the label 'hard-boiled' for his novels. See Sturak, in Madden (ed.), p. 147; Cain to some extent dissociates himself from the label in his 'Author's Preface' to *Double Indemnity*: 'I make no conscious effort to be tough, or hard-boiled. . . . I merely try to write as the character would write' (236).
8. Schickel, p. 30.
9. *Postman* was the source for both Pierre Chenal's *Le Dernier Tournant* (1939) and Luchino Visconti's *Obssessione* (1942). See Lee Richmond, 'A Time to Mourn and a Time to Dance: Horace McCoy's *They Shoot Horses, Don't They?*', *Twentieth Century Literature*, 17 (1971), p. 91; Hirsch, pp. 41–2. After the publication of the Gallimard edition (1946), McCoy was described in an American review as 'the most discussed American writer in France' (Robert Bourne Linscott, *New York Herald Tribune Weekly Book Review*, 9 February 1947, quoted in Richmond, 'A Time to Mourn', p. 92).
10. See Sturak, in Madden (ed.), p. 148.
11. Sturak, in Madden (ed.), p. 139.
12. Jon Tuska, *Dark Cinema: American Film Noir in Cultural Perspective* (Westport, Conn.: Greenwood Press, 1984), p. 97, rightly argues that Knight's novel is 'both a pastiche of the hard-boiled Hollywood novel *and* . . . an indictment of the California syndrome'.
13. He makes fun, for example, of Aimee Semple McPherson and of Upton Sinclair's 1934 EPIC (End Poverty in California) gubernatorial campaign.

14. Roy Hoopes, *Cain: the Biography of James M. Cain* (New York: Holt, Rinehart and Winston, 1982), p. 551; James Naremore, *More Than Night: Film Noir in its Contexts* (Berkeley: University of California Press, 1998), p. 83.
15. James M. Cain, 'Brush Fire' (originally published in *Liberty*, 15 December 1936), reprinted in Bill Pronzini and Jack Adrian (eds), *Hard-Boiled: an Anthology of American Crime Stories* (Oxford: Oxford University Press, 1995), pp. 144–5.
16. 'Author's Preface' to *Double Indemnity*, p. 235.
17. James Damico, in fact, in an overly ingenious effort to define the genre, takes this to be *the* narrative model of *film noir*: 'Film Noir: a Modest Proposal', in R. B. Palmer, *Hollywood's Dark Cinema: the American Film Noir* (New York: Twayne, 1994), pp. 129–40.
18. Schickel, p. 22.
19. Schickel, p. 58.
20. The first of the Woolrich 'black' series was the 1940 novel *The Bride Wore Black*. *Black Path of Fear* was adapted for the screen in 1946 as *The Chase*, directed by Arthur Ripley. Alain Silver and Elizabeth Ward (eds), *Film Noir* (London: Secker and Warburg, 1979, 1992), p. 55, class this as one of the best cinematic equivalents of the dark and oppressive atmosphere of Woolrich's novels, with its oneirism, eroticism, cruelty and ambivalence. It is significant, though, that the oneiric quality functions to mute the most disturbing aspect of the novel, the death of Eve (Lorna in the film), since in the adaptation she is only stabbed in a dream.
21. Silver and Ward, pp. 345–6, list 11 films adapted from Woolrich novels and stories.
22. W. M. Frohock, *The Novel of Violence in America* (London: Arthur Barker, Ltd, 1946, 1959), pp. 6–13.
23. For a fuller discussion, see Lee Horsley, *Fictions of Power in English Literature: 1900–1950* (London: Longman, 1995), Chapter 4, pp. 155–95. Another novel of the time dealing with the suppressed capacity for violent action is Geoffrey Household's *Rogue Male* (1939).
24. Sturak, in Madden (ed.), pp. 138–9.
25. George Orwell, 'Wells, Hitler and the World State' (1941), in *Collected Essays* (London: Secker and Warburg, 1961, 1975), p. 161.
26. E. M. Forster, 'The 1939 State', in *The New Statesman*, 10 June 1939, p. 888.
27. *Journey into Fear* (1943), directed by Norman Foster and (uncredited) Orson Welles, who also played Col. Haki. As well as a more upbeat ending, there is, as Silver and Ward observe (149), Graham's whimsical narration, which 'acts as a deflating counterpoint to the threatening noir atmosphere'. Ambler's 1939 novel, *Mask of Dimitrios*, was adapted in 1944, directed by Jean Negulesco; *Uncommon Danger* was adapted in 1943 as *Background to Danger* (Raoul Walsh), but is not classed as a *film noir*.
28. Graham Greene, *Journey without Maps* ([1936] Harmondsworth, Middx.: Penguin, 1980), p. 70.
29. Graham Greene, *Ways of Escape* (Harmondsworth, Middx.: Penguin, 1981), pp. 67–8.

Part II: 1945–70

1. Jean Pierre Chartier, 'The Americans Are Making Dark Films Too', in R. Barton Palmer (ed.), *Perspectives on Film Noir* (New York: G. K. Hall and Co., 1996), p. 25.
2. Nino Frank, 'The Crime Adventure Story: a New Kind of Detective Film', in Palmer (ed.), *Perspectives*, p. 23. Both the backlog of films and those being newly released were eagerly received by French intellectuals and cinema enthusiasts who found in them a 'radically different' vision of American life – of greed, criminality, violence, anomie. R. Barton Palmer, Introduction to Palmer (ed.), *Perspectives*, pp. 3–4.
3. Geoffrey O'Brien, *Hardboiled America: Lurid Paperbacks and the Masters of Noir* ([1981] New York: Da Capo Press, 1997), pp. 22–5; Lee Server, *Over My Dead Body: the Sensational Age of the American Paperback: 1945–1955* (San Francisco, 1994), pp. 34–5.
4. Jim Thompson, quoted by Max Miller in *San Diego Tribune*, 16 February 1949, in Michael J. McCauley, *Jim Thompson: Sleep with the Devil* (New York: The Mysterious Press, 1991), p. 125.
5. Mickey Spillane, the *Guardian* interview, National Film Theatre, 29 July 1999; Max Allan Collins and James L. Traylor, *One Lonely Knight: Mickey Spillane's Mike Hammer* (Bowling Green, Ohio: Popular Press, 1984), pp. 5–7; Server, *Over My Dead Body*, pp. 21–42; O'Brien, pp. 19–34. Although their great mass market impact was as paperbacks, most of Spillane's novels were first published in hardcover by Dutton.
6. Server, *Over My Dead Body*, p. 26.
7. O'Brien, p. 140. Goodis' *Cassidy's Girl* sold over a million copies. See Woody Haut, *Pulp Culture and the Cold War* (London: Serpent's Tail, 1995), p. 9.
8. Server, *Over My Dead Body*, jacket copy.
9. Frank, 'The Crime Adventure Story', in Palmer (ed.), *Perspectives*, p. 23.
10. Frank, in Palmer (ed.), *Perspectives*, p. 21.
11. James Naremore, *More Than Night: Film Noir in its Contexts* (Berkeley: University of California Press, 1998), p. 17.
12. Alain Silver and Elizabeth Ward (eds), *Film Noir* (London: Secker and Warburg, 1979, 1992), p. 120.
13. See Frank Krutnik's discussion of these films, *In a Lonely Street: Film, Genre, Masculinity* (London: Routledge, 1991), pp. 103–14 and 132–5.
14. Robin Buss, *French Film Noir* (London and New York: Marion Boyars, 1994), p. 13.
15. Some of the French imitators of the American style, most notably Albert Simonon, used French settings and gave considerable thought to coming up with a convincing body of French 'underworld slang' (see Ian Ousby, *The Crime and Mystery Book: a Reader's Companion* [London: Thames and Hudson, 1997], pp. 107 and 121; Buss, p. 32). The Gallimard series did not, however, include the most important European noir, such as the novels of Graham Greene and of the Belgian-French Georges Simenon, whose 1948 *La Neige Était Sale* [*The Stain on the Snow*], for example, written while he was living in America, is a powerfully disturbing exploration of the mind of a young murderer. None of the European writers published in the *Série Noire* were of the standard of Greene and Simenon.

16. Cheyney was in fact the first novelist translated for the *Série Noire* and also the only one whose novels became the basis for a series of French private eye movies. The Lemmy Caution films, starting with *La Môme vert-de-gris* in 1953, featured an 'authentic' American star, Eddie Constantine. Constantine's performances in the role were calculated to bring out the inherent self-mockery and comedy: 'You look at the camera and wink' (Eddie Constantine, quoted by Jill Forbes, 'The "*Série Noire*",' in Brian Rigby and Nicholas Hewitt [eds], *France and the Mass Media* [Houndmills: Macmillan, 1993], p. 90).
17. Naremore, pp. 22–3.
18. Malcolm Bradbury and Howard Temperley, *Introduction to American Studies* (London: Longman, 1981, 1998), p. 242.
19. Malcolm Bradbury, *The Modern American Novel* (Oxford: Oxford University Press, 1983, 1992), p. 165. Both Wright and Himes eventually moved to Paris.
20. Bradbury and Temperley, p. 262.
21. Sylvia Harvey, 'Women's Place: the Absent Family of *Film Noir*', in E. Ann Kaplan (ed.), *Women in Film Noir* (London: British Film Institute, 1972), pp. 23–5; and Krutnik, *In a Lonely Street*, pp. 60–1.
22. See Maltby, 'Politics of the Maladjusted Text', in Ian Cameron (ed.), *The Movie Book of Film Noir* (London: Studio Vista, 1992), p. 39.
23. For example, Richard Polenberg's *One Nation Divisible: Class, Race, and Ethnicity in the United States since 1938* (New York: Viking Press, 1988), cited by Dana Polan, *Power and Paranoia: History, Narrative and the American Cinema, 1940–1950* (New York: Columbia University Press, 1986), p. 41.
24. Bradbury and Temperley, pp. 256–8.
25. Irving Howe, 'The Age of Conformity', quoted in Bradbury and Temperley, p. 258.
26. Bradbury and Temperley, pp. 262–4.
27. Ibid.
28. Maltby, in Cameron (ed.), p. 47.
29. 'The last piece of true pulp-as-art was published circa 1965.' Bill Pronzini, 'Forgotten Writers: Gil Brewer,' in Lee Server, Ed Gorman and Martin H. Greenberg (eds), *The Big Book of Noir* (New York: Carroll and Graf Publishers, 1998), p. 193.
30. Krutnik, *In a Lonely Street*, p. 97.
31. Server, *Over My Dead Body*, pp. 12–14.
32. O'Brien, p. 26; Server, *Over My Dead Body*, pp. 12–18.
33. Naremore, p. 236.
34. Steve Holland, *The Mushroom Jungle: a History of Postwar Paperback Publishing* (Westbury, Wilts.: Zeon Books, 1993).
35. Holland, p. 28. Holland notes that James Hadley Chase and Harold Kelly, who (as Darcy Glinto) published *Lady – Don't Turn Over* in 1940, were the first two gangster novelists to have their work branded as obscene (in 1942) – but, as Holland says, 'they were certainly not the last'. The main legal action discussed by Holland (139–55) is the action taken against the publishers of Hank Janson for publishing 'obscene libels' in seven of the novels (*Accused, Auctioned, Persian Pride, Pursuit, Amok, Killer* and *Vengeance*).

36. The British market was still dominated by the work of such writers as Margery Allingham, Ngaio Marsh, Patrick Quentin, Edmund Crispin and, of course, Agatha Christie. See Julian Symons, *Bloody Murder, From the Detective Story to the Crime Novel: a History* (London: Pan, 1972, 1992), pp. 171–88.
37. Arthur Marwick, *British Society since 1945* (Harmondsworth, Middx.: Penguin, 1996, 3rd edn; 1982), p. 71.
38. Marwick, pp. 110–26.

4 Fatal Men

1. Jonathan Munby, *Public Enemies, Public Heroes: Screening the Gangster from Little Caesar to Touch of Evil* (Chicago: University of Chicago Press, 1999), p. 116, gives examples of some who argue in this way, such as James J. Parker, 'The Organizational Environment of the Motion Picture Sector', in Sandra J. Ball-Rokeach and Muriel G. Cantor (eds), *Media, Audience, and Social Structure* (Beverly Hills: Sage, 1986).
2. Mark Seltzer, *Serial Killers: Death and Life in America's Wound Culture* (New York: Routledge, 1998), p. 162.
3. Jack Shadoian, *Dreams and Dead Ends: the American Gangster/Crime Film* (Cambridge, Mass.: MIT Press, 1977), pp. 209–13; Chris Hugo, '*The Big Combo*: Production Conditions and the Film Text', in Ian Cameron (ed.), *The Movie Book of Film Noir* (London: Studio Vista, 1992), p. 249; Munby, *Public Enemies*, pp. 126–33; Alain Silver and Elizabeth Ward (eds), *Film Noir* (London: Secker and Warburg, 1979, 1992), pp. 28–9, 105–6, 142–3 and 226–7. And see Frank McConnell, '*Pickup on South Street* and the Metamorphosis of the Thriller', *Film Heritage*, 8 (1973), p. 15.
4. Bill Pronzini and Jack Adrian (eds), *Hard-Boiled: an Anthology of American Crime Stories* (Oxford: Oxford University Press, 1995), p. 348.
5. The other film adaptations of the Parker novels are *The Split* (Gordon Flemyng, 1968) and two French films, both released in 1967, Alain Cavalier's *Mise à Sac* and Godard's *Made in USA*.
6. Westlake talking to Charles L. P. Silet, 'Interview with Donald Westlake', in Lee Server, Ed Gorman and Martin H. Greenberg (eds), *The Big Book of Noir* (New York: Carroll and Graf Publishers, 1998), p. 269.
7. *The Man with the Getaway Face* is the second of the Parker novels; *The Outfit*, basis of the Flynn film, was published in 1971, and 13 other Parker novels appeared over the next three years (1971–4).
8. See the chapter on *Point Blank* in James F. Maxfield, *The Fatal Woman: Sources of Male Anxiety in Film Noir, 1941–1991* (Fairleigh Dickinson University Press, 1996), pp. 95–107; and Silver and Ward, pp. 229–30.
9. Max Allan Collins and James L. Traylor, *One Lonely Knight: Mickey Spillane's Mike Hammer* (Bowling Green, Ohio: Popular Press, 1984), pp. 4–6. 'Mike Danger' was revived for Tekno Comics in the mid-1990s. See James Naremore, *More Than Night: Film Noir in its Contexts* (Berkeley: University of California Press, 1998), p. 256, and Mickey Spillane, the *Guardian* interview, National Film Theatre, 29 July 1999.
10. Maxim Jakubowski, 'The Tough Guy Vanishes', in *The Daily Telegraph*, 2 May 1998; Geoffrey O'Brien, *Hardboiled America: Lurid Paperbacks and the Masters*

of Noir, expanded edn (New York: Da Capo Press, 1997), p. 104, quotes the 1953 New American Library boast that 'over 15 000 000 copies of his books have been published in Signet editions'. Server, writing in the mid-1990s, estimates that there have been '150 million or so' copies of Spillane's books sold to date. Spillane took up the series again in 1962, with *The Girl Hunters*.

11. Ed Gorman, quoted by Jakubowski, 'The Tough Guy Vanishes'.
12. Frank Krutnik, *In a Lonely Street: Film, Genre, Masculinity* (London: Routledge, 1991), p. 207.
13. Criticisms like that of Anthony Boucher, for example, who suggests that *I, the Jury* resembles 'required reading in a Gestapo training school'. See Jakubowski, 'The Tough Guy Vanishes'; and John M. Reilly (ed.), *Twentieth-Century Crime and Mystery Writers* (New York: St Martin's Press, 1980, 1985), p. 814.
14. *Guardian* interview with Spillane, NFT.
15. Ibid. On the connections between Hammer and Sapper's Bulldog Drummond, see Julian Symons, *Bloody Murder, From the Detective Story to the Crime Novel: a History* (London: Pan, 1972, 1992), p. 186.
16. William Ruehlmann, *Saint with a Gun: the Unlawful American Private Eye* (Washington, DC: American University Press, 1974), p. 98: Hammer's crusade 'is easy for an American to identify with; his vendettas are his readers'.
17. Harry Whittington, 'I Remember It Well', the author's introduction to *Web of Murder* (1987), p. xvii.
18. Wade Miller is the pseudonym for Robert Wade and Bill Miller, whose crime-writing partnership extended from the late 1940s until the beginning of the 1960s and who also produced a hard-boiled, though not particularly noir, detective series centring on the exploits of Max Thursday.
19. Rabe, one of the Gold Medal stalwarts from the mid-fifties on, published 16 novels just between 1955 and 1960, including the Daniel Port series, about a man who breaks with a crime syndicate (for example, *Dig My Grave Deep* [1956] and *The Out Is Death* [1957]).
20. O'Brien, pp. 145–50.
21. Whittington, 'I Remember It Well', p. xix.
22. Best known for creating the adventures of Travis McGee, John D. MacDonald also wrote many non-McGee novels, some of which, like *The Damned* (1952), *April Evil* (1956) and *Soft Touch* (1958), move towards more darkly ironic endings than are possible within the first-person narratives of a character as essentially good as Travis McGee.
23. One of the most successful writers of paperback originals, Brewer produced some 30 novels, mainly for Gold Medal and Avon, during the fifties and sixties, beginning in 1951 with one of his many femme fatale stories, *13 French Street*.
24. 'Patricia Highsmith im Gespräch mit Holly-Jane Rahlens', in Franz Cavagelli and Fritz Senn (eds), *Über Patricia Highsmith*, quoted by Tony Hilfer, *The Crime Novel: a Deviant Genre* (Austin, Texas: University of Texas Press, 1990), p. 129.
25. Hilfer, p. 136, contrasts Highsmith's novel with the film of it directed by René Clement, *Plein Soleil* (*Purple Noon*), which ends with Tom exposed when Dickie's body literally surfaces.

26. Reilly, p. 446.
27. Jon L. Breen, 'The Novels of Vin Packer', in Jon L. Breen and Martin Harry Greenberg (eds), *Murder Off the Rack: Critical Studies of Ten Paperback Masters* (Metuchen, New Jersey: The Scarecrow Press, 1989), p. 55.
28. Lee Server, *Over My Dead Body: the Sensational Age of the American Paperback: 1945–1955* (San Francisco: Chronicle Books, 1994), pp. 52–5; and Ed Gorman, 'The Golden Harvest: Twenty-Five-Cent Paperbacks', in Server *et al.* (eds), *Big Book of Noir*, p. 186.
29. Naremore, p. 34.
30. As Zizek points out, in the Hitchcock films focusing on 'transference of guilt' the main character accused by mistake is never straightforwardly innocent: though not guilty of the facts he is guilty of desire. Slavoj Zizek, *Everything You Always Wanted to Know about Lacan (But Were Afraid to Ask Hitchcock)* (London and New York: Verso, 1992), pp. 186–7.
31. Silver and Ward, p. 254.
32. James Sallis, *Difficult Lives: Jim Thompson, David Goodis, Chester Himes* (New York: Gryphon Books, 1993), p. 19. When Thompson died in 1977, all of his novels were out of print in the United States. Only in France had they remained generally available. He was not even one of the writers adapted for the screen: until the 1970s, Thompson's only connection with Hollywood *film noir* was his role in scripting Stanley Kubrick's 1956 film, *The Killing*, an adaptation of one of Lionel White's caper novels, *Clean Break* (1955).
33. Noel Simisolo, 'Notes sur le film noir', *Cinéma*, 223 (July 1977), p. 102, quoted by Hilfer, p. 137.
34. Seltzer, pp. 9–15.
35. Thompson's *Pop. 1280* was filmed in 1981 by Bertrand Tavernier as *Coup de Torchon*. *Killer Inside Me* was also filmed (1976, directed by Burt Kennedy), but this is a rather weak adaptation.
36. Robert C. Elliott, *The Power of Satire: Magic, Ritual, Art* (Princeton, NJ: Princeton University Press, 1960, 1972), pp. 3–15.
37. Frederic Wertham, *Dark Legend: a Study in Murder* (London: Victor Gollancz, 1947), quoted in Seltzer, p. 161.

5 Fatal Women

1. As we have seen, the novels of 1920–45 – of the 'pre-sex days of the detective pulps' (Harry Whittington, 'I Remember It Well', author's introduction to *Web of Murder* [1987], p. ix) – much less often resolved themselves into a gendered or sexual theme.
2. Jon Tuska, *Dark Cinema: American Film Noir in Cultural Perspective* (Westport, Conn.: Greenwood Press, 1984), p. 65.
3. See E. Ann Kaplan (ed.), *Women in Film Noir* (London: British Film Institute, 1972), *passim*; see also Foster Hirsch, *Film Noir: the Dark Side of the Screen* (San Diego: A. S. Barnes, 1981), pp. 152–7, on the role of the femme fatale.
4. Christine Gledhill, 'Klute 1: a Contemporary Film Noir and Feminist Criticism', in Kaplan (ed.), *Women in Film Noir*, pp. 15–18, and Frank Krutnik, *In a Lonely Street: Film, Genre, Masculinity* (London: Routledge, 1991), p. 97.

5. See Gledhill, 'Klute 1', and Janey Place, 'Women in Film Noir', in Kaplan (ed.), *Women in Film Noir*, pp. 15–18 and 43–5.
6. James F. Maxfield, *The Fatal Woman: Sources of Male Anxiety in Film Noir, 1941–1991* (Madison, Wis.: Fairleigh Dickinson University Press, 1996), pp. 9–13.
7. Ibid., and Gledhill, 'Klute 1', in Kaplan (ed.), *Women in Film Noir*, p. 18.
8. Place, 'Women in Film Noir', in Kaplan (ed.), *Women in Film Noir*, pp. 35–6.
9. Duff Johnson, *Easy to Take* (120); Ben Sarto, *Dread* (121).
10. Bardin's *Devil Take the Blue-Tail Fly* was finally published in the United States by Macfadden in 1967. Bardin's work was championed by Julian Symons, who also secured a reprinting of his books in England. See Julian Symons, *Bloody Murder, From the Detective Story to the Crime Novel: a History* (London: Pan, 1972, 1992), pp. 182–3, and John M. Reilly (ed.), *Twentieth-Century Crime and Mystery Writers* (New York: St Martin's Press, 1980, 1985), p. 54.
11. Maxfield, p. 45.
12. Lee Server, *Over My Dead Body: the Sensational Age of the American Paperback: 1945–1955* (San Francisco: Chronicle Books, 1994), pp. 51–5.
13. *Miss Otis Comes to Piccadilly* (1946) was Modern Fiction's first best-seller. Under the pen-name of Ben Sarto, Fawcett is estimated to have sold something like five to six million copies of his books. Steve Holland, 'I Kill 'Em Inch by Inch!', in Lee Server, Ed Gorman and Martin H. Greenberg (eds), *The Big Book of Noir* (New York: Carroll and Graf Publishers, 1998), pp. 214–16. See also Steve Holland, *The Mushroom Jungle: a History of Postwar Paperback Publishing* (Westbury, Wilts.: Zeon Books, 1993), pp. 28–31.
14. Server, *Over My Dead Body*, pp. 87–91, calls Ellson 'the incontrovertible king of jd fiction'.
15. Gledhill, 'Klute 1', in Kaplan (ed.), *Women in Film Noir*, pp. 15–17.
16. Woolrich first used the William Irish byline in 1942 for *Phantom Lady*. Nevins, p. 258, notes that it came to be better known than his own name, especially in France.
17. Place, 'Women in Film Noir', in Kaplan (ed.), *Women in Film Noir*, pp. 41–2, gives a good summary of the opposing types.
18. Whittington elsewhere – for example, *Murder is My Mistress* (1951) – creates female protagonists who do have a 'bad' past that catches up with them after they have become respectable.
19. Hank Janson was the pseudonym used in writing the longest-running and most popular series of British gangster pulps.
20. Geoffrey O'Brien, *Hardboiled America: Lurid Paperbacks and the Masters of Noir*, expanded edn (New York: Da Capo Press, 1997), pp. 92–3; and James Sallis, *Difficult Lives: Jim Thompson, David Goodis, Chester Himes* (New York: Gryphon Books, 1993), pp. 62–5.
21. Instead of 'a coherent realisation of the unstable, treacherous woman', there may be several partial characterisations that act to qualify one another (as, for example, in the Tay Garnett [1946] film of *The Postman Always Rings Twice*). Gledhill, 'Klute 1', in Kaplan (ed.), *Women in Film Noir*, pp. 15–18. Tuska, p. 208, suggests that another film in which the male discourse defining women is exposed as false is *The Blue Gardenia* (Fritz Lang, 1953).
22. Mary Ann Doane, *Femmes Fatales: Feminism, Film Theory, Psychoanalysis* (London and New York: Routledge, 1991), p. 2.

23. *Hell Is a City* was filmed with Stanley Baker as Inspector Martineau (Val Guest, 1960).
24. Server, *Over My Dead Body*, pp. 35–6.
25. O'Brien, p. 145.

6 Strangers and Outcasts

1. The extracts are taken from the last page of each novel.
2. For example, *The Blue Dahlia* (George Marshall, 1946) confronts the veteran Johnny (Alan Ladd) with loss of home due to his wife's unfaithfulness and with suspicion and pursuit. In Edward Dmytryk's *Crossfire* (1947) four soldiers on furlough are dangerously adrift in a world 'too used to fightin' (Sam Levene in *Crossfire*, quoted in James Naremore, *More Than Night: Film Noir in its Contexts* [Berkeley: University of California Press, 1998], p. 114). See also Michael Walker, 'Film Noir: Introduction', in Ian Cameron (ed.), *The Movie Book of Film Noir* (London: Studio Vista, 1992), pp. 35–6.
3. Nelson Algren, in David Ray, 'Walk on the Wild Side: a Bowl of Coffee with Nelson Algren', *The Reporter*, 20 (11 June 1959), pp. 31–3, quoted in James A. Lewin, 'Algren's Outcasts: Shakespearean Fools and the Prophet in a Neon Wilderness', *The Yearbook of the Society for the Study of Midwestern Literature*, 18 (1991), p. 107.
4. Albert Camus, quoted by Robert G. Porfirio, 'No Way Out: Existential Motifs in the Film Noir', in R. Barton Palmer (ed.), *Perspectives on Film Noir* (New York: G. K. Hall & Co., 1996), p. 126. The presence of existential motifs can be seen to unify *films noirs* as diverse as *Maltese Falcon, Detour, Brute Force* and *Woman in the Window*. See Porfirio, in Palmer, *Perspectives*, p. 117.
5. John M. Reilly (ed.), *Twentieth-Century Crime and Mystery Writers* (New York: St Martin's Press, 1980, 1985), p. 935.
6. Eric Lott, 'The Whiteness of Film Noir', *American Literary History*, 9, No. 3 (1997), p. 551, quoting Steve Fraser and Gary Gerstle, Introduction to *The Rise and Fall of the New Deal Order, 1930–1980* (Princeton: Princeton University Press, 1989), p. xix. See also Evelyn Gross Avery, *Rebels and Victims: the Fiction of Richard Wright and Bernard Malamud* (Port Washington, NY: Kennikat Press, 1979), pp. 3–4.
7. Lott, for example (pp. 542–8 and 561–2), urges a recognition of 'the informing presence of racial difference in the American imaginary', pointing to *film noir*'s use of 'otherness' of a moral and psychological kind: 'Racial borders are invoked and implicated in social and representational ones.' See also Julian Murphet, 'Film Noir and the Racial Unconscious', *Screen*, 39, No. 1 (1998), pp. 22–35, and Naremore's chapter on 'The Other Side of the Street', pp. 220–53.
8. Liam Kennedy, 'Black *Noir*: Race and Urban Space in Walter Mosley's Detective Fiction', in Peter Messent (ed.), *Criminal Proceedings: the Contemporary American Crime Novel* (London: Pluto Press, 1997), pp. 42–8.
9. 'Civil rights noir' is the label Lott, p. 561, gives to the film adaptation of McGivern's *Odds Against Tomorrow* (Robert Wise, 1959), which is the only example he finds of this.
10. Gilbert H. Muller, *Chester Himes* (Boston: Twayne Publishers, 1989), p. 21.

11. Other examples are *Phantom Lady* (Robert Siodmak, 1944) and *Deadline at Dawn* (Harold Clurman, 1946), both based on Cornell Woolrich novels, *Nightfall* (Jacques Tourneur, 1957, adapted from the Goodis novel), *The Big Clock* (John Farrow, 1948, adapted from Kenneth Fearing's novel), *Detour* (Edgar G. Ulmer, 1945) and *D.O.A.* (Rudolph Maté, 1950). See Walker, 'Film Noir', in Cameron, pp. 14–16.
12. Alain Silver and Elizabeth Ward (eds), *Film Noir* (London: Secker and Warburg, 1980), pp. 241–3.
13. Nicholas Blincoe, 'British Hardboiled', in Nick Rennison and Richard Shephard (eds), *Waterstone's Guide to Crime Fiction* (Brentford, Middx.: Waterstone's Booksellers Ltd, 1997), p. 13.
14. Paul Duncan, 'It's Raining Violence: a Brief History of British Noir', *Crime Time*, 2, No. 3 (1999).
15. *More Deadly Than the Male* is the only novel that Chase wrote under the name of Ambrose Grant; the argument that Greene had a hand in it is advanced by W. J. West, *The Quest for Graham Greene* (London: Weidenfeld and Nicolson, 1997), pp. 113–15.
16. Silver and Ward, pp. 209–10.
17. First published as *Detour*, but not to be confused with the earlier (1946) and much darker Edgar G. Ulmer film.
18. Sy Kahn, 'Kenneth Fearing and the Twentieth-Century Blues', in Warren French (ed.), *The Thirties: Fiction, Poetry, Drama* (Florida: Everett/Edwards, Inc., 1967, 1976), p. 133; Julian Symons, *Bloody Murder, From the Detective Story to the Crime Novel: a History* (London: Pan, 1972, 1992), p. 181.
19. Philippe Garnier's biography of Goodis, *Goodis: La Vie en Noir et Blanc* (Editions du Soleil, 1984), quoted in James Sallis, *Difficult Lives: Jim Thompson, David Goodis, Chester Himes* (New York: Gryphon Books, 1993), pp. 54–5 – discussing the response of the French to Goodis' existentialist qualities. See also Reilly, p. 385: 'Goodis is recognised in France as a master of the *roman noir Americain* second only to Woolrich.'
20. Bill Pronzini and Jack Adrian (eds), *Hard-Boiled: an Anthology of American Crime Stories* (Oxford: Oxford University Press, 1995), pp. 340–7 (quotation from p. 345).
21. The tactic of using a black character to deepen the novel's meaning is also used by the black novelist, Charles Perry, in his non-genre (but crime-centred and decidedly noir) *Portrait of a Young Man Drowning* (1962), which has a white protagonist but includes the inset narrative of a black labourer who digs his own grave – a story of loss, isolation and deprivation which in many ways foreshadows the fate of the narrator.
22. See the arguments of Woody Haut, *Pulp Culture and the Cold War* (London: Serpent's Tail, 1995), p. 142.
23. Schuyler's *Ethiopian Murder Mystery* was serialised in the thirties and reprinted as a novel in 1994; Paula L. Woods, *Spooks, Spies and Private Eyes: an Anthology of Black Mystery, Crime, and Suspense Fiction of the 20th Century* (Edinburgh: Payback Press, 1996), pp. 36–45, reprints 'The Shoemaker Murder', which Schuyler originally published in 1933 under the name of William Stockton.
24. Fisher's *Conjure Man Dies* was reissued by The X Press in 1995, and an extract is printed in Woods, pp. 20–35.

25. Wright wrote a dust-jacket blurb for Jim Thompson's grim, naturalistic *Now and on Earth* (1942), hailing it as 'an accurate picture of what happens to men and women in our time', and it is worthwhile to consider parallels between the two. Mark J. Madigan, 'As True and Direct as a Birth or Death Certificate . . .', *Studies in American Fiction*, 22, No. 1 (1994), pp. 105–10.
26. Wright, 'The Man Who Killed a Shadow', reprinted in Woods, p. 103. Wright's very influential *Native Son* (1940) also, of course, develops its racial theme through a melodramatically noir plot. See Ian Walker, 'Black Nightmares: the Fiction of Richard Wright', in A. Robert Lee (ed.), *Black Fiction: New Studies in the Afro-American Novel since 1945* (London: Vision Press, 1980), pp. 11–28.
27. Muller, pp. 4–7 and 13–14; Pronzini and Adrian, pp. 185–6.
28. Melvin Van Peebles, 'The Unconquered', introducing *The Harlem Cycle*, Vol. 1 (Edinburgh: Payback Press, 1996), p. xiii.
29. Stephen E. Milliken, *Chester Himes: a Critical Appraisal* (Columbia: University of Missouri Press, 1976), p. 212.
30. See Mike Davis, *City of Quartz: Excavating the Future in Los Angeles* (London: Vintage, 1990), pp. 42–3, on the brief appearance of 'Black *Noir*' in Los Angeles in the forties.
31. Michel Fabre, Robert E. Skinner and Lester Sullivan (compilers), *Chester Himes: an Annotated Primary and Secondary Bibliography* (Westport, Conn.: Greenwood Press, 1992), pp. 151–3.
32. Some otherwise good studies of Himes give misleading analyses of the relation between Himes' work and that of earlier noir/hard-boiled writers because of this tendency to define the existing tradition in too limited a way: see Robert E. Skinner, *Two Guns from Harlem: the Detective Fiction of Chester Himes* (Bowling Green State University Press, 1989); Stephen F. Soitos, *The Blues Detective: a Study of Afro-American Detective Fiction* (Univ. of Massachusetts Press, 1996); James Lundquist, *Chester Himes* (New York: Frederick Ungar, 1976).
33. Soitos, p. 145.
34. French obituaries for Himes, for example, stressed the importance of humour to both Himes and Thompson. See Fabre *et al.*, *Annotated Bibliography*, p. 175.
35. Fabre *et al.*, *Annotated Bibliography*, p. 162; James Sallis, 'In America's Black Heartland: the Achievement of Chester Himes', *Western Humanities Review*, 37, No. 3 (1983), pp. 191–206.
36. See Sallis, *Difficult Lives*, p. 73: 'if his people are monsters, misshapen, grotesque things, it is because the egg they formed in forced them to that shape'.
37. Shane Steven, 'Preface', *Blind Man with a Pistol* (New York: Morrow, 1969), quoted by Lundquist, pp. 116–17.
38. Chester Himes, 'Preface' to *Blind Man*, in *The Harlem Cycle*, Vol. 3 (Edinburgh: Payback Press, 1996), p. 193.
39. For example, Michel Fabre and Robert E. Skinner, 'Introduction' to *Plan B*, in *Harlem Cycle*, Vol. 3, pp. 383–400.
40. David K. Danow, *The Spirit of Carnival: Magical Realism and the Grotesque* (Lexington, Ky: The University Press of Kentucky, 1995), pp. 39–40.

41. 'Le Forum des livres: *Plan B*, par Chester Himes', *Var Matin*, 18 December 1983, quoted by Fabre and Skinner, 'Introduction' to *Plan B*, p. 390.

Part III: 1970–2000

1. The novels referred to are, respectively: Behm, *Eye of the Beholder*; Blincoe, *Acid Casuals*; Theroux, *Chicago Loop*; Frewin, *London Blues*; Ellis, *American Psycho*; Hjortsberg, *Angel Heart*; Dick, *A Scanner Darkly*; and Womack, *Random Acts of Senseless Violence*.
2. Alain Silver and Elizabeth Ward (eds), *Film Noir* (London: Secker and Warburg, 1979, 1992), p. 398.
3. Malcolm Bradbury and Howard Temperley, *Introduction to American Studies* (London: Longman, 1981, 1998), p. 269.
4. Arthur Marwick, *British Society since 1945* (Harmondsworth, Middx.: Penguin, 1982, 1996), pp. 121 and 174.
5. See the analysis of Bond as *the* Swinging Sixties hero in Michael Denning, *Mechanic Accents: Dime Novels and Working-Class Culture in America* (London: Verso, 1987), pp. 91–2.
6. Norman Mailer, *An American Dream* ([1965] London: Flamingo, 1994); Mailer's post-seventies noir crime novel, *Tough Guys Don't Dance* (London: Abacus, 1997), written at speed in 1984, is a less serious and less successful use of the form.
7. Marwick, p. 184.
8. Silver and Ward, pp. 336 and 440–3.
9. James Naremore, *More Than Night: Film Noir in its Contexts* (Berkeley: University of California Press, 1998), p. 37.
10. Silver and Ward, p. 398.
11. See Silver and Ward, p. 414.
12. Silver and Ward, pp. 108–9.
13. Ellroy, in an unpublished interview with Lee Horsley, London, 7 October 1995, quoted in Lee Horsley, 'Founding Fathers: "Genealogies of Violence" in James Ellroy's L. A. Quartet', *Clues*, 19, No. 2 (1998), pp. 139–40.
14. For discussions of recent developments in British noir, see: Mike Ripley and Maxim Jakubowski, 'Fresh Blood: British Neo-Noir', in Lee Server, Ed Gorman and Martin H. Greenberg (eds), *The Big Book of Noir* (New York: Carroll and Graf Publishers, 1998), pp. 317–22; Paul Duncan, 'It's Raining Violence: a Brief History of British Noir', *Crime Time*, 2, No. 3 (1999); and two recent Nicholas Blincoe articles, 'The Same Mean Streets Seen from a Fresh Angle', in *Murder, They Write* (*The Times*, 18 April 1998), p. 17; and 'British Hardboiled', in Nick Rennison and Richard Shephard (eds), *Waterstone's Guide to Crime Fiction* (Brentford, Middx.: Waterstone's Booksellers Ltd, 1997), pp. 11–13.
15. The settings of literary noir and *film noir* are discussed, respectively, by Ralph Willett, *The Naked City: Urban Crime Fiction in the USA* (Manchester: Manchester University Press, 1996), and Nicholas Christopher, *Somewhere in the Night: Film Noir and the American City* (New York: The Free Press, 1997).
16. James Sallis, 'In the Black', *Time Out*, 4–11 September 1996, p. 50, quoted

in Woody Haut, *Neon Noir: Contemporary American Crime Fiction* (London: Serpent's Tail, 1999), p. 112.

17. John M. Reilly (ed.), *Twentieth-Century Crime and Mystery Writers* (New York: St Martin's Press, 1980, rev. edn 1985), p. 589.
18. Reilly, p. 227.
19. Reilly, p. 228.
20. For example in *Blue Belle* ([1988] London: Pan, 1989).
21. Naremore, p. 39.
22. Fredric Jameson, 'Postmodernism and Consumer Society', in Peter Brooker (ed.), *Modernism/Postmodernism* (London: Longman, 1992), pp. 170–1.
23. Mike Featherstone, *Consumer Culture and Postmodernism* (London: Sage Publications, 1991, 1998), pp. viii–ix.
24. John Updike, 'When Everyone Was Pregnant', in *Museums and Women* (1973), quoted in Malcolm Bradbury, *The Modern American Novel* (Oxford: Oxford University Press, 1983, 1992), p. 158.
25. Richard Martin, *Mean Streets and Raging Bulls: the Legacy of Film Noir in Contemporary American Cinema* (Lanham, Md: The Scarecrow Press, 1997), pp. 52–3.
26. Peter York and Charles Jennings, *Peter York's Eighties* (London: BBC Books, 1995), p. 42.
27. York and Jennings, p. 40.
28. York and Jennings, p. 150.
29. York and Jennings, pp. 153–60.
30. David E. Ruth, *Inventing the Public Enemy: the Gangster in American Culture* (Chicago: The University of Chicago Press, 1996), pp. 63–81.
31. Laura Mulvey quoted by Naremore, pp. 196–7.
32. Naremore discusses this line of criticism, pp. 211–12, and refers readers to Anne Friedberg, *Window Shopping: Cinema and the Postmodern Condition* (Berkeley: University of California Press, 1993) for a fuller discussion of postmodern spectatorship and consumerism.
33. Naremore, p. 212.
34. The film is an adaptation of a John Gregory Dunne novel, *True Confessions* (1977), which is based on the Black Dahlia murder case (in LA in the 1940s). The novel and film (scripted by Dunne and his wife, Joan Didion) are compared in an article by Jon L. Breen, 'True Confessions', in Server *et al.*, *The Big Book of Noir*, pp. 149–52. Breen rightly classes *True Confessions* as 'one of the great films of the eighties, a classic of latter-day film noir' (149).
35. See John G. Cawelti, '*Chinatown* and Generic Transformation', in Gerald Mast and Marshall Cohen (eds), *Film Theory and Criticism* (New York: Oxford University Press, 1985), pp. 503–20, on nostalgic evocation not as an end in itself but as a means of ironically undercutting the generic experience.
36. 'Noir grotesque' is a useful category suggested by Rennison and Shephard (eds), *Waterstone's Guide*, p. 167: in addition to Hiaasen, it includes Ferrigno, Hjorstberg and Lansdale; see also Julie Sloan Brannon, 'The Rules Are Different Here: South Florida Noir and the Grotesque', in Steve Glassman and Maurice O'Sullivan (eds), *Crime Fiction and Film in the Sunshine State: Florida Noir* (Bowling Green, Ohio: Popular Press, 1997), pp. 47–64, which centres on the work of Carl Hiaasen and Charles Willeford.

37. See, for example, L. C. Thomas, *Games, Theory and Applications* (Chichester: Ellis Horwood, 1984), pp. 15–21.
38. For example, in the novels of Hammett and Paul Cain.
39. Michael Walker, 'Film Noir: Introduction', in Ian Cameron (ed.), *The Movie Book of Film Noir* (London: Studio Vista, 1992), p. 113.
40. See, for example, the discussion in Linda Hutcheon, *The Politics of Postmodernism* (London: Routledge, 1989), pp. 134–40.
41. See Sally R. Munt, *Murder by the Book? Feminism and the Crime Novel* (New York and London: Harvester Wheatsheaf, 1994), pp. 120–46, for a detailed discussion of lesbian crime fiction.
42. Ripley and Jakubowski, 'Fresh Blood', in Server *et al.* (eds), *Big Book of Noir*, p. 321.
43. Raymond Borde and Etienne Chaumeton, 'Toward the Definition of Film Noir', in R. Barton Palmer (ed.), *Perspectives on Film Noir* (New York: G. K. Hall & Co., 1996), p. 65.
44. Naremore, p. 276.
45. Borde and Chaumeton, in Palmer (ed.), *Perspectives*, p. 59.
46. Ibid.

7 Players, Voyeurs and Consumers

1. The discussion here is of Tarantino's original script, as published by Faber and Faber in 1995, not the Oliver Stone film (1994).
2. Mark Seltzer, *Serial Killers: Death and Life in America's Wound Culture* (New York: Routledge, 1998), pp. 169–70.
3. See Brenda O. Daly and Maureen T. Reddy, *Narrating Mothers: Theorizing Maternal Subjectivity* (Knoxville: University of Tennessee Press, 1991), pp. 12–13 and 21–2; Katharine Horsley and Lee Horsley, '*Mères Fatales*: Maternal Guilt in the Noir Crime Novel', *Modern Fiction Studies*, 45, No. 2 (1999), pp. 373–4.
4. Guy Debord, *Society of the Spectacle* (Detroit: Black and Red, 1983), thesis 1, quoted, for example, in Annette Kuhn (ed.), *Alien Zone: Cultural Theory and Contemporary Science Fiction Cinema* (London: Verso, 1990), p. 197, and Jim Collins, *Architecture of Excess: Cultural Life in the Information Age* (New York: Routledge, 1995), pp. 11–12.
5. The cinema 'makes voyeurs and fetishists of us all'. Arthur Asa Berger, *Cultural Criticism* (Thousand Oaks, Calif.: Sage Publications, 1995), p. 31.
6. Mike Featherstone, *Consumer Culture and Postmodernism* (London: Sage Publications, 1991, 1998), p. 101.
7. Dana Polan, *Power and Paranoia: History, Narrative and the American Cinema, 1940–1950* (New York: Columbia University Press, 1986), p. 219.
8. This contrasts, for example, with Walter Benjamin's notion of the gambler as 'not an agent but an object of an endless system'. See Polan, pp. 218–19.
9. L. C. Thomas, *Games, Theory and Applications* (Chichester: Ellis Horwood, 1984), p. 16.
10. This is suggested, for example, by the title of Ken Binmore's text on game theory, *Fun and Games: a Text on Game Theory* (Lexington, Mass.: D. C. Heath and Company, 1992).

11. Robert Dean Pharr, quoted by Graham Clarke, 'Beyond Realism: Recent Black Fiction and the Language of "The Real Thing"', in A. Robert Lee (ed.), *Back Fiction: New Studies in the Afro-American Novel since 1945* (Plymouth and London: Vision Press, 1980), p. 212.
12. See Jonathan Munby, *Public Enemies, Public Heroes: Screening the Gangster from Little Caesar to Touch of Evil* (Chicago: University of Chicago Press, 1999), pp. 26–38.
13. As game theorists stress, if threats are made there must be an understanding that they will be implemented: 'A reputation for toughness may be a very valuable asset in future play.' Binmore, pp. 263, 347.
14. The terms are from evolutionary game theory: see Binmore, p. 19.
15. Leonard's early stories and novels were Westerns which sometimes contained decidedly noir elements. See Bill Pronzini and Jack Adrian (eds), *Hard-Boiled: an Anthology of American Crime Stories* (Oxford: Oxford University Press, 1995), pp. 257–71, reprinting and commenting on Leonard's 'Three-Ten to Yuma' (a 1953 story for *Dime Western*). *City Primeval* was originally subtitled *High Noon in Detroit*. Woody Haut, *Neon Noir: Contemporary American Crime Fiction* (London: Serpent's Tail, 1999), p. 246.
16. See Andreu Mas-Colell, Michael D. Whinston and Jerry R. Green, *Microeconomic Theory* (New York and Oxford: Oxford University Press, 1995), pp. 243–9.
17. Jay McInerney, *Model Behaviour* (London: Bloomsbury, 1998, 1999), p. 71.
18. See Sally R. Munt, *Murder by the Book? Feminism and the Crime Novel* (New York and London, 1994), p. 125, on self-determination, integration and communality.
19. She is ultimately herself 'disarticulated' when, at the very end, she can no longer speak of herself in the first person. Her articulateness has enabled her to distance herself from disturbing realities, for example p. 137, 'I was thinking that it was an interesting use of the word "on," as in "cutting on her body". . . .'
20. See Christian Metz, *Psychoanalysis and Cinema: the Imaginary Signifier*, trans. Celia Britton *et al.* (London: Macmillan, 1977, 1983), p. 62.
21. Berger, p. 79.
22. Metz, p. 61.
23. Seltzer, pp. 182–3.
24. Seltzer, p. 184.
25. Lewis also published two 'Carter prequels', *Jack Carter's Law* and *Jack Carter and the Mafia Pigeon*. For an overview of his work, see Paul Duncan, 'All the Way Home: Ted Lewis', *Crime Time*, 9 (Spring 1997), pp. 22–6.
26. Seltzer, p. 64.
27. David J. Skal, *The Monster Show: a Cultural History of Horror* (New York: W. W. Norton, 1993), pp. 375–6.
28. Skal, p. 376.
29. Will Hutton, *The State We're In* (London: Vintage, 1995, 1996), pp. xi–xii and 54.
30. Nicholas Blincoe, 'The Same Mean Streets Seen from a Fresh Angle', in *Murder, They Write* (*The Times*, 18 April 1998), p. 17.
31. Willocks' subsequent novels are also set in America – *Green River Rising* (1994) in Texas, *Bloodstained Kings* (1995) in a Southern landscape that

stretches from New Orleans to Georgia. Mike Ripley and Maxim Jakubowski, 'Fresh Blood: British Neo-Noir', in Lee Server, Ed Gorman and Martin H. Greenberg (eds), *The Big Book of Noir* (New York: Carroll and Graf Publishers, 1998), p. 321, note that other contemporary British crime writers who have set novels in the USA include Philip Kerr, Michael Dibdin, Maxim Jakubowski and Christopher Brookmyre. Some, of course, just touch down there – like Ken Bruen, whose *Rilke on Black* (1996) ends with the narrator 'pushed into a cell' and wondering whether 'America was all it was cracked up to be' (151).

32. Jacket blurb on Cameron's *Vinnie Got Blown Away*.
33. Peter York and Charles Jennings, *Peter York's Eighties* (London: BBC Books, 1995), pp. 8 and 73.
34. Jeff Torrington, in *Scotland on Sunday*, 8 August 1993; and Irvine Welsh, interviewed in *The Times*, 25 July 1998, both quoted by Andrew Crumey, 'Irvine Welsh' on users.globalnet.co.uk, 28 September 1999, pp. 9 and 35.
35. Mark Fisher reviewing *Headstate* in *The Observer*, 9 October 1994, quoted by Crumey, p. 18.
36. Peter Millar, review of *Country of the Blind, The Times, Directory* (8–14 November 1997), p. 22. Irvine Welsh is an east-coast Scottish writer, originally from Leith – near Edinburgh but not to be confused with it ('Leith and Edinburgh are quite analogous to Scotland and England', Welsh says. Crumey, p. 2).
37. Iain Banks, Interview with Robin Eggar, *The Times*, 14 November 1997.

8 Pasts and Futures

1. Bruce Sterling (ed.), *Mirrorshades: the Cyberpunk Anthology* (London: HarperCollins, 1986, 1994), p. xii.
2. As, for example, in *Night Has a Thousand Eyes*, published under the name of George Hopley in 1945.
3. On *film noir* as a fusion of fantasy and realism, see J. P. Telotte, 'The Fantastic-Realism of *Film Noir – Kiss Me Deadly*', *Wide Angle*, 14, No. 1 (1992), pp. 4–18: 'Thanks to [a] style that calls attention to itself . . . the film noir can seem a nearly schizophrenic form, powerfully pulled in different directions by both realistic and fantastic impulses' (7).
4. James Naremore, *More Than Night: Film Noir in its Contexts* (Berkeley: University of California Press, 1998), p. 9.
5. See, for example, Brian Aldiss, *Trillion Year Spree* (London: Paladin, 1973, 1988): Aldiss argues that science fiction, poised between romance and realism, shares with the Gothic novel a reliance on suspense, mystery and 'a limited number of startling props', that it transforms standard Gothic character types (cruel father into scientist; seducing monk into alien) and reworks plot patterns, such as the descent into 'inferno or incarceration', where the protagonist must go to complete his search for secret knowledge. See also Mark Rose, *Alien Encounters: Anatomy of Science Fiction* (Cambridge, Mass.: Harvard University Press, 1981) and Fred Botting, *Gothic* (London: Routledge, New Critical Idiom, 1996).
6. This is, in part, simply a process of creating metaphoric representations of the various aspects of computer technology. A 'ghost self', say, is just a com-

puter-simulated self. But it is also a way of investing cyberspace with a spiritual dimension. As Samuel Delany says, Gibson's cyberspace 'is haunted by creatures just a step away from Godhead'. Samuel Delany, *Mississippi Review*, Nos 2 and 3, p. 33, quoted in Jenny Wolmark, *Aliens and Others: Science Fiction, Feminism and Postmodernism* (Hemel Hempstead, Herts.: Harvester Wheatsheaf, 1993), p. 119.

7. *Neuromancer*, for example, is discussed both by Douglas Rushkoff, *Cyberia: Life in the Trenches of Cyberspace* (London: Flamingo, 1994), pp. 225–31 and Botting, p. 163.
8. David Punter, *The Literature of Terror: a History of Gothic Fictions from 1965 to the Present Day* (London: Longman, 1980), p. 121; Rose, p. 5; Aldiss, pp. 42–56; and Edward James, *Science Fiction in the 20th Century* (Oxford: Oxford University Press, 1994), p. 110.
9. See Wolmark, pp. 111–14.
10. Chris Baldick, 'Introduction' to Chris Baldick (ed.), *The Oxford Book of Gothic Tales* (Oxford: Oxford University Press, 1992, 1993), p. xix.
11. In the significance it attaches to Hawksmoor's churches, Ackroyd's earlier novel draws heavily on Iain Sinclair's *Lud Heat*. Sinclair incorporates De Quincey's detailing of the Ratcliffe Highway murders and takes as his epigraph De Quincey's line, 'All perils, specially malignant, are recurrent', which is also one of Ackroyd's central themes.
12. Mark Seltzer, *Serial Killers: Death and Life in America's Wound Culture* (New York: Routledge, 1998), p. 186.
13. Scott Bukatman, *Blade Runner* (London: British Film Institute, 1997), pp. 19–21; J. P. Telotte, 'The Doubles of Fantasy and the Space of Desire', in Annette Kuhn (ed.), *Alien Zone: Cultural Theory and Contemporary Science Fiction Cinema* (London: Verso, 1990), pp. 154–5.
14. See Rushkoff, pp. 223–32.
15. Rushkoff, pp. 225–9.
16. Michael Hutchinson, quoted by Rushkoff, pp. 287–8.
17. *Observer Life*, 10 September 1995.
18. *Manga Video*, 1995, p. 13; Bob Cotton and Richard Oliver, *The Cyberspace Lexicon* (London: Phaidon, 1994), p. 52.
19. Sterling, *Mirrorshades*, p. xii.
20. Michael Grant, *Myths of the Greeks and Romans* (New York: Mentor, 1962), pp. 248–51. As Paglia says, Dionysus is 'the return of the repressed', appealing to the 'salacious voyeurism' of an audience that looks 'directly into daemonic fantasy, the hellish nightscape of dream and creative imagination'. Camille Paglia, *Sexual Personae: Art and Decadence from Nefertiti to Emily Dickinson* (Harmondsworth, Middx.: Penguin, 1990), pp. 5, 102–3.
21. *Random Acts* is part of Womack's New York quintet, the other novels being *Ambient* (1987), *Heathern* (1990) and *Elvissey* (1993), which take place in twenty-first-century New York; and *Terraplane* (1988), an alternate-world version of thirties New York. *Random Acts* is the final novel of the series and the one closest to our own time.

Bibliography

Primary

There are obvious difficulties involved in creating a useful bibliography of primary sources for a study in which so large a number of the texts is out of print. Many of the novels have been read in those libraries which have substantial popular culture holdings; many more have been picked up over the years from book fairs, dealers, market stalls and second-hand bookshops. The list that follows is therefore an idiosyncratic assortment of long out-of-print paperback reissues, the occasional paperback original, a few hardcover editions and a reasonable number of contemporary paperbacks and currently available reprints of the better-known noir crime writers (Hammett, Chandler, Thompson, Woolrich, Goodis and so on). Except where I have used a first edition, the original publication date is given in brackets, followed by the bibliographic details for the edition I have used. Page numbers in the text refer to the editions identified here. The titles after each writer's name are generally placed in order of publication.

I have included in this bibliography only those primary texts that I have mentioned in my study. For complete lists of the stories and novels of most of the writers discussed in Parts I and II (and some in Part III), see John M. Reilly's *Twentieth-Century Crime and Mystery Writers*. Readers who want to locate inexpensive copies of out-of-print titles will find a large range of second-hand crime paperbacks in the catalogues produced by Zardoz Books (Westbury, Wilts.); lists of other dealers are published in the newsletters of the BAPC (British Association of Paperback and Pulp Book Collectors).

Ackroyd, Peter, *Hawksmoor* (1985), London: Hamish Hamilton, 1986; *Dan Leno and the Limehouse Golem* (1994), London: Minerva, 1995

Algren, Nelson, *The Man with the Golden Arm* (New York: Doubleday, 1949)

Ambler, Eric, *The Dark Frontier* (1936), London: Fontana, 1988; *Cause for Alarm* (1938), London: Fontana, 1988; *Mask of Dimitrios* (1939), London: Fontana, 1988; *Journey into Fear* (1940), London: Fontana, 1989

Amis, Martin, *Night Train* (1997), London: Vintage, 1998

Anderson, Edward, *Thieves Like Us* (1937) in *Crime Novels: American Noir of the 1930s and 40s* (No. 94, The Library of America, 1997)

Appel, Benjamin, *Brain Guy* (1934), London: Constable, 1937; *Dock Walloper* (1934–35), New York: Lion, 1953; *Hell's Kitchen* (1934–39, 1952), New York: Berkley Books, 1958

Ballard, J. G., *High-Rise* (1975), London: Panther, 1985; *Running Wild* (London: Flamingo, 1988); *Cocaine Nights* (1996), London: Flamingo, 1997

Banks, Iain, *Complicity* (1993), London: Abacus, 1995

Bardin, John Franklin, *Devil Take the Blue-Tail Fly* (1948), New York: MacFadden, 1967

Bateman, Colin, *Cycle of Violence* (London: HarperCollins, 1995)

Beck, Robert [Iceberg Slim], *Trick Baby: the Story of a White Negro* (1967), Edinburgh: Payback Press, 1996; *Long White Con* (1977), Edinburgh: Payback Press, 1997

Behm, Marc, *The Eye of the Beholder* (1980), Harpenden, Herts.: No Exit Press, 1999

Blincoe, Nicholas, *Acid Casuals* (London: Serpent's Tail, 1995)

Bloch, Robert, *The Dead Beat* (1959), New York: Popular Library, 1961; *Psycho* (1960), London: Bloomsbury, 1997

Block, Lawrence, *The Mat Scudder Mysteries 2* (London: Orion, 1997), including: *A Stab in the Dark* (1981), *Eight Million Ways to Die* (1982) and *When the Sacred Ginmill Closes* (1986)

Bocca, Al [Bevis Winter], *City Limit Blonde* (London: Scion, n.d. [1950]); *She Was No Lady* (London: Scion, n.d. [1950])

Boyle, Kay, *Monday Night* (1938), Mamaroneck, NY: Paul P. Appel, 1977

Brackett, Leigh, *The Tiger Among Us* [aka *Fear No Evil* and *13 West Street*] (1957), London: Blue Murder, 1989; *An Eye for an Eye* (1957), London: Corgi, 1961

Brecht, Bertolt, *The Resistible Rise of Arturo Ui* (1941), London: Eyre Methuen, 1976

Brewer, Gil, *13 French Street* (1951), Bath: Chivers Press, 1989; *So Rich, So Dead* (1951), London: New Fiction Press, 1952; *77 Rue Paradis* (1955), London: Red Seal, 1959; *And the Girl Screamed* (1956), Manchester: Fawcett (Gold Medal), 1959; *Wild to Possess* (Derby, Conn.: Monarch, 1959); *Nude on Thin Ice* (New York: Avon, 1960)

Brookmyre, Christopher, *Quite Ugly One Morning* (1996), London: Abacus, 1997; *Country of the Blind* (1997), London: Abacus, 1998

Brown, Fredric, *The Fabulous Clipjoint* (1947), London: Sabre Books, 1967; *The Screaming Mimi* (1949), New York: Carroll and Graf, 1989; *The Lenient Beast* (1957), London: Corgi, 1959

Brown, Wenzell, *The Naked Hours* (1956), Manchester: World Distributors, 1959

Bruen, Ken, *Rilke on Black* (London: Serpent's Tail, 1996); *Her Last Call to Louis MacNeice* (London: Serpent's Tail, 1998)

Bunker, Edward, *No Beast So Fierce* (1973), Harpenden, Herts.: No Exit Press, 1995; *Little Boy Blue* (1981), Harpenden, Herts.: No Exit Press, 1995

Burke, James Lee, *A Stained White Radiance* (1992), London: Arrow, 1993; *Dixie City Jam* (1994), London: Phoenix, 1995

Burnett, W. R., *Little Caesar* (1929), London: Kaye and Ward, 1974; *High Sierra* (1940), London: Flamingo, 1968; *Nobody Lives Forever* (New York: Armed Services Edition, 1943); *The Asphalt Jungle* (1949), London: Corgi, 1964; *Underdog* (1957), New York: Bantam, 1958

Burroughs, William S., *Wild Boys* (1969), New York: Grove Press, 1992

Butler, Gerald, *The Lurking Man* (1946), New York: Lion, 1952; *Blow Hot, Blow Cold* [*Choice of Two Women*] (New York: Dell, 1951)

Cain, James M., *The Five Great Novels of James M. Cain* (London: Picador, 1985): including *The Postman Always Rings Twice* (1934), *Serenade* (1937), *Double Indemnity* (1945), *Mildred Pierce* (1943), *The Butterfly* (1949); *Love's Lovely Counterfeit* (New York: Avon, 1942); *Sinful Woman* (1947), Berkeley: Black Lizard, 1989

Cain, Paul [pseud. George Carrol Sims], *Fast One* (1932), Harpenden, Herts.: No Exit Press, 1989; *Seven Slayers* (1933–36, 1946), Los Angeles: Blood and Guts Press, 1987

Cameron, Jeremy, *Vinnie Got Blown Away* (1995), London: Touchstone, 1996; *It Was an Accident . . .* (1996), London: Touchstone, 1997
Capelli, Ace [Stephen Frances], *Yellow Babe* (London: Gaywood Press, n.d.)
Chandler, Raymond, *Trouble is My Business* (1933–39, 1946), Harmondsworth, Middx.: Penguin, 1952; *Three Novels* (Harmondsworth, Middx.: Penguin, 1993): including *The Big Sleep* (1939), *Farewell, My Lovely* (1940) and *The Long Good-Bye* (1953); *The Lady in the Lake* (1944), Harmondsworth, Middx.: Penguin, 1961; *The Little Sister* (1949), Penguin, 1969; *The High Window* (1943), Harmondsworth, Middx.: Penguin, 1971; *Fingerman* (1950), London: Ace, 1960
Chase, James Hadley [René Raymond], *No Orchids for Miss Blandish* (1939), London: Panther, 1961; *Eve* (1945), London: Panther, 1962; *More Deadly Than the Male* (1946), London: Panther, 1960; *The Wary Transgressor* (1952), London: Panther, 1969
Cheyney, Peter, *Dames Don't Care* (London: Collins, 1937); *Can Ladies Kill?* (1938), Harmondsworth, Middx.: Penguin, 1949; *You'd Be Surprised* (1940), London: Fontana, 1962
Coburn, Andrew, *Goldilocks* (New York: Charles Scribner's Sons, 1989)
Coburn, Sammy [Bevis Winter], *Uneasy Street* (London: Scion, n.d. [1950])
Conrad, Joseph, *Heart of Darkness* (1902), Harmondsworth, Middx.: Penguin, 1973; *The Secret Agent* (1907), Harmondsworth, Middx.: Penguin, 1981
Crumley, James, *The Wrong Case* (1975), London: Hart Davis MacGibbon, 1976; *The Mexican Tree Duck* (1993), London: Picador, 1994
Curtis, James, *They Drive by Night* (London: Jonathan Cape, 1938)
Daly, Carroll John, *The Snarl of the Beast* (London: Hutchinson, n.d. [1928]); *The Adventures of Satan Hall* (1932–34), New York: Mysterious Press, 1988
Dick, Philip K., *Do Androids Dream of Electric Sheep?* [*Blade Runner*] (1968), London: Grafton, 1990; *A Scanner Darkly* (1977), London: HarperCollins, 1996
Duffy, Stella, *Calendar Girl* (1984), London: Serpent's Tail, 1994
Ellin, Stanley, *Dreadful Summit* (1948), Harmondsworth, Middx.: Penguin, 1964
Ellis, Bret Easton, *American Psycho* (London: Picador, 1991)
Ellroy, James, *The Black Dahlia* (1987), London: Arrow, 1993; *The Big Nowhere* (1988), London: Arrow, 1994; *L.A. Confidential* (1990), London: Arrow, 1994; *White Jazz* (1992), London: Arrow, 1993; *American Tabloid* (London: Arrow, 1995)
Ellson, Hal, *Duke* (New York: Popular Library, 1949); *Tomboy* (1950), New York: Bantam, 1965
Estleman, Loren D., *The Midnight Man* (1982), London: Papermac, 1988; *Downriver* (1988), London: Papermac, 1989
Faulkner, William, *Sanctuary* (1931), New York: Vintage International, 1985
Fearing, Kenneth, *The Big Clock* (1946), London: Blue Murder, 1990
Ferrigno, Robert, *Dead Silent* (1996), New York: Berkley Books, 1998
Fischer, Bruno, *The Lady Kills* (New York: Gold Medal, 1951)
Fisher, Rudolph, *The Conjure Man Dies* (1932), London: The X Press, 1995
Fisher, Steve, *I Wake Up Screaming* (1941), Berkeley: Black Lizard, 1991
Frewin, Anthony, *London Blues* (Harpenden, Herts.: No Exit Press, 1997)
Gibson, William, *Neuromancer* (1984), London: HarperCollins, 1993; *Count Zero* (1986), London: HarperCollins, 1993; *Mona Lisa Overdrive* (1988), London: HarperCollins, 1994; *Virtual Light* (1993), Harmondsworth, Middx.: Penguin, 1994

Glinto, Darcy [Harold Ernest Kelly], *Lady – Don't Turn Over* (London: Wells Gardner, Darton & Co., 1940); *Protection Pay-Off* (Hove, Sussex: Racecourse Press, n.d.); *Dainty Was a Jane* (London: Robin Hood, 1948)

Goines, Donald, *Whoreson: the Story of a Ghetto Pimp* (Los Angeles: Holloway House, 1972); *Street Players* (Los Angeles: Holloway House, 1973)

Goodis, David, *Black Box Thrillers: Four Novels* (London: Zomba Books, 1983), including (in addition to *Down There* and *Nightfall*, for which separate editions were used): *Dark Passage* (1946) and *The Moon in the Gutter* (1953); *Nightfall* (1947), Berkeley: Black Lizard, 1987; *Cassidy's Girl* (New York: Fawcett, 1951); *The Burglar* (1953), London: Blue Murder, 1988; *Black Friday* (1954), Berkeley: Black Lizard, 1987; *The Blonde on the Street Corner* (1954), London: Serpent's Tail, 1998; *Street of No Return* (1954), Berkeley: Black Lizard, 1987; *Down There* [*Shoot the Piano Player*] (1956), New York: Vintage Crime, 1990; *Night Squad* (1961), New York: Vintage Crime, 1992; *Somebody's Done For* (1967), London: Blue Murder, 1990

Gorman, Ed, *Night Kills* (1990), Glasgow: CT Publishing, 1998

Greene, Graham, *A Gun for Sale* (1936), Harmondsworth, Middx.: Penguin, 1979; *Brighton Rock* (1939), Harmondsworth, Middx.: Penguin, 1971; *The Confidential Agent* (1939), Harmondsworth, Middx.: Penguin, 1971; *The Ministry of Fear* (1943), Harmondsworth, Middx.: Penguin, 1979

Gresham, William Lindsay, *Nightmare Alley* (1946), New York: Signet, 1962

Grimwood, Jon Courtenay, *neoAddix* (London: New English Library, 1997); *Lucifer's Dragon* (London: New English Library, 1998)

Hall, James, *Buzz Cut* (1996), London: Mandarin, 1997

Hallas, Richard [Eric Knight], *You Play the Black and the Red Comes Up* (1938), Berkeley: Black Lizard, 1986

Hamilton, Patrick, *Hangover Square* (1941), Harmondsworth, Middx.: Penguin, 1974

Hammett, Dashiell, *The Big Knockover and Other Stories* (1923–29, 1966), Harmondsworth, Middx.: Penguin, 1969; *The Continental Op* (1923–30, 1974), New York: Vintage Crime, 1992; *The Four Great Novels* (London: Picador, 1982): including *Red Harvest* (1929), *The Dain Curse* (1929), *The Maltese Falcon* (1930) and *The Glass Key* (1931); *The Thin Man* (1932), Harmondsworth, Middx.: Penguin, 1974; *Woman in the Dark* (1933), New York: Vintage Crime, 1989

Hansen, Joseph, *Nightwork* (1984), London: Panther, 1985

Headley, Victor, *Yardie* (1992), London: Pan, 1993; *Excess* (1993), London: Pan, 1994

Hemingway, Ernest, *To Have and Have Not* (1937), London: Arrow, 1994

Hendricks, Vicki, *Miami Purity* (1996), London: Minerva, 1997; *Iguana Love* (London: Serpent's Tail, 1999)

Hiaasen, Carl, *The Carl Hiaasen Omnibus* (London: Picador, 1994), including: *Tourist Season* (1986); *Double Whammy* (1988) and *Skin Tight* (1989)

Higgins, George V., *The Friends of Eddie Coyle* (1970), London: Robinson, 1988; *Trust* (1989), London: Sphere, 1991

Highsmith, Patricia, *Strangers on a Train* (1950), Harmondsworth, Middx.: Penguin, 1974; *Ripley* (Harmondsworth, Middx.: Penguin, 1992): including *The Talented Mr Ripley* (1955), *Ripley Under Ground* (1970), *Ripley's Game* (1974) and *The Boy Who Followed Ripley* (1980); *Deep Water* (1957), Harmondsworth, Middx.: Penguin, 1974

Higson, Charles, *Full Whack* (1995), London: Abacus, 1996
Himes, Chester, *If He Hollers Let Him Go* (1945), New York: Signet, 1949; *The Harlem Cycle*, Vol. 1 (Edinburgh: Payback Press, 1996), including: *A Rage in Harlem* (1957), *The Real Cool Killers* (1959) and *The Crazy Kill* (1959); *The Harlem Cycle*, Vol. 2 (Edinburgh: Payback Press, 1996), including: *The Big Gold Dream* (1960), *All Shot Up* (1960) and *The Heat's On* (1966); *The Harlem Cycle*, Vol. 3 (Edinburgh: Payback Press, 1996), including: *Cotton Comes to Harlem* (1965), *Blind Man with a Pistol* (1969) and *Plan B* [1983]
Hitchens, Dolores, *Stairway to an Empty Room* (New York: Dell, 1951)
Hjortsberg, William, *Falling Angel* (1978), Harpenden, Herts.: No Exit Press, 1996
Holden, Craig, *The River Sorrow* (1994), London: Pan, 1995
Homes, Geoffrey [Daniel Mainwaring], *Build My Gallows High* (1946), London: Blue Murder, 1988
Huggins, David, *The Big Kiss* (1996), London: Picador, 1997; *Luxury Amnesia* (London: Faber and Faber, 1999)
Hughes, Dorothy B., *Ride the Pink Horse* (1947), New York: Golden Apple, 1984; *In a Lonely Place* (1947), London: Nicholson and Watson, 1950; *The Expendable Man* (1963), New York: Avon, 1969
Izzi, Eugene, *Players* (London: Arrow, 1996)
Janson, Hank [Stephen Frances], *Menace* (London: Moring, n.d.); *Hell's Angel* (London: Moring, n.d.); *Devil's Highway* (London: Moring, 1957); *Hellcat* (London: Moring, n.d.); *Don't Cry Now* (London: Moring, n.d.); *Flight from Fear* (London: Moring, 1958); *Mistress of Fear* (London: Moring, 1958); *Kill This Man* (London: Moring, 1958); *Lose This Gun* (London: Moring, 1958); *Play It Quiet* (London: Roberts and Vinter, 1962)
Jeter, K. W., *Noir* (London: Orion, 1998)
Johnson, Duff, *Easy to Take* (London: Hamilton and Co., n.d.)
Kavanagh, Dan [Julian Barnes], The Duffy Omnibus (Harmondsworth, Middx.: Penguin, 1991), including: *Duffy* (1980), *Fiddle City* (1981), *Putting the Boot In* (1985) and *Going to the Dogs* (1987)
Keene, Day, *Notorious* (1954), Tel Aviv: Sharon Publications, 1964; *Dead Dolls Don't Talk* (1959), Manchester: World Distributors, 1972
Kerr, Philip, *Berlin Noir* (Harmondsworth, Middx.: Penguin, 1993), including: *March Violets* (1989), *The Pale Criminal* (1990) and *A German Requiem* (1991)
Kersh, Gerald, *Night and the City* (1938), London: Ace, 1959; *Prelude to a Certain Midnight* (1947), Harmondsworth, Middx.: Penguin, 1953
Lansdale, Joe R., *Savage Season* (1990), London: Indigo, 1996; *The Two-Bear Mambo* (1995), London: Victor Gollancz, 1996
Leonard, Elmore, *Three Novels* (1994): including *Swag* (1976), *Stick* (1983) and *Mr Majestyk* (1974); *City Primeval* (1980), Harmondsworth, Middx.: Penguin, 1988; *Gold Coast* (1980), Harmondsworth, Middx.: Penguin, 1988; *Split Images* (1981), Harmondsworth, Middx.: Penguin, 1988; *Rum Punch* [*Jackie Brown*] (1992), Harmondsworth, Middx.: Penguin, 1998; *Riding the Rap* (1995), New York: Dell, 1998
Lewis, Ted, *Jack's Return Home* (1970), London: Robinson, 1985; *Plender* (1971), London: Allison and Busby, 1997; *Jack Carter's Law* (1974), London: Sphere, 1976
Linton, Duke [Stephen Frances?], *Crazy to Kill* (London: Scion, n.d. [1950]), *Dames Die Too!* (London: Scion, n.d. [1950])

Lodwick, John, *Something in the Heart* (1948), London: Panther, 1959; *Brother Death* (1948), London: Panther, 1959

McCoy, Horace, *They Shoot Horses, Don't They?* (1935), Harmondsworth, Middx.: Penguin, 1965; *No Pockets in a Shroud* (1937), Harmondsworth, Middx.: Penguin, 1962; *I Should Have Stayed Home* (1938), Harmondsworth, Middx.: Penguin, 1966; *Kiss Tomorrow Goodbye* (1948), London: Serpent's Tail, 1997

MacDonald, John D., *The Damned* (1952), Manchester: Fawcett (Gold Medal), 1964; *The Neon Jungle* (Greenwich, Conn.: Gold Medal, 1953); *April Evil* (1957), London: Pan, 1960; *Death Trap* (1958), London: Pan, 1964; *Soft Touch* [*Man-Trap*] (1958), London: Pan, 1961; *The Crossroads* (1959), London: Pan, 1965; *The Executioners* [*Cape Fear*] (1959), London: Pan, 1961; *The Deep Blue Good-by* (1964), Greenwich, Conn.: Gold Medal, 1964; *The Girl in the Plain Brown Wrapper* (1968), New York: Fawcett Crest, 1995

Macdonald, Ross [Kenneth Millar], *Blue City* (1947), London: Allison and Busby, 1997; *The Doomsters* (1958), London: Fontana, 1971; *The Underground Man* (1971), London: Collins, 1971

McEwan, Ian, *The Innocent* (London: Picador, 1990)

McGivern, William B., *The Big Heat* (1953), London: Blue Murder, 1988; *Odds against Tomorrow* (1957), London: Blue Murder, 1991

Mailer, Norman, *An American Dream* (1965), London: Flamingo, 1994; *Tough Guys Don't Dance* (1984), London: Abacus, 1997

Millar, Margaret, *The Iron Gates* (1945), New York: Dell, 1960; *Beast in View* (1955), London: Hodder and Stoughton, 1967; *A Stranger in my Grave* (1960), London: Corgi, 1962; *Beyond This Point Are Monsters* (1971), London: Keyhole Crime, 1982

Miller, Wade [Robert Wade and Bill Miller], *The Killer* (1951), Manchester: Fawcett (Gold Medal), 1959; *Kitten with a Whip* (Greenwich, Conn.: Gold Medal, 1959)

Moore, Susanna, *In the Cut* (1995), London: Picador, 1997

Mosley, Walter, *A Red Death* (1991), London: Pan, 1993; *White Butterfly* (1992), London: Pan, 1994; *Black Betty* (1994), London: Pan, 1995

Nebel, Frederick, *Six Deadly Dames* (1930s, 1950), Boston: Gregg Press, 1980; *Sleepers East* (Boston: Little, Brown and Co., 1933); *The Adventures of Cardigan* (1933–35), New York: Mysterious Press, 1988

Nielsen, Helen, *Detour to Death* [*Detour*] (New York: Dell, 1953)

Nisbet, Jim, *The Damned Don't Die* [*The Gourmet*] (1981), Berkeley: Black Lizard, 1986

O'Connell, Jack, *The Skin Palace* (1996), London: Pan, 1997; *Word Made Flesh* (1998), Harpenden, Herts.: No Exit Press, 1999

Packer, Vin [Marijane Meaker], *The Damnation of Adam Blessing* (1961), Manchester: Fawcett (Gold Medal), 1962

Parker, Robert B., *Chance* (1996), Harmondsworth, Middx.: Penguin, 1997

Pelecanos, George P., *A Firing Offense* (1992), London: Serpent's Tail, 1997

Perry, Charles, *Portrait of a Young Man Drowning* (1962), Edinburgh: Payback Press, 1996

Pharr, Robert Dean, *Giveadamn Brown* (1978), Edinburgh: Payback Press, 1997

Procter, Maurice, *Hurry the Darkness* (New York: Dell, 1951); *Hell's a City* [*Somewhere in this City*] (1954), New York: Avon, 1956

Rabe, Peter, *Kill the Boss Good-by* (1956), Berkeley: Black Lizard, 1988; *Dig My*

Grave Deep (1956), Manchester: Fawcett (Gold Medal), 1957; *The Out is Death* (1957), Manchester: Fawcett (Gold Medal), 1959
Raymond, Derek [Robin Cook], *The Crust on its Uppers* (1962), London: Serpent's Tail, 1992; *How the Dead Live* (1986), London: Abacus, 1995
Reaves, Sam, *A Long Cold Fall* (London: Serpent's Tail, 1991)
Rucker, Rudy, *Software* (1982), Harmondsworth, Middx.: Penguin, 1985; *The Hacker and the Ants* (1994), New York: AvoNova, 1995
Sallis, James, *The Long-Legged Fly* (1992), Harpenden, Herts.: No Exit Press, 1996; *Moth* (1993), Harpenden, Herts.: No Exit Press, 1996
Sarto, Ben [Frank Dubrez Fawcett], *Dread* (London: Modern Fiction, n.d.); *Miss Otis Comes to Picadilly* (London: Modern Fiction, n.d., 1946, 1949); *Miss Otis Throws a Come-Back* (London: Modern Fiction, n.d. [1949]); *Miss Otis Blows Town* (London: Milestone, 1953)
Simenon, Georges, *The Stain on the Snow* (1948), Harmondsworth, Middx.: Penguin, 1972
Simmons, Herbert, *Corner Boy* (1957), Edinburgh: Payback Press, 1996
Smith, Karline, *Moss Side Massive* (1994), London: The X Press, 1998
Smith, Michael Marshall, *Only Forward* (1994), London: HarperCollins, 1998
Spillane, Mickey, *I, the Jury* (1947), London: Corgi, 1960; *My Gun is Quick* (1950), London: Corgi, 1960; *Vengeance is Mine* (1950), London: Corgi, 1960; *The Big Kill* (1951), New York: Signet, 1955; *One Lonely Night* (1951), New York: Signet, 1955; *Kiss Me, Deadly* (1952), London: Corgi, 1975
Stark, Richard [Donald E. Westlake], *The Hunter* [*Point Blank*] (1962), London: Allison and Busby, 1986; *The Parker Omnibus* (London: Allison and Busby, 1997), including: *The Man with the Getaway Face* (1963), *The Outfit* (1963) and *Deadly Edge* (1971)
Stephenson, Neal, *Snow Crash* (1992), London: Roc (Penguin), 1993
Sterling, Bruce, *Schismatrix* (1985), Harmondsworth, Middx.: Penguin, 1986
Symons, Julian, *The Players and the Game* (1972), Harmondsworth, Middx.: Penguin, 1974
Tarantino, Quentin, *Natural Born Killers* (London: Faber and Faber, 1995)
Theroux, Paul, *Chicago Loop* (1990), Harmondsworth, Middx.: Penguin, 1991
Thompson, Jim, *Nothing More than Murder* (1949), New York: Vintage Crime, 1991; *The Killer Inside Me* (1952), New York: Vintage Crime, 1991; *Savage Night* (1953), New York: Vintage Crime, 1991; *The Criminal* (1953), New York: Vintage Crime, 1993; *A Hell of a Woman* (1954), New York: Vintage Crime, 1990; *The Nothing Man* (1954), New York: The Mysterious Press, 1982; *A Swell-Looking Babe* (1954), New York: Vintage Crime, 1991; *The Kill-Off* (1957), London: Corgi, 1988; *The Getaway* (1958), London: Sphere, 1973; *The Grifters* (1963), Berkeley: Black Lizard, 1985; *Pop. 1280* (1964), New York: Vintage Crime, 1990; *Child of Rage* (New York: Lancer, 1972)
Timlin, Mark, *Find My Way Home* (1996), London: Vista, 1997
Trail, Armitage [Maurice Coons], *Scarface* (1930), London: Bloomsbury, 1997
Vachss, Andrew, *Blue Belle* (1988), London: Pan, 1989
Welsh, Irvine, *Filth* (London: BCA, 1998)
West, Nathaniel, *The Day of the Locust* (1939), Harmondsworth, Middx.: Penguin, 1991
White, Lionel, *The Killing* [*Clean Break*] (1955), Berkeley: Black Lizard, 1988
Whitfield, Raoul, *Green Ice* (1930), New York: Avon, 1971

Whittington, Harry, *Call Me Killer* (New Jersey: Graphic, 1951); *Murder is My Mistress* (New Jersey: Graphic, 1951); *You'll Die Next!* (1954), New York: Ace, 1982; *Web of Murder* (1958), Berkeley: Black Lizard, 1987; *Hell Can Wait* (1960), Manchester: Fawcett (Gold Medal), 1962

Willeford, Charles, *High Priest of California* (1953), New York: RE/Search, 1987; *Pick-Up* (1954), New York: Vintage Crime, 1990; *Wild Wives* (1956), New York: RE/Search, 1987; *The Woman Chaser* (1960), New York: Carroll and Graf, 1992; *Charles Willeford Omnibus* (Harpenden, Herts.: No Exit Press, 1995), including: *Pick-Up* (1967), *The Burnt Orange Heresy* (1971) and *Cockfighter* (1972); *Miami Blues* (1984), New York: Futura, 1990; *New Hope for the Dead* (1985), New York: Ballantine Books, 1989; *Kiss Your Ass Goodbye* (1987), London: Gollancz Crime, 1989; *Sideswipe* (1987), New York: Dell, 1996; *The Way We Die Now* (1988), New York: Dell, 1996; *The Shark-Infested Custard* (1993), New York: Dell, 1996

Williams, Charles, *A Touch of Death* (1953), Greenwich, Conn.: Gold Medal, 1963; *Hell Hath No Fury* [*The Hot Spot*] (1953), Harmondsworth, Middx.: Penguin, 1965; *The Big Bite* (1957), London: Pan, 1960; *Stain of Suspicion* [*Talk of the Town*] (1958), London: Pan, 1959

Williams, Gordon, *Straw Dogs* [*The Siege of Trencher's Farm*] (1969), London: Redemption Books, n.d.

Williams, Greg, *Diamond Geezers* (London: Fourth Estate, 1997)

Willocks, Tim, *Bad City Bues* (1991), London: Jonathan Cape, 1997; *Green River Rising* (1994), London: Arrow, 1995; *Bloodstained Kings* (1995), London: Arrow, 1996

Womack, Jack, *Random Acts of Senseless Violence* (1993), New York: Grove Press, 1995

Woodrell, Daniel, *Under the Bright Lights* (1988), Harpenden, Herts.: No Exit Press, 1997; *Give Us a Kiss* (1996), Harpenden, Herts.: No Exit Press, 1997

Woolrich, Cornell, *The Bride Wore Black* (1940), Montreal: Pocket Books, 1947; *Phantom Lady* [as William Irish] (1942), New York: Ballantine Books, 1982; *The Black Path of Fear* (1944), New York: Ballantine Books, 1982; *Night Has a Thousand Eyes* [as George Hopley] (1945), New York: Paperback Library, 1967; *Waltz into Darkness* [as William Irish] (1947), New York: Penguin Books USA, 1995; *I Married a Dead Man* [as William Irish] (1948), New York: Penguin Books USA, 1994

Zahavi, Helen, *Dirty Weekend* (1991), London: Flamingo, 1992

Secondary

Aisenberg, Nadya, *A Common Spring: Crime Novel and Classic* (Bowling Green, Ohio: Popular Press, 1979)

Aldiss, Brian, *Trillion Year Spree* (London: Paladin, 1973, 1988)

Alexander, Ric (ed.), *Cyber-Killers* (London: Orion, 1997)

Allen, Dick and David Chacko (eds), *Detective Fiction: Crime and Compromise* (New York: Harcourt Brace Jovanovich, 1974)

Ashbrook, John, *The Crime Time Filmbook: the Year in Crime Films* (Harpenden, Herts.: No Exit Press, 1997)

Ashley, Bob, *The Study of Popular Fiction: a Source Book* (London: Pinter Publishers, 1989)

Avery, Evelyn Gross, *Rebels and Victims: the Fiction of Richard Wright and Bernard Malamud* (Port Washington, NY: Kennikat Press, 1979)

Bailey, Frankie Y., *Out of the Woodpile: Black Characters in Crime and Detective Fiction* (New York and Westport, Conn.: Greenwood Press, 1991)

Baldick, Chris (ed.), *The Oxford Book of Gothic Tales* (Oxford: Oxford University Press, 1992, 1993)

Barson, Michael S., '"There's No Sex in Crime": the Two-Fisted Homilies of Race Williams', *Clues*, 2, No. 2 (1981), 103–11

Bell, Ian and Graham Daldry (eds), *Watching the Detectives: Essays on Crime Fiction* (London: Macmillan, 1990)

Berger, Arthur Asa, *Cultural Criticism* (Thousand Oaks, Calif.: Sage Publications, 1995)

Bergman, Andrew, *We're in the Money: Depression America and its Films* (New York: Harper and Row, 1971)

Bernstock, Bernard (ed.), *Essays on Detective Fiction* (London: Macmillan, 1983)

Binyon, T. J., *Murder Will Out* (Oxford: Oxford University Press, 1991)

Biskind, Peter, '"They Live by Night" by Daylight', *Sight and Sound*, 45, No. 4 (1976), 218–22

Bloom, Clive (ed.), *Twentieth-Century Suspense: the Thriller Comes of Age* (Houndmills: Macmillan, 1990)

Bloom, Clive, *Cult Fictions* (Houndmills: Macmillan, 1996)

Bogdanovich, Peter, *Fritz Lang in America* (New York: Praeger, 1967)

Bordwell, David, 'The Bounds of Difference', in David Bordwell, Janet Staiger and Kristin Thompson (eds), *The Classical Hollywood Cinema: Film Style and Mode of Production to 1960* (London: Routledge, 1985), 70–84

Botting, Fred, *Gothic* (London: Routledge, New Critical Idiom, 1996)

Bourdier, Jean, *Histoire du Roman Policier* (Paris: Editions de Fallois, 1996)

Bradbury, Malcolm, *The Modern American Novel* (Oxford: Oxford University Press, 1983, 1992)

Bradbury, Malcolm and James McFarlane (eds), *Modernism 1890–1930* (Harmondsworth, Middx.: Penguin, 1976, 1985)

Bradbury, Malcolm and Howard Temperley, *Introduction to American Studies* (London: Longman, 1981, 1998)

Breen, Jon L. and Martin Harry Greenberg (eds), *Murder Off the Rack: Critical Studies of Ten Paperback Masters* (Metuchen, NJ: The Scarecrow Press, 1989)

Broderick, Damien, *Reading by Starlight: Postmodern Science Fiction* (London: Routledge, 1995)

Brody, Meredith, 'Missing Persons: David Goodis' and 'Killer Instinct: Jim Thompson', *Film Comment*, 20, No. 5 (1984), 42–7

Brooker, Peter (ed.), *Modernism/Postmodernism* (London: Longman, 1992)

Bukatman, Scott, *Blade Runner* (London: British Film Institute, 1997)

Buss, Robin, *French Film Noir* (London and New York: Marion Boyars, 1994)

Cameron, Ian (ed.), *The Movie Book of Film Noir* (London: Studio Vista, 1992)

Caputi, Jane, 'American Psychos: the Serial Killer in Contemporary Fiction', *Journal of American Culture*, 16, No. 4 (1993), 101–12

Carr, Helen (ed.), *From My Guy to Sci-Fi: Genre and Women's Writing in the Postmodern World* (London: Pandora Press, 1989)

Cawelti, John G., *Adventure, Mystery and Romance: Formula Stories as Art and Popular Culture* (Chicago: University of Chicago Press, 1976)

Cawelti, John G., '*Chinatown* and Generic Transformation', in Gerald Mast and Marshall Cohen (eds), *Film Theory and Criticism* (New York: Oxford University Press, 1985), 503–20

Chibnall, Steve and Robert Murphy (eds), *British Crime Cinema* (London: Routledge, 1999)

Christopher, Nicholas, *Somewhere in the Night: Film Noir and the American City* (New York: The Free Press, 1997)

Clarens, Carlos, *Crime Movies: from Griffith to the Godfather and Beyond* (London and New York: Secker and Warburg/Norton, 1980)

Collins, Jim, *Uncommon Cultures: Popular Cultures and Postmodernism* (London: Routledge, 1989)

Collins, Jim, *Architecture of Excess: Cultural Life in the Information Age* (New York: Routledge, 1995)

Collins, Max Allan and James L. Traylor, *One Lonely Knight: Mickey Spillane's Mike Hammer* (Bowling Green, Ohio: Popular Press, 1984)

Copjec, Joan (ed.), *Shades of Noir* (London and New York: Verso, 1993)

Cotton, Bob and Richard Oliver, *The Cyberspace Lexicon* (London: Phaidon, 1994)

Cranny-Francis, Anne, 'Gender and Genre: Feminist Rewritings of Detective Fiction', *Women's Studies Int. Forum*, 11, No. 1 (1988), 69–84

Cranny-Francis, Anne, *Feminist Fiction: Feminist Uses of Generic Fiction* (Cambridge: Polity Press, 1990)

Crowther, Bruce, *Film Noir: Reflections in a Dark Mirror* (London: Columbus Books, 1988)

Daly, Brenda O. and Maureen T. Reddy, *Narrating Mothers: Theorizing Maternal Subjectivity* (Knoxville: University of Tennessee Press, 1991)

Danow, David K., *The Spirit of Carnival: Magical Realism and the Grotesque* (Lexington, Ky: The University Press of Kentucky, 1995)

Davies, Philip and Brian Neve (eds), *Cinema, Politics and Society in America* (Manchester: Manchester University Press, 1981)

Davis, Mike, *City of Quartz: Excavating the Future in Los Angeles* (London: Vintage, 1990)

Debord, Guy, *Society of the Spectacle* (Detroit: Black and Red, 1983)

De Jongh, James, *Vicious Modernism: Black Harlem and the Literary Imagination* (Cambridge: Cambridge University Press, 1990)

Denning, Michael, *Mechanic Accents: Dime Novels and Working-Class Culture in America* (London: Verso, 1987)

Dick, B. F., 'Columbia's Dark Ladies and the Femmes-Fatales of Film Noir', *Literature-Film Quarterly*, 23, No. 3 (1995), 155–62

Diemert, Brian, *Graham Greene's Thrillers and the 1930s* (Montreal: McGill-Queen's University Press, 1996)

Doane, Mary Ann, *The Desire to Desire: the Woman's Film of the 1940s* (Houndmills: Macmillan, 1987)

Doane, Mary Ann, *Femmes Fatales: Feminism, Film Theory, Psychoanalysis* (London and New York: Routledge, 1991)

Docherty, Brian (ed.), *American Crime Fiction: Studies in the Genre* (Houndmills: Macmillan, 1988)

Dooley, Dennis, *Dashiell Hammett* (New York: Frederick Ungar Publishing Co., 1984)

Dowdy, Andrew, *The Films of the Fifties: the American State of Mind* (New York: Morrow, 1973)
Duncan, Paul (ed.), *The Third Degree: Crime Writers in Conversation* (Harpenden, Herts.: No Exit Press, 1997)
Duncan, Paul, 'It's Raining Violence: a Brief History of British Noir', *Crime Time*, 2, No. 3 (1999)
Eden, Rick A., 'Detective Fiction as Satire', *Genre*, 16 (Fall 1983), 279–95
Elliott, Robert C., *The Power of Satire: Magic, Ritual, Art* (Princeton, NJ: Princeton University Press, 1960, 1972)
Ewing, D. E., '*Film Noir*: Style and Content', *Journal of Popular Film and Television*, 16, No. 2 (1988), 60–9
Fabre, Michel, Robert E. Skinner and Lester Sullivan (compilers), *Chester Himes: an Annotated Primary and Secondary Bibliography* (Westport, Conn.: Greenwood Press, 1992)
Featherstone, Mike, *Consumer Culture and Postmodernism* (London: Sage Publications, 1991, 1998)
Fine, David (ed.), *Los Angeles in Fiction* (Albuquerque: University of New Mexico Press, 1984)
Fisher, Phillip, *Hard Facts: Setting and Form in the American Novel* (Oxford: Oxford University Press, 1987)
Flanagan, Maurice, *British Gangster and Exploitation Paperbacks of the Postwar Years* (Westbury, Wilts.: Zeon Books, 1997)
Flinn, Tom, '*The Big Heat* and *The Big Combo*: Rogue Cops and Mink-Coated Girls', *The Velvet Light Trap*, 11 (1974), 23–8
Forbes, Jill, 'The "*Série Noire*"', in Brian Rigby and Nicholas Hewitt (eds), *France and the Mass Media* (Houndmills: Macmillan, 1993), 85–97
Freccero, Carla, 'Historical Violence, Censorship, and the Serial Killer: the Case of *American Psycho*', *Diacritics*, 27, No. 2 (1997), 44–58
Freiburger, William, 'James Ellroy, Walter Mosley, and the Politics of the Los Angeles Crime Novel', *Clues: a Journal of Detection*, 17, No. 2 (1996), 87–104
French, Warren (ed.), *The Thirties: Fiction, Poetry, Drama* (Florida: Everett/Edwards, Inc., 1967, 1976)
Frohock, W. M., *The Novel of Violence in America* ([Dallas: Univ. Press, 1946] London: Arthur Barker, Ltd, 1959)
Gamman, Lorraine and Margaret Marshment (eds), *The Female Gaze: Women as Viewers of Popular Culture* (London: The Women's Press, 1988)
Geherin, David, *The American Private Eye: the Image in Fiction* (New York: Ungar, 1985)
Glassman, Steve and Maurice O'Sullivan (eds), *Crime Fiction and Film in the Sunshine State: Florida Noir* (Bowling Green, Ohio: Popular Press, 1997)
Gorman, Ed (ed.), *The Black Lizard Anthology of Crime Fiction* (Berkeley: Black Lizard Books, 1987)
Gorman, Ed, Bill Pronzini and Martin H. Greenberg (eds), *American Pulp* (New York: Carroll and Graf Publishers, 1997)
Goulart, Ron, *Cheap Thrills: an Informal History of the Pulp Magazines* (New Rochelle, NY: Arlington House, 1972)
Grimes, Larry E., 'Stepsons of Sam: Re-Visions of the Hard-Boiled Formula in Recent American Fiction', *Modern Fiction Studies*, 29, No. 3 (1983), 535–44
Gross, Larry, 'Film Apres Noir', *Film Comment*, 12, No. 4 (1976), 44–9

Grossvogel, David A., *Mystery and its Fictions: from Oedipus to Agatha Christie* (Baltimore: Johns Hopkins University Press, 1979)

Hagemann, E. R., 'Cap Shaw and His "Great and Regular Fellows": the Making of *The Hard-Boiled Omnibus*, 1945–1946', *Clues*, 2, No. 2 (1981), 143–52

Hantke, Steffen, '"The Kingdom of the Unimaginable": the Construction of Social Space and the Fantasy of Privacy in Serial Killer Narratives', *Literature/Film Quarterly*, 26, No. 3 (1998), 178–95

Haut, Woody, *Pulp Culture and the Cold War* (London: Serpent's Tail, 1995)

Haut, Woody, *Neon Noir: Contemporary American Crime Fiction* (London: Serpent's Tail, 1999)

Hawkins, Harriet, *Classics and Trash: Traditions and Taboos in High Literature and Popular Modern Genres* (New York and London: Harvester Wheatsheaf, 1990)

Hilfer, Tony, *The Crime Novel: a Deviant Genre* (Austin, Texas: University of Texas Press, 1990)

Hiney, Tom, *Raymond Chandler: a Biography* (London: Vintage, 1997)

Hirsch, Foster, *Film Noir: the Dark Side of the Screen* (San Diego: A. S. Barnes, 1981)

Hoffman, Frederick J., *The Twenties: American Writing in the Postwar Decade* (New York: The Free Press, 1949, 1962)

Holland, Steve, *The Mushroom Jungle: a History of Postwar Paperback Publishing* (Westbury, Wilts.: Zeon Books, 1993)

Hoopes, Roy, *Cain: the Biography of James M. Cain* (New York: Holt, Rinehart and Winston, 1982)

Horsley, Katharine and Lee Horsley, '*Mères Fatales*: Maternal Guilt in the Noir Crime Novel', *Modern Fiction Studies*, 45, No. 2 (1999), 369–402

Horsley, Lee, *Fictions of Power in English Literature: 1900–1950* (London: Longman, 1995)

Horsley, Lee, 'Founding Fathers: "Genealogies of Violence" in James Ellroy's L. A. Quartet', *Clues*, 19, No. 2 (1998), 139–61

Hubly, Erlene, 'The Formula Challenged: the Novels of P. D. James', *Modern Fiction Studies*, 29, No. 3 (1983), 511–21

Hutcheon, Linda, *The Politics of Postmodernism* (London: Routledge, 1989)

Hutton, Will, *The State We're In* (London: Vintage, 1995, 1996)

Inge, M. Thomas, *Handbook of American Popular Literature* (New York and Westport, Conn.: Greenwood Press, 1988)

Irons, Glenwood (ed.), *Gender, Language and Myth: Essays on Popular Narrative* (Toronto: University of Toronto Press, 1992)

Jakubowski, Maxim (ed.), *London Noir* (London: Serpent's Tail, 1994)

Jakubowski, Maxim (ed.), *The Mammoth Book of Pulp Fiction* (London: Robinson, 1996)

James, Edward, *Science Fiction in the 20th Century* (Oxford: Oxford University Press, 1994)

Jayamanne, Laleen (ed.), *Kiss Me Deadly: Feminism and Cinema for the Moment* (Sydney: Power Publications, 1995)

Jensen, Paul, 'The Return of Dr Caligari: Paranoia in Hollywood', *Film Comment*, 7, No. 4 (1971–2), 36–45

Jensen, Paul, 'Raymond Chandler and the World You Live In', *Film Comment*, 10, No. 6 (1974), 18–26

Juno, Andrea and V. Vale, *Re/Search: J. G. Ballard* (Hong Kong: Re/Search Publications, 1984)

Kaminsky, Stuart, '*Little Caesar* and Its Role in the Gangster Film Genre', *Journal of Popular Film*, 1 (1972), 209–27

Kaplan, Cora, 'An Unsuitable Genre for a Feminist?' *Feminist Rev.*, 8 (1986), 18–19

Kaplan, E. Ann (ed.), *Women in Film Noir* (London: British Film Institute, 1972)

Kaplan, E. Ann, 'Is the Gaze Male?' in Ann Snitow *et al.* (eds), *Desire: The Politics of Sexuality* (London: Virago Press, 1984), 321–38

Kaplan, E. Ann (ed.), *Psychoanalysis and the Cinema* (New York and London: Routledge, 1990)

Kerr, Paul, 'Out of What Past? Notes on the B Film Noir', in Paul Kerr (ed.), *The Hollywood Film Industry* (London: Routledge, 1986), 220–44

Kinder, Marsha, 'The Return of the Outlaw Couple', *Film Quarterly*, 27 (1974), 2–10

Klein, Kathleen Gregory, *The Woman Detective: Gender and Genre* (Urbana and Chicago: University of Illinois Press, 1988)

Knight, Stephen, *Form and Ideology in Crime Fiction* (London: Macmillan, 1980)

Kracauer, Siegfried, *From Caligari to Hitler: a Psychological History of the German Film* (Princeton University Press, 1947, 1974)

Krutnik, Frank, 'Desire, Transgression and James M. Cain: Fiction into *Film Noir*', *Screen*, 23, No. 1 (1982), 31–44

Krutnik, Frank, *In a Lonely Street: Film, Genre, Masculinity* (London: Routledge, 1991)

Kuhn, Annette, *The Power of the Image: Essays on Representation and Sexuality* (London: Routledge, 1985)

Kuhn, Annette (ed.), *Alien Zone: Cultural Theory and Contemporary Science Fiction Cinema* (London: Verso, 1990)

Landrum, Larry N., Pat Browne and Ray B. Browne (eds), *Dimensions of Detective Fiction* (Bowling Green, Ohio: Popular Press, 1976)

Lang, R., 'Looking for the Great Whatzit: *Kiss Me Deadly* and *Film Noir*', *Cinema Journal*, 27, No. 3 (1988), 32–44

Leary, Timothy, *Chaos and Cyber Culture* (Berkeley: Ronin Publishing, 1994)

Lee, A. Robert (ed.), *Black Fiction: New Studies in the Afro-American Novel Since 1945* (London: Vision Press, 1980)

Leibman, N. C., 'The Family Spree of *Film Noir*', *Journal of Popular Film and Television*, 16, No. 4 (1989), 168–84

Lenz, K., 'Put the Blame on "Gilda": Dyke-Noir Versus Film-Noir', *Theatre Studies*, 40 (1995), 17–26

Lewin, James A., 'Algren's Outcasts: Shakespearean Fools and the Prophet in a Neon Wilderness', *The Yearbook of the Society for the Study of Midwestern Literature*, 18 (1991), 97–114

Lott, Eric, 'The Whiteness of Film Noir', *American Literary History*, 9, No. 3 (1997), 542–66

Lundquist, James, *Chester Himes* (New York: Frederick Ungar, 1976)

McArthur, Colin, *Underworld USA* (London: Secker and Warburg, 1972)

McCauley, Michael J., *Jim Thompson: Sleep with the Devil* (New York: The Mysterious Press, 1991)

McConnell, Frank, '*Pickup on South Street* and the Metamorphosis of the Thriller', *Film Heritage*, 8 (1973), 9–18

McHale, Brian, *Constructing Postmodernism* (London: Routledge, 1992)

Madden, David (ed.), *Tough Guy Writers of the Thirties* (Carbondale, Ill.: Southern Illinois University Press, 1968)

Mahan, Jeffrey H., 'The Hard-Boiled Detective in the Fallen World', *Clues*, 1, No. 2 (1980), 90–9

Margolies, Edward, 'The Thrillers of Chester Himes', *Studies in Black Literature*, 1, No. 2 (1970), 1–11

Marling, William, 'On the Relation Between American *Roman-Noir* and *Film-Noir*', *Literature/Film Quarterly*, 21, No. 3 (1993), 178–93

Marling, William, *The American Roman Noir: Hammett, Chandler, Cain* (Athens, Ga: Univ. of Georgia Press, 1995)

Martin, Richard, *Mean Streets and Raging Bulls: the Legacy of Film Noir in Contemporary American Cinema* (Lanham, Md: The Scarecrow Press, 1997)

Marwick, Arthur, *British Society Since 1945* (Harmondsworth, Middx.: Penguin, 1982, 1996)

Maxfield, James F., *The Fatal Woman: Sources of Male Anxiety in Film Noir, 1941–1991* (Madison, Wis.: Fairleigh Dickinson University Press, 1996)

Messent, Peter (ed.), *Criminal Proceedings: the Contemporary American Crime Novel* (London: Pluto Press, 1997)

Metress, Christopher (ed.), *The Critical Response to Dashiell Hammett* (Westport, Conn.: Greenwood Press, 1994)

Metz, Christian, *Psychoanalysis and Cinema: the Imaginary Signifier*, trans. Celia Britton *et al.* (London: Macmillan, 1977, 1983)

Milliken, Stephen E., *Chester Himes: a Critical Appraisal* (Columbia: University of Missouri Press, 1976)

Modleski, Tania, *The Women Who Knew Too Much: Hitchcock and Feminist Theory* (New York and London: Routledge, 1988)

Moore, Lewis D., *Meditations on America: John D. MacDonald's Travis McGee Series and Other Fiction* (Bowling Green, Ohio: Popular Press, 1994)

Most, Glenn W. and William W. Stowe (eds), *The Poetics of Murder: Detective Fiction and Literary Theory* (New York: Harcourt Brace Jovanovich, 1983)

Muller, Gilbert H., *Chester Himes* (Boston: Twayne Publishers, 1989)

Munby, Jonathan, '*Manhattan Melodrama*'s "Art of the Weak": Telling History from the Other Side in the 1930s Talking Gangster Film', *Journal of American Studies*, 30 (1996), 101–18

Munby, Jonathan, 'The "Un-American" Film Art: Robert Siodmak and the Political Significance of Film Noir's German Connection', *iris*, 21 (Spring, 1996), 74–88

Munby, Jonathan, *Public Enemies, Public Heroes: Screening the Gangster from Little Caesar to Touch of Evil* (Chicago: University of Chicago Press, 1999)

Munt, Sally R., *Murder by the Book? Feminism and the Crime Novel* (London and New York: Routledge, 1994)

Murphet, Julian, 'Film Noir and the Racial Unconscious', *Screen*, 39, No. 1 (1998), 22–35

Naremore, James, *More Than Night: Film Noir in its Contexts* (Berkeley: University of California Press, 1998)

Neale, Stephen, *Genre* (London: British Film Institute, 1980)

Nelson, Raymond, 'Domestic Harlem: the Detective Fiction of Chester Himes', *Virginia Quarterly Review*, 48, No. 2 (1972), 260–76

Neve, Brian, *Film and Politics in America: a Social Tradition* (London and New York: Routledge, 1992)
Nevins, Francis M. (ed.), *The Mystery Writer's Art* (Bowling Green, Ohio: Popular Press, 1970)
Nevins, Francis M., *Cornell Woolrich: First You Dream, Then You Die* (New York: Mysterious Press, 1988)
O'Brien, Geoffrey, *Hardboiled America: Lurid Paperbacks and the Masters of Noir*, expanded edn (New York: Da Capo Press, 1997)
Orwell, George, 'Raffles and Miss Blandish', in *Collected Essays* (London: Secker and Warburg, 1961, 1975)
Osteen, M., 'The Big Secret: *Film Noir* and Nuclear Fear', *Journal of Popular Film and Television*, 22, No. 2 (1994), 79–90
Ottoson, Robert, *A Reference Guide to the American Film Noir: 1940–1958* (Metuchen, NJ: The Scarecrow Press, 1981)
Ousby, Ian, *The Crime and Mystery Book: a Reader's Companion* (London: Thames and Hudson, 1997)
Palmer, James W., '*In a Lonely Place*: Paranoia in the Dream Factory', *Literature/Film Quarterly*, 13, No. 3 (1985), 200–7
Palmer, Jerry, *Thrillers: Genesis and Structure of a Popular Genre* (London: Edward Arnold, 1978)
Palmer, Jerry, *Potboilers: Methods, Concepts and Case Studies in Popular Fiction* (London and New York: Routledge, 1991)
Palmer, R. Barton, *Hollywood's Dark Cinema: the American Film Noir* (New York, Twayne: 1994)
Palmer, R. Barton (ed.), *Perspectives on Film Noir* (New York: G. K. Hall and Co., 1996)
Panek, LeRoy Lad, *Probable Cause: Crime Fiction in America* (Bowling Green, Ohio: Popular Press, 1990)
Payne, Kenneth, 'Pottsville, USA: Psychosis and the American "Emptiness" in Jim Thompson's *Pop. 1280*', *International Fiction Review*, 21 (1994), 51–7
Pendo, Stephen, *Raymond Chandler on Screen: His Novels into Films* (Metuchen, NJ: Scarecrow Press, 1976)
Phillips, Gene D., 'Kubrick, *Killer's Kiss, The Killing*, and *Film Noir*', *American Classic Screen*, 4, No. 3 (1980), 13–18
Pierce, Hazel Beasley, *A Literary Symbiosis: Science Fiction/Fantasy Mystery* (Westport, Conn.: Greenwood Press, 1983)
Polan, Dana, 'Blind Insights and Dark Passages: the Problem of Placement in Forties Film', *Velvet Light Trap*, 20 (1983), 27–33
Polan, Dana, *Power and Paranoia: History, Narrative and the American Cinema, 1940–1950* (New York: Columbia University Press, 1986)
Polito, Robert, *Savage Art: a Biography of Jim Thompson* (New York: Alfred A. Knopf, 1995)
Porter, Dennis, *The Pursuit of Crime: Art and Ideology in Detective Fiction* (New Haven: Yale University Press, 1981)
Powers, Richard Gid, *G-Men: Hoover's FBI in American Popular Culture* (Carbondale, Ill.: Southern Illinois University Press, 1983)
Prassel, Frank Richard, *The Great American Outlaw: a Legacy of Fact and Fiction* (Norman: The University of Oklahoma Press, 1993)
Priestman, Martin, *Crime Fiction from Poe to the Present* (Plymouth: Northcote House, 1998)

Pronzini, Bill and Jack Adrian (eds), *Hard-Boiled: an Anthology of American Crime Stories* (Oxford: Oxford University Press, 1995)

Punter, David, *The Literature of Terror: a History of Gothic Fictions from 1965 to the Present Day* (London: Longman, 1980)

Rader, Barbara A. and Zettler, Howard G. (eds), *The Sleuth and the Scholar: Origins, Evolution and Current Trends in Detective Fiction* (New York and Westport, Conn.: Greenwood Press, 1988)

Raymond, Derek [Robin Cook], *The Hidden Files: an Autobiography* (London: Warner Books, 1992, 1994)

Reddy, Maureen T., *Sisters in Crime: Feminism and the Crime Novel* (New York: Continuum Books, 1988)

Reilly, John M., 'Chester Himes' Harlem Tough Guys', *Journal of Popular Culture*, 9, No. 4 (1976), 935–47

Reilly, John M. (ed.), *Twentieth-Century Crime and Mystery Writers* (New York: St Martin's Press, 1980, rev. edn 1985)

Rennison, Nick and Richard Shephard (eds), *Waterstone's Guide to Crime Fiction* (Brentford, Middx.: Waterstone's Booksellers Ltd, 1997)

Reynolds, Quentin, *The Fiction Factory: from Pulp Row to Quality Street* (New York: Random House, 1955)

Richardson, Carl, *Autopsy: an Element of Realism in Film Noir* (Metuchen: Scarecrow Press, 1992)

Richmond, Lee, 'A Time to Mourn and a Time to Dance: Horace McCoy's *They Shoot Horses, Don't They?*', *Twentieth Century Literature*, 17 (1971), 91–9

Rose, Mark, *Alien Encounters: Anatomy of Science Fiction* (Cambridge, Mass.: Harvard University Press, 1981)

Rosenbaum, Jonathan, 'Black Widow: Cornell Woolrich', *Film Comment*, 20, No. 5 (1984), 36–8

Routledge, Christopher, 'A Matter of Disguise: Locating the Self in Raymond Chandler's *The Big Sleep* and *The Long Good-Bye*', *Studies in the Novel*, 29, No. 1 (Spring 1997), 94–107

Rowson, Martin, *The Waste Land* (Harmondsworth, Middx.: Penguin, 1990)

Rubin, Martin, *Thrillers* (Cambridge: Cambridge University Press, 1999)

Ruehlmann, William, *Saint with a Gun: the Unlawful American Private Eye* (Washington, DC: American University Press, 1974)

Ruhm, Herbert (ed.), *The Hard-Boiled Detective: Stories from 'Black Mask' Magazine, 1920–1951* (New York: Random House, 1977)

Rushkoff, Douglas, *Cyberia: Life in the Trenches of Cyberspace* (London: Flamingo, 1994)

Ruth, David E., *Inventing the Public Enemy: the Gangster in American Culture* (Chicago: The University of Chicago Press, 1996)

Sallis, James, 'In America's Black Heartland: the Achievement of Chester Himes', *Western Humanities Review*, 37, No. 3 (1983), 191–206

Sallis, James, *Difficult Lives: Jim Thompson, David Goodis, Chester Himes* (New York: Gryphon Books, 1993)

Schickel, Richard, *Double Indemnity* (London: British Film Institute, 1992)

Selby, Spencer, *Dark City: the Film Noir* (Jefferson, NC: McFarland, 1984)

Seltzer, Mark, *Serial Killers: Death and Life in America's Wound Culture* (New York: Routledge, 1998)

Server, Lee, *Danger is My Business: an Illustrated History of the Fabulous Pulp Magazines: 1896–1953* (San Francisco: Chronicle Books, 1993)

Server, Lee, *Over My Dead Body: the Sensational Age of the American Paperback: 1945–1955* (San Francisco: Chronicle Books, 1994)
Server, Lee, Ed Gorman and Martin H. Greenberg (eds), *The Big Book of Noir* (New York: Carroll and Graf Publishers, 1998)
Shadoian, Jack, *Dreams and Dead Ends: the American Gangster/Crime Film* (Cambridge, Mass.: MIT Press, 1977)
Shaw, Joseph T. (ed.), *The Hardboiled Omnibus: Early Stories from 'Black Mask'* (New York: Simon and Schuster, 1946)
Shelden, Michael, *Graham Greene: the Man Within* (London: Heinemann, 1994)
Silver, Alain and James Ursini (eds), *Film Noir Reader* (New York: Limelight Editions, 1996, 1999)
Silver, Alain and Elizabeth Ward (eds), *Film Noir* (London: Secker and Warburg, 1979, 1992)
Skal, David J., *The Monster Show: a Cultural History of Horror* (New York: W. W. Norton, 1993)
Skinner, Robert E., *Two Guns from Harlem: the Detective Fiction of Chester Himes* (Bowling Green, Ohio: Popular Press, 1989)
Sklar, Robert, *Movie-Made America: a Cultural History of the American Movies* (New York: Random House, 1975)
Slusser, George and Tom Shippey, *Fiction 2000: Cyberpunk and the Future of Narrative* (Athens, Ga: The University of Georgia Press, 1992)
Smith, Murray, '*Film Noir* and the Female Gothic and *Deception*', *Wide Angle*, 10, No. 1 (1988)
Snyder, Stephen, 'Rescuing Chandler: Crime Fiction, Ideology and Criticism', *Canadian Review of American Studies*, 14, No. 2 (1983), 185–94
Soitos, Stephen F., *The Blues Detective: a Study of Afro-American Detective Fiction* (Amherst: University of Massachusetts Press, 1996)
Sterling, Bruce (ed.), *Mirrorshades: the Cyberpunk Anthology* (London: HarperCollins, 1986, 1994)
Svoboda, Frederic, 'The Snub-Nosed Mystique: Observations on the American Detective Hero', *Modern Fiction Studies*, 29, No. 3 (1983), 557–68
Symons, Julian, *Bloody Murder, From the Detective Story to the Crime Novel: a History* (London: Pan, 1972, 1992)
Tani, Stefano, *The Doomed Detective: the Contribution of the Detective Novel to Postmodern American and Italian Fiction* (Carbondale, Ill: Southern Illinois University Press, 1984)
Telotte, J. P., *Voices in the Dark: the Narrative Patterns of Film Noir* (Urbana and Chicago: University of Illinois Press, 1989)
Telotte, J. P., 'The Fantastic-Realism of *Film Noir – Kiss Me Deadly*', *Wide Angle*, 14, No. 1 (1992), 4–18
Telotte, J. P., 'Fatal Capers: Strategy and Enigma in Film Noir', *Journal of Popular Film and Television*, 23, No. 4 (1996), 163–71
Thomson, David, *America in the Dark: Hollywood and the Gift of Unreality* (London: Hutchinson, 1978)
Touraine, Alain, *Critique of Modernity*, trans. David Macey (Oxford: Basil Blackwell, 1995)
Turim, Maureen, 'Flashbacks and the Psyche in Melodrama and Film Noir', in Maureen Turim (ed.), *Flashbacks in Film: Memory and History* (New York: Routledge, 1989)

Tuska, Jon, *Dark Cinema: American Film Noir in Cultural Perspective* (Westport, Conn.: Greenwood Press, 1984)

VanDover, J. K. (ed.), *The Critical Response to Raymond Chandler* (Westport, Conn.: Greenwood Press, 1995)

Walker, Ronald G. and June M. Frazer (eds), *The Cunning Craft: Original Essays on Detective Fiction and Contemporary Literary Theory* (Macomb: Western Illinois University Press, 1990)

Warshow, Robert, 'The Gangster as Tragic Hero', in *The Immediate Experience* (New York: Atheneum, 1970)

Webster, Duncan, *LookaYonder: the Imaginary America of Populist Culture* (London and New York: Routledge, 1988)

West, W. J., *The Quest for Graham Greene* (London: Weidenfeld and Nicolson, 1997)

Willett, Ralph, *The Naked City: Urban Crime Fiction in the USA* (Manchester: Manchester University Press, 1996)

Williams, John, *Into the Badlands: Travels through Urban America* (London: Flamingo, 1991, 1993)

Wilson, Edmund, *A Literary Chronicle, 1920–1950* (Garden City, NY: Doubleday Anchor Books, 1952)

Winks, Robin W. (ed.), *Detective Fiction: a Collection of Critical Essays* (Woodstock, Vt: Countryman Press [1980], 1988)

Wolfe, Peter, 'The Critics Did It: an Essay-Review', *Modern Fiction Studies*, 29, No. 3 (1983), 389–433

Wolmark, Jenny, *Aliens and Others: Science Fiction, Feminism and Postmodernism* (New York and London: Harvester Wheatsheaf, 1993)

Wood, Robin, *Hitchcock's Films Revisited* (London: Faber and Faber, 1989)

Woods, Paula L., *Spooks, Spies and Private Eyes: an Anthology of Black Mystery, Crime, and Suspense Fiction of the 20th Century* (Edinburgh: Payback Press, 1996)

Worpole, Ken, *Dockers and Detectives: Popular Reading: Popular Writing* (London: Verso, 1983)

York, Peter and Charles Jennings, *Peter York's Eighties* (London: BBC Books, 1995)

Zizek, Slavoj, *Everything You Always Wanted to Know About Lacan (But Were Afraid to Ask Hitchcock)* (London and New York: Verso, 1992)

Zizek, Slavoj, *Looking Awry: an Introduction to Jacques Lacan through Popular Culture* (Cambridge, Mass.: The MIT Press, 1992)

Index